CROSS
The LINE

A Holly Novel

By C.C. Harris

Books by C.C. Warrens

The Holly Novels
Criss Cross
Winter Memorial (a short story)
Cross Fire
Crossed Off

Seeking Justice Series
Injustice for All
Holly Jolly Christmas
Imperfect Justice

Stand-Alone Novels
Firefly Diaries

RECOMMENDED READING ORDER

Criss Cross

Winter Memorial

Cross Fire

Crossed Off

Injustice for All

Holly Jolly Christmas

Imperfect Justice

Cross the Line

CROSS
The LINE

A Holly Novel

By C.C. Warrens

THIRTEEN MONTHS AFTER *CROSSED OFF*

(To read more about the events that occurred between *Crossed Off* and *Cross the Line*, read the Seeking Justice Series.)

The streets named in this book are fictional and not representative of any real street with the same or similar name.

Acknowledgements

I am grateful to God for this creative journey. I couldn't do it without Him. And I'm grateful for the love of my life, who supports me through every stage of writing a book. You, my dear husband, are my sounding board, my encourager, my partner in laughter, and without you, these books wouldn't be possible.

1

*F*lush against the wall, I peered around the corner and up the staircase at the hallway. The second floor was quiet except for muffled voices coming from one of the apartments.

I tugged my fluffy hat further down over my red braids, as if it could do anything to mask my identity if I was spotted, and crept up the steps.

My black flats were silent as I tiptoed my way to the top, but the leftover change from my hot chocolate at the café jingled like an alarm bell in my knapsack.

Way to be stealthy, I thought.

I pulled my lips between my teeth and looked around, paying close attention to the apartment on my right. If anyone was going to catch me . . .

A man on his phone stepped out of a room at the far end of the hallway. "She said to meet her at the restaurant. I'm on my way now." He didn't even glance my way before climbing into the elevator.

I relaxed, turning to the door on my left. I had a shrinking window of time to carry out my plan, so I had to make this quick.

I grabbed what I needed from the pocket of my bag and went to work on the lock, wincing when the clunk of the releasing dead bolt resounded in the silence.

Someone would've heard that.

Heartbeat quickening, I turned the knob and squeezed through the gap into the unlit apartment, barely managing to re-latch the door before the one across the hall groaned inward.

The strap of my camera bag slipped down my shoulder, and I snagged it before it could knock into the table against the wall next to me. I hiked it back up, grimacing at the weight.

Floorboards creaked beneath shifting feet, and a crackling female voice let out a suspicious "hmm."

Did she see me? Was she going to call the police?

I stretched onto my toes to see through the door's peephole and caught a flicker of pink before the door across the hall clicked shut. Releasing a breath, I lowered my bag to the floor and rubbed at my tense shoulder muscles.

I'd made it undetected.

A quick check of the alarm panel revealed that it wasn't armed. Someone needed a lecture about the purpose of home security systems. If he didn't arm it, *anyone* could sneak in.

Navigating around the bulky silhouettes in the living room, I fumbled with the lamp on a side table. A warm glow lit the room, and I found myself surrounded by enough open cardboard boxes to make a litter of cats giddy.

I turned up a cardboard flap and smiled at the label scrawled across it in barely legible handwriting. Contents and room destination. Not the least bit surprising.

Most of the boxes were partially filled, and I picked up one of the movies from the media stack. *WALL-E*. Marx told me once that the little robot reminded him of me—lovable, socially awkward, fiercely loyal, and prone to eating junk.

I definitely enjoyed my junk food.

I returned the movie to the box and padded into the tidy kitchen. A fancy coffeemaker with individual pods sat on the countertop. Everything about it declared, "I entrust my coffee to no one but myself."

I grinned. "Such trust issues."

Mounting my hands on my hips, I turned in a slow circle, considering the possibilities. There was no clutter in the apartment, which limited my options. My gaze landed on the cupboard above the stove.

Mischievous plans are best carried out with snacks, I silently reasoned.

"Now all I need is . . ."

Aha. The step stool was tucked beneath the peninsula. I placed it in front of the stove and climbed up, grateful for the extra eight inches of height.

I opened the cupboard doors and perused the snackables that lined the shelves. Granola bars, vegetable chips, beef jerky. I shuffled things around until a package of cherry licorice appeared.

"Hello, tasty." I snatched the package and hopped down.

Tearing open the plastic, I fished out one of the sweets and popped it in my mouth as I wandered down the hall to the spare bedroom.

This had been my room before I moved out three weeks ago, and memories, some beautiful and some painful, gathered around me as I stood in the doorway.

I had shed a lot of tears into the purple pillows on this bed, but the beautiful lining to that dismal cloud was that I felt safe enough to let down my guard and release them. I sobbed, I prayed, and I fought to pull the fractured pieces of myself back together in this very room.

Home, my heart whispered.

In a few weeks, I would lose this place completely, but I took comfort in the fact that I wouldn't lose the man who made it safe and comfortable. At least I hoped I wouldn't.

Marx had become the father I craved since I lost my family at the age of nine, and seeing him twice a week since moving back into my apartment didn't feel like enough.

I suspected I would see him even less once he remarried his ex-wife and moved back into the house they used to share. Shannon and I were on good terms—I was even going to be her maid of honor in the upcoming wedding—but I didn't imagine she would appreciate me spending the night or keeping her husband up until dawn with goofy movie marathons. And she certainly wouldn't let me come over and bake in her magazine-cover kitchen.

I caught sight of the perpetually crooked picture frame hanging on the wall to my right, my gift to Marx last Christmas. It needled his desire to have everything in perfect order.

Perfect order went out the window when he let me into his life, but rather than getting upset about it, he embraced it. I smiled and tipped the frame a bit more.

Would Shannon let him hang it up at their house, or would she stuff it in the attic because it didn't fit her style?

A tendril of worry and sadness curled around my heart. Mending his relationship with Shannon was a good thing for Marx, but I wasn't sure where a not-quite daughter would fit into his reclaimed life.

I pushed away the insecurities that had been growing in the back of my mind with the wedding approaching, and tugged off a bite of licorice. I had two and a half weeks before those changes swept through all our lives, and I wasn't going to waste them worrying.

I returned to the kitchen to work a little mischief and then made my way into the bathroom. When I was finished, I left my calling card on Marx's nightstand.

Considering he was a hyper vigilant police detective with an addiction to order, he would notice the changes two seconds after walking through the door. I expected a visit first thing in the morning.

I turned off all the lights, leaving the place *mostly* the way I'd found it, and slung the strap of my bag over my head.

I reached for the knob on the front door, but paused at the sound of voices. The peephole revealed the self-appointed hall monitor in a pink flower-patterned housecoat and slippers.

Mrs. Neberkins.

She was a strange old woman, and she was always popping out of her apartment like those creatures in that whack-a-mole game.

Pop: "Quit making so much noise."

Pop: "Pull your pants up."

Pop: "Quit being such a mary-jew-anna-selling hooligan."

I smiled as I reflected on all my awkward and unexpected interactions with the woman. She liked me well enough, but she was convinced Marx was evil incarnate. No evidence to the contrary could change her mind.

She wasn't wagging a disapproving finger or flinging insults at anyone tonight, though. She was smoothing the top buttons of her housecoat and . . . smiling. I never realized her facial muscles could do that.

"Good afternoon, Henry," she said, in a tone I had never heard her use before. "Are those new slippers?"

The old man, whose back was to me, pushed a foot forward to model his blue slippers. "You betcha. Memory foam and all. It's like walking on clouds."

"They make you even more handsome."

The edges of his ears turned pink, and he ducked his head. "You're beautiful as always, Margie. Like a glass of ice water on a hot day."

I tucked my lips between my teeth, smiling at this unexpected yet adorable exchange. Mrs. Neberkins was *flirting*.

She smoothed her housecoat. "Henry, are you making eyes at me?"

"I might be." His ears turned even pinker, and my heart melted at his bashfulness. Could he be any cuter? "I was hoping you might wanna have a date with me. Maybe a movie and . . . well, I can't have popcorn anymore because of my dentures, but I have Jell-O."

Mrs. Neberkins leaned forward and whispered, "I have chocolate pudding."

5

"Even better."

"How does a Western sound?"

Henry fidgeted with a hearing aid. "We'll have to turn it up pretty loud so I can hear the talking bits between the showdowns. That won't bother your neighbors?"

Mrs. Neberkins waved an age-spotted hand. "The Zimmermans are on vacation till Sunday. I overheard them talking about it. And that one's off selling drugs to school kids out of his car."

Henry turned and looked directly into the peephole, and I resisted the urge to drop my head against the door. There was the Mrs. Neberkins I knew, always equipped with an outlandish accusation. But selling drugs to school children? Really, what would she dream up next?

"Isn't he an officer?" Henry asked.

"He's the worst sort. A closet criminal. You remember that girl he was forcing to stay with him like some slave. I confronted him, and then she disappeared in the night."

Or during the day with a packed bag.

"Probably dead," she added, and I almost choked at the offhand way she threw that possibility out there.

Now might be a bad time to pop out and say hello. Poor Henry's heart might give out from shock.

Mrs. Neberkins invited the old man inside, and as she closed the door, I heard her ask, "Did you know that drug-dealing scoundrel stole my dog?"

I waited for the snap of her dead bolt and then released a breath. Time to go.

Marx would be home from work soon, and I couldn't be late for my weekly therapy appointment. I snuck out of the apartment and relocked the door, tiptoeing down the steps to catch the bus.

2

Nervous energy flowed through my fingers into a foil candy wrapper as I sat in my therapist's office.

Verbalizing my pain wasn't one of my strengths. Years of abuse and isolation taught me to keep it hidden, and I was only now learning how to put it into words.

Silence was easier, but to move forward, I had to surrender the skills that helped me survive in favor of the skills that would help me live, or so Annette had said. She still did most of the talking, but I offered a handful of words every now and then.

"And then I sorta freaked out," I said, filling her in on the incident at the library yesterday evening.

Everything had been fine until a man brushed past me down the aisle. It wasn't his nearness that rattled me; it was the cologne he wore—*his* cologne. Before I even knew what was happening, memories surged up and coiled around my rib cage, squeezing the breath from my lungs.

"You had a panic attack," she said.

"Yeah."

The admission tasted like failure, and I couldn't meet the eyes of the woman sitting in the chair across from me. The sympathy that always softened her face during these discussions would threaten my control over the tears pressing against the backs of my eyes.

The bits of my story she hadn't gleaned from the media, she'd coaxed out of me one agonizing detail at a time over the past year. She probably knew more about me than I did.

"It's only been two weeks since the guilty verdict in Pennsylvania. Give yourself some time to come to terms with the fact that you're safe," Annette advised.

"I know he's in prison, that he can't hurt me anymore, but I still couldn't breathe, and I ran out of the library like a crazy person."

She uncrossed her legs and leaned forward, nudging the bowl of sweets on the coffee table closer to me. "Yes, he's in prison, but that doesn't mean the wounds you've suffered are suddenly gone. What it does mean is that you're safe enough to stop and care for those wounds properly."

I grabbed a few more chocolates and mounded them on the pillow in my lap. After my third visit to Annette's office, she made note of my slight sugar addiction and made sure there were always sweets.

"I haven't had a panic attack in months. I thought . . . I was hoping that maybe I was getting better."

"Healing isn't a straight line, Holly. Like any path in life we travel, there will be hills and valleys. There's no reason to be ashamed about an unexpected valley." Graying hair brushed her shoulder as she tilted her head, studying me. "But now you're doubting how far you've come?"

"Last night I felt like . . ." I searched for the right words. "Like I was back where I started."

"Do you remember when we first met?"

I nodded. I had wanted to be anywhere but this office, with its shelves of stuffed animals, fluffy pillows, and warm gray walls. The soothing space and the middle-aged woman with kind eyes had been a stark contrast to the despair and anger devouring me from the inside out.

"You were severely traumatized," she said.

Dying, I mentally corrected, as the foil in my hands began to take shape.

The doctors had stitched my body back together and pumped air into my collapsed lungs, but there was nothing they could do to stop my soul from bleeding out. It wasn't long before I hit rock bottom and found myself holding a handful of pills. That was how

I ended up here. Marx was terrified he was going to lose me, and he begged me to talk to someone.

"I could barely get a word out of you," Annette continued. "And the mere mention of Collin's name made you physically ill."

I had hurled all over her carpet. Now an empty trash can sat beside the chair, waiting to catch my stomach if it decided to jump out of my throat again.

"I worried about that girl. She was so fragile and consumed by fear and hopelessness. But I'm not worried anymore, because you, Holly, you are miles apart from the girl who curled up in that chair, paralyzed by fear and trauma."

"Sometimes it doesn't feel like it."

"*Sometimes* it doesn't feel like it. What about the rest of the time?"

I bent part of the candy wrapper into a butterfly wing. "Most of the time I feel . . . more like me before he . . . took me." Convincing my tongue to speak the other things he'd done to me was still a work in progress.

"Good. And as you heal, those moments of anxiety will become less frequent. *Sometimes* will become occasionally, and occasionally will become rarely."

"What about never?" I asked. "Is there a never-have-another-panic-attack option? Because I like that one."

Deep lines crinkled around her eyes as she smiled. "I hope you'll eventually reach a point in your healing that panic attacks will be a thing of the past, but for now let's work toward making them less frequent. We still have a lot to process."

It wasn't the answer I wanted, but Annette never told me what I wanted to hear if it conflicted with the truth.

"When you do hit another valley, give yourself the same grace you would offer any other woman in your position. You have an abundance of love and understanding for others, and you deserve the same."

I set the candy wrapper on the table next to twelve other foil butterflies.

Annette leaned forward to examine my miniature creations. "I see you're making good use of the origami book I gave you. But I'm curious—why butterflies?"

I shrugged a shoulder. "They always seem so free and happy."

She made a thoughtful noise. "I want you to try something this week. Last month we worked on a list of things you've longed to do but couldn't while your foster brother was still a threat. I know you're feeling discouraged right now, so I would like you to pick one of the activities from that list and do it. It will remind you of the freedom and happiness you're working so hard for."

"Okay."

She smiled and made a note in her notebook, a reminder to herself to follow up on it during our next meeting.

I pushed up from the chair and tucked my uneaten candy into the pouch of my sweatshirt for later. After all that chocolate, I had more sugar in my veins than blood.

"Are you heading to work from here?" Annette asked.

I nodded and scooped my camera bag off the floor. If tonight followed the trend of the past couple of weeks, it would be a slow evening at JGH Investigations, and I would have more than enough time to sort through my photos.

"Remember to be careful," she said, genuine concern for my well-being in her eyes. "And keep in mind that I have a few emergency hours every day. If you find yourself in another valley, come see me."

"Okay. Thanks."

We said our good-byes, and I slipped out of her office into the hall. I paused to free the hood of my sweatshirt from beneath my bag strap, and Annette's soft voice carried through the closed door.

"Lord, you are mightier than the waves of hardship and pain that crash against us each day. You are our shield against the world.

I know that you adore Holly. Help her heal so she can burst forth from the cocoon of her past and spread her beautiful wings like the butterflies she admires."

I listened, captured by her prayer.

"She has such a compassionate heart and a propensity for brightening the lives of the people around her. Wrap her in protection as she heads out into the world, Father. I pray for the next client who walks into my office, that you blanket them with comfort . . ."

My eyes burned with moisture as I backed away from the door. I had never heard anyone pray like that for me. There was love and passion in her voice as she connected with God.

Maybe someday I would be able to pray like that.

. . . .

Curled up in the oversized chair in my office, I nibbled on a piece of cherry licorice and clicked through the photos on my laptop.

The overcast sky at the church today wasn't ideal, but I still managed to snag a few beautiful shots of the couple celebrating fifty years of love.

They were too cute with their white hair and matching sweaters, and adoration gleamed in the old man's eyes as he gazed at his wife.

Was it possible to adopt old people? I was in the market for some cuddly grandparents, even if wearing ugly blue-and-pink plaid sweaters was a requirement.

A knock drew my attention past the computer screen to my office doorway. A tall blonde man leaned against the door frame— Jordan, my full-time friend and part-time employer.

"Mind if I come in?"

I waved the licorice wand in invitation.

He straightened, his grin deepening the dimples in his cheeks. "What happened to trying to eat healthy?"

I ignored the trash can where the carrot sticks and celery stalks had been . . . laid to rest. "I did try. It was gross."

Marx was a bit of a nutrition nag, and he insisted I supplement my sugar intake with vegetables and whole grains. If they would help me grow upward, I would eat carrot sticks all day long. Unfortunately, after three weeks of nibbling on rabbit food, I was still five foot two—well, almost—so I didn't see the upside to the taste bud torture.

"Not a celery fan, huh?" Jordan asked.

"It's like gnawing on a stick of dental floss." I tugged off a piece of licorice with my teeth to chase away the grotesque memory on my tongue.

"It's not too bad if you stuff it with raisins and p—" He bit off the words *peanut butter* with a barely perceptible wince.

I used to love peanut butter, but now it turned my stomach and dredged up memories of my abduction. It had been thirteen months since the warehouse, but sometimes the horrors that happened there still haunted me.

"So . . ." I closed my laptop, smoothing my fingers around the edges while staring at the "Marshmallow is a food group!" sticker on the cover. I didn't want to think about the warehouse right now. "I heard the phone ring. Do we have a new case?"

As much as I enjoyed my freelance photography, my heart longed for something more fulfilling, like finding the lost and forgotten.

Jordan slid to a crouch against the wall on my right, hands resting between his knees. "A case, yes. New, not so much."

"Mrs. Muriel again?"

"Yeah. She wandered off while the family was preparing dinner, and they haven't been able to find her."

Mrs. Muriel was an eighty-six-year-old woman with dementia. Occasionally, her mind slipped into the past and she wandered away in search of familiar places and people, some of whom no longer existed.

I could only imagine how frightening and disorienting it must be for her to find herself in a different time, surrounded by unfamiliar faces and details. Her son was reluctant to place her in a nursing home, so he called us whenever she snuck away.

"Do you think she went to the ceramics place with all the creepy garden gnomes or that bakery that makes the s'more brownies?"

Jordan huffed a laugh. "You *would* remember that detail."

"I never forget a good s'more." Or brownie, for that matter. I reached for one of my flats. "Should we split up to cover more ground?"

"There's only a handful of places she usually goes, so it shouldn't be too hard to find her. Why don't you stay here and finish up your photos."

My shoe dangled from a finger as I absorbed the unexpected suggestion. He never left me alone at the agency after dark. "Are you sure you're okay with that?"

"Yeah." He checked his watch. "We're technically still open for another ten minutes, but I'm gonna lock up. I don't like the idea of anyone and everyone being able to walk in when you're here alone at night."

I had no objections. This neighborhood wasn't the safest, especially after dark, and I would prefer to choose who came through the door.

His blue eyes drifted past me to the darkness seeping between the slatted blinds of the window, uncertainty churning in their depths.

I wasn't the only one still dealing with fallout from my abduction. Jordan blamed himself for not being there to keep me safe, and he was struggling to find a balance between protecting me from every potential threat and giving me space to stretch my wings.

"Riley and I will be fine," I assured him.

Riley, my German shepherd snoring in the lobby, was my companion as much as he was my guardian, and he would attack anyone he perceived as a threat to me.

We had been taking care of each other for over a year, but he had only officially become mine a few months ago. His original owner passed away from a heart attack, and Marx finally managed to get in touch with the man's only living relative—an estranged son who lived overseas and wanted nothing to do with anything that belonged to his father.

Jordan pushed to his feet and shuffled his keys between his hands. "I won't be far away if you need me."

"Okay."

After he closed and locked the front door, I tucked my fuzzy-socked feet between the edge of the cushion and the arm of the chair, covered myself with a throw blanket, and wiggled into a more comfortable position before reopening my laptop.

That was all the further I made it into my task before the business phone on my desk trilled. I frowned at it. I really didn't feel like getting up now that I was cozy.

Stretching, I pawed at the receiver with my fingertips, but I was too far away to wrap my fingers around it. With a sigh, I climbed out of my chair and snatched the phone from its cradle.

I adopted the professional voice I had begun practicing when Jordan hired me last spring. "JGH Investigations, this is Holly speaking. How can I help you?" Dead air stretched, and I tried again. "Hello?"

An older woman's voice filled the silence. "Are you even old enough to be answering a business phone?"

I squinted at a splotch of purple paint on the white ceiling and tried to tamp down my indignation before replying. "Yes, can I help you with something?"

If she asks to speak to an adult, I'm hanging up.

"Is the manager or supervisor available?"

14

"He's not in right now, but I can take a message and have him give you a call as soon as he's back in the office."

"I suppose that's fine." She gave me her information, and I jotted it on a sticky note before disconnecting.

I practiced my phone greeting as I carried the note to Jordan's office, trying to deepen my voice and enunciate my words. Maybe I should mimic my friend Sam and answer the phone in monotone, using as few syllables as possible. "JGH Investigations. What?"

I snickered as I stuck the note to Jordan's desk calendar, but the amusement faded when I saw one of our bills peeking out of the manila folder by his half-empty coffee mug.

Past due.

He hadn't mentioned financial troubles, but clients had been scarce. Opening the folder, I sifted through a few more loose leaves of paper—water, electric, insurance. They were all overdue, and the meager check from Mrs. Muriel's family wouldn't come close to covering these expenses.

I reached into my back pocket and pulled out the paycheck Jordan had given me today. If he couldn't pay the business expenses, then he was paying me out of his personal savings.

I spread out the bills to compare the amounts due. My paycheck would cover at least one of them. Jordan would argue with me, but I had my photography and monthly percentage from my father's bookstore as income. Neither would sustain me for long, not unless I picked up more photography clients, but it was still more income than Jordan had right now.

Lord, I don't know what the plan is here, but please help us through this. I trust you.

I placed my paycheck in the folder and closed it. I would have to be more cautious with my money, but that was better than watching my friend struggle.

As I left his office, I turned off the lobby lights to save on electricity.

I snuggled into my chair with my laptop and clicked through the remaining images, adding the best ones to the print folder. Typically, I provided digital samples for my clients, but the elderly couple would appreciate hard-copy samples.

My printer groaned and clunked to life, as grouchy and disagreeable as my friend Jace in the mornings. Maybe if I poured three shots of espresso into it, it would perk up too.

An odd clicking sound grew louder as the printer chugged out images. I'd never heard it make that noise before. Was it struggling to grab the paper, or was the clicking coming from—

Something smacked the outside of my office window, and I jumped, nearly falling out of my chair onto the floor. I gaped at the blinds, one foot on the carpet and the other still tangled in the blanket.

What was that?

Heart slamming against my ribs, I placed my laptop on the desk and shifted onto my knees, parting the blinds with two fingers. Darkness between our building and the business behind us glared back.

Maybe it was the wind. It could've blown a stray piece of garbage into the window. Our neighbors never did secure their trash bags properly. They seemed to think the drawstrings were there for decoration.

But there was something on the glass. Wrapping fear-chilled fingers around the string, I tugged up the blinds, revealing several oily smudges.

Was that part of a handprint?

Who would be running through an unlit alleyway in this neighborhood at night? I leaned forward to see as far as I could, but there was no one.

The telltale rattle of a locked door snapped my attention toward the front of the building, and my window blinds crashed back to the sill, startling a squeak from me.

I fumbled off the chair and wrapped both hands around the hockey stick propped against the wall. I didn't play hockey, but I couldn't bring myself to touch a baseball bat. Not after . . .

Well, I just didn't like bats.

The hard rattling came again, followed by a rumbling growl from Riley. Someone had circled the building and was trying to force their way in.

3

*T*here had been a robbery at one of the businesses down the street last week, and visions of a masked gunman ricocheted around in my head as I tiptoed toward my office doorway.

The hours posted on the front window made it clear we were closed, and with no cars in the lot and the main lights off, the place was a prime target for burglary.

Except we had nothing worth stealing.

The rattling gave way to pounding, and I leaned forward to peer past the reception desk, a fixture from when this building had been a private doctor's office, toward the wall of windows at the front of the lobby.

A girl stood on the sidewalk, her details shrouded in shadow. She pounded her palm on the door one last time before dropping her forehead against it.

Concern chased away my lingering fear.

Was she hurt? In danger? Stranded?

Riley gravitated to my side, and together we walked toward the front door. Our unexpected visitor was a young woman, barely more than a child, and not much taller than me.

She had pink-blonde hair styled in a feminine cut around her ears, which sported a row of silver studs and hoops. The scant clothing she wore, which would do nothing to shield her from the chilly bite of the spring night, emphasized her overly thin frame.

I grabbed the dead bolt, prepared to twist it, when instinct whispered, *She could be the bait to get you to open the door. And the real threat is lurking in the shadows, waiting.*

Life had taught me to be cautious and distrustful of other people and their motives and tactics, but I couldn't let fear smother my compassion. I scanned the dark parking lot to make sure she was alone, and then unlocked the door.

Her head snapped up at the clunk of the dead bolt, and her coffee-brown eyes, outlined in pink glitter, widened when she saw the large German shepherd by my side.

I took in the stiletto heels dangling from one hand, the bloody scrape on her knee, and her bare feet on the cold sidewalk as I opened the door. "Are you okay? Are you hurt?"

"Tripped and broke a heel in the alley." She scrutinized Riley and then me. "You don't look like an investigator."

I followed her gaze to my feet. Right . . . my fuzzy toe socks didn't exactly scream "professional." But in my defense, I thought she was a burglar, so I didn't take time to change into my flats.

She gestured to my weapon of choice. "What's with the hockey stick?"

"I wasn't expecting anyone this late." I leaned the stick against the window and flipped on the interior lights so I could see her better.

"I know you're closed and all, but I saw the light coming through the blinds back there, so I was hoping someone was still around." She smoothed a hand over her jean skirt, tugging at the frayed hem, as though trying to make its miniscule length stretch to cover more of her.

She had to be cold. I was covered from collarbone to toes, and I could still feel the thirty-something chill nipping at the skin beneath my layers.

I crossed my arms for warmth. "Is everything okay?"

"You guys find missing people, right?" She dug through the phone-sized purse slung across her body. "I found this on a sidewalk."

She held up our business card, which had been reduced to a kissing stamp—the edges decorated with wild shades of lip prints.

Across the bottom, in between pumpkin-orange and burgundy lip prints, was our slogan: "We find missing people."

Simple and to the point. It might need a little more flare to lure in customers.

"I need you to help me find someone." She thrust a folded picture toward me. "My friend Cami's been missing since last night."

I took the picture, straightening it out. On the left side of the crease was the girl in front of me, and on the right was a girl with a blend of African American and Asian features. While the girl on my doorstep looked young, her missing friend was definitely under eighteen.

"Why don't you come in for a few minutes. I'll make some hot tea and you can tell me what happened."

She scratched around the sparkling stud in the side of her nose. "I work the night shift, and time is literally money for me, so I can't stay."

"I can't help unless you tell me more. Like the rest of her name, what happened, where it happened." Riley pressed forward to catch a scent on the air, and I snagged his collar. "Does she have family she might've gone to stay with?"

She dragged her fingers through her hair, leaving tufts of it poking in every direction. "Her name is Camilla Chen. She got a raw deal in the family department, like most of us, you know? She ran away, and here we are."

A runaway, like I had been at seventeen. I wasn't on the streets long before the sharks started circling, trying to draw me into the nightlife. With this girl's clothing, her comment about working nights, and the "time is literally money" remark, I had my suspicions about why she'd come here instead of going to the police about her missing friend.

"Were you with Cami around the time she disappeared?" I asked.

She folded her arms over her bare stomach and nodded. "We were working like we do every night over on Brush. We try to stay close to each other, but I was . . . busy when it happened."

Brush must be short for Brushwick Avenue. The street was full of warehouses, repair shops, and pawnbrokers, but after those businesses closed down for the night, an entirely different business filled the streets. I had stumbled across it once when I was homeless and then made a point to avoid it.

The girl's expression hardened as she braced for judgment and disgust. My heart ached at the thought of how badly she must be treated on a daily basis, if she needed to steel herself against cruelty.

"You two look out for each other," I said.

The defensive stiffness in the girl's shoulders softened. "Yeah. Usually we get a feel for who's crazy. Most guys are fine, but some come there looking to hurt somebody. Cami and me, we watch each other's back." Light glinted off the moisture gathering in her eyes. "I knew something was wrong when she didn't come back after an hour and didn't answer my texts. That ain't like her. Something happened to her."

Riley's posture tensed, his attention fixed on something in the distance, but all I could see were pockets of shadow between street lamps. What did he see that I couldn't?

Trying not to dwell on my growing unease, I asked, "Did Cami get into a car with someone, or did she leave on her own?"

"Dorina said the guy pulled up around midnight in a fancy car with darkish paint, and Cami got in."

And the guys thought *I* was a bad eyewitness. This Dorina was even more vague than I was when it came to vehicle descriptions. At least I listed the number of doors and a color group. What did darkish even mean?

"License number?" I asked doubtfully.

"Nah."

"I don't suppose you told the police you think something might've happened to Cami."

Her upper lip curled away from her teeth in a sneer. "Cops don't care if a hooker goes missing. We don't matter to them. If we turn up dead in a gutter, the city's that much cleaner."

Her impression of cops wasn't too dissimilar from mine before I met Marx and Sam. I wanted to tell her that none of the cops I knew would think of her as less, but divulging my police connections might spook her.

"I don't got a lotta money," she said, tugging a wad of crumpled bills from her purse and offering it to me. "If it ain't enough, I'll have more by morning, and I'm sure I can work out some sort of payment arrangement with the boss man. As long as he ain't into anything too weird."

My stomach twisted as I realized what she meant. "You don't have to—"

"I'll do whatever it takes. Cami is one of the few people who cares about me, and I care about her, and no one else is trying to find her. That creep . . . he took her, and I don't want her to end up dead. Please."

I'd been that missing person no one was looking for, the invisible girl society didn't care about. I wanted to assure her that I would find her friend, but that wasn't a promise I could make.

"Keep your money. At least until I figure out what we can do."

Anger snuffed out the flicker of hope in her eyes. "Fine." She stuffed the bills back into her purse. "If you decide you care, come find me on Brush. Ask for Pixie."

When she turned to leave, I stepped outside, the cold leeching through my socks. "Wait. You can't walk around the city without shoes."

She shrugged the hand with her broken high heels. "Ain't a lotta shoe stores open at this hour, so I don't got much choice."

"Give me one second." I fetched my black flats from my office. She would need them more than I did tonight. "Here."

She eyed the offering. "Schoolgirl shoes?"

They weren't as stylish and flashy as the red pair of heels she'd intended to wear, but it was these or a night of dodging broken glass and filth. "They should fit. We're about the same size, and they're better than nothing."

Her tongue piercing poked between her top teeth. "How much you want for them?"

"Nothing, and there's no strings attached. Promise."

After a moment of skeptical hesitation, she took them. "You're a strange sorta person, Nancy Drew, giving a hooker your shoes."

"My name's Holly, and I'm giving my shoes to a woman who needs them. What she does in them is her business."

She slipped them on and wiggled her toes. "A little tight, but they'll do the job." She readjusted the strap of her purse and considered me. "Word of advice. If you do come by Brush tonight, bring some muscle. Some of the guys that hang around . . . they ain't the nice sort."

I folded my arms against the chill that curled around my spine. "Got it. Be safe out there."

"Safe is for the rich. I just try to make it home in the morning." She walked away, turning down the alley between our building and the abandoned one next door.

A familiar feeling crept along my skin like a swarm of ants as I watched her go, and my focus shifted to the gaping black window of the empty building.

Was someone inside?

It wouldn't be the first time troublemakers set up shop. But it was quiet tonight—no chattering voices or blaring music.

I visually scanned the parking lot. A Styrofoam cup rolled over the blacktop in the breeze, catching up with a pair of napkins that escaped from a crumpled fast food bag, and a utility pole wire bobbed above the sidewalk.

I didn't see anything out of the ordinary, but after being stalked by my twisted foster brother for over a decade, I had learned never to dismiss my internal alarm.

I locked the door and grabbed my hockey stick, clutching it tight. Riley remained alert, nose fogging the glass as he stared at the darkness. Someone or something was out there in the shadows.

4

I tapped my pen against my knee as I reviewed the information I had jotted down in my pocket-sized notebook.

It was nothing I couldn't remember, but every good detective needed a place to consolidate names, leads, and theories.

Marx kept a notebook pertaining to each of his cases, though his contained a lot more details than mine, and it probably wasn't splattered with hot chocolate.

I rubbed at a chocolate stain with a finger, frowning at one of the words that was now warped: *kidnapped.*

Pixie was convinced her friend had been taken against her will, but I hoped she was wrong. I was intimately familiar with the horrors that could happen to a kidnapped girl.

As painful as it would be for Pixie, it would be better if her friend *chose* to disappear. I had made that same decision more than once in my past, and always with a good reason.

What might've motivated Cami?

Supposedly, she climbed into that last car willingly, something I would need to confirm with the witness, but anything could've happened after those doors closed.

Was she in trouble? Was she trying to escape her life of prostitution? Would a pimp come searching for her?

I wrote the word *pimp* and added a question mark. Some women were manipulated or controlled by pimps, while others operated independently, still enslaved by the lie that they didn't deserve or couldn't have a better life.

My attention drifted to Riley, who trotted into my office. He'd finally relinquished his post by the lobby door in favor of sprawling at my feet.

I stretched out a leg and rubbed his side with my toes, my touch drawing a contented sigh from him.

Whatever, or whoever, had him on edge the past ten minutes must be gone. It could've been a stray animal prowling around next door, but my instincts told me it had been a person.

A person who happened to be hanging around at the exact time Pixie came by to ask for help and who happened to leave shortly after she did.

Coincidence?

Doubt nibbled at me. If I had something more than slippers to wear, I might hook Riley up to his leash and follow the most likely path Pixie would've taken to be sure she made it safely to her destination.

Like her destination is any safer, my mind offered, complete with flashes of Pixie following random men into dark alleys and creepy cars.

Even the thought of being alone in an alley with a lustful man made my palms sweat, and I dried them on my jeans. That horrifying situation was life for girls like Pixie and Cami.

With a sigh, I leaned my head against the backrest of my oversized chair and stared up at the web of twinkling lights on my office ceiling.

Where would Cami go if she was on the run or in hiding?

I knew a few good places to lie low. Certain areas of the city were safer at night. She might try the homeless shelters, but for a young woman those could be more dangerous than the streets. There was an assortment of people crammed into those buildings, some of whom were mentally unstable and others who were predatory.

When I was homeless, I preferred abandoned buildings. It meant being dirty and cold, but it also meant no one could corner me in a shower or crawl under my blankets in the middle of the night.

Cami had other options. She might not have an ideal relationship with her parents, but that didn't mean they would slam the door in her face if she needed a safe place to stay. If I could get in touch with them and confirm that she was there, it might put Pixie's fears to rest.

I grabbed my computer and nestled it in my lap. I didn't know much about social media, except that everyone seemed to have it nowadays and their lives were on full display. It was mind-boggling how freely people shared their whereabouts, plans, and relationships.

Two years ago, sharing even a fraction of that information would've gotten me killed. Or worse, trapped in an endless nightmare.

A metal door creaked in my memory, rusty hinges screaming, and goose bumps skated along my skin. I released a shuddering breath and threw up a mental wall against the intrusive memories.

"Focus on Cami."

Her relatives were likely listed on one of her social media sites. It couldn't be that hard to find a profile for Camilla Chen.

I typed her name into the search engine. A stream of social media links and business profiles flooded the screen. Yoga instructor, baker, college student, doctor of something that had to do with rhinos.

After scrolling through two dozen more links, I closed the laptop to give my overwhelmed brain a break. My eyes would glaze over trying to sort through all those people without something to narrow the results.

Jace was familiar with every social media site in existence. She shared pictures of everything, from a hole in her favorite shirt to the winning scoreboard at her athletic events, one of which would be starting any minute.

I grabbed my phone to call her, and she picked up on the second ring.

"Hey, Holly Pocket."

I crinkled my nose at the greeting. Polly Pocket was a favorite toy of hers as a kid—miniature dolls and dollhouses that fit in your pocket. Apparently, she considered me pocket-sized.

"Hi, I know you can't talk long, but I was hoping you could help me with something really quick."

"Sure, what's up?"

"How can I find a specific person on Facebook, Twitter, and TikTak?"

"It's TikTok, Holly. Like a clock, not a poppable mint." I could practically see her rolling her eyes. "And you log into the media site and type in the person's name. Then you can search through the pictures and location information until you find them."

"Log in?" I had to have a membership to the site to find other people? "Um, how do I . . ."

"Oh, hey, my sled hockey game is about to start. Can I help you with this tomorrow? I gotta go crush some people. Love you." Before she disconnected, I heard her shout, "Hey, those are my hockey sticks. Yes, both of them. Don't—"

My best friend was an interesting soul. I set my phone aside and contemplated my next step. Jordan knew how to run a search and track down hard-to-find people, but I couldn't ask him to work on a case that would bring in next to no money. Not when he was already stressed about finances.

Did I dare try to solve this myself?

I wasn't a licensed investigator, and I didn't know the first thing about navigating digital trails, but I was an excellent snoop.

Dorina, the witness, would be a good place to start. She had to know more than Pixie relayed. But first I needed reliable transportation to and from Brushwick.

Bus pickup times slowed down at night, stretching from fifteen minutes to two hours, and if something went wrong, I didn't want to be stranded for hours.

Setting aside my notebook and laptop, I stepped over Riley to reach my desk. I riffled through the drawers for the prepaid debit card Marx had given me on my birthday. It was inside a sparkly box with a note that read, "In case you need to get somewhere in town, and I'm busy."

He didn't love the idea of me taking the bus, and he all but forbade me from taking the subway after someone was murdered there recently.

No box in the top drawer.

I opened the second drawer, my snack cubby, and rummaged through the sweets and bags of chips.

Ooh, a package of purple Peeps. I forgot about those. I checked the expiration date: last year. I squeezed one of the marshmallows. Still squishy, still good. I tucked the package back into the drawer and continued the search.

"Aha."

The box I was hunting for was behind a bag of chips. I snatched it and popped off the lid, relieved to find the card inside. Now I could afford a taxi.

My cell phone made a water-drop sound, and I grabbed it off the chair to find a text from Jordan:

Muriel wasn't at any of the usual places. I'm going to drive around until I find her. Want me to see if Marx or Sam can give you a ride home?

Marx had a date with Shannon, and Sam would be at Jace's game, supporting her with his statuesque presence. I couldn't imagine him pushing enough inflection into his voice to actually cheer.

I told Jordan I would take a cab and then closed my phone. Riley lifted his head from his paws, his big brown eyes seeming to spear me with disapproval.

"What? I'll explain everything to him later, when he's less stressed."

If I told him now, he would abandon the search for Mrs. Muriel and insist on coming with me. Finding her and getting her home safe was more important.

"You know you can't come with me either." As much as Riley's company would comfort me, his protectiveness would endanger his life. If he attacked someone for scaring me, the law might label him dangerous and demand I put him down.

I wouldn't risk losing him.

I was on my own for this trip. I grabbed my computer and looked up the number for a taxicab company.

5

*A*n air freshener dangled from the rearview mirror of the cab, the flat yellow lemon swaying as the car turned a corner.

The driver, a man in his sixties with deep-set eye sockets and a nose that hooked down over wiry facial hair, peered at me in the rearview mirror.

He'd taken me home to drop off Riley and grab my sneakers, but when I climbed back into the backseat with a request for him to drive me to Brushwick, he twisted around to face me.

"You sure that is right place?" he asked in a thick Russian accent. "Maybe you have wrong address."

When I confirmed the street name, he shook his head and pulled away from the curb outside my apartment. He didn't say anything more about it, but he glanced at me in the rearview mirror every few minutes, as though hoping I might come to my senses.

Maybe this *was* reckless.

I didn't have Sam's badge or Jordan's formidable presence to discourage threats. All I had was my pepper spray and a box cutter. I extended the stubby blade, not sure it would do much more than tick someone off, and then retracted it, stuffing it into my sweatshirt pouch.

I studied the map I'd printed out before leaving the agency, making note of the businesses in the area. Some of them were open late, which meant they were possible safe spaces if something went wrong.

"Excuse me, um . . ." I searched my memory for the driver's name, but I wasn't sure he'd given it to me.

"Andrei," he supplied.

"Do you know anything about the businesses where we're going?" I had collected the names and hours of operation, but none of their questionable practices would be listed online. "Are there any I should avoid?"

Brown eyes met mine in the mirror. "You should avoid whole area." He returned his attention to the traffic, signaling the end of the conversation.

I sighed and refocused on my map. If I needed immediate help, I would have to take a chance on one of the businesses and hope the owners were good people.

The cab turned onto Brushwick and drifted to a stop behind a traffic jam of vehicles idling alongside the sidewalk, red taillights stretching into the distance.

Women, and even a few young men, huddled beneath building awnings and in recessed entryways to avoid the impending rain, flirted with passersby.

Andrei grunted in disgust and gestured to the van in front of us. "Man like this wonders why his family falls to pieces, all the while he is here."

Plastered across the rear window in front of us were generic family stickers, depicting a husband, wife, and three children. The man could be home reading bedtime stories to his little ones or spending time with his wife.

A catcall cut through the air, and a young man in flashy clothes, who couldn't have been more than eighteen, sidled up to a truck and climbed into the cab.

The hot chocolate in my stomach curdled, and I dragged my eyes from the scene, reaching into my bag for my card. "How much for the fare?"

Andrei twisted in his seat to study me. "I can't leave you here. You're scared. I see it."

I tried to steady my hand as I slid the card into the backseat card reader to pay the total that appeared on the screen. "This is where I need to be right now."

"You are young, kind girl." His brows dipped in thought. "I have cousin who owns restaurant. You waitress for him."

I blinked in confusion, and then understanding dawned. He thought I was here to work as a prostitute. "Oh, I'm not . . . here for the reason you think."

I couldn't blame him for coming to the wrong conclusion, considering most of the workers were women and the customers were men. Why else would I be here?

"You don't like waitress job." He rubbed at his beard. "I have friend who is delivery driver. He can put in good word. This . . ." He waved a hand at the heartbreaking transactions taking place. "It is no place for you. No place for anyone."

His passion to save a stranger from a path that held only pain and degradation kindled a spark of hope in this dark place. I hadn't expected to bump into another compassionate soul tonight.

"I appreciate your concern, but I'm not here to work the street. I'm here to find out what happened to a missing girl who *does* work this street."

Doubt crossed his face. "Truly?"

I grabbed one of our business cards from my knapsack and handed it to him. "Truly."

He read the card and then cast me a doubtful look. "If I leave you here alone, *you* will end up missing girl."

That was a terrifying possibility, and it was one of the reasons I had sent Jace a text to let her know where I was going and when I planned to be back. I asked her not to call anyone unless I didn't make it home by my deadline. If she respected my wishes, I had about ninety minutes. If she checked her phone during the game and panicked, I had about thirty before she called everyone.

"I'll be fine. Thank you. For the ride and for caring."

"This is bad idea."

Great. Even strangers were critiquing my plan-making skills now.

"I can take care of myself."

Andrei released a phlegmy scoff. "I have nine-year-old grandson bigger than you."

33

Of course he did.

"Since your mind will not be changed . . ." He scribbled a number on the bottom of a receipt and passed it to me. "I can come back if you need quick getaway."

He said *getaway* like I was about to rob a bank. All things considered, that might actually be safer than what I was about to do. I accepted the slip of paper and stuffed it into my knapsack. "Thank you."

"Good luck, little investigator."

I climbed out, readjusted my knapsack over my shoulder, and closed the door.

6

*A*nxiety wrapped around me like a weighted blanket as I stood alone and motionless on the sidewalk.

I used to pass through a street like this when I lived in Darby. It was the shortest and most well-lit path to the all-night diner where I waited tables. During the day it was an ordinary street, but it transformed as shop owners flipped the "Closed" signs in their windows.

In Darby there had been more foot traffic. Here, vehicles crowded the curb as men window-shopped for girls. Frantic bees swarmed my stomach when I caught a couple of men visually appraising me, and my fingers tightened around the canister of pepper spray.

Don't panic. You can do this.

I dragged in a slow breath to steady my nerves, cigarette smoke burning my airway, and retrieved the picture of the girls from my sweatshirt pouch.

I wished I could say that seeing someone their age working the streets was unusual, but I had seen even younger girls in Darby. Many were runaways making a living the only way they knew how.

I lifted my eyes from the picture and searched the unfamiliar faces. I needed to find the witness to Cami's disappearance, but which one of these women was Dorina?

It sounded like an older name, something given to a baby born four or five decades ago, but that was only a guess.

I should've thought to ask for more details—the woman's age, ethnicity, maybe even where she usually set up shop.

Something that would've narrowed down the spectrum of ages and skin colors on this street to a handful of possibilities.

If I could find Pixie, I could ask the questions I hadn't thought to ask before. Unfortunately, I didn't see her pink hair anywhere. Was she with someone, or . . .

The earlier concern that someone was in the parking lot during Pixie's visit crept through me. What if someone *had* been there, following her, and something happened before she made it here?

No. I cut that frightening thought off before it could branch into rabbit trails of horrifying possibilities like predators and murderers. Pixie was with someone, and Cami ran home to her family to escape this life.

Until I found evidence to the contrary, I would cling to those theories.

"Some fine vanilla right there," a man purred from behind me, and I stiffened. He plucked a sucker stick from between his lips and drank me in from head to toe as he inched by. "If I only had time tonight."

He grunted appreciatively before returning his attention to whoever was on the other end of the phone pressed to his ear.

Relax and breathe, I told myself as he walked away, trying to soften the muscles that had locked up and left me standing there like an opossum in front of an oncoming car.

In a place like this, fear and vulnerability were like blood in shark-infested waters.

A breath shivered from my lungs, and I tugged my sweatshirt lower, trying to add an extra layer to anything that might garner attention. Unfortunately, being a woman on this street was all it took to draw unwanted attention.

My gaze snagged on a girl who, unlike some of the other women flirting with passersby, sat on a bench, her posture unapproachable.

"Prepare to be approached," I mumbled.

36

Releasing another anxious breath, I peeled my shoes from the spot where the cab left me and started toward her.

I sidestepped a woman in spiked heels who didn't seem to notice me as her fingers flew across the keyboard of her phone, detoured around a guy staring at the sky in a drug-induced haze, and bumped into someone else who shoved me away with a sharp "Watch it!"

By the time I reached the bench, the nerves in my stomach were twisted so tight that I felt queasy. Navigating this sidewalk was like a panic-inducing game of hopscotch.

The girl, who couldn't be more than midtwenties, raised her head when I approached the bench. Her eyes, one brown and the other a deep blue, were devoid of emotion.

"You're not my usual customer." She turned a silver dollar between her fingers as she regarded me. "It's fifty bucks for twenty minutes."

Her tone was as lifeless as her eyes as she gave me the price for her body, and my stomach twisted even tighter.

"I just wanna talk."

She flipped the coin with a thumb and caught it, the move practiced and effortless. "Talking is what people *don't* come here to do."

"I guess I'm breaking the mold then." I sat down on the open stretch of bench beside her.

"It's still fifty bucks for twenty minutes. And if you're not buying, you can't sit on my bench." As if she expected me to challenge her claim to the bench with something juvenile like "Is your name on it?" she pointed to a name scratched into the wood. "Ownership stamp."

I tilted my head to read the letters: Tandi. I'd never heard that name before. It was unique, like the girl with two different-colored eyes.

"What's it gonna be, Red? You wanna rehearse a breakup with your lover? Confess where you buried a body? Practice how to tell your strict Catholic mom you're secretly an atheist?"

"No lovers, no dead bodies, and I'm definitely not an atheist." I watched as she flipped the silver dollar into the air again, light catching it midturn. "What's the story behind the coin?"

She slapped it down on the back of her hand and then lifted her fingers to see whether it was heads or tails. "No story, really. Old guy tossed it out the window to me my first night. It landed upside-down in a disgusting puddle, sort of like my life."

Her tone was cavalier, but I didn't buy it. I was intimately familiar with trying to hide shame and pain behind a mask of indifference.

I managed to avoid being lured or forced into prostitution when I was on the run for ten years, but I knew how it felt to be valued as nothing more than an object for a man's entertainment. It was . . . soul-shredding.

"I'm surprised you kept it," I said.

Tandi paused before admitting, "Not really sure why I did." Then she cast me a sideways glance. "You're still sitting on my bench."

Right, payment for her time. Unfortunately, I didn't have the currency she was accustomed to, but I did have sweets. Every girl had a sweet tooth. "If I share a snack, can I talk to you a while longer?"

"Depends on what you got." She wrapped her fur jacket around her bare stomach as a cold gust of air whipped down the street.

I shifted my bag into my lap and rummaged around until I found the open licorice package. I held it up for her approval.

A hint of interest lit her eyes, confirming our shared weakness for sugar. "I prefer white peanut butter cups, but these'll do." She snagged a piece and popped it into the corner of her mouth like a cigar. "You got five minutes. But when Spike comes back, you shouldn't be here."

"Spike?"

"Bald guy, tattooed knuckles, neck thicker than my head. Can't miss him. Rumor has it he stabbed a guy with a spike once, and the nickname stuck, but who knows?" She bit off one end of the licorice. "Maybe it's all a story to keep us in line. Spike's got a lotta girls to keep in line."

I set the package of licorice on the bench between us. "Spike's the guy who makes you do this?"

A defensive edge slid into her voice. "Spike helped me when no one else would. I lost my job and got evicted all in the span of two months, and I was digging through trash for leftovers and stuff to stay warm. He gave me a roof, clothes, and all the food I need."

And all he asks for in return is this. She didn't speak the words, but they hung in the air between us.

If Tandi believed Spike was being generous with this arrangement, then she had no idea what "help" truly was. When I was on the brink of living on the streets again, Marx had given me a place to stay and food to eat without asking for *anything* in return. He helped me because it was the right thing to do.

"You don't have to do this, Tandi. There are people who will help you get out of—"

She cut me a sharp look. "Stop talking like that. If it gets back to Spike that I'm even thinking about what you're talking about, he'll lose it. And I don't need that kinda drama. I'm doing fine with my life the way it is."

Her vehement reaction made the rest of my words stick in my throat. I wanted to help her, not put her at risk.

Tandi finished her licorice and reached for another. "This isn't really your kinda neighborhood, so why are you *really* sitting on my bench, Red?"

"I'm looking for someone." I showed her the picture of Cami and Pixie. "Have you seen either of these girls around?"

"Not tonight."

My heart sank at her answer. Pixie should've arrived well before me, and she would stand out with her pale skin and pink hair. "What about Dor—"

My phone alerted me to a text, sidelining my question. I flipped it open to find a message from Jordan. He'd found Mrs. Muriel and returned her safely home. That was one worry resolved.

"If that's your boyfriend, you should have him pick you up before Spike sees you," Tandi suggested. "He collects unique girls. A little doe-eyed ginger with your complexion, you could bring in real good money for him."

My fingers tightened around my phone, and I checked the area for the intimidating man she described.

"I'm not interested in being some guy's meal ticket," I said, pushing the words past the lump of fear in my throat.

"It's not so bad once you learn to block it out."

I knew all about enduring painful moments by blocking them out, and it was something I never wanted to experience again. "Um, if Spike likes unique girls, what about these ones?" I indicated the snapshot of Cami and Pixie.

She tapped Cami's half of the picture with her licorice. "Don't see many people with her blend of features. Spike's been watching her real close ever since he heard her pimp got himself offed last year."

If Cami's pimp was dead, that eliminated one suspect in her disappearance, but Spike's interest in her added another.

"Did Spike try to recruit her?" I asked.

"She turned him down. She'd rather be a free agent. He was real mad about that."

"Mad enough to make her disappear?"

Tandi tugged off a piece of licorice. "What do you mean?"

"She got in a car and didn't come back last night."

"Oh. That happens to girls sometimes."

There was something profoundly sad about the way she delivered that statement, as though it were normal.

I needed to find out if Spike was involved in Cami's disappearance, but I wasn't sure how to handle that interview. If Tandi's warning held even a grain of truth, being alone with the man long enough to have a conversation could be dangerous.

My ponderings about Spike skidded to a halt as a man approached. He was in his late forties, and the buttons of his shirt strained against his bulging stomach. He wiped at the sweat on his forehead as his hungry stare devoured both of us.

My heart slammed into my ribs, and my fingers squeezed the canister of pepper spray beneath my bag. If he tried to touch me, I was going to mace him in the face.

He must've been less than impressed with me in my sweatshirt and jeans, because he turned his attention to Tandi, who wore considerably less. "How much?"

"Fifty for twenty."

He scowled at the number, reconsidered me, and then said, "Fine. My car's around the corner."

Tandi sighed and tucked her silver coin into a fold of clothing before pushing to her feet. I released the pepper spray and grabbed her hand.

"Tandi, please don't go with him."

The man cleared his throat impatiently.

Tandi eased her fingers from mine. "Thanks for the licorice, Red."

In a blink, her body language shifted from resigned to flirtatious, and the glimmer of personality I'd seen in her eyes during our conversation died. Tandi was gone before she even linked her arm through the man's and strode off.

Tears burned my eyes, and I blinked them away before they could betray weakness.

No one should have to do this to survive, but there was nothing I could do to rescue Tandi. I pulled a pen and business card from my bag and wrote on the blank side of the card, "If you ever want help." I slipped it into the licorice package and left it on the bench for her.

7

I tried to commit the information Tandi had given me to memory, because this wasn't the place to pull out my notebook and record it.

I had missed my opportunity to ask her about Dorina, but surely someone else could point me in the right direction.

Running my fingers along the edges of the photograph, I fixed my attention on a pair of women leaning against a metal gate securing one of the closed shops.

The older woman wore a leopard-print mini dress with matching heels, her lips crinkling with age as she puffed on a cigarette. She was around the age I expected my witness to be.

She eyed me as I made my way toward her and leaned over to mutter to her friend, "This stupid girl wandering round here like she on a school field trip."

Her shorter friend grunted in amusement as she picked at something beneath one of her fake fingernails. "Girl gonna get herself snatched up and tricked out."

Her words sent a stab of fear through me, and I scanned the people in my vicinity, but no one seemed to be paying much attention to me. Clearing the nerves from my throat, I approached the two women. "Hi."

Cigarette Cindy, for lack of a better name, plucked the lipstick-stained cigarette from her mouth, smoke swirling lazily from her parted lips. "Beat it. We workin'."

"Yeah, we workin'. Beat it," the shorter woman echoed, placing a hand on her curvy hip. Her blonde beehive wig tilted with the aggressive cock of her head, and she readjusted it before it could topple off.

"I need to speak to Dorina. Do you know where I can find her?"

Cindy's eyes narrowed with suspicion, and she flicked smoldering ash at me. "Whatchu want with Rina?"

I swatted the ash from my sweatshirt before it could burn a hole through the fabric. "I was told she was one of the last people to see a girl who went missing."

"You a cop or somethin'?"

Beehive Beatrice took my measure. "Too scrawny to be a cop. What are you, a size nothing?"

I ignored the curvy woman's jab at my lack of shape, determined not to feel self-conscious. "I'm someone who wants to help."

"You some kinda do-gooder, that it?" Cindy asked, her tone mocking. "Try doing yourself some good. Run back to your cute little house in your safe little neighborhood 'fore it's too late."

"But I need—"

"You heard her. Be gone." Beatrice shooed me away with her talon-sharp fingernails. "Nobody wanna talk to you."

Cindy flicked her cigarette again, and I backed away to avoid the ash. I turned to find someone else to answer my questions, but Beatrice was right—none of the women wanted to speak with me. They turned away or shrugged me off without letting me finish my questions.

"Excuse . . . could I . . . I just need to . . ."

I released a frustrated breath and planted myself in the middle of the sidewalk, searching for anyone who seemed marginally approachable. There had to be *someone*.

A man leaning against an alley wall straightened and rubbed at his nose. "I can take you to Dorina. I know where she hangs out." He smoothed back oily hair and jerked his head toward the depths of the alley. "Follow me."

Follow a strange man down a dark alley by myself. Nope.

Even if he was telling the truth, I had no doubt he would expect some form of payment for the information. But more than likely, the only thing I would find at the end of that alley was a nightmare.

I shook my head and stepped closer to the street. "No, thanks."

"What, you don't trust me?" He pressed both hands to his chest and adopted a wounded expression. "I'm trustworthy. *And* a gentleman."

The woman near the alley huffed in amusement, earning a scorching glare from the man. She met my eyes and tipped her head toward an auto repair shop nearby.

I opened my mouth to thank her, when a man called from behind me, "Hi, uh . . . excuse me."

The woman's attention moved past me, and she flipped her hair behind her freckled shoulders as she sashayed toward the beckoning voice. My focus gravitated to the Jesus fish sticker on the rear passenger window of the car she approached, and my stomach soured.

"I uh . . . I'm not sure how this works, but if you're free . . . not *free,* free. I mean if you've got time, if you're not busy . . . I could use some company," the man in the driver's seat stammered. "I've, uh, I've got cash. And the seats are . . ." He brushed off the passenger seat. "They're clean if you wanna . . ."

He took in the beautiful woman who opened the passenger door, and then his gaze slid past her to me. Panic bleached the color from his face.

I knew him from somewhere, but I couldn't place him.

Snapping out of his shock, he said, "I'm sorry, this was a mistake." He leaned over and snapped the door shut before the girl could climb in. He jerked the car away from the curb and swerved around the other vehicles.

The girl spat a curse and stomped back to the building to wait for another interested party.

I stared after the man's receding taillights, trying to figure out where I knew him from, but I couldn't make the connection. It would come to me eventually.

I approached the business entrance of the auto shop, unsure whether I would find answers or trouble if I knocked on the door. It was my only lead, so I had to take the chance.

There was a "Closed" sign glowing in the window, and I peered through the metal grate into the dark interior. On the off chance that someone was still here, I reached through the window bars and knocked on the glass.

A masculine figure shifted inside. Or was that the reflection of someone staring at me from the street? I whirled to face the man who cast the blurry reflection, half-expecting the man with the oily hair, but there was no one there.

My nerves and imagination must be playing tricks on me.

A car window whirred down, drawing my attention to the line of vehicles along the curb. The pane of glass disappeared to reveal a handsome man with sandy blonde hair and a prominent square jaw.

"Hey there." He draped an arm across the passenger window opening, eyes raking over me in a way that felt like a threat. "Gorgeous."

That single word, an endearment only my foster brother used, brought bile bubbling up my throat.

"I haven't seen you before. I like the college girl look." He reached out the window and tapped the rear door. "Hop in. We'll make sure you get paid well."

Fear twisted my tongue into knots. "No, I'm . . . I'm . . . not for sale."

He bared his unnaturally perfect teeth in amusement. "You're all for sale. That's why you're here. Didn't your pimp explain that during whorientation?"

The cold bars pressed against my back as I instinctively put more space between me and the car. How could I make it clear that

I wasn't someone he could buy? Maybe he was the kind of man who believed everyone had a price.

"I think this one's a little slow, guys," the man joked. "Must be her first night."

Coming here was a mistake. I'd gleaned next to nothing from this community, and all I had to take away with me was more fuel for my nightmares.

The rear window dipped partway down, revealing another man in the backseat. He considered me, uncertainty creasing his face. "I don't think she's interested, Erik. Leave her alone. We can go to a club or—"

"All she needs is a little incentive." The man with the square jaw, Erik, held up a hundred-dollar bill between two fingers. "Make room for her in the back."

I tensed, prepared to make a run for it if one of them tried to force me into the car. There should be a late-night grocery store one street over where I could hide and wait for my ride. I could make it there.

Something snapped behind me, and I jumped as the door to the auto shop opened.

A dark-skinned woman in her fifties stood in the gap, dressed in a red blouse and knee-length skirt. Her dark eyes lingered on my face for a long moment, as though she were memorizing my features, and then settled on the men.

She motioned me inside with her fingers, but addressed them. "You boys, go find a girl on another street."

Erik glared at her. "We found one on *this* street."

"I know the kinda trouble you are, and I'm not letting another girl disappear into your car."

I gasped as her words penetrated my fear. Was this the vehicle Cami climbed into last night? Before I could grab the details of the car or the men, she pulled me inside and closed the door.

8

The interior of the auto repair shop reminded me too much of an empty warehouse, the cement floor and cavernous echo leaving a chill in my bones.

I hugged myself as I lingered by the door to the street, attention divided between the passing cars in front of me and the darkness behind me.

The suspicious car had squealed away, taking my hope for answers with it, but if those men had something to do with Cami's disappearance, maybe it was for the best. I was here to gather information, not confront a car full of suspects.

Goose bumps skated across my arms as I remembered the way the man in the passenger seat had looked at me. What would've happened if my mysterious rescuer hadn't pulled me into this building?

I knew nothing about the woman, except that she *might* be Dorina. I didn't have a chance to confirm anything before she clomped away into the darkness with a remark about turning on the lights. She invited me to follow her, but I had no intention of following a stranger deeper into an unfamiliar building.

For all I knew, she was no safer than the men in that car. After one woman helped my foster brother abduct and imprison me, and two other women conspired to kill me, there was no avoiding the fact that threats came in all sexes and sizes.

I preferred to stay beside the exit, in case I needed to make a quick escape.

The overhead lights blazed to life with a resounding thump, like a breaker being flipped, and I squinted at the high ceilings.

A scuff on the cement behind me prickled the hairs on the back of my neck, and I twisted in time to see a shadow shrinking

48

down a hallway. Either the woman had slipped off her heels, or we weren't the only people in the building.

The sound of my own nervous breathing filled the silence that followed, and I tried to calm my heart as I visually dissected the freshly lit space. A desk was sandwiched between two tool chests against the wall, and I padded over for a closer look.

Invoices, food wrappers, and half-crushed soda cans cluttered the surface. I studied the contents without touching any of the grimy papers, then followed the pile of junk to the poster of a woman tacked to the wall.

Was the guy who hung this inappropriate picture here tonight? Was it his shoes that scuffed the cement floor after the lights came on?

That was not a man I wanted to meet.

I dragged my phone from my pocket and sent a text to Jace, letting her know where I was, and another to Andrei. I would come back during the day, when it was safer, and talk to Dorina then.

Need that quick getaway. I gave Andrei the name of the business, and since he wouldn't recognize the number, I added reluctantly, *From the little investigator.*

A man's hushed voice drifted down the hall and through the cavernous space. "I put up with a lot because we're family, but you can't keep bringing your trouble here. What am I supposed to do with that little white girl in my garage?"

My thumb stilled on the keypad of my phone as the man's question registered. What was he supposed to *do* with me?

"You don't need to worry about her," a female voice replied—the same one that had invited me inside. "She won't be here long. I'm gonna have someone come get her."

Their conversation tripped a warning in the back of my mind. "Girl gonna get herself snatched up and tricked out," Beatrice had said.

My gaze darted to the door. I had no way of knowing how long it would take for Andrei to return, but it was time to cut my losses and leave now.

I tucked my phone into my pocket and scampered to the glass door. I gripped the dead bolt, but before I could twist it, a bald man with a thick neck strutted into view. As he lifted a hand to press a shrinking cigarette between his lips, I noticed the tattoos on his fingers.

Spike.

He paused to observe one of the girls flirting with a driver, then flicked away the smoldering nub of his cigarette, grinding it into the sidewalk with a boot. He glanced toward the shop, noticing me, and I stiffened.

Even without Tandi's warnings, one look at this man would've told me I didn't want to be alone with him long enough to ask a question.

"Don't tell me this isn't your problem. If something happens to her on this street, it is *all* of our problem, Clayton," the woman said, her voice reminding me that I needed to find another exit.

I backed away from the front door and searched the garage for options. Three rolling doors opened onto the street, but they would dump me out too close to Spike, who seemed to be in no hurry to move on. Going out the back would likely lead into an equally dangerous alley.

How do I get myself into these situations?

If I couldn't find a safe exit, I was going to have to hide and call one of the guys. That was my absolute last resort. I had gotten myself into this mess, and there had to be a way to get myself out of it.

"You might not remember what happened last spring, but I do," the woman said, her voice fading as I made my way to the back of the garage and squinted through a grimy window into the alley.

There were no visible threats.

Maybe I could crawl out the window and sneak around the side of the building to wait for my ride. I unlocked the window and wiggled it up, but the moment I released it, it dropped like a guillotine. I hissed in a breath, catching it before it could slam and crack the glass.

"The cops were all over the streets, shoving pictures in people's faces," the woman continued. "Harassing us for information about that pretty red-haired girl who got taken. You ended up in lockup for being drunk with an attitude."

Surprise washed over me along with the cool night air. That was why she stared at me so long after she opened the door; she recognized me.

"I remember. You're saying that girl in my garage is . . ." The man trailed off, and when he spoke again, doubt tinged his voice. "Are you sure?"

"You know I remember faces. It helps that hers was plastered all over the media a few months ago. I don't remember the specifics, but she's got some sort of connection to the cops."

"What do you mean *connection*?"

"The boys in blue don't get that worked up over a missing woman in this city unless she's some kinda important. Like family."

"And you brought her into my shop? Are you crazy?!" he demanded, his volume rising with fear. "What if her blue-blooded father or brother kicks down my door, searching for her again? One look at me and they'll assume I kidnapped her. Then it's off to prison. Clayton behind bars. Already has a TV movie ring to it."

"Calm down. She'll be gone soon enough. The cops won't have any reason to come looking here. I'm gonna go deal with her, and then we need to make sure that car doesn't come around again. I can't be a hundred percent certain it's the same one as last night, but until I know, I don't want any of my girls getting into it."

My girls. The faces of the women I passed on the street flashed through my mind. Did some of them work for her?

Footsteps echoed down the hallway, each clack of high heels tightening the tension in my spine. If this woman made a living selling human beings, then I needed to tread carefully.

She entered the garage bay, pausing when she spotted me by the window. "I wouldn't go out that way. You won't like what you find at this hour."

I settled the window back into place. There was no squeezing out of something that wouldn't stay open anyway.

"Coffee?" She offered me one of the two mismatched mugs she carried. "It's decaf, since I assume you prefer to sleep at night."

I shook my head.

She set the second mug on the tool chest and leaned against the desk. "I think it's time we call you a ride."

I rolled the pepper spray in my sweaty hand. I wasn't getting into any vehicle she called. "My cab will be here soon. And my friends know where I am."

"They're not very good friends if they let you come here alone. Most people navigate this street fine, and most of the johns are decent enough, but there are dangerous people here looking for easy prey. And here you are, wandering around like a lost and frightened little lamb."

"I'm not lost. I'm looking for Dorina."

She considered me. "And how would a nice girl like you know that name?"

"Someone mentioned it."

"And which one of the girls is passing my name around to anyone who asks?" Her tone was saccharin sweet, but irritation glinted in her dark eyes.

I withheld Pixie's name for her protection and demanded, "How many of them are you forcing to work for you?"

Sure, accuse her of being a pimp outright. That's treading carefully.

She wrapped both hands around her mug, manicured nails clinking against the handle. "What makes you think I'm forcing anyone to do anything?"

"You said 'my girls.'"

"Ah, and now you think I might've slipped a roofie into your coffee so I could transport you to some sort of brothel." She nodded in understanding, and when she spoke again, there was a note of sadness in her voice. "It does happen, more than you might think, but never here. I don't bring girls into this life. I only help them survive it."

"What do you mean?"

"I've been in this business for longer than some of the girls out there have been alive. When the new ones show up, clueless and desperate, I offer to teach them the basics of survival. Skills I had to learn the hard way."

She tugged aside the collar of her blouse, revealing a long, faded scar on her shoulder. My hand went to my stomach, where I bore three similar scars. From a knife.

"Always be alert for weapons. Always know your exits. Don't get in a vehicle with more than one man, and never let him take you anywhere you're not familiar with," she said.

"What happens when something goes wrong?"

"Something *will* go wrong eventually. It's unavoidable. Most of these women have been attacked with a knife, beaten, or assaulted by a john at some point. Surviving with as few injuries as possible is the goal."

Nausea rolled through my stomach as Pixie's parting words rang through my mind: *Safe is for the rich. I just try to make it home in the morning.*

What a heartbreaking way to live.

"Now," Dorina said, taking a sip of her coffee. "Who gave you my name, and why?"

Pixie seemed to trust this woman and must've known I would speak with her, so withholding her name likely wouldn't help anyone.

"Pixie." I retrieved the folded picture from my sweatshirt pouch and crossed the room to show it to her. "She gave me this."

Long lashes feathered Dorina's round cheeks as she looked at the image, and a sigh slipped from between her red lips. "This is about Cami."

"She's worried about her, and I wanna help."

"If you wanna help, then do Pixie a kindness and don't give her false hope."

"I'm not trying to give her false hope."

"Girls who get taken from places like this end up dead and dumped like trash. We all lose a friend out here eventually. It's hard, but it's life. We move on."

"But—"

"She's gone, and she's not coming back. There's no point in trying to find her."

Frustration sharpened my voice. "You don't know she's dead. If someone will tell me what happened, I might be able to find her before . . ."

Before what, my mind offered in challenge. *Before something bad happens to her?*

Unspeakable things had happened to me within an hour of my abduction, and Cami had been missing for almost a day.

"Is there a chance she got out of that car somewhere else and went home to her family, or maybe ran away because she wanted out of this life?" I asked, reluctant to abandon the hope that she was somewhere safe.

"Cami adores Pixie, follows her around like one of those baby ducks. She would never abandon her."

My hope deflated. "Then please, help me find her. I heard you talking back there. You know my story, which means you know that sometimes the girl gets found before it's too late. All it takes is for people to care enough to try to find her. I know I'm only one person, and I don't have the power of law enforcement to search every street, but I care."

She stared at me for a long second before saying, "I believe you mean that." She set aside her coffee and folded her arms. "There's not much I can tell you, unfortunately. A fancy car like that one pulled up, and Cami got in. That might've been the same man in the passenger seat, but I was too far away to see him clearly last night. I know he had the same entitled, rich-boy attitude. They think they can get away with anything, and they usually do."

"I don't suppose you saw the license plate."

"I don't remember details like that. People are my business."

I tried to mask my disappointment, even though I expected her answer. "Were there a lot of guys in the car Cami got into?"

"Only one. Otherwise, she wouldn't have gotten in. Cami was young, but she wasn't a fool."

Dorina's use of the past tense drove home the point that she thought it was too late and that I was wasting my time trying to find a girl who was already dead.

"The guys tonight, have you seen them around before?" I asked. "Do they come by at regular times?"

If I could anticipate when they would return, I could be ready to record the license plate. Finding someone to run it who wouldn't ask me a bunch of questions would be an issue, though.

"They come around from time to time, but they never come knocking on my door, so I can't say when or how often they drop in. I have my own schedule to keep." Dorina checked the clock on the shop wall. "Speaking of schedules, I have a widower in need of company arriving in five minutes. How long until your cab gets here?"

"Any minute. But can you tell me anything more about Cami before I leave? Where she lives, anyone she might've had problems with, how to get a hold of her family?"

Dorina fixed a piece of hair that slipped free from the knot on top of her head. "When Cami first showed up a couple of years ago, she had a pimp who housed her and some of the other girls. She has her own place now."

"Do you have the address?"

A cab pulled up outside, and I caught a glimpse of Andrei straining to see the sign on the building. Dorina grabbed a pen and paper from the desk and wrote down the address, tearing it off the corner of a bill.

She offered it to me, but jerked it out of my reach when I grabbed for it. "Don't come back here. It's not safe, and I won't save you twice."

Her statement removed any misperception that she helped me because she cared about my well-being. She intervened because she wanted to protect herself and her family member's business from police complications. Nothing more.

"I'll try to bring someone if I have to come back," I assured her.

She handed me the address. "For all the good it will do. She won't be there."

"One more thing. Did Pixie show up tonight? She left the agency on foot about two hours ago, and I thought I might find her here, to ask her some more questions."

"I haven't seen her tonight, but that doesn't mean much. She's usually pretty busy."

Worry gnawed at me as I folded the slip of paper and tucked it into my sweatshirt. "Okay, thanks."

I checked the sidewalk for Spike before pushing open the door and dashing to my cab. I slumped in the seat and locked the door, ready to be anywhere but here.

9

*T*he cab slowed to a stop along the curb outside the apartments. My home was considered part of the apartment complex, but it sat alone twenty feet from the brick tower where the other tenants lived.

Most of the structure was underground, leaving the windows at ground level, but the builders fashioned a set of steps that descended to my recessed front door, where my patio light blazed in the night.

My fingers stilled on the rear door handle when I spotted a familiar figure seated on the steps leading up to the main building.

My hesitation drew Andrei around in his seat. "If he is problem, I will walk you to your door." The keys in the ignition jingled as he prepared to turn off the engine.

"I appreciate that, but he's a friend."

There was only one reason Jordan would be sitting there. My eyes drifted upward to the tenth-story window framed by decorative blue lights. The sheer curtains swished, and a face ducked out of view.

Jace had snitched on me.

She hadn't responded to any of my messages, so I assumed she hadn't read them yet. I should've known better. Her phone was an extension of her being, and she would've read the messages the moment she took a water break during the game.

She could've at least sent me a courtesy text that said something like, *I tattled. Brace yourself for unhappy visitors.*

Steeling myself, I tugged the handle to open the door and climbed out of the cab. A utility van breezed by on a mission, whipping a few loose strands of hair into my face, and I tucked them behind my ears.

Jordan took me in from a distance, and his stiff posture relaxed, his head dipping between his shoulders in relief. How long had he been sitting in the cold, waiting for me to come home?

I slung my bag strap over one shoulder and started for the main building. I trudged up the steps and sank down beside Jordan, letting my bag slide to rest between my feet.

A puff of steam left his mouth, and he watched the yellow taxi disappear down the street. "I'll take a cab home. That's what you said in your text. Was that before or after you took a cab to this Brushwick Avenue?"

I puckered my lips between my teeth. I was a grown woman, and I didn't owe him an explanation for what I did in my personal time, but I felt guilty for withholding my true intentions when I sent him that message. "I came home first, and then I went to Brushwick."

He shook his head and lifted his eyes to the cloudy night sky. "I'm not a New York City native, and even I know certain streets aren't safe after dark, especially for a woman."

I didn't suppose now would be a good time for show and tell: *Look, I had a map, pepper spray,* and *a box cutter, so I was perfectly safe.*

Except no one was perfectly safe on a street where people were bought and sold, a place where human decency and respect were scarcer than sunshine in a rainstorm.

"Jace told you about the text messages?" I asked.

"The game ended early, she told Sam as soon as she read them, and he called me. You have no idea how hard it was to sit here and wait to see if you would make it home all right." Jordan looked me over again, more thoroughly this time. "*Are* you all right?"

I tugged the sleeves of my sweatshirt over my fingers and nodded, but I couldn't shake the unsettled feeling that place left in my spirit.

"Holly," he said, the gentleness of his voice drawing my gaze to him, "I can tell something's wrong."

What *wasn't* wrong? A teenage girl surviving as a prostitute was missing, women and girls were selling their bodies because they were imprisoned by lies, threats, and false beliefs, and men with everything to lose were trapped in a cycle of corrosive desire.

"There were so many men there, Jordan, and so many girls."

He released a long breath, the steam dissipating as silence stretched. "The first time I encountered prostitution was during college, when one of my friends brought a prostitute to our room to celebrate passing finals."

A knot tightened in my stomach.

"Her body language said one thing, but her eyes said something else. We were criminal justice majors, learning how to spot those kinds of discrepancies. I asked Ethan how he couldn't see it, but then I realized he didn't *want* to see it. That girl didn't wanna be doing what she was doing."

"What happened?"

"Ethan and I got into an argument. We had no choice but to room together, but we didn't speak to each other for months." He rubbed his cold hands together. "A man who buys a woman isn't a man, in my opinion, and I didn't hesitate to share that opinion. He was acting like an impulsive boy, only thinking about what made him feel better. Unfortunately, the world is full of boys who grow old but never grow up."

"What happened to the girl?"

"I asked her if she needed help, she said no. I was too young to know what to do at that point, so I accepted her answer at face value and moved on."

"You said something, you asked. That's more than most people would do." I paused before adding, "And thanks for not being one of those boys."

He smiled. "I would rather earn the love and affection of an amazing woman."

"Your mom made you do chores for hugs and kisses, didn't she?"

He laughed. "I am definitely not talking about my mom, who would stand outside with a Free Hugs sign if Dad would let her."

Mrs. Radcliffe was one of those people who was sweet-natured and quick to love, and she always had a hug for me when I was a child.

Jordan's amusement faded. "Should I even ask why you went to Brushwick?"

"You can ask, but I don't think the explanation is gonna make you feel any better."

"I'm listening."

I tugged the folded picture from my pouch and handed it to him, tapping a finger on Cami's face. "She's been missing for almost twenty-four hours." I relayed what little information I had and waited for his response.

"You . . ." He pressed his lips together and rubbed at his temple, visibly trying to temper whatever words wanted to come out of his mouth. "This teenage girl disappeared from Brushwick, likely kidnapped, and you went there alone to chat up pimps, drug dealers, and potential kidnappers."

It sounded really bad when he said it like that.

I sucked on the inside of my cheek for a long second before confessing, "Yes, but it's what you would've done."

"You really think that's a fair comparison? I have law enforcement experience, martial arts training, a gun, an extra eighty pounds, and eleven more inches to work with."

"Maybe I was going for discreet."

"Yeah." He dragged out the word as he considered my purple sneakers, pink sweatshirt, and fluffy hat. "I'm sure you fit right in." He returned his attention to the photo. "Who came by to tell you this girl is missing?"

"A friend . . . slash coworker."

He ran a hand over his hair. "I don't like this, Holly. Prostitution can be a dangerous thing to get involved in, and when I offered you this job, I promised Marx I wouldn't send you to interview any pimps."

"You didn't send me. It was my choice."

"I don't think he's gonna see it that way." He stared at the two girls in the worn photo. "She's so young. She shouldn't be anywhere near that street." After a moment he released a long breath. "Okay. If you can hold off on any more death-defying trips tonight, we'll dig deeper into this tomorrow."

"Really?"

"I know you well enough to recognize when no amount of reason or logic will make you hit the brakes, and I'm not letting you investigate something like this alone. Aside from the fact that it's rife with risk, you have a tendency to attract weirdos."

My eyebrows arched in amusement, and he sighed as his own words registered.

"I just insulted myself, didn't I?"

I grinned. "Yep."

Air swished as one of the glass doors behind us opened, and Sam pushed out onto the landing. His dark, expressionless eyes scanned me, and if I didn't know his feelings for me were strictly brotherly, it would've made me uncomfortable.

"Do we need to arrest anyone?"

"No. Miraculously, she's fine," Jordan said.

"Good." Sam turned to go back inside, then reconsidered, pinning me with a look that made me squirm on my step. "The next time you run off to a dangerous part of the city where you're at risk of being assaulted, abducted, or killed . . ."

61

I braced myself for the painful conclusion of his statement.

"We're not waiting to come get you."

It took a moment for his words to register, and then my defenses crumbled. "I thought you were gonna say I'm on my own."

"You're never on your own anymore."

And with that statement, delivered as an unquestionable fact, my stoic friend disappeared back into the building.

My heart overflowed. "He was almost warm and fuzzy there for a second."

"Yeah, he's warm and fuzzy now. You should've seen him when I told him we shouldn't go after you right away. I thought he was gonna bulldoze through me."

"Why did you decide to wait?"

"I don't ever want you to feel like I'm trying to control your decisions. Even if they are bad ones." He cast me a displeased glance to make sure I knew his thoughts on my latest decision. "But in all honesty, you had about three more minutes to get home safe, or Sam and I were coming there to *bring* you home safe. And on that note . . ." He rose and offered his hand to me. "Permission to cross the border and escort you home, milady."

There was a time when the thought of his touch terrified me, and I kept him at arm's length, but over the past year, the invisible boundary between us had become more flexible, allowing for moments like this.

I placed my fingers in his palm and let him help me to my feet. The moment I found my balance, he released me.

"I can cover those twenty feet on my own, you know," I said, scooping my bag off the step.

"It's dark and treacherous. You could get lost on the way to your door."

His playfulness brought a smile to my lips. "I could get intercepted by sinister ninjas in the shadows."

"Or garden gnomes."

I shuddered at the creepy painted gnomes people peppered around their flower beds and porches. Some of their maniacal smiles made them look like miniature serial killers with garden spades.

"That reminds me, where did you find Mrs. Muriel, if not the ceramics place or the bakery?" I asked, falling in step beside him.

"The cemetery."

"The one where her husband's buried?"

"Yeah. She was standing by his grave, confused about why his name was on a gravestone when he was supposed to be fighting in the war." A pinch of sadness formed between his brows. "When I approached her, she thought I was her husband. She told me I shouldn't play such mean pranks."

"What did you do?"

"What *could* I do? She was already so upset and confused. Trying to explain a reality that didn't match hers would only hurt her. So I took her hand and we strolled back to the car as husband and wife in 1940. And then I drove her home."

The situation must've been awkward for him, but he handled the old woman's confusion with patience and grace.

"You have a very kind heart, Jordan Radcliffe."

"If I do, it's only because you're rubbing off on me."

"I don't think I'm the best example to follow. I've got a bit of a criminal history."

"Oh yeah? Like what?"

"I stole a Bible once."

He laughed. "Something tells me you're gonna get a pardon for that one."

"I break into Marx's apartment once or twice a week."

"It's technically not breaking in when you have a key, the alarm code, and an open invitation. Although, when he told you to come visit every week, I don't think he meant sneak in while he's at work and play pranks on him."

"Then he should've been more specific."

"I'm afraid to imagine what you would do to my apartment if you had an open invitation and a key."

"There's nothing in your apartment to do anything *with*." His living space was practically a barren wasteland.

"I'll have you know, I bought a toaster, and it even matches the can opener in the drawer."

He sounded so proud of his ability to coordinate kitchenware that I couldn't help but laugh. Nothing in my kitchen matched, not even the silverware.

I retrieved my keys as we descended the steps onto my patio. "Thanks for walking me home and keeping me safe from the garden gnomes."

"Always."

He lowered his eyes before I could see the longing in them, but I knew it was there. It was always there when he walked me to my door—a desire for something more than a brisk "good night."

He never voiced or acted on that desire, and on nights like tonight, when it seemed to burn a little hotter, he afforded me more space.

Stuffing his hands into his pockets, he stepped to the edge of my patio. "I'll hang out until you're inside with the doors locked. Say hello to little J for me."

I smiled. It amused Jordan that even though I had forgotten him for most of my life, I had named my blue-eyed cat after him. "I'm actually calling him Sausage now because it's less confusing."

"Sounds more confusing for him."

"He responds to my voice, not a name, and Sausage suits him."

"When you subconsciously named him after me, he was trim and agile, right? That was before he puffed out like a jumbo marshmallow."

That startled a laugh out of me. "He was actually skin and bones and really unfriendly, if that makes you feel any better."

Movement in the corner of my vision drew my attention to a figure in the shadows near the main building. He watched us as he thrust a shovel into the ground and slammed a booted foot against it.

Jordan's demeanor shifted from relaxed to guarded when he heard the man's foot strike the metal, and he zeroed in on the sound. "Who's that?"

"The maintenance man and groundskeeper."

"What's he doing here this late at night?"

"He always works nights. Unless someone has something that needs fixed during the day. He doesn't . . . people well." I tried not to judge, but the way he crept around the property at night could be disconcerting. I kept my distance from him when I took Riley out after dark.

"When did he start working here?"

"Sometime while I was staying with Marx."

The man thrust the shovel into the soil of the flower bed again, his attention fixed on us. Judging by how deep he was digging, he was either planting a bush or burying a body. Or planting a bush *over* a body.

"I think we should get you inside," Jordan suggested.

Riley's tail thumped the interior wall, and he whined with impatient excitement as I unlocked the dead bolts. Hand on the knob, I turned back to Jordan. "I'll see you after my appointment tomorrow."

"Sounds good."

I retreated into my small but cozy apartment and relocked the door. My knapsack slid to the floor, and I sagged against the counter. My energy reserves were depleted, but before I could climb into bed, I needed to record my notes for the evening and take a shower.

After documenting the information I gathered tonight, I hopped in the shower. I scrubbed away the sorrow and hopelessness of Brushwick Avenue that clung to me as heavily as

Cindy's cigarette smoke, and then I crawled beneath the blankets with my journal.

Cracking it open, I pressed my purple pen to the blank page, the ink stain growing as I searched my heart for gratitude. Most days, gratitude came easily, but on nights like tonight, after what I'd seen on Brushwick, I had to peel back layers of heartache and disappointment to find it.

Dear Jesus,

> *Thank you for always being there for me when I was desperate and scared, for always making a way and offering me hope so my desperation didn't drive me to a path similar to Tandi's.*

Remembering Sam's unexpected comment on the steps, I added,

> *And thank you for bringing genuine and beautiful friendships into my life. They make everything better.*

10

Sunrise brightened the horizon as Riley and I jogged our usual route through the still-slumbering city, past dark shop windows and across empty streets.

Anxiety from last night's haunting dream seeped from my pores and beaded my skin as I pushed myself, determined to sweat out every drop.

Most of the dream's details faded after I woke up, but I remembered enough. A shadowy figure had lunged out of the line of cars on Brushwick and chased me into an abandoned warehouse with a stone block room, and that was where the unpleasant dream twisted into a familiar night terror.

No matter how they began, my nightmares always took me back to that room.

My screams had roused Riley, and he licked at my face, startling me awake a second before the metal door could slam shut and trap me in that torturous prison.

Another early riser pounded the pavement in our direction, the pulse of loud music seeping from the large headphones beneath his hood. Riley let out a warning growl, and I wound his leash around my hand a few more times to reel him in as we stepped into the grass to give the man the right-of-way.

To my dismay the jogger plodded to a stop beside us rather than taking advantage of the open walkway, and I drew Riley even closer to my side.

The man flipped back his hood and slid the headphones from his ears, breath puffing from his mouth. "Holly, hey. It's been a while."

His face was familiar, but his name escaped me. It started with . . . a consonant. Yep, that narrowed it down. "Hi," I said, not bothering to hide my uncertainty.

"Luke," he offered.

The memories came trickling back—the jogger who used to try to catch up with me, the man who sent a muffin to my table at the café Jace and I used to frequent, the paramedic who tended to me at my apartment.

"Sorry, I'm bad with names."

He flashed a blindingly white smile. *That* I remembered. He could be a poster boy for whitening toothpaste.

"It's okay. The last time we saw each other, you had a severe concussion, and I think you were seeing two of me."

He had witnessed the unfortunate aftereffects of the roofie Edward slipped into my fruit punch. I didn't remember everything, but what I did remember made me want to shrink between the sidewalk slabs in embarrassment. "That wasn't my best day."

"I tried to come check on you after I dropped you at the hospital, but your detective friend kicked me to the curb."

That sounded like something Marx would do. "He's protective."

"And who's this handsome fellow?" Luke crouched and stretched a hand toward Riley.

"Um, I wouldn't do that. He's protective too." I doubted Riley would bite him without provocation, but I didn't want to take the chance.

Luke dropped his hand and stood. "Thanks for the warning." He scratched at the skin around his fitness band. "There's something that's been on my mind since I saw you on the news a few months back."

My fingers tightened apprehensively around Riley's leash. "Oh?"

"That day in your apartment, when I was buckling you to the gurney, you said something I haven't been able to forget. You said,

68

'Nobody ever comes when Collin hurts me.' That guy who kidnapped you a year ago, is that the one you were talking about?"

I looked down at my sneakers, focusing on the unevenly tied laces, as I nodded.

"I'm glad he's finally where he belongs, but I'm sorry it wasn't soon enough," Luke said. "You didn't deserve to go through any of that."

No one deserved to go through that. It wasn't an experience I would wish on the worst human beings I knew.

"Don't take this as me flirting, because that's not my intention, but you're an incredible woman, Holly. And I don't just mean the fact that you seem to have more lives than a cat. Not many women find the courage to stand up and confront the men who hurt them, and the day you walked into the courtroom despite what happened on the front steps . . . I think you became a hero to a lot of women."

I fidgeted at the praise. I didn't think of myself as a hero, and I certainly didn't feel like one. Paramedics like him were more deserving of that title.

"I'll let you get back to your run," he said. "And if you ever decide you're craving a muffin, catch up with me and let me know."

"Before you go, can I ask you something about your work?"

He paused with his fingers on his headphones. "Sure."

"On any of your ambulance runs the past couple of days, have you picked up a teenage girl? Pretty, with a mixture of black and Asian features."

"No, why?"

"She's missing. My friend Jordan and I are trying to find her."

Concern pulled at the corners of his mouth. "I'll ask around. If I find out something, or even if I find out nothing, I'll let you know. I suggest checking the hospitals too, in case someone drove her there in a personal vehicle."

"Thanks." I rubbed Riley's head as Luke flipped up his hood and jogged away. That had been a surprisingly normal and pleasant interaction with a man I barely knew.

Maybe my therapist was right, and I was making more progress than I realized. Her advice to do something I had been longing to do drifted through my mind, and I checked the time on my phone. After this exhausting run, I knew exactly what I wanted to do.

. . . .

I sprawled in the grass outside my apartment, coolness against my back while the intermittent sunlight warmed my face and set my eyelids aglow.

I stretched my arms further out at my sides and released a contented sigh. I hadn't lain outside like this since I was a little girl. Collin had awakened my awareness of the evils in the world, and relaxing out in the open with my eyes closed and music in my ears would've left me too vulnerable to attack.

But my monster was trapped behind bars now, and I didn't have to spend every moment on guard, wondering when I would have to run for my life.

I could sink into the moment with every fiber of my being—the crisp morning air, the sweet scent of flowers, the breeze stirring the baby hairs that curled wildly beside my ears. I dug my fingers into the cool bed of grass, a smile on my lips. Was this what freedom felt like?

Dear Jesus, today I'm grateful just to be able to lie in the grass.

Soon, spring would melt seamlessly into summer, and then I could lie in the *warm* grass and get a tan. Okay, maybe that was an unrealistic hope, considering fifteen minutes in the sun turned my skin from porcelain to fried tomato.

Coldness stretched across my body, and my eyelids snapped open. A silhouetted figure blocked the sun. I yanked the earbuds from my ears, but before I could draw my legs up and scramble away from the potential threat, a familiar Southern voice quieted my fear.

"It's only me, sweet pea."

I dropped my head back to the ground with a shaky exhale and pressed the earbuds to my chest, the worship song vibrating through my rib cage. "Hi."

Marx crouched beside my head, his features sharpening with his nearness—salt and pepper hair, eyes the color of the grass between my fingers. "Did you fall over?"

"No, I didn't fall over." I wasn't *that* uncoordinated. Usually. "I'm relaxing."

"In the damp grass?"

"I'm sweaty from my run, so I didn't even notice." Or care, to be honest. This moment was . . . wonderful.

Marx studied my face. Could he see the shadows under my eyes from too little sleep or intuit the nightmares that pushed me out of bed before dawn?

As the lines around his eyes deepened with concern, I decided to shift the subject away from the question no doubt forming in his mind. "Why are you dressed for work on a Saturday?"

He was wearing a suit jacket and jeans rather than the plain T-shirts he typically wore on the weekends. As a detective, he was supposed to wear dress slacks, but Marx wasn't one to conform without a fight.

"I have a few interviews to conduct today. I had to work around their busy schedules, which are apparently more important than mine."

"And what brings you by before work?" I asked, feigning innocence even as mischievous anticipation bubbled up.

"A funny thing happened last night. It seems the marshmallow bandit struck again. Left a callin' card on my nightstand." He reached into his jacket pocket and then held up a mini marshmallow between his thumb and forefinger.

I pulled my lips between my teeth to hide a smile. "What did he steal?"

"*She* uncurled my toothpaste container and squished the contents around the tube. I had to squeeze it all back up to the top and reroll it."

"How obnoxious."

A smile twitched across his lips, letting me know he found that unpleasant surprise amusing rather than irritating. "But it didn't stop there." He stretched out in the damp grass, his head next to mine with his legs in the opposite direction. "I opened my kitchen drawer to grab a butter knife for my jelly toast, like I do every mornin', and imagine my surprise when I found the silverware organizer missin'. There were butter knives fraternizin' with the steak knives, spoons bumpin' elbows with the forks."

I tried not to laugh at the scene he painted, but it bubbled out of me. I covered my mouth to keep from disrupting the quiet morning.

"It was complete anarchy." Marx gave me a pointed look. "Where is it?"

My hand slid from my mouth to my chest. "What makes you think I took it?"

He placed the mini marshmallow on the tip of my nose. "Evidence."

I grabbed the marshmallow and popped it into my mouth with a grin. "What evidence? You can't prove a thing."

"I could ask Mrs. Neberkins."

"She didn't even see me."

He chuckled. "And you just placed yourself at the scene of the robbery."

Oh. Oops.

"Don't ever commit a crime. You'll be found out in two sentences," he said. "And there are no miniature marshmallows for snacks in prison."

"That's cruel and unusual punishment."

He smiled. "A good deterrent for your criminal impulses. Now, where's my silverware organizer?"

"Under your bed."

"Mmm. Right where it belongs." The breeze blew a strand of my hair into his face, and he peeled it away. "You know, if you wanted to see me, you could've called."

"Where's the fun in that? Besides, you're moving in with Shannon in a few weeks, and I don't have a key, so I've gotta get all my fun out of the way now."

"What makes you think you're not gonna have a key? It doesn't make sense for you not to have a key when you have a bedroom."

"I have a bedroom in the house?"

"Of course." He pulled something from his pants pocket, and light glinted off the metal key. "All of your things from my apartment will go into your room at the house. That way if you ever feel lonely or you're havin' a rough night, you can come over."

I bit my bottom lip as emotion swelled. Sometimes it was hard to wrap my mind around how much he seemed to love me. I hesitantly took the key. "Are you sure Shannon's okay with this?"

"She suggested it before I could."

"Why? She doesn't owe me anything, and we're not exactly close." We'd barely spoken to each other since the trial concluded in January.

"There's somethin' you need to understand about Shannon. She grew up in a dysfunctional household. There wasn't a lot of love, and she doesn't attach to people very easily. Apart from her friend in law school, you and I are the only ones who've managed to breach the walls she still hides behind. But I know for a fact she adores you."

I folded my fingers over the key. "Really?"

"Mmm hmm. She's not very demonstrative, most likely because nobody ever showed her how to be, but she cares very deeply for you."

I crinkled my nose in confusion. "She's not what?"

"Demonstrative. It means openly affectionate."

I narrowed my eyes in skepticism. "I think you made that word up."

"If you don't believe me, look it up in your dictionary. D-e-m." He pushed up onto his elbows. "I gotta get to work. They don't pay me to lie around in the grass and watch the clouds roll by. What are your plans this mornin'?"

"I have a meeting with my photography clients around eight fifteen at Jumping Bean Café. Hopefully, they'll buy the pictures." I *needed* them to buy the flash drive of pictures.

"I have no doubt they will." Marx pressed a kiss to my forehead. "Love you, peanut."

"Love you too. Thanks for coming to visit."

"Don't stay out too long. Rain's comin'."

Gray stretched across the sky in the distance, sweeping closer with every second. Spring was in full swing.

I turned the unfamiliar key over between my fingers after Marx's car pulled away from the curb, still uncertain about how pleased Shannon would be with me having it. I wouldn't be surprised if she made a copy for me simply to appease the man she loved.

Pushing to my feet, I dusted grass clippings from my clothes and went inside to fetch the fat dictionary from my bookshelf. I flipped through the pages.

"D-e-m." I slid my finger down the alphabetical list, searching for Marx's make-believe word. "D-e . . ." My finger stilled. "Openly showing feelings, particularly affectionate. Huh."

It was a word.

I closed the dictionary and returned it to the shelf. I needed to clean up before my meeting and put on something more professional than my shenanigans sweatshirt.

I showered and changed, then grabbed my knapsack with sample photos, my laptop, and my driving book, and slung it over my shoulder. I kissed Riley on the head.

"I'll be back for you later."

I scratched Sausage between his ears, and he slanted a glare my way, still bitter that I had brought home another furry housemate. My cat held on to a grudge tighter than Scrooge held on to shiny coins.

"There's gotta be forgiveness stored away in those squishy layers somewhere. Maybe under the chin?" I rubbed his favorite spot. His head lifted to allow better access, and a purr rumbled through his chest.

Ah, the sound of momentary forgiveness.

It was a start. I poked his adorable pink nose and then hurried out the door.

. . . .

Ordinarily, I walked to the café, but I couldn't tote my laptop and book that distance in the drizzle that had broken out.

I lifted my eyes from the driver's manual in my lap as the bus doors hissed open at another stop, and passengers flowed both ways.

A man dropped into the vacant seat by the doors. He was around my age, with brown eyes and an oddly round face for someone as trim as he appeared to be.

He smiled at me with obvious interest, and I jerked my attention back to my studies. I failed my driver's test last week, but really, how was I supposed to know I was driving the wrong way down a one-way street? And who wouldn't shriek and swerve all over the road to avoid the truck coming straight at them?

I scared ten years off my instructor, and her voice was a shrill squeak when she demanded, "Didn't you see the sign?!"

There were so many signs in New York City. Who could pay attention to them all? That explanation got me booted from the driver's seat. A bit of an overreaction, in my opinion, but she wasn't open to negotiation.

I doubted reviewing the book content again would help matters. I closed it with a sigh.

Buying a car wasn't in my budget, but getting my license wasn't really about the independence of driving myself. It was about achieving a milestone my foster brother had stolen from me, like graduating from high school or going to prom.

I was *going* to get my license, and then I was going to get my GED. The bus rocked under the weight of more boarding passengers, and I caught the round-faced man watching me.

"I couldn't help but notice your book on driving," he said, as if my passing glance was the invitation he'd been waiting for. "Not a fan of public transportation?"

I shrugged. "It's fine." Until someone decided to make things awkward by breaking the unwritten rule of keep-to-yourself.

"I actually like taking the bus," he said, leaning forward. "Everyone's so busy in this city, so focused on being somewhere else. Sometimes I ride around just to meet new people."

The way he assessed my ringless left hand suggested he rode around on the bus to meet single women.

I should've walked. Sure, I had run six miles this morning, and the rain was steadily increasing to a downpour, but it would be better than the messy destination this conversation was hurdling toward.

"My name's Cole."

"Hi," I replied, stuffing my book into my bag and squinting out the window to catch the name of the street we passed. The bus was traveling in slow motion today.

"Do you usually ride at this time?"

"No, my schedule's pretty irregular." I picked at a stain on the fabric of my bag. Was that salsa? It was probably salsa.

"When you have time, maybe I could take you out for coffee," he offered.

Little did he know I was headed to a coffee shop right now. I certainly wasn't going to volunteer that information.

"How about I text you and we can set something up?" Cole grabbed his phone from his jeans pocket, thumbs poised over the wide screen. "What's your name and number?"

I didn't want to give him either piece of information and encourage his interest, but I didn't want to hurt his feelings either.

"I don't . . . I mean, I'm not . . ."

My therapist's advice drifted through my mind as I struggled for a response: *It's okay to be assertive to rebuff unwanted advances. You can be honest without being unkind, but do not put yourself in an uncomfortable or unsafe situation to spare his feelings.*

"I'm not . . . looking for a relationship," I managed to squeeze out, hoping the words were kind but assertive enough to convey my lack of interest.

Disappointment and defeat rippled over his features, and he muttered, "Figures." He dropped back in his seat with a scowl, his attention on his phone screen.

The dramatic shift in his mood and manner caught me off guard, and an apology sprang to my lips, but I bit my tongue. I didn't want to give him the impression that there was a chance.

The bus hissed to a stop at my drop-off, which was down the street from the café, and the doors folded open.

Thank goodness. I tugged my hat down to shield more of my hair from the rain, double-checked that the flap of my bag would keep my laptop dry, and exited the bus. A fat droplet of icy rain splashed on my nose as my sneakers hit the sidewalk.

Spotting the cute elderly couple hiding from the rain beneath the café awning, I sprinted down the sidewalk to join them.

11

I folded the check from my photography clients and tucked it into the side pocket of my knapsack. The amount would cover the rest of my rent for the month, but there wouldn't be much left for groceries.

I wasn't out of food yet, but if I waited until my next paycheck to go shopping, I would be slathering saltine crackers with ketchup and topping them with pickle slices for dinner.

I opened my laptop and used the café's wireless internet to search for nearby food pantries. Two of the ones I went to before moving in with Marx were still around, but the third had closed its doors. I recorded the dates, times, and locations in my notebook.

A woman bumped my table on the way to the door and muttered an apology around the straw of her iced beverage.

There were too many people crammed into this small café on a Saturday morning, jostling each other with overstuffed purses and elbows.

For most of these people, Jumping Bean Café was a pit stop on the way to weekend adventures, and they would leave as soon as their caffeine fix was warming their fingers.

A well-dressed man knocked into a skinny kid rising from a nearby chair and didn't bother to apologize. The boy stumbled off balance into his table, and his coffee tipped off the edge, along with the rest of his belongings.

I glared after the retreating man's back—there was no excuse for rudeness—and rose to help the flustered boy gather his things. With his youthful features, he couldn't be more than seventeen or eighteen. I expected to find schoolbooks, but as I scooped up the first one, I realized it was a self-help book on social anxiety.

I felt a pang of empathy for him. I understood anxiety all too well, and I doubted this situation was going to help him. "Here."

He gaped at me with shell-shocked eyes as I held out the book. His mouth opened, moving silently before he managed, "You're . . ."

Dreaded anticipation squeezed my insides. *Please don't recognize me from the news.* I wanted to melt back into the masses of the city, another unfamiliar face.

A blush crawled up his neck and infused his cheeks. Whatever he'd intended to say died on his lips as he ducked his head and took the book.

I retrieved his open notebook from the molten pool of coffee, passing it back to him. "I'm sorry that guy was a jerk."

He grimaced. "I'm used to jerks. Pretty girls being nice to me is a twist, though. Usually all they do is laugh at me." The moment the words left his mouth, the red in his cheeks burned even hotter.

And now I felt awkward.

He stood at the same time I did, shuffling his belongings in his arms. "I'm sorry, that was probably one of those thoughts I should've kept to myself. Sometimes I blurt things out. And other times I can't make my tongue say anything at all. I'm trying to . . . I mean, I'm working on fitting in and being more normal."

I glanced at his social anxiety book. "Most of the people who leave an imprint on the world don't do it by fitting in. In my experience, it's okay to be a little abnormal, and it's okay to struggle with things."

"Thanks."

"You're welcome. You might wanna let an employee know about the spilled coffee so no one slips."

I stepped around him and made my way to my table beside the gas fireplace. I sank into the chair closest to the window and resumed my search for food pantries. There was a new one at a Baptist church two miles from my apartment, and it was open from noon to two today.

"Morning, Holly."

I stiffened, startled to find a person standing beside my table—a six-foot-tall woman with the build of someone who could throw a full-grown man across the room. "Oh hey, Zoey."

She was the barista who had been making my drink every Wednesday and Saturday morning for the past six months, and while we didn't know each other well enough to be friends, I liked her.

She smiled, two diamond studs emphasizing the natural dimples in her cheeks. "I know you get jittery trying to make your way through all the people, so I figured I would bring this to you instead of calling you to the counter."

She set a covered mug on the table, the scent of sweet chocolate and vanilla wafting from the hole in the lid.

"I appreciate that, but I didn't order it."

I couldn't afford to order it.

"Someone called in, requested your usual, and paid over the phone. He asked me to make sure you got it."

Wariness curled around my spine. "Did he leave a name?" The last thing I needed or wanted was a mysterious admirer who knew my habits and preferences.

"Name on the credit card receipt was Richard Marx, and he said to tell you that either way, you're a great photographer."

My spine relaxed, and I smiled. I couldn't put into words how much Marx's thoughtfulness meant to me. I wrapped my fingers around the warm mug. "Thank you."

"Not a problem, hon." She jerked her chin toward the window behind me. "You got company."

The door opened, and chilly, damp air swirled around me. A familiar voice muttered a thank-you, and then Jace wheeled into the café.

Zoey flashed a diamond-studded grin and raised a fist. "Morning, Hot Wheels."

81

Jace tapped her waiting fist with her own. "What's up, Dimple Pierce?"

"Zo!" one of the other employees called from behind the busy counter. "We're getting behind on orders."

"Sounds like they need a bit of my coffee magic." Zoey winked and then excused herself.

Jace rolled up to the table with an exaggerated shiver. "I think this might be the coldest April in the history of ever. Feel my fingers. I can't."

She reached toward my neck, and I leaned as far away as possible without falling out of my chair. "Don't touch me with those icicles." I exited out of my internet browser and closed the laptop. "You and Zoey seem to know each other well."

"She comes into the library for science fiction books almost every week. Who knew she was a sci-fi nerd too? She's team Star Trek, though, and obviously, I'm team Star Wars."

"There are teams?"

"There are teams for everything. For example, I'm team coffee bean, and you're team cocoa bean. Different but complementary."

"And you happened to come here for your coffee beans at this hour?"

"Oh no, I schemed. Total schemery, which isn't a word, but it should be. This is your favorite café, and I was hoping you would be here so I could help you with that social media search and maybe talk."

"You could've texted before making the trip."

"It's not that far. Besides, I know you're sorta mad at me, and I didn't want you to bail before I got here. Now . . . espresso. I need like three shots and a blueberry scone stat, or I'm gonna face-plant on this table. It's so early, even God's still in bed."

"It's eight-thirty."

"Yeah, I just said that, but like . . . with more syllables." She eyed the line that was steadily dwindling. "How many toes do you think I would run over if I hopped in line?"

"A lot."

A man gripped the back of Jace's wheelchair as he paused behind a group filing out the door, and she shot him a glare. "Dude, I am not a railing. Hands off the chair."

He snatched his hand away with a muttered apology and hurried out the door after the others.

Irritation tightened Jace's lips as she turned back around. It wasn't the first time she encountered something like that, but she usually took it in stride.

"Is everything okay?"

"Totally. I just hate when people do that. It's not like I would use *his* back as an armrest." She scooted my computer over in front of her. "So about last night."

She opened my laptop and peered over the screen at me as her fingers pecked at the keyboard.

"I know you were mad about me telling Sam where you were. But you're my best friend, and you went somewhere alone at night, someplace shady enough that you wanted someone to know you were there. After I looked up that street's reputation online, I wanted to call everyone. Mission save-Holly-from-traffickers. But I restrained myself and only told Sam. He told Jordan, so that part's not my fault. But you understand, right?"

I traced the Jumping Bean logo on the side of my paper mug with a thumb. "I'm a grown woman, Jace, and I'm allowed to go places without everyone knowing. A heads-up before you snitch next time might be nice."

Her shoulders drooped. "Sometimes you make risky decisions without thinking through everything, Holly. And I know it's because you're following your heart, but your heart is like crazy reckless, and it needs a time-out."

"I'm pretty sure if my heart took a time-out, I would no longer be among the living."

She squinted. "Right, with the whole blood-pumping thing. Forget I said that. Your heart is grounded until someone with a gun can go with you. Now, what's this girl's name?"

"Camilla Chen."

She logged into one of her social media accounts and typed the name into the search bar. "Hello, hundreds of results. Yikes. I can narrow it by location, but there's a chance we'll miss her if she has a different state plugged in, so let's do a broad search. You know what she looks like?"

I placed the picture in front of her.

"Huh, she's only half Chinese, like me. Except my dad's white, and I'm guessing since her last name is Chen, it's her mom who's black. Super jealous of how thick her hair is compared to mine."

She turned the laptop back toward me.

I stared at the list of names and faces that filled the screen. "What do I do now?"

"Look for a match."

"But some of these don't have pictures."

"It's the selfie generation. No way a teenage girl doesn't have pictures of herself. Unless she's weird like you. Poke around while I order the goods."

She wheeled away to run over some toes, and I puffed out a breath, resting my chin on my fist. This could take hours.

I began scrolling through the results. There were a lot of women with the same name, but few had the darker coloring. The features of the girls began to blur as they rolled by, and I almost missed Cami's picture.

Straightening, I backtracked and clicked on the small image. It redirected me to another page with an enlarged version of the headshot. There was no doubt it was Cami.

Jace breezed up to the table and plopped a chocolate muffin beside me and a blueberry scone in front of herself. "Dimple Pierce said it'll be a minute for my large, iced fudge latte with espresso and extra whip, so breakfast first."

I blinked at the complexity of her drink. Marx would make fun of her until the end of time if he learned about that order. He always seemed to get stuck in line behind people like her, when all he wanted was a black coffee.

"Any luck finding your girl?" she asked around a bite of scone.

"Yep." I scooted closer to her and angled the laptop so we could both see the screen. "Now what?"

Jace slid a finger over the mousepad, viewing the page contents. "Her profile's public, so we can see everything she's posted, and there's nothing since Thursday night."

"That's when she went missing."

"When you create a social media account, make sure you set it to private so creepers can't see everything."

"*When* is a bit presumptuous."

"If you're gonna do investigative work"—she cast me a pointed look—"of the non-dangerous variety, social media can be an invaluable tool. I use it to snoop on people all the time."

Somehow, that didn't surprise me.

"Let's see what kind of personal info Cami's got listed." She tapped the mouse pad. "She's supposedly from Virginia, her favorite movies are zombie films. Yuck. No family listed. Lucky her."

My gaze bounced from the screen to my friend as I wiggled a chocolate chip loose from my muffin. "Your mom called you before you came here this morning, didn't she?"

Her face twisted with annoyance. "At seven o'clock. She *invited* me to a business gala, in true fascist dictator fashion."

"You're not allowed to say no?"

"Not with the agreement we made. She said that if I want the responsibility of handling Scott's medical decisions, then I need to take more responsibility in the family businesses and social events. She can retake control of his medical decisions at any time."

Jace wanted nothing to do with the empire her family had built, but she would do almost anything to keep her mother from removing her comatose brother from life support. Years had passed with no improvement, but Jace wasn't ready to let him go. She fought with her mother to keep him on life support, and this was the uneasy arrangement they had come to.

"You could still take her to court," I said.

Her face fell. "I can't beat her in court. Even if I could afford a lawyer half as good as hers, which I can't, she's his mom, and she's paying his hospital bills. No one's gonna award me power of attorney over his health care. Jumping through her hoops is the only way I can protect him." She picked at her scone. "I have to be there at seven tonight, but she told me I'm not allowed to bring Sam."

"What does she have against Sam?"

"He's a civil servant, and every time I see her, she makes it a point to bring up how she doesn't think he's good enough for me. She doesn't care that I . . ."

When she didn't continue, I prompted, "That you what?"

She ducked her head. "Doesn't matter right now. He's not allowed to come with me tonight, so I was hoping you might."

"Uh, your mother doesn't just disapprove of me, she *hates* me." I lowered my voice. "She thinks I'm a prostitute."

"Yeah, but she didn't say I couldn't bring you. She doesn't think I would do something that audacious. Won't she be surprised?"

"What if she has me thrown out?"

"I'd like to see her try. The county DA is on the guest list, and I bet you can guess who her plus one will be."

Shannon would bring Marx, which meant Mrs. Walker couldn't do anything but grit her teeth and tolerate my presence. If she got on Marx's bad side, she would be on the district attorney's bad side, and she was too concerned with appearances and connections to burn that bridge.

"There's a dessert table and all the cheese you can eat," Jace said, trying to bribe me with tasty treats.

When she looked at me again, I noticed a shadow hiding behind the usual sparkle in her eyes, and it took me a moment to identify it—grief. She was struggling with something today, and she was doing everything she could to conceal it.

"Okay, I'll go," I agreed.

"Sweet. I was thinking you could—"

"I'm not wearing heels."

"What about—"

"Or a dress."

She snapped her mouth shut, lips dipping in a pout. "Terms begrudgingly accepted, but you can't wear jeans. It's a black tie gala."

"I don't have any black ties." Or ties of any color, for that matter. Why was that even a dress code requirement?

Jace coughed around another bite of scone. "It means dress formal, like people did at the police memorial. But please don't wear that red sweater that makes you look pregnant."

"I did not look pregnant."

Jace cleared her throat and returned her attention to the computer screen. "Cami follows several diabetes pages. I don't know anyone with diabetes, but doesn't that usually mean bottles of insulin and needles and stuff?"

I shrugged. "One of my foster brothers had diabetes, but he had a pump attached to his side. Maybe Cami has one of those?"

"Let's check her pictures. Maybe we'll see something there."

I leaned closer as she clicked through photos. Most of them were of Cami by herself, posing with different hairstyles and makeup. Good grief, how many pictures could there possibly be?

Jace clicked to the next picture. "Hold up, familiar face alert." She slapped the creased photo on the table and dragged it closer, comparing it to the girl in the digital photo with Cami.

Pixie's hair was covered with a hat, and she wasn't wearing as much makeup, but it was her. Jace hovered the mouse arrow over her face, and a name popped up.

"Hope Carmichael," I read aloud.

Did someone else give her the name Pixie, or did she choose it as a way to protect some small part of herself from a life that took too much?

Zoey bellowed for Jace, and her head snapped up. "Finally. I'm two seconds from literally dying of fatigue." She wheeled away from the table to grab her drink.

I texted Jordan the information about Cami's possible diabetes as well as Pixie's real name, then snapped my phone shut, watching the rain as it streamed down the café windows. I hoped that wherever Cami was right now, she was safe and warm.

Lord, please help us find her.

12

The rain dwindled to a sprinkle, with ribbons of sunlight peeking through the gray clouds. If we were lucky, the temperature would tiptoe above forty in the sunshine today.

Jace leaned over as I climbed out of the passenger side of her car into the agency parking lot. "Tell second-place best friend I said hi."

I smiled and shook my head, closing the door. I was not getting in the middle of that never-ending battle.

The passenger window dropped, and warmth from the heater swirled around me. Jace called out, "Come by my place around three so we can hang out before we figure out what to wear."

I didn't relish playing dress-up to find an outfit, but the nicest thing I owned was the sweater I'd worn during my testimony, and I couldn't wear it without remembering that day in court.

Jace whipped out of the lot, intending to spend the rest of the morning and afternoon at the hospital with her brother. If I didn't have a missing girl to track down, I would keep her company and help break up the hours of painful silence.

There was no telling how much longer Scott would cling to this world, but I had noticed the guarded smiles and careful words of the nurses the last time we visited him.

I dreaded the day he passed, because Jace would be inconsolable. It had been almost twenty years since my precious sister's death, and I still felt the sting of her absence.

As I turned toward the agency, I caught my reflection in a puddle, my features rippling with every raindrop that kissed the surface. The sight released a beautiful memory from a time before I was familiar with trauma and loss.

Gin, wearing one of her flowery dresses and polka-dot rubber boots, laughed as we splashed through rain puddles in the backyard, dancing in the sprinkles that dripped off the tree leaves.

Her laughter always reminded me of bubbles—floating and carefree. We used to puddle-jump after every rainstorm and then whirl through the house like the tornado that barely missed our small Kansas town.

Mom would huff with amused exasperation, "Who needs tornadoes when we have these two?"

Dad would say, "I know how to stop these little twister sisters in their tracks." And then he would scoop us up midtwirl and smother us with kisses until we giggled ourselves breathless.

The sweet memories left an ache in my chest, and I tipped my face toward the drizzling sky. "I miss you, Gin-Gin."

Heaven was lucky to have her.

I passed an unfamiliar car parked beside Jordan's as I strode toward the agency entrance.

"Please be a paying client."

A hissing sound cut through the air, drawing me up short of the sidewalk, and I scanned the parking lot. What was that?

A thump, followed by a pained groan, came from the abandoned building next door. Someone was inside, and it sounded like they were having a rough morning.

Squeezing the strap of my knapsack with both hands, I crossed the parking lot to the front of the building, pausing on the sidewalk at the foot of the steps.

"Are you all right in there?"

The door had been kicked off its hinges long ago, leaving a gaping void crisscrossed with plywood and weathered boards, and I squinted, trying to see inside without venturing any closer.

Half of a shadowed face appeared in the opening, and my heart fluttered in my chest. The woman stared at me with one large eye. She shifted, revealing more of herself, and I recognized her as the homeless woman who wandered this street.

"Are you okay? I heard you fall in there."

Her short, gray-streaked brown hair was pasted to one side of her head, like she'd just woken up. Had she slept here last night? With no door and most of the windows busted out, she must've been freezing.

She pressed her lips together and looked around before leaning through the opening. "Did you know?"

"Did I know what?"

Her voice dropped to a whisper. "Your parking lot is haunted. I saw a ghost here last night."

I wasn't sure what to say to that since the only ghost I believed in was the *Holy* Ghost, and he didn't drift around parking lots after sundown.

"What did this ghost look like?"

"A watcher."

She pointed to the place where darkness formed a pocket at night, the very spot Riley had fixated on while Hope and I were speaking.

A chill crawled across my skin. "What was he watching?"

"Who," she corrected and then disappeared from view.

"Wait." I leaned forward, trying to see her, but all I could see was the shadowed destruction of the interior. She'd apparently said all she intended to say on the matter.

I didn't believe she'd seen a ghost, but she'd seen someone. Thoroughly spooked, I kept an eye on my surroundings as I walked back to the agency. Before I could reach the door, a woman burst out of it.

"Ridiculous. Filthy, cockroach-riddled hole in the wall." She clomped to her car in alligator-skin heels and wrenched open the driver's door. "Useless."

I took exception to that string of insults.

Our business might be a hole in the wall, but it was not filthy or riddled with roaches. I scattered the dust bunnies regularly and even washed the windows.

Well, the parts I could reach.

I eyed the obvious zigzag of grime that coated the top half of the glass. I needed a squeegee and a step ladder to reach that.

The woman slammed her car door and peeled out of the parking lot, flinging grimy water with her tires. I back-stepped, avoiding most of the spray.

"I bet she sucks the joy out of any room she stomps into," I muttered, wrapping my fingers around the door handle.

From this position, I had a direct line of sight into Jordan's open office. He sat with his elbows on his desk and his face in his hands, weariness and frustration in every line of his body.

He'd left our hometown, his family, and a stable career because he wanted to be a regular part of my life, and now he was struggling to keep the lights on.

Guilt tried to slither in, but he'd reminded me more than once that moving here was his decision, not mine.

I opened the door and stepped on the mat to dry my boots. Jordan straightened, his hands dropping from his face. In an instant, all vulnerability vanished, and he summoned a smile.

"Morning."

He crumpled a piece of paper in his fist, leaned back in his office chair, and let it fly. It bounced off the door frame instead of the trash can and rolled into the lobby.

I scooped it up. "Whiff."

His forced smile spread into an easy grin. "Nice try, but *whiff* is a baseball term, meaning you swung and missed the ball entirely. In basketball, missing everything is called an air ball."

"Well, you definitely air-balled." I tossed the crumpled paper back, and he snatched it, taking a second shot that sent it straight into the can.

"It's more of a noun."

"That wasn't the message I left on your desk, was it?"

"No, the lady you spoke with wanted details on our success rate before sending a friend our way. The woman who left a minute ago was a walk-in."

"Walked in and stomped out. That can't be a good sign."

"She wanted dirt on her soon-to-be ex-husband. She had an affair, he cut her off financially, and now she wants something she can leverage against him for money. I told her we don't do that kind of work."

"Clearly, she takes rejection well."

Jordan moved his coffee so I could sit on the side of his desk, my favorite spot for discussing cases. It made me feel more involved and capable than the squat guest chairs on the opposite side.

I hopped up. "What are we gonna do for cases?"

"I wish I knew. I've left business cards everywhere and even checked news articles for people who might be interested in our services. All that's left to do now is pray."

I tilted my head at his choice of words.

I'd heard a lot of Christians use the phrase "All that's left to do is pray." It seemed odd to me that prayer was a last resort for people who claimed to believe in a God capable of making the impossible possible.

"I feel like prayer should come first, not last," I said. "Anything we do to try to fix our situation will pale in comparison to what God can do, so why wait until we're desperate and out of options before we turn to Him?"

"I guess I hadn't really thought about it like that. It's in my nature to try to fix things under my own power."

"I'm pretty sure that's *human* nature."

A frown line appeared between his eyebrows. "I've never been all that good at praying."

"It's just talking to God. It doesn't have to be anything fancy. There aren't any magic words or phrases." I rubbed at a muddy spot on my jeans from Cruella's tires. "You should . . . come to church with me tomorrow morning."

"You mean come to church with you and Marx."

"He'll behave. Probably."

"I doubt that." He leaned back in his chair and propped a leg over his knee, considering my invitation. "As long as no one's gonna quiz me on the Bible and I don't have to sing, I'll be there."

"Good." I snagged a paper clip from the bowl by his stapler, twisting it between my fingers. "Would you mind checking the front door camera for the period of time you were gone last night?"

"Sure." He opened his laptop, bringing up the video clips from the motion-activated camera. "What are we hoping to see?"

"There's a lady in the abandoned building next door, and she says she saw someone loitering."

His mouth tightened. "I wish the city would tear that place down. Having it vacant makes me nervous."

I leaned over to study the screen as he played the recordings. "She said the person was in this area." I circled it with my finger.

It was strange, watching the interaction between me and Hope. Outside of the occasional hand gesture and the moment when I passed her my shoes, I was out of the frame.

"I don't see anything there. Hope shows up, you two talk, you give her your shoes." He cracked a smile. "Somehow that doesn't surprise me. She leaves, and there's nothing else until your cab arrives."

"Hmm."

It was possible the woman had mistaken a passerby or even a moving shadow for the person she believed was a ghost, but my instincts and Riley's senses suggested otherwise. And yet the camera showed nothing. Maybe he was too far away to trip the sensor.

I straightened. "Did you find any information about Cami that might be helpful?"

"I found information, but no telling how helpful it will be." He swiveled in his chair to grab the documents from the printer, clipping them into a folder. "You can review it on the way. Cami's apartment manager agreed to answer whatever questions he can about her."

"Do you think we can get in and look around her place without breaking any laws?"

"We can try to convince him to let us in. But before we get to all that"—he reached into the bill folder and pulled out my paycheck—"any idea how this ended up here?"

I puckered my lips between my teeth and shrugged.

"Yeah, that was almost convincing." He slid the check across the desk to me, and the moment he lifted his fingers, I slid it back. "Holly, you have to take your paycheck."

"No, I don't. I'm . . ." I tried to think of a good excuse. "I'm on vacation."

"You're not, but even if you were, that doesn't affect your paycheck for the past two weeks."

I left the check where it lay on the desk. "I know it won't cover much, but the electric bill is around three hundred dollars. Maybe you could use it for that and some of the water bill."

He stared at me, his expression unreadable. "I'm not using your check to pay the business bills."

"And I'm not cashing it, so . . . you can use it or . . . it can hang out there collecting dust."

"You having enough food and staying warm at night is more important to me than paying the electric and water bill."

"I know, and I have faith that God will work all that out." When his stubborn expression didn't soften, I added, "You help me all the time. Now it's my turn. Please let me do this."

He swallowed, and I glimpsed a sheen of moisture in his eyes before he looked away. "I don't . . ." He blew out a breath and ran a hand over his hair. "I don't know what to say."

I turned my attention back to my deformed paper clip. "I'm sure you'll pay me back with a lifetime of trips to ice cream shops, so you don't need to say anything."

"A lifetime, huh? You sure you wanna spend that much time around me?"

I shrugged, heat creeping up my face. "I'm warming up to the idea. But no more ice cream strolls in February. It's freezing. In fact, I think we should wait until it's above sixty degrees." I set the twisted paper clip on his desk. "Ready to go track down a missing girl?"

Jordan closed his laptop and opened his top drawer to retrieve his gun. He clipped the holster to his belt and grabbed his keys. "Let's go see what we can find out."

13

*M*usic from the car radio softened the harsh sounds of the city as Jordan drove, and I rested a folder against my propped knees as I perused the information he'd pulled together on our missing girl.

He was faster at gathering information than I was, overshadowing the meager details I collected from Cami's Facebook. We still needed to scour her other social media accounts.

Camilla Chen was first reported missing two years ago at the age of fourteen, a suspected runaway from Virginia. Her father passed away when she was eleven, but her mother was still alive.

"Why do you think she ran away?"

"Kids run away for all kinds of reasons. Rebellion, pursuing dreams, meeting up with someone they think they love." Jordan glanced my way, leaving off one of the more common reasons children ran away from home—to escape an abusive or hostile environment.

Had Cami packed her bags in fear and dashed away in the dead of night, or had she snuck away to chase her dreams?

"Shortly after I started working with my dad as a deputy in Stony Brooke, this eleven-year-old boy ran away from home," Jordan said. "I found him in a hideout he'd made in the woods. He built it out of cardboard boxes, branches, and a camouflage blanket."

"Almost like what we made."

When we were children, we built a cardboard fort in the woods, using the last of Dad's duct tape to stitch it together, and then glued leaves to it, hoping to make it invisible to everyone else.

"Yep, and we argued over the password."

I searched my memories. "You wanted it to be some guy's name."

"Kevin Appier, only the best pitcher to ever throw a ball for the Kansas City Royals. I didn't realize at the time that they were a Missouri team, not a Kansas team, but still, it was better than what you and Gin picked."

I couldn't keep the grin from spreading across my lips. "Sprinkles?"

"Rainbow sprinkles, to be precise, and Gin told me that since we now had a hidden castle in the woods, I could be the sprinkle king."

I laughed. I must've missed that part of the conversation, but that comment was perfectly Gin. With her love of sprinkles, she would've thought it was a compliment.

"She cried when I told her that was a stupid name," Jordan said, wincing with remorse. "I felt like the worst friend ever. At that point, I had no choice but to accept rainbow sprinkles as the password."

Talking about Gin kept her alive in my memory, and those precious moments filled my heart with warmth. "She loved you."

Sadness edged his smile. "I loved her too."

I rested my head against the seat. "So, what happened with the little boy and his cardboard fort?"

"His parents argued almost constantly, and he felt invisible and unwanted, so he stashed food and water in his hideout and planned to live there with his pet hamster. When I found him and took him home, I suggested that the family get counseling. Of course, they didn't, and they were actually shocked when their son left town with some of his friends at sixteen and never returned. Parents don't realize that the way they treat their spouse affects their kids too."

My parents had adored each other, but some of my foster parents flung verbal jabs at each other like opponents in a boxing match, creating an atmosphere of chaos and hostility that made us kids feel like the floor was made of eggshells.

"Hope told me that Cami got a raw deal in the family department," I said. "I somehow doubt she ran away from home and into this life because her parents argued."

"I didn't have a chance to dig very deep into her family situation, but at first glance I didn't see anything concerning."

"You wouldn't have seen anything concerning if you'd dug into my childhood living situations either."

His fingers tightened on the steering wheel at the reference to my difficult childhood, but his voice remained steady. "You think she was being abused by her family and didn't tell anyone?"

"Working as an underage prostitute while trying to get a hold of and pay for insulin has to be a nightmare. If home was a safe option, I think she would've gone back a long time ago."

"A fourteen-year-old girl, alone and desperate on the street. I bet she was recruited by a pimp within a week." His jaw hardened. "Sometimes I hate this world."

"Me too. But then I remember all the good that's in it, like friends, rainbows, pets, French fries."

He smiled at that. "I knew there would be food in there somewhere. I was banking on tacos."

"Oo tacos. Love tacos."

His smile faded as we turned onto the street listed on the slip of paper Dorina had given me. "If it's all right for me to ask, how did you survive all those years with no identification for a job or housing? I know part of that time you were a minor."

I closed the folder and rested it against my knees. "It's not exactly a Hallmark story."

"If you'd rather not talk about it—"

"No, it's fine." As long as I could skirt around the more difficult moments, I didn't mind sharing about my past. "The first few years after I ran away from my last placement were really rough. Even though I was older than Cami, I didn't look it, and I couldn't prove it. No one wanted to hire me, even under the table, and I couldn't provide for myself. There were people who tried to convince me that prostitution was my only option if I wanted to survive, but it wasn't something I could do, wasn't something I was *willing* to do to survive."

He chanced another look at me. "What did you do?"

"I lived on the street, ate at soup kitchens, got boxed foods from food pantries. I even slept in the basement of a church one night because someone forgot to lock the door."

"Why not stay in a homeless shelter?"

"I tried that a couple of times, but . . . it wasn't for me." I wiggled my socked toes closer to the dashboard heater. "There were times when I felt like giving up, when I was a breath away from hopeless, and then God would show me a way forward. Sometimes the paths He provided involved waiting tables for sixteen hours a day strictly for tips, sweeping parking lots for ten dollars, or sleeping in abandoned places. Things weren't easy or ideal, but He made them possible."

That was why I had fallen in love with the verse, "I can do all things through Christ who strengthens me." It described my life. God's strength made it possible for me to keep moving forward despite everything against me.

Jordan maneuvered the car into a parallel parking space and switched off the engine. "Is that why you're so sure God's gonna help us through this financial issue?"

"Yep." I peered out at the impoverished area as I tugged on my sneakers.

Some of these apartments buildings weren't just low-income housing. They were barely held together by strips of tape, boards, and sheets of plastic. I wouldn't be surprised if the handrails were attached with gum.

My gaze trailed over the vehicles parked along the street, snagging on a white van with a cross sticker on the side. A community outreach vehicle maybe?

Violent music pounding from the speakers of a car caught my attention, and the driver sized us up as he cruised by.

"This place is . . ."

"Yeah," Jordan said, checking to make sure his gun was securely clipped to his belt as we exited the car. "Do me a favor and don't wander off."

Why did everyone always say things like that? It wasn't like I frolicked after every dust particle that floated by.

Jordan tipped his head. "Should be this building here."

An older man stood at the top of the steps, brushing a layer of mismatched paint onto the chipped and splintering frame of the front door.

"Excuse me," Jordan said as we approached. "Are you Mr. Brenneman?"

The older man lowered his arm and twisted to face us. "Might be. Who are you?"

"Jordan Radcliffe. I'm the private investigator who called earlier to discuss Camilla Chen. This is Holly, my partner."

"Right." Mr. Brenneman dropped the paintbrush into the tray, then swiped a sleeve across his forehead, smearing paint all the way to his temple. "I don't know what you think I can tell you."

"When was the last time you saw Cami?" I asked.

"Last I saw her . . . Thursday before she left for the night. Around six."

"Do you know where she was headed?"

"Work, I suppose. That's where she goes most nights." He snagged a towel from his utility belt and wiped at the wet paint on his fingers.

"Did you see any indication Cami might have plans to stay somewhere else when she left on Thursday?" Jordan asked.

"Nope." Brenneman's eyebrows were so thick and wild that they almost touched when they pinched with concern. "In the eight months she's been here, she always comes home before dawn and takes a long shower before other people get up for work. I live in this crumbling pile of bricks, too, and I'm usually up by then."

"Have you noticed anyone hanging around the neighborhood or paying too much attention to her?" Jordan asked.

"Plenty of people hang around, but I can't speak to whether or not they're paying attention to anyone in particular."

"Is there anything you can tell us about her?" I asked.

Brenneman worked the rag between his fingers. "She lied about her age on her apartment application, even provided a fake ID and employment history. I don't know how old she is, but she's still a minor."

Jordan's eyebrows lifted. "And knowing that, you rented an apartment to her anyway?"

"She's a kid trying to survive on her own. Somebody had to give her a break. Honest, I expected I would have to kick her out at the end of the first week for not paying rent. Eight months later, she's the best tenant in the building. Keeps to herself, never complains, and always pays her rent on time. Except this week."

"When was it due?" Jordan asked.

"Rent is due every Saturday morning before noon. Used to be Monday, but people would blow their paychecks over the weekend and have nothing left for rent. Cami always hands me her rent by eight o'clock sharp, which is how I know something's wrong and why I'm gonna let you into her apartment to see what you can see." He tossed the stained rag beside the paint tray and opened the door. "Follow me."

We trailed after him into the building and up to the fifth floor. He led us to a door that had been freshly painted, but the crude insults scrawled in black marker lingered like pale shadows beneath the thin layer of white.

I touched the door. "Who did this?"

Brenneman sighed. "Wish I knew. One of the male tenants recognized Cami from her place of business, and the word spread through the building. Some of the other residents started hassling her, but when she's off the clock, she wants to be left alone like everyone else. It was probably one of them."

Poor Cami. Her life was hard enough.

"Did any of that hassling turn aggressive?" Jordan asked.

"Not that she told me." He sifted through his labeled keys until he found the correct one. "I'm letting you in to look around, but don't go taking anything."

"We won't," I assured him.

He unlocked the door and pushed it inward. "I've got window frames to paint. Come get me if you need me."

"Mr. Brenneman," I called after him, and he paused halfway down the hall. "Thank you for giving a desperate teenage girl a chance. Thank you for showing her kindness."

He pressed his lips together and jingled his keys, emotion clinging to his voice when he spoke. "You find her." And with that, he left us to our search.

Jordan gestured to the open doorway. "Ladies first."

My apartment was small, but Cami's living space was claustrophobic. If she sneezed in the entrance, she would have to wipe sneeze spray off every wall. It couldn't be more than 150 square feet.

The kitchen was a single counter with a sink and two cabinets. No oven or stove top, only a tiny microwave and a mini fridge designed to hold drinks.

I inched inside, fighting against the butterflies in my stomach whipping themselves into a frenzy at the confined space.

Clothes hung from a wire strung between two walls, similar to the setup over my bed, and a folding wall partitioned the sleeping area from the kitchen and clothes.

Confused, I said, "There's no bathroom or shower."

"I saw them at the end of the hall. Looks like they're communal for the floor, like a college dormitory."

I knew nothing about the setup of college dorms, but sharing a bathroom and shower with men on the same floor sounded terrifying. Unfortunately, a place like this was probably all Cami could afford.

Jordan crouched in front of the mini fridge, opening it. "Diet sodas, a handful of fruits, and . . . two vials of insulin." He held them up for me to see.

"What about syringes?"

"Maybe she keeps those somewhere more secure. A diabetic's needles would be an instant draw for drug addicts." Jordan returned the vials to the fridge and stood, searching the cupboards and drawers.

I studied the collage on the wall. It had been formed in the shape of a star—a collection of photos, magazine cutouts, quotes, posters of places she probably longed to visit. Over the top of all that were sporadically placed music notes, as if someone blew them off a sheet of music and onto the collage.

This was a wall of dreams.

I traced my fingers over a quote she'd taped up: "Never let the world dull your sparkle." This cruel world we lived in tried to destroy every sparkle, sanding them away one heartbreak, one trauma, one criticism at a time. It took strength to hold on to them.

We're gonna find you, Cami.

And somehow we would help her. She couldn't come back to this life.

Jordan moved behind the bedroom partition, and a thump sent the folding wall tumbling toward the kitchen. It hit the clothesline, and I yelped as Jordan crashed to the floor on top of it in a shower of shirts and dresses.

I barely had time to process the fact that someone had shoved him, because that same blur slammed into me and knocked me into the hallway. Impact with the floor punched the breath from my lungs, and a heavy weight landed on top of me.

A man. There was a man on top of me, his legs straddling mine. For a moment I was paralyzed by fear, staring into brown eyes visible through oval holes in his mask. And then my desperation never to be hurt again flushed the lead from my limbs, and I attacked, slapping and punching at his face.

He flinched away from my blows and, in a matter of a few rapid heartbeats, was on his feet and running.

I scooted up against the wall, chest tight with fear, and tried to catch my breath. My fingers bumped something on the floor, and I realized there were needles scattered around me.

"Holly." Jordan dropped to a crouch beside me. "Are you okay?"

I nodded and used the door frame to steady me as I stood. "We need to catch him."

Jordan's expression told me what his words didn't: he didn't want me chasing after a potentially dangerous person. But he was going to have to get used to the fact that I had no interest in sitting on the sidelines.

"Are you coming with me?" I asked.

He nodded, and we sprinted after the man, our chances of catching him slipping away with every passing second. Would he force his way into another apartment or head for the street?

Jordan pounded down the steps with me on his heels and shoved through the entryway door onto the stoop. I spilled out into the gray morning beside him.

Chest heaving, I scrutinized the retreating figures and cars in the distance. Had he jumped into a vehicle or taken off on foot? My gaze landed on an open space along the opposite curb. What kind of vehicle had been parked there when we went inside?

Was its absence a coincidence?

A door squeaked, drawing my eyes to a mini mart on the corner, but it was only a patron leaving. The man was gone. In the time it took us to pull ourselves together and make the decision to pursue him, he had melted into the urban landscape.

14

Questions about the masked man consumed my thoughts as we rounded the corner onto Brushwick on foot, leaving Jordan's car parked on a street where it wasn't likely to be stolen.

The responding officers dismissed the incident at Cami's apartment as a burglary, a junkie scavenging for drugs or valuables he could sell. The needles he dropped after we collided supported that theory, but the place wasn't trashed from a frenzied search. Until we arrived and started rummaging around, nothing seemed disturbed.

Even more curious, the man was in the apartment with us the entire time, crouched soundlessly next to the bed on the other side of the divider. I had never encountered a drug addict that still or quiet while conscious.

And how did he get inside?

We wanted to speak with the neighbors, to see if anyone heard or saw the man let himself into Cami's apartment, but the officers dismissed us with, "Let us do our jobs."

"This place seems deserted," Jordan said, bringing my attention back to the present.

Brushwick was a ghost town during the day—no cars clogging the street, no shouting voices or people loitering against the buildings. If not for the glow of lights in the windows, I would assume the businesses were closed.

"It's kind of eerie," I admitted.

My attention lingered on the empty bench where I'd sat with Tandi last night. Had she gotten the sweets and the card I left for her? Would she call if she needed help?

"We're not as alone as we seem," Jordan said, inhaling through his nose.

An odor clung to the air—marijuana mixed with cigarette smoke. It wafted from an alley ahead of us, along with quiet voices. As we neared the mouth of the alley, the disquiet I felt in this place intensified.

A group of men lingered in the alley, chatting and laughing as they smoked. Their differing skin tones and clothing colors meant they likely weren't a gang, but that didn't mean they wouldn't be interested in stirring up trouble.

"Hey, vanilla," one of them called out, and the familiarity of his voice made my muscles tighten. The man pulled a joint from between his lips and purred, "I got time to hook up now."

I inched closer to Jordan, almost stepping on him.

"Do me a favor and walk on my other side," he said, guiding me to his left to put himself between me and any threats. It also left his gun easily accessible if someone decided to get aggressive.

I tried to keep my attention on our destination, but I could feel several pairs of eyes on our backs as we walked. On impulse, I tucked my icy fingers into Jordan's hand, stealing warmth and confidence.

He looked down in surprise.

"For protection," I explained. "So none of those guys take advantage of you."

He grinned, dimples deepening. "I feel safer already." He closed his fingers over mine, keeping his grip featherlight so I could pull away if my anxiety got the better of me.

"Why do we need to talk to Dorina again? She already told me what she knows."

"I'd like to interview her myself, if she'll talk to me. Often times, people know more than they realize." Jordan nodded to the repair shop. "Is this the place?"

"Yep."

He checked to make sure we weren't being followed, and then we ducked under the partially raised garage door into the bay.

Soft jazz music played from a portable radio on the cluttered desk, adding warmth to the drab space.

A car sat in the bay, hood raised as someone tinkered with the engine. I caught a glimpse of gray overalls as the mechanic shifted, and the man muttered to the engine, "Oh, come on, baby, don't do me like that. Be nice to Clayton."

I had heard his voice last night, and considering this was Clay's Auto Repair, it was safe to assume he was the owner. I inched forward, my fingers slipping from Jordan's. "Excuse me. Clayton?"

He straightened so fast he thumped his head against the raised hood, and the tool in his hand clattered into the engine. "Who the devil . . ."

He stepped out from behind the car, rubbing the top of his head, and my breath caught. He had to be six foot three or more, with broad shoulders and hands bigger than my face.

Clayton's eyes bounced from me to Jordan, and then to the gun on Jordan's hip. He held out his hands, and the oil-stained rag dropped from his fingers. "I knew this was gonna happen. Look, I never touched your girl. Didn't even think about touching her. In fact, we weren't even in the same room last night. She's not even my type. I don't like skinny girls." He flicked a glance at me. "No offense."

I blinked.

"Okay," Jordan said, his tone conveying his confusion. "Is Dorina around?"

"Put your hands down, Clayton," Dorina said, sashaying into the garage in a flowery dress and sandals. "You look like a bank hostage."

"I told you one of her blue-blooded connections was gonna come here for revenge. And there's the boyfriend with a gun."

"And? You have a gun in your overalls."

Clayton dropped his arms with a scowl. "Don't tell everyone my business."

"Why not? You do." She snapped open the can of orange soda she carried. "I know my cousin's size can be a shock, but the only thing he's a threat to is a six pack of beer and a bag of Doritos."

"That's right. Sure, I got a magazine problem and sometimes I drink a little too much, and I fudge the numbers when I work on people's cars, but I don't hurt nobody." Clayton's eyes drifted sideways, pulling his mouth with them. "You didn't need to know all that, but now you do, so . . ." The man shrugged his big shoulders. "Everybody's got flaws."

"He also talks too much when he's nervous." Dorina tapped a fingernail on the soda can as she fixed me with a censuring look. "I told you not to come back here."

I tucked my fingers into the pockets of my jeans and shrugged. "I did say if I had to come back, I would bring someone with me."

She took Jordan's measure. "Cop?"

"Ex-sheriff," he corrected, extending a hand. "Jordan Radcliffe."

Dorina rested a manicured hand in the one he offered, the row of bracelets on her wrist jangling as they shook.

"Holly mentioned that you helped her last night. Thank you."

"She didn't give me much choice. I didn't want a repeat of last spring. Business is hard enough without cops swarming the place and searching for one of their own."

Jordan released her hand, his blonde eyebrows dipping ever so slightly with curiosity. "Don't take this the wrong way, but you're not what I envisioned when Holly told me what you do for a living."

Dorina smiled. "You mean because of how I speak and dress?" At his nod, she clarified. "I wasn't raised in this life. I was a married woman, halfway through nursing school, when my husband died and left me with a heap of debt and three children that I needed to find a way to take care of. With no help to fall back on and no job that could cover my bills, well . . . here we are."

"I keep reminding her that her kids is grown, and she should get a job in a department store or something. And then I get this." Clayton gestured to the exasperated look Dorina threw his way.

"If I leave, who will help these girls?"

"They ain't your responsibility."

"Someday I'm gonna buy a house and create a safe place for the girls who want out of this life, but until then I'm gonna do what I can to teach them how to stay alive. And that's the end of it. I don't wanna discuss it anymore."

Clayton grumbled something under his breath that sounded like, "Unless you get snatched or dead first."

Dorina sighed. "Stop overreacting."

"Overreacting?" His eyes widened until the pupils were engulfed in white. "I almost had to shoot someone. Tell them about that fool last night."

"They're here about Cami. What happened last night had nothing to do with her."

Clayton made a noise with his lips that reminded me of air seeping out of a balloon and turned to us. "Last night, around two, she went out for a smoke, and some lowlife tried to force her to go with him. I put a couple bullets in his van. He's lucky it was his hubcaps and not his kneecaps."

I sucked in a breath. "What?!"

Dorina waved off my concern with another jangle of bracelets. "I'm fine. A rough night every now and then is inevitable. It's best to move on."

Cami's disappearance and then an attempted abduction on the same street, two nights apart? That couldn't be a coincidence, could it?

"You've had some bad encounters, but you have never almost been kidnapped before," Clayton challenged. "That knife incident was bad enough, but the only kinda people who kidnap hookers is serial killers."

"What did you notice about the van?" Jordan asked, and I grabbed my notebook and pen to take notes.

"White, with two rear doors. One of those utility vans, with a wall between the storage compartment and the cockpit," Dorina said.

I finished writing and lifted my head. "Any designs or logos on the outside?"

"The doors were open. I couldn't see."

"Did either of you get a look at the guy?" Jordan asked.

"Freak was wearing a ski mask," Clayton said. "Gotta have something to do with what happened to Cami. Rina ain't got no enemies who might wanna hurt her, and she ain't exactly a baby-faced girl some pimp might wanna snatch up and force to work for him."

"Between the darkness and his mask, I didn't see much," Dorina admitted. "But I did elbow him in the face. Whoever he is, he's got an ice pack on his eye."

Clayton nudged her shoulder. "That kid that came by this morning had a bruise on his face. Right here." He tapped a finger on his cheekbone.

"Kid?" Jordan prompted.

"One of those richy riches, walking around here like it's a strip mall his daddy owns. Strolled in here and started asking questions. He wanted to know if the 'Asian black girl' had been around lately. I told him not since Thursday. He ran his hands through his hair and started muttering something about mistakes, then left."

"On foot?"

"As rich as he looked, any car he parked on this street would get picked clean in less than an hour." Clayton cleared his throat and scratched behind his ear. "Not that I use stolen car parts for repairs."

"The kid was in his twenties, dark hair, hazel eyes, broad nose," Dorina said.

I recorded the information in my notebook. I supposed it was pointless to ask if they had called the police about the attempted kidnapping.

"Have you ever seen him before?" Jordan asked.

"Last night, actually. He was in the backseat of the car full of guys your girl was having trouble with. They're the reason I pulled her inside."

Jordan's glance told me he was going to ask for more details about this "trouble" when we were alone. "And then he came here asking about Cami and seemed stressed that she hadn't been back since Thursday."

Dorina nodded. "I thought the car last night might've been the one that picked up Cami Thursday, but I wasn't a hundred percent sure. After his visit this morning, though—"

"They're a car full of kidnappers. That's what they are," Clayton cut in.

"Did you notice anything we can use to identify at least one of the men in the car?" Jordan asked. When they both shook their heads, he added, "Cameras?"

Clayton made another leaky balloon sound. "People on this street can't afford that stuff. Our security is barred windows, locks, and guns, which I most certainly do not keep in my overalls."

Jordan pressed his lips together, thinking. "Who else might know this group? What other girls have they interacted with?"

Dorina shrugged. "I help the girls when they need it, but I don't monitor them. You're welcome to come back tonight and ask around. They seem to go for the pretty girls closer to their age. Maybe ask Tandi or Pixie if they've been approached."

"Did Hope show up last night?" I asked.

If Dorina was surprised that I knew Pixie's real name, she didn't show it. "A short while after you left."

"And she was okay?"

"She was still upset about Cami. I told her you were here poking around for answers."

112

"Do you know where I can find her or how I can get a hold of her? She was in a hurry last night and forgot to give me her contact info."

"I don't have her address or her number, but she came by again this morning, about thirty minutes ago. She said something about returning some shoes to Nancy Drew, whatever that means."

I stuffed my notebook and pen into my bag. "Hope's headed to the agency. We should go before we miss . . ."

A man ducked beneath the partially raised garage door and straightened, his bald head reflecting the overhead fluorescent lights. His cold eyes cut through the others to me, and my breath snagged in my lungs.

With a flick of his wrist, Spike sent something fluttering through the air. A JGH business card landed on the floor near my feet. I bent to pick it up and then flipped it over to find the message I had written for Tandi: "If you ever want help." Only now there was a smear of dried blood in the corner.

My heart crawled into my throat.

I had left this note to help her, but what if Spike had hurt her because of it? The card trembled in my hands as I looked back at him.

Before I could ask him what he'd done to Tandi, Dorina stepped forward. "You need to leave, Theodore."

A vein throbbed in Spike's forehead. "Don't call me that."

"You know the rules. You don't set foot in this building."

"Rules," he sneered. "Your little friend tried to steal one of my girls right out from under me. Putting ideas in her head I had to knock loose." He cracked his tattooed knuckles for emphasis.

Throat dry, I asked, "What did you do to her?"

"Reminded her she owes me. She gave up your description in less than a minute. I saw you in here last night, and the boys saw you come in here this morning. Seems like you're starting to like it around here."

"Did you hurt Cami too?"

"What use do I got for a girl with a busted-up pancreas? Her drugs cost more than what I give my girls to keep them happy. She ain't worth the trouble."

Clayton shouldered past Dorina. "Get out of my shop."

"Don't boss me, old man. I tolerate you and your *rules* 'cause Rina here patches up the girls from time to time. But don't push your luck. Besides . . ." He jerked his head toward me. "I got business with this one."

Jordan angled his body in front of me. "No you don't."

"She messed with my business. There are consequences for that. And if my money maker walks out on me, you better believe I'm gonna replace her with this—"

"That's not a fight you want." Jordan's hand moved to rest on his gun.

"You think you're the only one with a gun?" Spike reached under the front of his T-shirt, but Jordan drew his sidearm and aimed before the man's fingers could even curl around the handle of the weapon protruding from his waistband.

"Don't," Jordan said, and there was a plea as much as a demand in his voice. He didn't want to have to shoot him.

Clayton fumbled his gun from his overalls, pointing it at Spike, and I fished my weapon from my bag, popping out the blade of my box cutter.

Spike stilled when he realized he was at a disadvantage, though I doubted it was my one-inch blade with a neon pink handle that made him rethink his life decisions.

Dorina stepped forward. "Dealing in unwilling girls is trouble, Theo. Even thinking about it is trouble. You know the others who tried it on this street got locked up. And this girl comes with so many strings attached, you'll hang yourself trying to escape them."

"Yeah? What sorta strings?"

"Blue strings," Clayton clarified. "Little Red here's got cops in the family. 'Hunt you down, shoot you in your own crib, and cover it up' family."

If that was Clayton's idea of cops, it was no wonder my presence made him nervous.

Spike's jaw shifted, as though he were silently chewing on that information, and then he lifted one finger at a time from the gun, finally dropping his hand to his side. "You better stay away from my girls, princess, or it won't matter who your daddy is. I don't stand for nobody messing with what I worked hard to build."

He sneered at Jordan, then ducked under the garage door and walked away, his words leaving a chill in my body.

Jordan holstered his gun, but tension lingered in his shoulders. "How dangerous is he? Is he gonna come after Holly?"

Dorina sighed and readjusted her bracelets. "I've known Theo since he was thirteen, running through these streets and stealing whatever he could get his hands on. The only person Theo cares about is Theo, and he'll do anything to protect himself. He's angry right now, but I don't think he'll pick a fight if it means putting himself in the NYPD's crosshairs. Holly should be safe as long as she doesn't wander around here by herself."

Should be safe. That wasn't as comforting as she meant it to be.

I looked at the bloodstained business card in my hands. Tandi's blood. Leaving this card for her was a mistake. I could only imagine how scared she was when Spike discovered it.

Dorina rested a hand on my shoulder. "That's not your fault, if that's what you're thinking. Tandi chooses to stay with him, despite the way he treats her. One day she'll get tired of his bullying and leave him."

"If you see her, tell her I'm sorry."

Dorina took the card from me. "I'll do that."

Clayton scowled as he returned his weapon to his overalls. "Tandi might be able to run away from him, but I got a business here. I told you this girl was trouble when you bought her here. Now you've put me and my shop in the middle of a mess."

Dorina shot him another exasperated scowl. "Don't pretend you didn't pull out that gun to keep him from coming after her."

Clayton's scowl deepened to a full-face grimace. "That ain't the point." He stomped to the car in the bay and bent under the hood. "I got work to do. Everybody get out."

"Thank you," Jordan told Dorina.

Clayton popped up. "I helped. You could thank me too."

I smiled. "Thank you, Clayton."

"Well, couldn't just let him take you, now could I? A man's gotta be able to sleep at night." He disappeared back under the hood, muttering to himself.

Still shaken by Spike's visit, I twined my cold fingers through Jordan's. Amusement glinted in his eyes as he looked down at the box cutter in my other hand, stubby blade still extended.

"Are you planning to carry that all the way to the car?"

"Yep. Gotta defend you from creepers."

His lips curled up at the corners, and he led me to the garage door, bending down to peer out. Satisfied it was safe, we slipped under it and hurried back to his car two streets over.

15

*A*n ambulance whooped and passed us as we idled at a traffic light, reminding me of Luke's advice this morning.

"Do you think we should call the local hospitals to see if anyone matching Cami's description has been brought in?"

"I do. I already compiled a list of hospitals and clinics to call this afternoon. I'd like to be sure the girl we're trying to find hasn't already been found," Jordan said.

If she was badly injured, unconscious, or scared, she could be lying in a hospital bed, unidentified.

I rested my head against the seat. "When we were in her apartment, I noticed the collage on her wall. It looked like a collection of dreams, places she wants to go, love stories she might wish were hers, things she wants to try."

"I saw that."

I angled toward him in my seat. "What are your dreams?"

He paused for so long that he was either trying to come up with dreams, or he was debating which ones to share with me. "Number one came true when I found my missing best friend. Number two I can't tell you."

"What? Why not?"

"For the moment, it's something I'm not ready to share. Maybe someday, when the time is right."

I couldn't read his expression, but there was something in his tone that made my nose tingle with curiosity. It was hard not to pry, but everyone was entitled to private dreams.

"Is there a number three?"

"I want my business to succeed, and number four, if you can keep a secret, I wanna beat Sam at arm wrestling."

"Mmm, I don't think that last one's gonna come true."

Sam was obscenely strong. He was the person I would call if I needed help moving my refrigerator or lifting a car off a trapped kitten.

"Thanks for the vote of confidence."

"I can lie if it'll make you feel better."

"We both know you couldn't tell a lie to save your life." He threw a grin my way. "I can take Sam in almost every sparring match, but when it comes to brute strength, he's got me beat." Sam had everyone beat in that department. "Your turn."

"I'd like to beat Sam at arm wrestling too."

He snorted a laugh. "Sounds reasonable. What else?"

I had my private dreams, like falling in love and having children, but I wasn't comfortable sharing those. "I wanna get my license and my GED, and . . . I wanna go to a prom."

Jordan glanced at me, sadness creeping into his voice. "Those are all things you missed out on because you had to run, aren't they?"

I shrugged, my mind traveling back to the day I came home from school and found Collin sitting in the living room with my foster mother. There had been rumors of a winter formal at school that day, and I had even flirted with the idea of going.

"I do have another dream," I said, forcing my thoughts away from the difficult memories. "I wanna invent marshmallow ice cream."

"I'm not sure if this'll come across as good news or bad news, but marshmallow ice cream already exists."

I gasped. "It does?"

"It does. I came across it at one of those chain ice cream places during college. I can't remember the name of it."

"I need to try it and test their flavor accuracy."

"We'll go marshmallow ice cream hunting on one of those ice cream trips I owe you for the rest of my life."

We turned into the agency parking lot, and I dropped my feet to the floorboard, wiggling my sneakers on without bothering to untie and retie the laces.

Hope sat on the sidewalk in front of the door, my shoes resting beside her. She was no smaller than I was, but at the moment, she looked tiny and defeated.

The makeup around her eyes was smudged into dark shadows, and her hair poked out in every direction like hedgehog spikes, a sign that she'd been running her fingers through it and tugging at the strands.

She lifted her head and squinted at the car as a beam of sunlight glinted off the windshield. Pushing to her feet, she tried to smooth her hair against her scalp, but it was untamable.

Jordan assessed her with a quick once-over as he shifted the car into park. "Anything I should know?"

"She's not like me."

He smiled. "Nobody's like you."

My cheeks warmed. "I mean, she's used to men interacting with her in a certain way, and she's learned to use it to her benefit. Flirting and touching are second nature to her." And they were far from second nature to me.

"Don't worry, I won't take advantage of her."

"I'm not worried about *you* taking advantage of *her*," I said, thinking about the payment arrangement she'd alluded to last night. I flung off my seat belt and climbed out of the car.

"I was starting to wonder if you were ever coming back to your office," Hope said, relief softening her shoulders. "I thought I should bring your shoes back now that I got some from my place."

I took the offered shoes. "How are you?"

"Wiped. Rough night and morning, you know?" She started to drag her hand through her hair again but stopped herself, curling her fingers into her palm. "I heard you came around asking about Cami, but you came by yourself."

There was an unspoken concern in her comment—she doubted I was capable of finding her friend on my own.

"Yeah, um, Jordan was busy, and I thought it was too important to wait. But he's on board now."

When Jordan's car door slammed, I caught the subtle slackening of Hope's jaw. "You get to work with that guy every day? Man, I'd pretend to be lost just so he could find me."

I bit back a smile. Jordan was handsome, especially when he wore a shirt that accentuated the blue of his eyes—like today—but I wasn't going to tell him that and make things awkward between us.

He joined us on the sidewalk. "You must be Hope."

The flirty curve to her lips flattened when he said her name. My instinct was right; her name was something she guarded closely, a part of herself she didn't share with everyone. "Yeah, that's me. I guess I shoulda known you'd figure that out."

Jordan unlocked and opened the door. "Ladies."

Hope strode into the office, narrow hips swinging like a pendulum, and I blew out a flustered breath before following. This was going to be an interesting meeting.

Jordan ignored her sensual strut as he flipped on the lights and excused himself to make coffee.

Hope planted her hands on her hips, lips puckered to one side as though his behavior perplexed her. Spinning toward me, she whispered, "Are you two an item?"

"No."

Her eyebrows pinched. "What's wrong with him?"

"Nothing."

"So there's something wrong with you?"

"No."

"Is he gay?"

That question threw me, and I blinked a few times before responding. "No, definitely not."

"Then what's the problem?"

120

I folded my arms, frustrated with her questions. There were a lot of problems standing between me and Jordan becoming anything more than friends, and none of them were easy to fix. Besides, he deserved a woman without so many . . . issues. I couldn't even sleep without a knife in my nightstand and a night-light attached to the wall.

Hope's gaze dipped from my face to the locket resting against my chest. "I had something like this when I was a kid." She reached out and touched it, sliding her fingers over the smooth metal and charms. "Mind?"

"Go ahead."

She popped it open to see the picture inside. "This your family?"

"Yeah."

"You got a twin, huh?" She squinted. "Which one of you is the one who looks like she licks all the cookies and puts 'em back in the jar?"

I grinned. "That would be me."

"I figured you for the one in the cutesy dress and ribbons. Seems to match your personality."

Boy, wouldn't she be surprised when she got to know me. Gin had always been the sweet one. I, on the other hand, had been a cookie-thieving, rough-and-tumble mischief monster. Despite our matching features, no one in town ever confused us.

"My locket wasn't super nice like this one, but it had a picture of me and my best friend. Livy and me were like sisters," Hope said. "You and your sister still close?"

My heart cracked at the question. "No, she, um . . . she died a long time ago."

"Tough break." She clicked my locket shut and released it.

"What happened to *your* locket?"

"Mom stole it while I was swimming at the lake and hocked it so she could buy her sleazy boyfriend beer and cigarettes."

"That's awful."

"I suppose it's my own fault for not expecting it." Hope wandered away to study the photos on the wall. Jordan had several of my photographs enlarged and framed, using them to decorate every wall of the lobby, even his office.

"What happened with your friend?" I asked, joining Hope as she studied the close-up of a bird launching from a branch and sending fall leaves showering down.

"All good things come to an end, right?" She twitched a shoulder to convey her indifference, but her tone betrayed the pain she still felt. "I don't got the best of luck with friends. First Livy, and now Cami."

"We'll do everything we can to find Cami," Jordan said, returning with two mugs of coffee. He offered one to Hope.

Her flirtatious attitude returned with his arrival, and she winked as she took the offering. "Thanks, handsome."

"There's cream and sugar on the counter if you want some. Help yourself."

She nodded but made no move toward the counter. "I wanted to say thanks for taking the case and all. I'm sure Holly told you, I don't got a lotta money to pay you, but . . . there are other ways."

She laid a suggestive hand on Jordan's arm. I tensed, wanting to rescue him from her unwanted advances. *If* they were unwanted. Hope was beautiful, even with her wild hair and smudged makeup.

Instead of pushing her hand away, Jordan stepped back beyond her reach, letting her arm drop back to her side. "Sorry, but no. I don't consider that a form of payment."

"Why not?" She sidled closer. "Holly said you two aren't together, so she won't mind, and I promise I know how to—"

He caught her wrist when she reached for him again, and I could see his struggle as a beautiful woman's temptation collided with his morals. "Don't take this as a slight, because it's not personal, but I'm not interested, and that needs to be the last time you offer."

Hope pulled her wrist free and stepped away, confusion and hurt in her voice. "What, I ain't good enough for you? You think I'm trash or something?"

Her response had the ring of old wounds, insults that had been flung at her so hard they left scars.

I touched her shoulder. "Hope—"

She wrenched away from me, coffee sloshing over the rim of the mug. "Don't touch me. I wouldn't want you to get your hands dirty handling the trash."

The tears in her eyes squeezed my heart. "I don't know who told you you're trash, but they lied. And you don't have to do that here."

"Do what?" she snapped.

"Use your body like it's something to be sold and traded. You're not a method of payment or a piece of merchandise. You're a human being."

She huffed. "Yeah, tell that to every other guy I've met."

"Point them out, and I will."

She stared at me. "Why do I get the feeling you're not bluffing?"

"She's not," Jordan confirmed, a twinkle of admiration in his eyes as he took a sip of his coffee.

Hope regarded me with wary curiosity. "I don't understand you. You're too nice to be a real person. What are you hiding? What's the angle?"

"No angle." I tucked my fingers into the back pockets of my jeans. "You don't have to be Pixie here. You can just be Hope."

"Yeah, well, I don't exactly know who that is anymore." She sank into one of the lobby chairs left over from the former doctor's office, and I caught a glimpse of the vulnerable child she must've been before this life began eating away at her innocence.

Her brown eyes held a world of uncertainty, curiosity, and even a speck of hope that people might not be as cruel and heartless as she believed five minutes ago.

Jordan, seeming to sense that his presence would be more of a hindrance than a help, said, "I'm gonna make you some chocolate milk with marshmallows." He walked to the counter by the mini fridge, giving us space.

I took the chair beside Hope, waiting to see if the silence would coax her into opening up. Finding Cami might be our goal, but helping this lost and broken girl was no less important to me.

"I was pregnant when I got caught up in all this," she finally said, tracing the rim of her mug with the pads of her thumbs. "No money, nowhere to go, and this guy caught me trying to pick his pocket. He told me I was gonna work for him. Next thing I know, I'm three months pregnant and turnin' tricks."

"What happened?"

"Had my baby, took a couple of weeks off to, you know, recover, and then got back to work. Little man's five now." Love softened her face. "I know I don't deserve him, but he's the best thing in my life. Before him, I was a nobody with nuttin' who lived in a trailer."

"There's nothing wrong with living in a trailer."

"There was a whole lot wrong with living in that sardine can," she said, and pain flitted through her eyes.

A nauseating possibility struck me as I realized how young she must've been when she got pregnant. What had she called her mom's boyfriend? Sleazy?

I swallowed the question on my tongue and chose a different one. "What's your son's name?"

"Tyler. Kid loves dinosaurs. He goes straight for the dinosaur books at the library so he can look at the pictures. He's real smart, gonna be real successful one day. He's gonna meet a nice girl his age and have a good family and a good home life."

Silence stretched before I asked, "What more can you tell me about Cami's home life? We know she ran away two years ago when she was fourteen, but we don't know why."

Hope took a sip of her coffee. "Her mom got remarried to some religious nut. He called Cami a filthy sinner every time she wore or did something he didn't like, and he used to lock her in a closet until she *repented*. Can you even imagine?"

Unfortunately, being locked in a small space was something I was intimately familiar with, and my stomach churned at the thought of little Cami trapped in a closet, sobbing and pounding on the door.

"Her mom was so in love that she didn't believe Cami when she told her what her stepdad was doing. That's why she ran away."

"Is it possible her mom or stepdad realized she was here and came to take her home?" I asked.

"I was thinking about that all last night. Cami hasn't talked to her mom in years. She felt real betrayed. But if that psycho figured out what she's been doing the past two years and came here to get her . . ." She pinched her lips. "I know she wouldn't go with him willingly, and she definitely wouldn't *not* text me back."

She retrieved a crumpled slip of paper from her skirt pocket and passed it to me.

"This is her mom's number. Cami gave it to me in case anything ever happened to her, but I can't talk to those people. Maybe you could call, and if you find out she's there, you could send a rescue party or something."

Jordan returned with my cup of chocolate milk and marshmallows and handed it to me. "Did I get the marshmallow to milk ratio right?"

I peered into the thick layer of bobbing marshmallows. "I mean it could use one m . . ." He plopped another marshmallow into it, and I laughed. "How did you know I was gonna say that?"

"Because I know you."

Hope peered into my cup. "That's nasty."

"No, *that's* nasty." I pointed to her coffee before taking a sip of my drink and chewing on a marshmallow. Who cared if no one else understood this combination of sweet perfection?

Jordan dragged another chair over and sat across from us, seriousness chasing away the lighthearted moment as he said, "We spoke with Dorina this morning, and she said a man came around asking for Cami."

Hope tensed. "Her stepdad?"

"This guy was in his twenties, comes from money, well educated." He repeated the physical description Dorina had given. "Does he sound at all familiar?"

She shrugged. "You got any idea how many guys come through there every night?"

"This guy was in a car with a group of friends last night, when they tried to pick up Holly. Dorina thinks they may have been driving the same car Cami climbed into Thursday night."

Hope turned to me. "Who are they?"

"We don't know yet," I said. "That's what we need to figure out. Dorina thinks these men could've approached other young women on the street. Have any groups of guys tried to pick you up?"

"You're kidding, right? College boys, sometimes high school boys, bachelor parties. I don't do groups, but they ask."

Jordan leaned forward, elbows on his knees. "Have you noticed anyone suspicious hanging around?"

"There's always creeps hanging around. Sometimes they get out and make trouble, and sometimes they sit in their cars and get their fix by staring at us like we're zoo animals."

"Did Dorina tell you what happened to her last night?" I asked.

Hope's gaze bounced between us. "What are you talking about? I saw Dorina this morning, and she was fine."

"A man grabbed her and tried to shove her into a van around two a.m.," I explained.

Hope's eyes widened. "She didn't say nuttin' about that earlier."

"We're not sure there's a connection with what happened to Cami, but the timing and . . ."—Jordan hesitated—"the profession of both women makes it hard to dismiss."

"Hang on." Hope set her coffee mug on the side table. "Don't get me wrong. I really like Dorina. I might even consider her a friend, but she's like fifty. Whoever tried to take her is not the same person who took a sixteen-year-old girl. You need to forget Dorina and focus on finding Cami."

"We have to consider every angle, Hope," I said, drawing on a phrase Marx had used on me when I questioned the direction of his investigation.

"That's not an angle. That's the wrong direction. This guy . . . either Cami's stepdad sent him 'cause there was no way she would get in the car with him, or he's a random psycho, and he did something to her. Or maybe he left her somewhere and somebody else did something to her. She could be locked up in some crazy guy's basement, and you have to find her."

"We're trying," I said.

"Well, try harder." Hope leaned forward and stared at the floor, taking a moment to calm her temper. She sniffed and rubbed at her nose. "I was supposed to look after her. From the moment TJ brought that fourteen-year-old girl over to my spot on Brush and told me to show her the ropes, I've been watching her back."

"This isn't your fault. Sometimes bad things just happen."

"Yeah, they sure do." She straightened and blew out a breath. "I wanna help however I can, but right now I gotta go home. I'm dead on my feet, and I only got a few hours to get some sleep before I pick up my son from day care." She stood. "I don't suppose either of you might wanna give a girl a ride home."

Jordan rose and set his mug on the reception counter. "Sure." He glanced at me. "You coming?"

"I can't. I have another appointment."

I couldn't tell him that my appointment was the food pantry, because it would add to the weight on his shoulders, and it would lead to another round of bickering about my paycheck.

"Okay. I'll talk to you later." Jordan held open the door to the parking lot.

Hope grabbed a pen and one of the business cards from the reception counter, scribbling down her number before passing it to me. "In case you learn something about Cami."

She walked past Jordan with barely a fraction of the hip action she'd displayed while entering, and it gave me hope that she might tamp down her flirtations while he drove her home.

As they turned out of the lot onto the street, I flipped open my phone and dialed the number on the slip of paper Hope had given me. The phone rang and then rolled over to a generic voice mail.

Telling the woman over voice mail that her daughter had possibly been kidnapped seemed inappropriate, so I left a vague message. Hopefully she would be the one to return my call and not her husband.

I wasn't telling that man anything.

Grabbing my knapsack, I shut off the lobby lights and locked up before walking to the bus stop to catch a ride to the food pantry.

16

I shifted the box of food in my arms as I descended the steps onto my patio, wariness crawling up my spine when I spotted the note taped to my apartment door.

The last time I found a message like this, it was from a homicidal stalker with fantasies of murdering me.

Letting the box slide onto the steps, I searched the grounds for anyone who might be watching and then peeled the note free. Steeling myself, I slipped my thumbs under the fold and opened it.

There was a handwritten message inside, and I skipped the paragraph to see who had signed the note.

Every vertebra in my spine relaxed when I saw Luke's name at the bottom, and I sat down on the step beside the box to read it.

Holly,

It was really nice seeing you again this morning. I was serious about the muffin, if you ever decide you want to reenact and improve upon our first meeting.

As thoughtful as his invitation was, I would never take him up on it. He'd made it clear he was attracted to me, and I didn't feel the same.

I checked around, but none of the paramedics in my circle picked up a girl fitting the description you gave me. There are a lot of ambulance companies in the city, though, so maybe one of them picked her up. Good luck, and sorry I couldn't do more. See you sometime. — Luke

I hadn't expected him to find anything, but I still felt a trickle of disappointment. Cami had been missing for almost two days, and we had no clues to point us in her direction.

Rising to my feet, I tucked the note into my pocket and unlocked my apartment. I stared at the box of groceries with a mixture of appreciation and weariness.

After hauling it to and from the bus stop, my arm muscles were limp noodles, and the last thing I felt like doing was picking it up again. But I couldn't kick it the rest of the way.

With a sigh, I hefted the box off the ground and lugged it inside. I dropped it onto the kitchen counter and nearly collapsed on top of it from exhaustion.

Who knew one box of groceries could weigh so much? I'd given up trying to carry it from the church to the bus stop and started dragging it like a dead limb.

A volunteer from the food pantry offered to help, but he set off all kinds of internal warning bells. I couldn't pinpoint *why* he unsettled me, but he did.

Maybe it was the way he watched me while I packed my box or the way his fingers grazed mine when he tried to take it from me and carry it outside. It could've been his offer to drive me home . . . after I politely declined three times or the way he talked about his "mission to convert those sinners in poor neighborhoods."

I could've misunderstood, but it sounded like he thought less of people who hadn't accepted Jesus, and it bothered me. Some of the people I loved most weren't Christians yet.

I blew a strand of hair from my face and straightened to examine my groceries. Other than the apple juice and a package of hot dogs, the rest could go in the cupboard.

Marx wouldn't approve of the crackers, cookies, and white bread, but I did grab jam and peaches. He was from Georgia. He had to approve of peaches, right?

I tucked away the groceries and set the box on the floor for Sausage to play with. He hopped off the couch with a chortle of excitement and waddled over to his kitty castle.

I dropped into one of the kitchen chairs to rest from the exertion of grocery shopping. I barely stretched out my legs when my phone in my knapsack on the counter rang.

Maybe it was Cami's mom returning my call. I hopped up and grabbed my phone, but the name that flashed across the screen was Jordan's.

Uh-oh.

Maybe I should've skipped the food pantry today and ridden with him and Hope. It wouldn't surprise me if she'd put him in an uncomfortable position. I couldn't blame her for being forward. She was a child when she found herself alone on the unforgiving streets of New York City, and she adapted to survive. I just didn't want my friends to have to fend off her advances.

I flipped open my cell. "Hey, did everything go okay?"

"Yeah, I dropped Hope at home. She's got our business card with my cell number in case she needs to reach us tomorrow while the office is closed. How did everything go with your appointment?"

"No problems," I said, rubbing at a muscle spasm in my forearm.

"Did you have a chance to call the number Hope gave you?"

"Yeah, I left a message. I was actually hoping it was Cami's mom returning my call." I paused before voicing one of my concerns. "What if Mrs. Chen has a different number than the one Cami gave to Hope? It's been two years."

"If someone you love goes missing, you do everything in your power to make sure you keep the methods of communication they're familiar with. Phone number, email, home address. You don't wanna chance missing that call or that message. If she doesn't get back to you tonight, try her again in the morning."

I scuffed my sneaker on the floor. "Speaking of tonight, I don't suppose you wanna sneak into a gala."

Amusement colored his voice. "While I appreciate the unofficial invite, I'm gonna call around to the hospitals and see what more I can dig up on Cami's social media accounts. I'll check in on you, though. See how you're holding up."

"Thanks. Talk to you later." I disconnected and crouched to give my animals some love. "All right, fur babies. I'm gonna go spend some time with your auntie Jace. Be good while I'm gone."

17

I tried to put thoughts of the case aside for the afternoon as Jace and I rummaged through her enormous closet for party clothes. Every time I thought we were almost finished, she whipped open another section.

The closet that came with the apartment wasn't nearly big enough to accommodate her shopping addiction, so she had the wall-to-wall storage unit shipped and assembled shortly after moving in.

The shoe section in the center took up more space than my entire wardrobe. For someone who couldn't feel her feet, my best friend had a die-hard obsession with shoes.

My attention drifted to the Darth Vader slippers on an upper shelf. I doubted Sam ever wore them when he was here, but the visual in my head was enough to make me smile.

Lifting a lid to one of the shoe boxes closest to me, I peered inside. I found a pair of knee-high, flat-bottomed boots whose color I could only describe as crusty mustard. Oddly, they gave me a craving for hot dogs from the vendor down the street.

"What do you think?" Jace asked, distracting me from thoughts of lunch, which I hadn't had time to eat.

"About the mustard boots?"

She threw me an indignant scowl. "The color is dandelion gold."

"Oh, so it's dandelion paste they squeeze onto hotdogs and cheeseburgers," I teased, my stomach letting out a quiet but desperate rumble for food.

"Ha-ha, you're hilarious." She swung a yellow dress from the metal rod and held it in front of her, waving a hand toward it as if she were a game show host. "This is mustard."

Amusement tickled my lips as I studied the feathers that trimmed the obviously yellow dress. "You killed Big Bird for that dress, didn't you?"

Her jaw dropped with indignation. "This is an extra small, so no, I killed Tweety Bird, and it was for a good reason."

There was *no* reason for that dress, even on a deserted island, but I kept that judgment to myself. While I preferred to blend in, Jace enjoyed standing out in a crowd, and we dressed accordingly.

She returned the hanger to the closet and plucked another option free—a green dress that flared out like a parachute midthigh. "What about this one for tonight?"

My eyebrows inched up. "Is that designed to slow you down if you fall out of a plane?"

"Never hurts to have a dress that doubles as a safety device."

Safety and dresses didn't belong in the same sentence, in my opinion.

"Did you know they even make dresses with inflatable sleeves in case you fall off a party yacht? Can you imagine one of them accidentally inflating at a party?" Jace asked with a grin, but there was something forced about the broad smile on her face.

"That would be awkward," I said, watching her out of the corner of my eye as she wiggled the dress back into the closet.

The smile dissolved from her lips, and pain crawled across her features before her black curtain of hair fell over the side of her face.

My friend was hurting, and I didn't know why. Did it have something to do with her brother, or was it the gala?

"Any news on your Cami case yet?" she asked.

"We're no closer to finding her, but Jordan had a showdown with a pimp who might be involved."

Her wide blue eyes snapped to me. "Are you serious? Like an actual flesh-peddling thug with gold teeth and a villainous temper?"

Sometimes I forgot how sheltered her upbringing was. I had navigated the same streets as these "flesh peddlers" before, but her exposure to pimps was limited to characters in TV shows and movies.

"No to the gold teeth, yes to the temper. But he calmed down when Jordan pulled his gun," I said.

"That's crazy."

My stomach rumbled. I needed a snack, preferably cheesy crackers. "I'm gonna grab some snackers." I blinked at the word that popped out of my mouth, a mangled combination of *snacks* and *crackers*. "Um . . . snacks."

"There's broccoli in the fridge." At my scowl, she grinned. "What? I'm trying to help you eat more rounded, like Mr. Southern suggested. You are kind of a sugar addict."

"Says the caffeine addict."

"Touché, my pocket-sized friend, touché."

I made my way to the kitchen and rummaged through the cupboard for a snack, settling on a box of multigrain crackers and sliced cheese. I placed a few cracker sandwiches on a plate and strode back into the bedroom.

Jace sat in front of the closet, her hand lingering on a floor-length, deep blue gown with beaded sleeves, and I could see the agitated rise and fall of her chest.

I set the plate of snacks on the bed, hunger forgotten.

"That's a beautiful dress," I said, coming up beside her. It was something I would've been thrilled to wear in another life.

"It was my junior prom dress," Jace said, easing it from the closet. She stared at it as though it held ghosts. "I danced for hours with my friends."

Clouds of grief gathered around her as she smoothed the fabric over her stomach and lap, the material spilling from her knees and down over her wheels like a shimmering waterfall.

My heart twisted as I realized she was remembering a time before the accident, when the gown poured down her straight body to conceal elegant shoes rather than wheels, a time when she'd been able to dance around the room with whatever boy worked up the nerve to ask her.

I crouched in front of her. "Talk to me, Jace. I know something's wrong." For as long as I'd known her, there was something about this time of year that made her withdraw.

Tears spilled over the rims of her eyes. "It was April . . . when the accident happened. April twenty-ninth, eight years ago."

Which meant it was less than a week until the anniversary of the event that altered her life forever. The crash, followed by the devastating news that she would never walk again.

"I hate this month, and of all the times to host a gala with dancing, my mother chooses April." Her chin quivered. "I don't know if she's being cruel or if it really didn't occur to her."

"Your mom can be a bit . . . self-absorbed," I said. Which was better than cruel, I supposed.

"Yeah, if by a *bit* you mean chronically. It's amazing she knows there are other people on the planet." She swiped at her damp face. "I've been trying so hard not to think about the accident, about the things I can't do anymore, and now this. I feel . . . like . . . I'm gonna burst."

"It's okay to cry."

"Says the strongest person I know. You've been through things I can't even imagine, and you hardly ever break down."

Her words surprised me. I didn't think of myself as strong, especially considering my mini meltdown at the library two nights ago. I hated letting people see my vulnerability, but maybe that was exactly what she needed.

"Last month was hard for me," I admitted. "With it being . . ."

"Your abductiversary?"

I crinkled my nose. "Let's not call it that. But yeah, it was painful."

The days of anxiety and depression leading up to that horrible anniversary culminated in sleepless nights and a flood of tears heavy enough to drown a village.

Marx had spent every available minute of those four days with me, surrounding me with love and comfort when I could barely function.

"And two nights ago, I had a panic attack at the library because I smelled his cologne. I sort of ran out with a bag of books I didn't check out. Alarms were going off, and I was dry heaving on the sidewalk."

The elegant gown pooled in Jace's lap as she released it and reached for my hands. "You should've called me. I would've come to help you through it." A breath shuddered from her. "But I get why you didn't. Some things are hard to talk about."

"They are, but letting another person in on that pain can make it less overwhelming. I'm guessing you haven't talked to Sam about all this, and your family probably isn't the most understanding."

She let out a watery scoff at the mention of her family. "Dad cares, but I can't talk to him. He tells my mother everything, and then I would get a call lecturing me about being overly dramatic. She's not the one who has to live the rest of her life in this chair."

I squeezed her fingers. "I'm sorry your mom is the way she is, but you always have me to talk to."

"You have so much of your own pain, Holly, and I—"

"Friends lean on each other when they're having a hard time. I'm trying to be . . . more open, and I want you to know you can do the same."

She lowered her head and released a quivering breath. It took her a moment to collect her words. "Sometimes . . . it makes me furious that the man who rear-ended my car and knocked me into oncoming traffic is walking around like nothing happened. My life changed in an instant, but he walked away with a few bruises. I know it was an accident, and I try not to hate him, but it's hard when I'm faced with things I can't do anymore because of his actions. Today is . . ." Her voice cracked. "Today is hard."

I wrapped my arms around her, and she buried her face in my shoulder, the salty wetness of her tears soaking into my shirt as she broke into sobs.

My throat burned with the pressure of my own tears, and I looked up at the ceiling. *God, I know Jace doesn't really know you, but you love her, and you ache for her. Please bring her some comfort.*

I wished there was something *I* could do to soothe her pain, but all I could do was hold her and let her know that this was no longer a battle she had to fight alone.

"I know that accident changed everything for you, and you struggle with how it turned out, but this you, the one you are now, is the amazing person I've come to know and adore. I'm grateful you survived, because it means I have you as a friend."

She was quiet for a moment before saying, "If I hadn't survived, you'd be stuck with Jordan as a BFF."

"It's not nice to call him my big fat friend. You know how sensitive he is about his figure," I teased.

She let out a snort that was half-laugh, half-sob and no small amount of snot, her arms tightening around me. "I love you, Holly."

I squeezed her back. "Love you too."

She pulled away and brushed at her face with her fingers. "We still need to find you something to wear tonight." She lifted the hanger with the beautiful gown. "And I think this needs a new home."

I pushed to my feet. "Don't look at me. I don't do dresses."

"It would look really pretty on you. Except . . ." Her gaze traveled the length of the gown and then the length of me. "You're like nine inches too short. I wonder if Miracle-Gro works on people."

"I'm sure someone's eaten it, hoping it would."

"Right?! But seriously, I think I can have this fitted to your height for the wedding. That way you can wear something other than jeans."

I folded my arms over my stomach. "I can't, Jace." Wearing anything that left me vulnerable during an attack was an anxiety I hadn't managed to work through.

"Man, we're quite the messed-up pair. I'm over here having a nervous breakdown because it's April, and you wear like ten layers of clothes every day because . . . you know."

"Isn't everybody kind of a closet disaster?"

"Not me. I can't fit in the closet with my wheels. I am front-and-center-stage disaster."

I admired her attempt to joke about her circumstances on a day like this. She was trying to recover and move forward.

She returned the gown to the closet. "I'm still gonna have this fitted for you in case you're feeling courageous the day of the wedding, but I have a few ideas for tonight." She collected several items from the closet and handed them to me. "One of these should work." She pulled out her phone. "Now, I have a very important message to send."

"To who?"

"Jordan. I need to let him know I'm your best friend forever, which leaves him as the big fat friend."

"Do not send that." I grabbed for her phone and missed. "Jace."

She grinned up at me, fingers flying across the virtual keyboard. "Relax. I'm texting Sam to see when he's gonna be here with coffee. I need caffeine and sugar if I'm gonna survive this night."

"I'm not sure caffeine will help."

"Of course it will. I'll let you try stuff on."

She glided out of the room and closed the door behind her. I locked it and then tossed the clothes onto the bed with a sigh. There had to be seven different outfits.

Reluctantly, I stripped and began the miserable process of putting on clothes only to take them off sixty seconds later. All but one pair of dress pants were too long. The last time I saw Jace wear them, the bottoms reached her calves. Their stretchy material hugged my ankles.

A knock sounded on the apartment door as I was changing back into my clothes, and Sam's flat, muffled voice drifted through the apartment.

"I know you wanted espresso, but I got you a decaf mocha. Spending the evening with your mother raises your blood pressure, and caffeine won't help."

"The woman's a walking stress test for anyone who crosses her path. Decaf won't make much of a difference, but thanks."

"Where's Holly? I brought her a tea."

"She's in the bedroom, trying on clothes for the gala. I suggested some dresses, but you were right. She's not ready."

Fully clothed, I unlocked the bedroom door and padded into the living room to find Sam sitting on the arm of the couch. "Hey, Sam."

He tipped his head in greeting. "Holly." He held out the drink tray with one cup remaining.

"Thanks." I took it and sipped at the straw, sweetness coating my tongue.

"I'm gonna go shower so I have time to try on twenty dresses and style my hair." Jace kissed Sam and rolled into the bathroom.

I sank onto the opposite arm of the couch. "I'm sorry you're not invited tonight."

"Jace's mother makes no secret about her dislike for me. I think you might be the only person she dislikes more."

I pondered that as I sipped my tea. "If an unlikable person dislikes you, is that a compliment?"

A hint of a smile curved his lips. "I'm not sure it works that way, but she has reason to dislike me. I explained the monumental errors in her parenting style the last time we were in a room together."

"Oh, I wish I had been invited to that conversation. Did she press her lips together so hard they turned white?"

"She did." He waited for the shower to turn on before continuing. "I'm not sure how well you know Mrs. Walker, but she has a tendency to use her wealth and power to control the people around her."

"I've noticed." The woman's husband was a submissive turtle.

"Jace has a hard time standing up to her, especially when her brother's life is on the negotiating table."

I cringed inwardly at his phrasing. He wasn't wrong, but it brought the reality of the situation into the light—Mrs. Walker believed her son was dead, and she had no problem leveraging Jace's love for him to influence her actions and decisions.

"Jace is the only heir to her family's wealth and businesses," Sam said. "Mrs. Walker has plans for her future, and unfortunately, I don't think you and I are a part of them."

His words left a queasy knot in my stomach. If Mrs. Walker was willing to use Scott to influence Jace's activities, it was only a matter of time before she used him to control where she lived and whom she spent time with.

"She banned you from the party because she can't control you, and you would be a voice of reason in the face of whatever she tries to push Jace into doing next," I realized.

"I suspect that's why she doesn't care for you either. We're wild cards. I'm guessing she doesn't know you're coming."

"Nope."

"Good. That means Jace won't be alone whenever her mother makes a move."

And if it was within my power, I would not let that woman force my friend into a life she didn't want.

18

J gaped at the ornate doors looming at the top of the exterior staircase. They had to be ten feet tall, and the glistening windows that spanned the first floor were equally large.

As I climbed the steps, I felt like Jack shimmying up the beanstalk to knock on the giant's door. Would they even let me in without an invitation?

A few couples passed me, exquisite gowns and sleek heels peeping beneath the bottoms of the women's coats. They dressed and carried themselves with elegance.

Elegant was nowhere in my DNA. If I made it through the night without tripping or stepping on someone's foot, it would be a miracle.

"Good evening, ma'am." A man in a uniform stepped away from the wall and opened one of the doors as I reached the top of the steps.

Jace was working her way up the ramp, so I stepped inside, the warmth of the hall wrapping around me as a shiver from the chilly night clacked my teeth together.

I drank in the extravagant space—a chandelier glittering overhead, floral wallpaper, wood floors that gleamed in the warm artificial light. And this was only the hallway. How fancy would the bathrooms be? I would bet they had really expensive soap.

An endless rack of black, gray, and cream-colored jackets stretched out before me, and I unzipped my purple puff coat with a fake fur lining. At least I wouldn't have any trouble finding it at the end of the night.

As I shrugged free of my warm layer, another man in a uniform appeared out of nowhere, extending his arm. "May I take your jacket, miss?"

Oh, this was one of those weird rich-people customs, where you weren't allowed to hang up your own coat. Reluctantly I handed it over, watching where the attendant placed it in case I needed to escape early.

Chilly air swirled through the entryway as the door opened again, and Jace rolled in. "That ramp is definitely steeper than it should be. I rolled backward twice." She twisted out of her jacket and tossed it to the attendant.

She had chosen a sleeveless sapphire gown that grazed her ankles, leaving her sparkly shoes on display. It also left the deep bruise on her right bicep visible.

"That looks like it hurts."

She twisted her arm to see the bruise. "It does, but I kinda like it. It's like my battle wound."

"Didn't you get it during sled hockey practice?"

"Yep. From Warren, my archnemesis. He's *almost* as good as me, so the coach never puts us on the same team during practice. He slapped the puck, and it nailed me right between the padding."

"Your mom's gonna freak out."

"Only because of how it looks, not because she's concerned. But she'll be too busy freaking out about your presence to notice." She eyed the doors into the ballroom and puffed air through her lips. Reaching over, she snagged my hand. "Thanks for coming with me. I don't think I could do this without at least one ally."

I squeezed her hand and smiled.

"Okay, let's go pretend-party." She passed her invitation to the bouncer with the overhanging brow and informed him I was her plus-one. He opened the door to let us through.

The vast room could've been plucked from a castle—decorative tiles on the high ceiling, gold trim, another crystal chandelier, and tables draped in white cloth around the edges of the dance floor, where everyone mingled.

I slid a look at Jace. "You said your family has a lot of money. I think they have more than a lot if they can afford this."

"I might've undersold that a teensy bit. They're *super* rich, and they like to mingle with the well-offs in the city. Hence the ballroom and the table with enough food to feed the starving children of a third world country."

There were so many people—and far too many men in one room. My anxiety spiked, and my steps forward faltered.

Jace squeezed my hand. "You're having man anxiety, aren't you? I totally understand, but you're gonna be fine. If you could handle the degenerates on You-Know-What Avenue, you can handle the walking wallets."

She was right. I made it through Brushwick unscathed. I could handle an upscale dance party.

"Let me introduce you to some people from a distance." Jace pointed at random individuals in the room. "That guy runs a charity for inner-city youth. Super nice and thoughtful. That lady there is married to some millionaire who makes smart cars that one of our companies provides an essential piece of the technology for. Almost certain that guy in the blue tux is a closet serial killer."

"He . . . what?"

"Just making sure you're paying attention. He's actually the police commissioner. He'll be here for like five minutes before he makes an escape."

"Your mom invited a cop?"

"His role is more political, I guess. Nothing like what Sam or Marx do. But I guess he hates mingling at things like this."

"I can relate," I muttered.

"I see my dad. I'll be back in a sec."

"But . . ."

And she was gone, weaving her way across the crowded room. Great. I closed my fingers around my locket and tried to ignore the curious and occasionally judgmental glances from guests. Even in Jace's borrowed clothes, I was out of place among shimmering floor-length gowns and tailored suits, and I could read the questions on some of their faces.

Yes, I was invited. No, I didn't wander in off the street to steal your jewelry and wallets. I might stuff food into my pockets before I leave, however, I silently retorted, as I meandered toward the food table.

I didn't recognize some of the fancier foods, so I grabbed a fruit-and-cheese kabob and two chocolates. I nibbled on my snacks as I traveled the edges of the room, hoping I might come across Marx. We could hide in a corner together.

I stilled when I spotted a familiar face—a petite Asian woman in a navy dress, her black hair coiled on top of her head, diamond earrings swinging like pendulums over her bare shoulders.

Mrs. Walker.

There weren't many people in the world I disliked with every fiber of my being, but Mrs. Walker was one of them. She treated people like they were beneath her, and she didn't have an ounce of warmth or affection for her daughter.

"I think the two of you would be a sensible match," she said to a man whose back was to me. "Jacelyn is a bit free-spirited, but that's nothing the right marriage can't fix. An engagement to a congressman's son would be quite an achievement for her, and of course, we would take care of all the expenses."

Engagement? She was trying to arrange a marriage for her daughter, with no regard for what Jace wanted?

"She's not seeing anyone else?" the man asked.

"She is, but he's little more than a passing interest."

Jace and Sam were growing closer every day, and there was no way she would leave him for another man, no matter how *sensible* the match. Unless . . .

My swallow of cheese cube landed in my stomach like a brick. Was the woman ruthless enough to use Scott's life to force Jace into a relationship that aligned with her goals?

"It might take her a few months to warm up to the idea, but I'm sure you can win her over, and of course I'll nudge her in the right . . ." Mrs. Walker trailed off when she spotted me, and I could see her brain trying to come to terms with my presence. "What is she doing here?"

The man turned, and the breath in my lungs hitched. Chiseled cheekbones, long hair combed back, and a wolfish smile.

It was the man from the passenger seat of the car outside Clayton's shop, the car Dorina suspected might have something to do with Cami's disappearance. Erik.

The smile melted from his face, and his complexion paled with shock before anger brought the blood rushing back to his cheeks.

What did *he* have to be upset about? I was the one he and his friends had tried to rent for an hour. I needed to ask him about Cami, but judging by the outrage smoldering in his eyes, that conversation wouldn't be productive.

He excused himself and stormed off in the other direction. The breath eased from my lungs, and the ball of nerves in my stomach uncurled.

Who was he? And what would a congressman's son be doing on a street with a reputation like Brushwick?

A blur of blue brought my attention back to the petite Asian woman covering the distance between us with brisk steps, a thunderstorm raging in her eyes.

She stopped so close to me that her perfume burned my nose, and her high heels put her several inches above me. "How dare you show up here?"

I matched her glare, unintimidated by her venomous tone. "Your daughter invited me."

"This event is for civilized society."

I flicked a glance in the direction Erik had gone. "And you think that man you were talking to is civilized?"

"The congressman and his son are respectable and accomplished, something I expect you know little about."

"You can't force Jace to marry someone you picked out. It doesn't work that way anymore."

"I'm not *forcing* my daughter to do anything, but I will encourage her to do what is best for her and this family."

"Encourage . . . by making her choose between the life of her brother and her own future? Are you really that cold and unfeeling?"

Her eyelids fluttered in surprise, but the moment passed, and her expression turned granite. "I will not allow my only living child to spend her life in poverty, with a man who will never be anything more than a civil servant. I have worked too hard to provide her with a future to allow her to throw it away. Not that our family affairs are any of your concern."

I gestured after Erik. "That man isn't a good person, and he certainly isn't what's best for her."

"And you know him how?"

I opened my mouth and then closed it. If I told her about his proposition on Brushwick, it would only confirm her belief that I was a prostitute. "It doesn't matter how I know him. What matters is, she deserves someone who loves and treasures her, and right now, that person is Sam."

"There is more to life than love."

"Love is the most beautiful thing you can have in this life. Everything else falls short."

"Mother." Jace wheeled over to join us, eyes narrowing at her mom's confrontational posture.

Mrs. Walker pressed her shoulders back. "I expected you to have the sense not to invite her, Jacelyn. I'm disappointed in you."

The disapproval radiating from her was so heavy that even I could feel the weight of it.

Jace's shoulders dropped a fraction. "She's my friend, Mother."

"She is a corrupting influence in your life, drawing your focus and ambition away from where it should be. As your mother, it's my duty to save you from reckless choices and dangerous influences, even if you don't like it."

She motioned someone forward, and I twisted to see two stone-faced men in suits break away from the wall.

Oh crud, security guards. She was going to have me forcibly removed from the gala. The possibility of being dragged or carried out launched my heart into my throat.

"You can't do this, Mother." Jace locked an arm around my waist.

Mrs. Walker ignored her and addressed the summoned guards. "This woman isn't on the guest list, and she isn't welcome. Escort her out without making a scene."

One of the men reached for me, and Jace slapped his hand away before his fingers could wrap around my arm. "Don't touch my friend."

The guard blinked in surprise, then silently deferred to Mrs. Walker for instructions on how to proceed with her daughter.

"If these mall cops touch Holly, you're the one who's gonna create a scene, Mother. You invited the district attorney, who adores Holly, and the man she brought with her is a homicide detective who thinks of Holly as a daughter. If anyone lays a finger on her, there will be a scene, and it'll be one your shallow guests will whisper about for years."

"I doubt that very much," Mrs. Walker said, but I couldn't see the expression on her face because I was too concerned with the men hovering in my personal space.

Neither of them made another move to grab me as they waited for instructions, one hand clasping the opposite wrist in front of them, but they watched me.

"If you had bothered to show up to the trial in January, you would already know how close Holly is with Shannon and Marx," Jace said. "And you would've realized that what you think you know about my best friend couldn't be further from the truth."

Mrs. Walker lowered her voice. "I know she is the reason you were abducted and nearly killed by one of her disgruntled ex-lovers."

"If you had even watched the trial, you would know that's not true either. I saw Daddy in the courtroom during my testimony, but you were nowhere to be found."

"There was a problem at one of the companies. We had to—"

"You have people for that. Just admit that you were embarrassed by the attention the trial brought to our family. For a second, I thought *maybe* you might be proud of me for standing up to the psycho who threatened to kill me, but that was too much to ask."

Mrs. Walker waved away the security, and the men retreated to their positions along the wall. "You know better than to use *maybe* and *might* in the same sentence, Jacelyn. It makes you sound uneducated."

Tears gathered in Jace's eyes. "That's what you took away from everything I said? My improper sentence structure?"

Mrs. Walker sighed. "I'm weary of your theatrics and childish rebellions. As the daughter of the host and hostess, I expect you to put your best face forward and mingle. As for you"— The hostile glance she threw my way suggested she considered my presence one of those childish rebellions—"try to avoid drawing attention to yourself."

What did she think I was doing by skirting the edges of the room and talking to no one?

Mrs. Walker smoothed her hands over her dress and then turned to address Jace once more. "With enthusiasm and a smile."

She waited for Jace to plaster on a fake smile before nodding and striding back into the throng of guests.

Jace's lips fell flat, and tears clung to her eyelashes. "Mingling is part of the agreement. You don't have to talk to anyone, but please don't run off and leave me."

"I'm not going anywhere, but we need to talk about your mom. She's up to something."

"She's always up to something." She squeezed my hand and then set off to appease the woman whose love and acceptance always seemed out of reach.

I dropped into a chair at one of the empty tables and blew out a breath. The music from the live band in one corner of the room grew louder, and clusters of chattering people broke into dancing.

The sequined purse Jace had lent me for the night made a water-drop sound, and I unsnapped the clasp to retrieve my phone. Jordan had sent me a message.

No luck with hospitals. How's the party?

I grunted and typed in reply, *You remember the birthday when Gin had the stomach flu, and we entertained her with skits and games, only to catch the same upchuck-y bug later that night? That was more fun.*

I could understand why Jace hated attending these events. There might be delicious food and live music, but what good was it when you had to pull on a mask and pretend to be someone you weren't?

"How much for a dance?" a familiar voice asked, and my attention snapped to the man who approached my table. Erik offered me a sneering smile as he dragged out the chair next to mine and sat.

Fear spread its wings in my chest, and I looked around the room. There were over a hundred people here, and Marx was somewhere in the crowd. Even if this man was responsible for what happened to Cami, he couldn't hurt me here.

"I realize talking isn't what you do best," he said, not bothering to hide the disgust in his voice. "But try, because we have something important to discuss."

He shifted so his legs were a hairsbreadth from mine, and panic whispered across my nerve endings. I scooted my chair away from his, bumping into the empty chair behind me.

The screech of wood on the floor drew a few sets of eyes, including the security, and Erik's mouth tightened. No doubt he wanted to have this conversation somewhere more private, but I wasn't going anywhere with him.

He lowered his voice. "You can quit the shy, innocent act. We both know you've been a lot closer to a man than this. *Holly*."

I stiffened, and smugness curled his lips.

"Mrs. Walker was happy to give me your name, as well as a detail or two that confirm what I already suspected. You're not supposed to be here. I can only think of two reasons a girl like you would be at a party like this. Either you're hoping to snag the attention and wallets of a few wealthy, unhappily married men, or you're here to blackmail me." His jaw hardened. "If you think I'm going to pay you to keep quiet about my extracurricular activities, think again. I'm not giving you a cent that isn't earned."

Desire overshadowed his irritation for a second, and my stomach squeezed. Jordan was right about men like him. He was close to my age, but he was nothing but a disrespectful boy driven by his urges and wants.

I twisted the remains of my cheese kabob in my grip. If he touched me, the pointy end would turn his hand into a kabob. "What did you do to Cami?"

"Who's Cami?"

I shouldn't be surprised he didn't know her name. "The girl who got in your car Thursday night. Black and Asian features."

Recognition lit his eyes. "I didn't do anything to that basket case. She freaked out when we stopped to pick up my friends, something about not liking groups, and got out of my car."

Dorina had warned her about being in a car with more than one man. They had a tendency to feed off each other's emotions and behaviors, and sometimes people got hurt.

Skepticism laced my voice. "And you let her go?"

"It was either her or my guys, and she wasn't worth the trouble. We found our entertainment elsewhere."

"She didn't make it back that night."

"That's her problem. We didn't do anything to her, so if you're here to accuse me of something, you're wasting your time." He leaned forward, dropping his voice to barely above a whisper. "To avoid any misunderstanding, you're not getting any money from me or my family, and if you go around spreading rumors, I will make your life—"

"Don't threaten me." I glared at him, bolstered by the familiar presence at the edge of my vision. Marx had slipped out of the dance crowd and was standing by a far table, monitoring the situation while giving me space.

One wrong twitch, and Erik would be kissing the dance floor.

"I don't want your money," I informed him. "I want you to back out of the arrangement you're making with Mrs. Walker."

He scoffed. "You want me to pass up a promising opportunity with one of the wealthiest and most influential families in this city."

"If you wanna marry someone for money, go for it," I said. "But stay away from my friend."

"You expect me to believe Jacelyn Walker is friends with a prostitute."

"She prefers Jace, and I don't care what you believe. She's a wonderful person, and if there's anything I can do about it, I won't let her mother force her into a relationship she doesn't want. She deserves better."

If Mrs. Walker intended to use Scott's health care as a bargaining chip again, Jace might choose her brother's life over her future, and this man would dull the sparkle in her eyes and squeeze the bubbles from her spirit.

Erik huffed. "This has to be a joke."

"I don't wanna hurt you, and I don't want my friend to get hurt, but if bringing your despicable behavior out of the shadows and into the light is the only way to save her from a heartbreaking decision, then I will."

His face reddened. "You realize I have enough influence and power to destroy your life, pathetic as it is."

The sound that escaped my throat was somewhere between a sad sigh and a laugh. "Scarier men than you have tried."

One had nearly succeeded. I had no doubt Erik could be dangerous, but he wasn't even in the same terrifying hemisphere as Collin.

"Please, tell Mrs. Walker you're not interested. If you don't, I'll have to tell her where I know you from. In this judgmental world, once one person knows, I imagine it doesn't stay secret long." I pushed to my feet, sliding my phone back into my purse.

Erik rose, fingers curling into fists at his sides, and I stepped back. He might not be the kind of evil who locked a girl up and tortured her for days, but his punch would still knock me flat.

"Holly." Marx's voice wrapped around me like a warm sweater on a winter evening, pure comfort and safety. He approached, his attention fixed on the man towering over me. "And who might you be?"

Erik forced his fingers to relax, but his face was still flushed. "I was about to ask her to dance."

"Mmm hmm. How unfortunate for you she already has a dance partner." He offered his hand. "Sweetheart."

I left my kabob on the table and slipped my fingers into his, letting him lead me away from the threat and out onto the dance floor. "You look nice in a suit."

The charcoal suit and forest-green undershirt brought out the green of his eyes. He would blend into the wealthy crowd, except for the way his gaze continually swept the room—absorbing details and assessing situations. Always a cop.

"It feels like a straitjacket," he admitted. "But I'll wear it for Shannon. You look extra pretty tonight. Blue's a good color for you." When I blushed at the compliment, he added, "It goes with that adorable shade of pink your face just turned."

"Oh hush," I said, flustered, and he chuckled.

"Here's a good spot." He found an opening for us and guided me around to face him.

"Um, you know I've only ever danced that once. In your mom's kitchen."

"Just do what I tell you to."

"I'm not very good at that."

Amusement twinkled in his eyes. "I know." He guided my arms up and onto his shoulders, then rested his hands above my hips. "Now we move to the rhythm of the . . ."

I stepped on something and stumbled.

"That was my foot."

I winced. "Sorry."

"You wanna tell me who . . ." He trailed off when I stumbled again. "That was my other foot. What are you doin' down there, an Irish jig? Glide, don't stomp."

I dropped my head against his chest, which vibrated with silent laughter. Trying to keep my fidgety feet still, I swayed to the music with him.

"You wanna tell me who that man was and why he was mean-muggin' you?" Marx asked.

Ooh, dangerous territory. If I told him the whole truth, he would flip out about me going to Brushwick, and then he would lecture me until the end of time.

"He's an obnoxious guy who wasn't getting his way. Where's Shannon? Shouldn't you be dancing with her?"

The slight pinch of Marx's lips told me I had tripped his detective radar. He knew I was withholding important information. "She's talkin' to some politician. Why, I don't know. Politicians

155

can't tell the truth if it's written on a teleprompter in front of their faces."

If that was true, could I trust what Erik said about Cami, or was he as skilled at lying as his politician father likely was?

"Is that man you were talkin' to a problem?"

"Nothing I can't handle." *I hope.*

"If that changes, you call me. Immediately."

We danced through two slow songs while Jace mingled, and contentment twined around my heart. Collin had robbed me of the opportunity to attend prom, but I imagined it would be like this—swaying to soft music in the arms of someone special. I might not be wearing a beautiful gown, and we might not be romantically interested in each other, but this moment felt perfect.

A gentle smile curved Marx's mouth as he studied my face. "You look happy."

"I am." I met his warm green eyes, so full of affection. "Thanks for loving me."

Amusement crinkled the skin near his temples. "You don't have to thank me for that, sweetheart."

I shrugged and changed the subject to something that wouldn't make my eyes burn. "The past few days, I've been thinking about your wedding cake."

"You thinkin' about sweets. I'm shocked."

I scrunched my nose at him. "I saw this one online with pastel M&M's around the outside that spell the word *love*. I think it would be cute for a wedding reception. Or there was this other one. The layers were cut so it kinda looked like a leaning tower of flowers."

"A crooked cake."

"With flowers."

He chuckled. "As amusin' as that might be, Shannon already picked out a cake. It's a simple white cake with white frostin'."

"That's it? No pretty colors or candies or sprinkles?"

"That's how she wants it."

"Well . . . she has terrible taste."

"Thank you," he said, deadpan.

I laughed. "I don't mean you."

"Mmm hmm."

A commotion broke out at the front of the room, and even though the band continued without a hitch, many of the dancers around us paused, frozen in their poses.

"Stop, okay?!" Jace's shout carried through the ballroom, and all other conversation dropped away.

I moved for a better view of the dispute, and I caught sight of Jace and her mother in front of the buffet table, a metal tray of snacks scattered across the floor. Jace turned away from her mortified mother and wheeled from the room, guests hastening to clear a path.

Crap.

I looked up to see that Marx had followed me. I stretched onto my toes to kiss his cheek. "I gotta go. Thanks for the Irish jig."

I skirted the edge of the room, offering a wave to Shannon as I made my way to the double doors. I spilled into the entryway to find Jace jerking the sleeves of her jacket over her arms.

She sniffled. "I was gonna text you that we need to leave early."

The attendant brought my coat, and I thanked him before tugging it on. "Your mom said something to you."

"When doesn't she have some kind of critical commentary on my life decisions?" She released a long breath that shivered with pent-up tears and wheeled toward the exit.

I wished I could console her, but there were no words to take away the pain of her mother's rare and conditional acceptance. I couldn't even call it love.

The attendant opened the door, and a man's hushed voice drifted in with the chill that bit at our faces. "It's an unexpected problem, but . . ."

The muscles in my body knotted when I saw three men huddled against the outside of the doors, drinking glasses of champagne.

Erik's gaze swept past his friends and over Jace's head to me as he finished the statement our exit interrupted. "Thankfully, it's a *small* problem."

My heart pounded harder in my chest as we squeezed past the men to reach the ramp that led to the parking lot. Jace offered a polite "excuse us," but I kept my lips pressed together.

I had said everything there was to say to this man in the ballroom, and I wanted nothing more to do with him.

Erik's searing stare followed me down the ramp, making it hard to focus on Jace's words as she launched into a tirade about her mom. Mrs. Walker was pressuring her to break things off with Sam and spend more time with men of "higher standing."

Higher Standing was a petty man-child who, at last glance, looked like he wanted to shove me off the side of the ramp. One of his friends had a hold of his arm, discouraging him from pursuing us.

I fixed my sights on Jace's car in the handicapped parking space and ushered her forward every time she paused to rant with her hands. If she didn't stop doing that, I was going to grab her wheelchair handles and push her.

By the time we reached the car, the top of the staircase was empty. I released a breath of relief and sank into the passenger seat.

19

Perfect yet disastrous, I thought, reflecting on the gala as I closed my apartment door and tossed my keys on the kitchen counter.

I never thought I would get to experience a dance, and it meant the world to me that Marx had been my partner. His presence enveloped me in safety, letting me sink into the moment.

If only the evening had gone as well for Jace. We were barely on the road before her composure crumbled beneath a flood of tears. Her heartache was so heavy that it filled the car.

Why couldn't her mother love her the way she deserved to be loved, even if she didn't approve of her choices? God doesn't approve of all of our choices, but He doesn't withhold His love from us. When we need it, need Him, He is waiting with open arms.

By the time we reached our street, Jace's tears had dried, and the only sound was the heat rattling through the car vents. I offered to come up to her apartment and keep her company, but she wanted solitude.

I sighed and kicked off my dress shoes. It had been a long day, and I was ready to change into pajamas and curl up on the couch with one of my library books. I had started one about a mysterious murder on the beach yesterday.

Maybe I would be able to unravel the mystery before the author made it obvious. My investigative skills were sharpening every day.

I shrugged off my puffy coat, draping it across the kitchen table, and went to gather my clothes for the night.

Riley stalked my heels as I dressed for bed, twisted my hair into a messy pile on top of my head, and returned to the kitchen to warm water for tea.

As I picked up my library book, the greeting card I'd used as a bookmark slipped from between the pages, bringing a smile to my lips. It had come in the mail two days ago, dropped into the metal box mounted beneath the light on my patio.

Now that I was no longer hiding, I had an address, and there was something delightful about having my own mailbox. It made me feel like an official New Yorker.

I had been expecting a letter from my friend Thomas at the psychiatric facility, but it was going on two and a half weeks since I'd written to him with no response.

This card had come in an envelope postmarked from Georgia. Marx's mom, whom I'd met over Christmas, loved sending me greeting cards with cute sayings and recipes.

The saying on this one read, "Life will never be perfect, but it is in those stretches of darkness that we learn to appreciate the light." I opened the card to reread the handwritten note inside:

> Hi baby,
>
> I am so happy you've been able to move back home. I hope to see your cozy place when we're in the city. I wanted to send this double fudge brownie recipe, because as soon as I saw it in my magazine, I thought of you. Now, be careful not to overbake it, and make sure you let it cool all the way before digging in or it'll fall to pieces. I miss you, sweet girl, and I look forward to seeing you at the wedding.
>
> All my love,
> Martha

She included a Bible verse on a slip of paper inside the envelope, like she did with every letter and card, and it hung from a magnet on my freezer door.

"And our hope for you is firm, because we know that just as you share in our sufferings, so also you share in our comfort."

I smiled and turned my attention to the recipe.

"Double fudge brownies. We could try substituting marshmallow peeps for eggs and peaches for butter." I glanced at Riley for his input, but he didn't seem too enthusiastic. "You're right. It's better to wait until we get more groceries."

None of the "minimal ingredients" recipes Jace and I found on that Pinterest site ever worked out. Sawdust, bricks, or snot was usually the result.

The microwave beeped, and I returned the card and recipe to the book so I could fix my mug of tea. I shuffled to the couch with my warm drink and cozy murder mystery and snuggled in for a couple hours of reading.

Barely ten chapters later, Riley let out a whine by the door.

I dropped the book to my chest, pages splayed. "Now?"

Thunder rumbled in the distance, and darkness pressed against the windows. Now was better than later, when the skies opened up.

I dragged my tired body off the couch and noticed my cat eyeing my empty mug on the floor. Was there kibble dissolving into goo on his tongue, waiting to be dropped into my mug the moment I walked away?

"Forget it, fuzz butt." I scooped up my cup, and the piece of kibble tumbled out of Sausage's mouth onto the floor in disappointment. "I know your sneaky plans."

My cat was a plotter, which was a little scary.

I set the cup on the counter and pulled on my jacket and shoes before attaching Riley's leash. Wind and mist smacked me in the face the moment I opened the door, and Riley led me up the steps into the grass.

I watched the sky as he sniffed around for the perfect spot. It was too bad the coming downpour couldn't save the dead and dying plants in the flower bed that wrapped around my apartment. I had tried my hand at gardening, but I was like the grim reaper for plants.

I needed the flower equivalent to goldfish—hardy and difficult to kill. A cactus maybe. Though, with my luck, I would drown it.

The bulb on my patio buzzed and blinked out, sucking away all the light with it. My fingers tightened reflexively around Riley's leash as fear unfurled in my stomach.

I hated the darkness, especially when there was a chill in the air. The combination churned up memories that leached every drop of warmth from my body.

Stay calm. Don't freak out.

Most of the light fixtures sprinkled along the apartment walkways and staircases were unlit because the landlord was too cheap to replace the bulbs or fix the bad wiring, but my vision would adjust to the dim glow of streetlights in a minute.

The sound of something skipping on the sidewalk, like a bottle cap bouncing off the tip of a shoe, made my heart jump, and I whirled toward it.

It was something the wind picked up, I told myself. *There's no one out here.*

But the raised hairs on the back of my neck refused to relax. I searched the shadows that gradually sharpened as my eyes adjusted, seeing nothing but empty cars and rustling bushes.

I tugged Riley's leash after he finished watering the lawn. "Come on. I wanna go inside."

He sniffed the air, and I waited for a growl to confirm my fear that someone was out there, but he only snorted and then trotted alongside me down the steps.

I closed the door, and the last of my fear fled, leaving exasperation in its wake. The only threats outside were my memories crawling out of the darkness after the patio light blew out.

It was no surprise the bulb had finally kicked the bucket, considering I never turned it off. But couldn't it have waited until morning?

I unhooked Riley, and he bounded over to the couch to stretch out. My phone alerted me to an incoming text. It was from Jace.

Need your help in the laundry room.

The laundry room? It was nine o'clock at night, and she was doing laundry in the creepy basement of the apartment building? A second text came through from her.

Pretty please with sprinkles.

The soft patter of rain against the kitchen window drew my attention. The tension in the sky had finally broken. Stifling a sigh, I snagged my keys and opened the door. I hesitated on the threshold of my patio, but my friend needed me. Drawing in a breath of courage, I stepped into the cold, dark drizzle.

. . . .

The basement door screeched on old hinges as I pushed it open, and I stepped into the musty length of hallway.

There was something spooky about this level of the building—all of the storage and utility rooms, the clunking pipes, the black and green tile adding to the air of "abandoned insane asylum."

I hated doing laundry here, but it was better than loading my clothes into plastic bags and riding the bus to a laundromat.

Rubbing at my arms, I started toward the laundry room at the far end. I drew in a breath to call out to Jace, but a door opened ahead of me, startling the words back down my throat.

A yellow cleaning bucket rolled into the hall, soapy water splashing over the edges onto the tile. A man followed, his hands gripping the wooden handle of the mop he used to steer the bucket.

The maintenance man lifted his head, staring through me as if I were no more solid than a ghost.

Haunted—that was the look in his eyes, one I had seen reflected back at me enough times to recognize it. What unimaginable horrors had this man experienced?

Without a word, he lifted the mop from the water, squeezed it out, and sponged up the overflow on the tile.

"Are you coming or what?"

I flinched at Jace's unexpected voice as it bounced down the hallway. She sat in her wheelchair in the doorway of the laundry room, watching with a puzzled expression.

"I'm coming."

I skirted past the mop bucket, but compassion for the man who had experienced some kind of life-altering trauma tugged me back around. He had already returned the mop to the bucket and was making his way toward the elevator.

"Good night, Spencer," I said.

He stilled at his name, and I clutched my locket between my fingers as I waited for his response. He gave a curt nod before moving into the elevator.

Air seeped out between my lips. I had hoped he might respond to my greeting with words, but the man had no interest in connecting with other human beings.

You were there once, I reminded myself. Jace practically had to use a crowbar to pry an interaction out of me when we first met.

"Why were you talking to spooky Spencer?" she asked as I approached.

My nose wrinkled. "I hate that everyone calls him that."

164

She lifted her eyebrows and rocked back on her hind wheels. "You're telling me Stone-Cold Steve Eye Sockets doesn't give you the jeebies?"

"Of course Spencer makes me uneasy. Along with every other man I don't know and trust. That's no reason to be unkind."

Jace's wheels tapped back down on the tile, guilt creasing her face. "You're right, it's not. I guess I'm still a little punchy from the thing with my mother."

"Understandable. So what did you need help with?"

Jace rolled over to the top-load washer, which was level with her eyebrows, and grabbed the long grippers she used to grab items that were out of her reach. She squeezed the button, but nothing happened. "The spring broke, and I have a washer full of bras and underwear."

Oh, that would explain why she didn't ask one of the neighbors to help her. I walked over to the washer, the bane of my laundry existence, and peered into its depths. The machine was nearly four feet tall, and I was barely five. I practically had to crawl inside to drag my clothes out twice a week.

"I don't have my stool."

"You could stand on my lap."

I shot her an incredulous look.

"Seriously." Jace snapped her brakes into place and patted her legs. "Let's do this. I'll hug you like a teddy bear so you don't fall."

"I am not standing on you."

"Fine." She stared at the floor in thought and then snapped her fingers. "Oh, I have an idea. I'll be back in like three, maybe five minutes." Jace disengaged her brakes and wheeled out before I could ask her for specifics.

I puffed out a breath and unzipped my rain-slicked jacket, tossing it on the wall-length counter before hopping up beside it to wait for Jace's return.

The clouds visible through the basement windows ignited with blue light, and a few seconds later, thunder rumbled overhead. The basement lights flickered, and my fingernails dug into the underside of the counter as anxiety sparked in my stomach.

I didn't want to be down here in the dark.

Old hinges screeched, and I watched the doorway, expecting someone to appear with a basket of laundry. Seconds ticked by. Maybe they went back up to grab something they forgot, like quarters for the machines.

Except . . .

Was that a whisper of footsteps?

The lights flickered again as thunder cracked overhead, so violent that I could feel it vibrate through my body.

I flexed my fingers on the edge of the counter and called out, "Hello?"

When no one responded, I scooted off the counter and padded to the doorway, peering into the hall. The eerie corridor stretched in both directions, but the only sign of life was a confused fly buzzing around an exposed ceiling bulb.

"Spencer?"

He must've returned to one of the storage rooms for more cleaning supplies. That would explain why no one responded when I called out.

An unexpected sound came from behind me, and I flinched, belatedly realizing it was my phone. I rolled my eyes—what was wrong with me today?—and returned to the counter to check it.

There was a text from Jace, informing me that she'd found tongs and would be back in a couple of minutes.

She had to be joking.

I was not hauling her clothes out of the washer one item at a time with hot dog tongs. My hand cramped just thinking about it.

I surveyed the room for something to stand on, but the counters were bolted to the wall, Jace's "clothes basket" was a bag

166

she slung over her handlebars, and I didn't feel like sprinting back and forth through a storm to grab my stool.

"Old school it is."

Setting my phone on the counter, I planted my hands on the washer and bounced on my toes. With a grunt, I heaved myself up onto the machine, grabbing the far edge to keep from toppling into the drum headfirst.

I missed Marx's front-load washer. It didn't try to eat me.

I grabbed what I could in one hand and dropped back to the floor, transferring the clothes to the dryer. I climbed up for another handful, but the strap of one of Jace's bras snagged, tangled with two other pieces of clothing around the agitator in the center. Aptly named, because it left me feeling deeply agitated as I tried to untangle three different straps without losing my balance.

"Oh come on, how does this even happen?" I squeezed out, my breath labored as the washer dug into my midsection.

Rubber squeaked in the hall.

Jace must be back with her oh-so-helpful cookout utensils. But then a disconcerting question whispered through my mind. *Why didn't the elevator ding?*

And why did I smell Froot Loops?

Before I could lift my head to investigate, something pressed against the backs of my legs, and a hard hand wrapped around the nape of my neck, shoving my head deeper into the washing machine. The force sent a bolt of pain across my shoulders and down my spine into my legs.

I yelped and twisted, trying to kick the person behind me, but my legs were trapped between the front of the machine and a solid body.

Fear punched against my ribs, and I groped desperately at the wet drum, the agitator, anything I could use to push myself up and away from whoever was behind me.

"Don't make this harder than it has to be," the man whispered. He leaned more weight against me, pinning my hips.

I screamed, my terror reverberating around the metal drum. I pushed at the edge of the opening with both hands, but I wasn't strong enough to lift his weight off me.

"Get off!" I cried out. I tugged and raked at the fingers squeezing my neck, but I couldn't peel them away.

"Stop screaming." He pushed down while keeping my hips pinned.

My body cried out from the overstretched position, but his weight forced the edge of the washing machine deeper into my stomach, and the only sound that escaped my throat was a wheezy whimper.

Tears trickled into my hair as I hung suspended, unable to see anything but the tangles of clothes at the bottom of the washer, unable to do anything to defend myself.

What was he going to do?

God, please don't let him hurt me.

"Listen carefully," he said, his whisper growing muffled with the building pressure in my head. "You need to stay . . ." He stiffened at the distant ding of the elevator, then released my neck and stepped away.

I gripped the edge of the washer to keep from falling in and sucked in a desperate breath. I dropped onto trembling legs and stumbled into the corner.

The hooded man turned out of the room and out of sight without a backward glance.

I slid down the wall to the floor and tried to breathe as panic burned a path through my body.

20

I dragged my way out of the disoriented fog like a zombie from a grave, clawing at my surroundings.

The stone wall was icy against my back, and the pen stain on my pink lounge pants blurred in and out of focus as I blinked. I was huddled in a corner, face buried in my knees.

Warm tears trickled down my face, and a breath shuddered from my lungs, stirring a loose strand of hair. I lifted my head enough to see the green-and-black tile floor of the laundry room between my sneakers.

That small movement awakened every ache in my body—my head, my neck, my back. I touched the tender spots where the man's fingers had dug in, shivering as the experience replayed through my mind.

My fingertips grazed rough material below my neck, tracing the edge of it to my shoulders. Someone had draped a wool blanket around me.

I looked up, brushing tears and sticky strands of loose hair from my face, and my heart backflipped in my chest at the sight of a man sitting nearby.

I pressed my hands to the tile to scoot away from the threat, but his familiar, soothing voice stilled me.

"Whoa, it's just me."

A few blinks cleared the tears from my vision, and Jordan's features sharpened. He sat against the wall, far enough to give me space, but close enough to catch me if I passed out and dropped like a dead bird.

I stared at him, trying to make sense of his presence. "How . . . when did you . . ."

"About five minutes ago. Jace called Sam, and he snagged me from my apartment." His arms rested on his knees, his relaxed posture at odds with the storm of emotions in his eyes. He nodded to the blanket. "I'm sorry I crossed the border without consent, but you were shaking."

My body was still trembling, but it was from the aftershocks of fear rather than the damp chill in the basement. I tugged the blanket tighter around me. "Thanks."

He rubbed his hands together, his lips pressed tight with concern. "I haven't seen you have an attack that bad in almost a year."

Some of my panic attacks were so intense that I couldn't remember what happened when they consumed me. Just terrifying, debilitating fear, then coming around sometime later. Dissociation, my therapist called it.

"There was . . . a man." I had seen him leave, but my eyes skipped around the room anyway, as if he could blend into the corners like a chameleon.

"Yeah, Jace saw him coming out of the laundry room in a hurry. He went out the back exit, the opposite direction she was coming from, so she didn't see his face."

I noticed the silver tongs lying on the floor. "Is she okay?"

"She was kinda freaking out. Sam sent her upstairs to make some calming tea. He said it was for you, but really, I think it was for her." He offered a half-smile that faded a second later. "You wanna tell me what happened?"

I glanced at the washing machine and puckered my lips between my teeth. I didn't want to talk about that humiliating ordeal.

"Did he hurt you?" One look in his eyes revealed protective anger churning beneath a thin layer of self-control.

Every ache in my body throbbed, demanding to be acknowledged, but most of them were a result of my own frantic struggle.

"I um . . ." I swallowed and instinctively reached for the locket at my chest, longing for the comfort of it against my palm. It wasn't there. I felt around my collarbone and throat. "I can't find my locket."

It contained one of the only two pictures I had of my family. I couldn't lose it.

"Your necklace is in the washer," a voice said, snapping my attention to the doorway. Sam. He wore sweatpants and a hooded sweatshirt rather than his police uniform, but he still exuded authority.

I cast an uneasy glance toward the machine that had nearly swallowed me. The chain must've slipped over my head in the struggle.

Sam motioned for Jordan to join him across the room. Jordan pushed to his feet. "I'll be right back, Holly."

Sam's body language was no more emphatic than his speech, and his stiff posture betrayed nothing of their hushed conversation. Something he said etched a line of concern between Jordan's eyes, and his gaze trailed to the washing machine.

I followed his attention, seeing for the first time what an investigator must see. Dirty indentations from shoes digging at the front of the machine about a foot off the floor, laundry divided between the open dryer and washer, bloody smears on the inside lid.

I removed my hands from the shelter of the blanket and studied them. The nail of my right middle finger was torn, with blood dried in the creases. I had been fighting so hard to free myself, I hadn't felt it tear away from the skin.

That, paired with my necklace at the bottom of the washer, they knew what had happened.

Flames of humiliation licked up my face. *They* would never have been that vulnerable and helpless. Somehow they would've fought back.

I gripped the counter and dragged myself to my feet, wincing as it pulled at strained muscles. What I wouldn't give for a heating pad I could wrap around my entire body. But I would have to settle for a hot bath and a soft bed.

I folded the unfamiliar blanket, placing it on the counter, and approached the washing machine, every step strengthening the residual trembling in my body. I had been so certain the man was going to hurt me, and there would've been nothing I could do to stop him.

I hugged myself and peered into the depths of the drum at my necklace, and then back at the tongs Jace had dropped on the floor.

Maybe . . .

Jordan broke away from Sam to join me, keeping his movements slow and quiet so he didn't startle me when my nerves were already tap-dancing on the edge of a cliff.

He reached into the drum to retrieve my necklace and coiled the chain into the palm of my hand.

"You should leave everything where it is," Sam said. "This is a crime scene."

I bit my bottom lip as I looped the chain over my head, the simple movement reigniting the fire in my muscles. "I'm not letting one of the few things I cherish get locked up in an evidence room for months or years."

Sam's disapproval was obvious in the press of his lips, but he didn't argue. "Officers are on the way to secure the scene. And they need to take your statement."

Another report with my name on it. At this rate, I would have my own filing cabinet at the precinct by the end of the year. I may as well bedazzle my name on it.

"Can't I talk to you?"

"I'm off duty."

If I couldn't talk to my men in uniform, I didn't want to give a report. My trust in law enforcement had grown from zero officers to a handful over the past year and a half, but that trust was hard earned on a case-by-case basis.

"I don't think there's much point in a report," I said, rubbing my locket between my fingers. "There's nothing I can say that will help the cops find this guy."

"You would be surprised by what kinds of details are helpful," Sam said, his mouth tightening as his attention fixed on my neck.

My hand moved to rub at the tender spots that would no doubt darken to bruises. "I don't have any details. He was behind me the whole time. I didn't see anything but the bottom of the washer, and he spoke so softly, I couldn't identify his voice even if I knew him."

"Have you had any unusual or awkward interactions with men lately?"

"Outside of you guys, every interaction I have with men is unusual and awkward."

A whisper of a smile softened his lips. "*Abnormally* unusual."

I mentally sifted through my interactions the past couple of days, but there were so many. "I don't know."

"Could this be a random attack, some guy who saw an opportunity and took it?" Jordan asked Sam.

"It's possible he saw her come into the building and followed her, hoping for an opportunity to get her alone. But it could just as easily have been targeted. Are you working any cases that may have stirred up trouble?"

"We're investigating a missing prostitute," Jordan said. When I threw him a disapproving scowl, he amended his description. "A missing girl who *works* as a prostitute. We believe she was kidnapped."

Cami and all those other women were so much more than what they did to pay their bills, even if they could no longer see it. They were mothers, daughters, sisters. Survivors. They were precious, and I wouldn't diminish their value and their uniqueness by summing them up with one demeaning word.

"Is it possible the man who took this girl came after Holly tonight?" Sam asked. "Maybe you're getting too close to the truth."

"We're nowhere near close."

"That might not be . . . completely true," I said, casting Jordan an apologetic glance. "You remember me mentioning Erik, the guy in the car? He was at the gala."

Jordan tensed, but before he could respond with whatever question or concern he was forming, Sam asked, "Who is Erik, and what car?"

I explained about my interaction with Erik and his friends last night, and filled him in on what Dorina and Clayton had said.

"It sounds like this guy is your prime suspect," Sam said. "Did he recognize you from your run-in on Brushwick?"

"Unfortunately. He accused me of being there to blackmail him and said he could destroy my life."

Jordan rubbed his hands over his face and blew out a breath. Apparently, something I said stressed him out.

"You might've started with that important detail," Sam said. "What's his last name?"

"No idea, but Mrs. Walker would know. She invited his father. Some congressman."

And she's trying to set him up with her daughter. But I kept that thought to myself for now. It would only hurt Sam and potentially inspire him to do something he shouldn't—like storm the penthouse where Jace's parents lived.

"Who knew you were gonna be down here?" Jordan asked.

"No one. Jace sent me a text that she needed my help in the laundry room. I came over, and . . ." My words stalled as I remembered the interaction with Spencer in the hallway. He was the only other person who knew I was down here.

"And what?" Sam prompted.

I sighed, reluctant to bring more hardship into the man's life. "The maintenance man. He came out of the storage closet with a mop bucket as I was walking down the hall."

"This is the guy who was watching us last night?" Jordan asked.

I nodded. "But he wasn't wearing a hooded sweatshirt, and him attacking me doesn't make sense. I've barely said two words to him, and he's never spoken to me."

"That doesn't mean he didn't take advantage of you being alone down here, and he could've easily thrown on a sweatshirt to conceal himself." Sam tapped notes into his phone. When the stairwell door screeched, he approached the hall to see who was coming. "Marx is here."

"You called Marx?"

"I didn't."

Jordan scratched the back of his head. "That would be me. I wasn't sure how long your panic attack would last, and I didn't know how to help you, so I called him for advice. His advice was, 'I'm on my way.'"

I bit back a groan. He was going to storm in with a ten-foot strip of bubble wrap, roll me up like a burrito, and carry me off to the safety of his apartment.

I shuffled into the hall to meet him.

Marx had stripped out of his jacket and tie, the top few buttons of his green dress shirt undone and his sleeves rolled up to midforearm.

The stress lines in his face softened when he saw me, and he swept me into a hug, his sigh of relief ruffling my hair. "Hey, peanut."

Fresh tears pricked my eyes as I huddled against his chest, the sense of safety he brought with him enveloping me. I hated that Jordan had called him away from his evening with Shannon, but I appreciated his presence.

He released me and cupped my face, his thumbs caressing my cheeks. "Jordan called and said you were havin' a really bad panic attack. What happened? Are you okay?"

He didn't know about the laundry room incident. If I didn't tell him, maybe I could convince him to go back to his date.

"Someone grabbed her in the laundry room," Sam said, blowing my plan into itty bitty pieces before I could even finish formulating it. He was never going to leave now.

"Define *grabbed*," Marx demanded. "Do I need to break somebody's fingers?"

"Not that kind of grabbed." Sam must've indicated his neck, because Marx gently lifted my chin with his thumb and examined the attacker's finger marks on my skin.

Fury bubbled beneath his tightly controlled tone. "Who did this?"

"I don't know," I admitted.

"He came up behind her while she was doing laundry," Sam said. "The ding of the elevator returning to the bottom floor scared him off."

Marx turned his anger on Jordan. "And this just slipped your mind when you called me?"

Jordan's mouth tightened. "I didn't know about the attack when I called you. All I knew was she was having a panic attack."

"Please don't argue," I pleaded.

Marx sighed and smoothed a hand over my hair. "I want you to come stay with me tonight."

Running back to the safety of his apartment was tempting, but I had been in my home for less than a month, and I wasn't going to let fear evict me again.

"I know you're worried, but I'm not running and hiding again."

"Sweetheart, we don't know who this man is or what his intentions are. He might come back and try to finish what he started."

"I'll be careful. And besides, my apartment is a bunker, remember?"

"Mmm hmm. A bunker you have to leave to walk your dog."

His statement reminded me of the unsettling feeling that Riley and I hadn't been alone outside when the patio light blew out. Had my attacker been outside then, waiting for me to be alone?

"I'm gonna need a pillow and a blanket," Marx said, dragging me from my thoughts.

I leaned back to look up at him. "You're not sleeping on my patio."

"Unless you're uncomfortable with me bein' in your apartment at night, I'm gonna sleep on your lumpy eggplant of a couch."

I opened my mouth to argue, but there was no point. The set of his jaw told me that if I refused and tried to send him home, he would sleep in his car by the curb.

The stairwell door opened, and the crackle of radios preceded the two uniformed officers into the hall. I sighed and rested my head against Marx's chest. This long day was turning into a long night.

21

$\mathcal{S}$team from a long, hot shower filled my bathroom, and I cleared the mirror above the sink with a rag.

I studied my neck. The man's hand had wrapped more than halfway around, leaving darkening finger marks an inch and a half below my jaw. I couldn't even hide them with my hair.

I sighed and checked my other aches—a broken fingernail and bruises on my elbows from repeatedly hitting the inner edge of the washer during my frantic attempts to push myself out.

The worst wound, though, was the one left behind by the panic attack. It had been a long time since I had a breakdown that severe, and humiliation, disappointment, and frustration smoldered in my chest.

What next? A flashback on the bus? A panic attack in the middle of a church service?

Annette's advice cut through my harsh thoughts: *When you hit another valley, give yourself grace.*

This certainly constituted a valley. I leaned against the sink and stared at my reflection in the mirror.

It's not your fault, and you have nothing to be embarrassed about or ashamed of. I willed those words to sink deep into my bones. I was never going to move forward if I kept dwelling on every setback.

"Grace," I whispered.

Marx's voice carried through the paper-thin wall that separated my bathroom and living room as he spoke on the phone. "Unfortunately, we don't know what the man's intentions were or if the attack was planned or opportunistic."

What had the man intended to say before the elevator spooked him? Would it have been another demand for me to stop screaming and fighting while he carried out his plan, or would it have been a threat?

Had I stepped on someone's toes during this investigation, wounded a man's pride this week, or was this a random incident that could've happened to any woman alone in a secluded place?

"I realize it's not our case because there's no dead body, but I'll remedy that when I find the guy," Marx said.

He must be on the phone with his partner. I didn't know Michael well, but his upbeat personality seemed to balance Marx's temper. And he enjoyed the muffins I baked and brought to the precinct.

Riley snorted at the bottom of the door, complaining that I'd left him alone with Marx and his moody feline roommate for too long.

"I'm coming."

I winced as I wiggled my arms into the long sleeves of my green T-shirt. The hot water and ibuprofen had done almost nothing to relieve the pain and tension in my body. I finger-combed my damp hair, letting it hang loose, and opened the door to find Riley sprawled on the floor like roadkill, mourning his mistreatment.

"I see your Aunt Jace is teaching you to be theatrical."

Jace had been nearly hysterical about what happened in the laundry room. She had interrupted my statement to the police with calming tea, which she clearly hadn't drunk any of, and expressions like "You could've been kidnapped" and "He could've been some laundry room serial killer who murders people by stuffing them in dryers and then steals their clothes to wear later."

Unfortunately, after everything we had been through, neither possibility sounded far-fetched. Except the part about him wearing her clothes. No guy was squeezing into her extra small clothes.

"I'll talk to you tomorrow." Marx disconnected his call and set his phone on the arm of the couch as I stepped over my dramatic dog. "Hey, sweet pea."

"Were you talking to Michael?"

"Mmm hmm. He's up late with their baby, so he texted to see how the gala went, and I called to fill him in." He watched me as I shuffled to the couch. "You're movin' like I usually do after wrestlin' with a suspect twice my size."

I sank onto the cushion beside him, drawing my feet up. "Who was the last suspect you wrestled with?"

"A man I arrested a couple of weeks ago. He murdered his neighbors with an axe he nicknamed Kindness."

My brain took a moment to process that. "He killed them with kindness?"

"Mmm hmm. Seems he took that nugget of advice a bit too literally. When we showed up at his door to arrest him, he made a run for his weapon. I tackled him, Michael handcuffed him, and we arrested him."

My mouth parted. "You wrestled with an axe murderer. A literal axe murderer?"

"He wasn't armed when we were rollin' around on the floor."

"Why didn't you tell me?"

"You have enough worries ricochetin' around in that little head of yours without me tellin' you about every case I work." He wrapped an arm around me and tucked me against him so he could plant a kiss in my hair.

My attack had rattled him—I could feel it in his tense posture—and I had no doubt dark possibilities were spinning through his mind. I snuggled closer, trying to comfort him even as he comforted me.

"I'm sorry if I ruined your night with Shannon."

"You didn't. I love her, but spendin' the evenin' with a room full of entitled, narcissistic self-promoters is enough to give me indigestion."

I couldn't argue with that.

"Can we talk about what happened tonight?" he asked.

I picked at the Band-Aid over my broken fingernail. "You were there when I spoke with the cops. You know everything they know."

"Which is next to nothin', since you ration details like a stranded person rations matches."

"Who uses matches anymore?"

"I do, and that's beside the point. You were arguin' with that man at the gala tonight. I was too far away to hear the conversation, but I could read your body language. You were angry and scared, and you looked ready to stab him with a shish kabob stick."

The thought had crossed my mind.

"And his posture suggested he was a breath away from violence. A couple of hours later, you're attacked. I'm not inclined to believe that's a coincidence."

"It's my problem. I can handle—"

"Do not make me go around you to keep you safe, sweetheart." His tone left no room for negotiation. He *would* go around me to find the man's identity, and then he would confront him. "I tried to let you handle him in your independent way, but now somebody hurt you. Who is he, and what's the problem?"

I sucked my lips between my teeth. There had to be a way to explain this without triggering a volcanic eruption. "Promise you won't freak out or get mad."

"Now I'm even more concerned."

I sighed. "I'm working on a missing person's case, a sixteen-year-old girl from Brushwick, and she might've been kidnapped."

"Tell me you didn't."

"I was careful. I took pepper spray and my box cutter, and I texted Jace to let her know where I was going so someone would know."

"You went by yourself?" he shouted, and Riley's head snapped up with a soft growl. Marx pointed a finger at him. "Don't even think about bitin' me."

"I didn't have a choice."

181

"Don't give me that. You know any of us would've dropped whatever we were doin' to make sure you were safe. You didn't even ask."

Indignant, I shifted on the cushions to face him. "Jordan was out trying to find an elderly woman with dementia, and if I had asked Sam, he would've told you, and we both know you would've tried to keep me from going."

"To Sodom and Gomorrah where a girl was kidnapped, where you could be kidnapped or worse? You're absolutely right I would've stopped you from goin'."

"You're proving my point." Ignoring the pain in my back and shoulders, I pushed up from the couch. "I had to go look for her. Everyone is convinced that she didn't run away. Someone took this sixteen-year-old girl, and every minute she's with him . . ." My throat squeezed with memories. "Every minute counts, and you know that."

Sadness clouded his eyes. "I do know that."

"I had you to come look for me when Collin took me. Cami has no one. And if she's . . . still alive, I doubt she has any hope of being rescued, because to society she's nothing but a runaway teen and a prostitute, someone who doesn't even matter." Tears burned my eyes. "I've been the girl living on the fringes of society, overlooked and unwanted, trying to survive. I won't overlook her, Marx. I won't let her disappear like she doesn't matter."

He rose from the couch to brush the tears from my cheeks with his thumbs. "Sometimes I forget how big your heart is."

My chest shuddered as I exhaled. "I know that what I'm doing is uncomfortable for you, but . . . I've worked really hard to reclaim my life so I can live it however I choose. I choose this—helping the overlooked and forgotten. And I want this girl to know that someone cares enough to look for her."

"Okay." He folded me into his arms and rested his chin on the top of my head. "I understand your reasonin', and even though it goes against my instincts, I will do my best to accept your decision. Now, tell me about the man at the gala."

"He's a jerk."

"I'm gonna need a bit more than that."

I told him what little I knew about Erik and filled him in on our meeting and argument.

"I think this Erik and I need to have a conversation," he said. His voice might seem calm and collected to someone who didn't know him, but I could hear the anger simmering beneath the surface.

"I don't know his last name."

"Shannon introduced me to Congressman McCallister at the gala, and now that I think about it, I can see a resemblance between this Erik and the congressman."

Erik McCallister. I needed to write that down. I slipped free of Marx's embrace and retrieved my pen and notebook.

"What's this?" Marx asked, as I cracked open my miniature pink notebook.

"Maybe you didn't know, but detectives carry notebooks to record information."

He smiled. "You don't say."

I turned the page to "Suspects" and added Erik's full name to his description. "And I'm kind of a detective now."

"A fact about which I am immeasurably unhappy," he said dryly. "But let's see what you've got."

I passed him my notes, a flutter in my stomach. I knew they were sparse and scattered, amateurish to someone who had been a detective for so many years, but I was learning.

Marx fidgeted with my little notebook in his large hands. "Why is this thing so tiny?" He paused, glanced at me, and then muttered, "Never mind."

He brought the notebook closer to his face to read my microscopic font, skimming Erik's name and physical description.

His lips twitched. "'Entitled jerkface. Also a creeper. Maybe a kidnapper.' If you ever have to recite your notes in court, that'll be an entertainin' day for the jury."

I rolled my pen between my fingers. "I still need to add stuff from our conversation at the gala, but I'm not sure how much truth there is to Erik's version of events."

"Make sure you keep the facts separate from the witness and suspect statements. You can flip back and forth to compare details, but don't mix them together. Also, keep your hunches separate from the facts."

I nodded, soaking up his advice.

He turned the pages, eyes dancing across my notes. "You haven't interviewed any of these potential suspects yet?" he asked, but before I could answer, his mouth dipped down at the corners. "Please tell me you didn't speak to a pimp named Spike by yourself."

"Of course not." I snatched my notebook back. "I thought about it, but he looked . . ."—*sleazy, terrifying, homicidally vicious*—"unfriendly."

"Then how do you know he likes unique girls and had an interest in your victim?"

"From one of the girls who works for him. And he popped in for a visit when Jordan and I were following up with Dorina. He said he didn't want anything to do with Cami because of her diabetes, but I don't know if I believe him."

Marx closed his eyes and rubbed his forehead. "Can't you find lost puppies? Why does it have to be missin' teenage girls with 'unfriendly' pimps?"

"Can't you work more robberies and fewer homicides?" I challenged.

"No, I work the cases that land on my desk."

"And we work the cases that knock on our door."

Marx sighed. "Fair enough. I think it's time to call it a night." He glanced at the bedding I had placed on one arm of the couch, just in time to see Sausage drop a soggy piece of cat food on top of the pile. "Your cat threw up on my pillow."

"He didn't throw up. He left you a . . . gift."

"Why?"

"Probably because he wants to sleep on your face."

He grimaced and slapped the food onto the floor. "Too bad for him I don't like cats."

I could've dropped the fur ball at Jace's for the night. She enjoyed his company, and he would appreciate time away from Riley, but I didn't want to deal with it at this hour.

"You two will work out the space issue."

"He can sleep on the floor, where animals belong." He kissed the top of my head. "Good night."

"Night. Come on, Rye."

He followed me into the alcove where my bed rested, and I tugged the thick purple drapes shut to partition the bedroom from the living room. I burrowed beneath the blankets and rested a hand on Riley's back.

Tiredness tugged at my eyelids, and I let them drift shut. I was on the edge of sleep when Marx's frustrated and muffled protest cut through the quiet. "Get off my face."

I laughed into my pillow. It was going to be a hilarious night with those two battling it out on the other side of the curtain. Unfortunately for Marx, Sausage wasn't one to surrender.

. . . .

A graze of fingers on my cheek ripped me from sleep, and my eyes popped open to see a dark figure looming over me. A scream gathered in my throat, and I fumbled for the knife I kept in my nightstand.

"It's me, sweetheart."

Marx's voice chased away the panic, and my galloping heart slowed as I scooted up against the pillows. "What's wrong?"

Did I wake him with one of my night terrors? I remembered dreaming, but the details dripped through my fingers like water as I tried to grab hold of them.

"Somebody's outside," he said.

My gaze darted to the dark ribbon of windows that stretched well beyond the curtain cordoning off my bedroom. I didn't see any sign of movement, but as I listened, I could hear a repetitive noise coming from the other side of the wall at my back.

"What's that sound?"

It wasn't the storm. It had swept through and moved on, taking the patter of rain and gusting winds with it.

"I don't know. The same pair of men's shoes walked past the window four times, and that noise has been goin' on for about ten minutes now. I'm gonna check it out."

I threw aside my blankets and swung my legs out of bed. "I'll come with you."

"No, you're stayin' put."

"But—"

"You were attacked six hours ago by a man we know nothin' about. I want you safe behind this locked door."

I looked back at the windows. If the source of the sound was actually a threat, Marx wouldn't be any safer than me without his gun.

I opened my nightstand drawer and grabbed my butcher knife, offering it to him handle-first. "Take this." When he made no move to grab it, I pointed out, "You don't have your gun. Either I come with you as backup or the knife does."

He sighed and grabbed the handle. "Fine." He tucked it into the back waistband of his slacks.

I scooted off the bed and followed him to the door, nerves swarming my stomach. "Please be careful."

"Stay inside, no matter what happens."

186

He was kidding, right? If whoever was out there attacked him, there was a zero percent chance I would stay inside. I was coming to the rescue with the first heavy object I could find.

I locked the door after he left and rubbed my hands together. What should I do? Shoes. I should put on some shoes in case he needed help.

I slid my feet into my flats and then scampered to the windows, listening as I scanned the darkness. There was probably nothing to worry about. More than likely, it was someone going for a walk.

At three in the morning?

Maybe they had to take their dog out.

And they're doing laps around the apartment property?

Outside, grunting broke out, and I stretched onto my toes, straining to see what was happening. A pair of feet stumbled into view, and then two bodies collapsed into the grass at the edge of the flower bed.

An elbow collided with the window, and I flinched back.

Marx was on the bottom of the pile, and the man on top of him held something sharp in one hand as they grappled.

Icy fear washed over me.

Was that a weapon?

I sprinted to the kitchen to grab the frying pan from the stove top and shot out the door, flinging it shut behind me to keep my pets safe. The grass was slick from the rain, and I nearly fell twice as I darted around the building to the back.

Marx and the man were still wrestling on the ground—arms and elbows flailing. Marx was trying to gain the upper hand, but the man on top of him seemed to anticipate every swing. The weapon in the attacker's hand was a garden tool with three prongs, and it was positioned over Marx's chest.

"Get off him!" I drew the skillet back and whacked the man across the side of the head. The impact sent painful vibrations through my fingers and up into my wrists.

The man tumbled off Marx with a groan, a hand pressed to his head, and dragged himself through the grass until his back hit the windows of my apartment.

I gripped the handle with both hands, keeping it aimed at the threat in case he decided to lunge. If he tried to tackle me next, he would get to smell the burnt bottom of my skillet up close.

Marx gathered his legs beneath him and scooped up the knife that must've fallen from the waist of his pants when the attack started. Breathing hard, he kicked the gardening tool out of the man's reach. "Don't move."

"Are you okay?" I asked.

"Better than he is. Nice swing."

Arms trembling, I lowered the skillet to my side. This thing was heavier than I expected.

Marx crouched in front of the man who had lowered his head, fingers buried in his hair. "You wanna tell me why you attacked me?"

The man dropped his hands and looked up, the moonlight turning the tears on his cheeks silver. "I thought you were a threat."

I sucked in a breath of recognition. Spencer. I'd never heard him speak before. I stepped forward, but Marx held out a hand to discourage me from coming any closer.

"I barely had a chance to speak to you before you lunged at me, so I'm not sure I buy that. Why are you lurkin' around out here at three in the mornin'?"

Spencer rested his head against the side of my building, offering no explanation for his actions.

"He does the groundskeeping and maintenance. He usually works nights," I said, though that didn't explain why he was lingering outside *my* apartment.

"Did one of the officers speak with you about Holly bein' attacked in the laundry room?"

Spencer's jaw shifted side to side, but he said nothing.

"You were the only man who knew she was gonna be down there, and considerin' the way you attacked *me* without provocation—"

Spencer's body remained perfectly still, but there was a chill in his voice. "Are you accusing me of hurting her?"

"Did you?"

"No."

Marx let the silence stretch, but if he hoped Spencer would fill it, the tactic was wasted. Jace's nervous rambling could go on for an hour without a single word from another person, but Spencer didn't seem the nervous type.

"Where were you between nine and nine thirty?" Marx pressed.

"Mopping the ninth and tenth floors. You can ask the woman in the wheelchair. I had to move so she could reach her apartment."

"Did you see or hear anythin'?"

"If I had, I would've intervened."

Marx sighed and looked down, tilting his head to study the tattoos on Spencer's forearm. I was too far away to make out the designs. "You were in the army."

Spencer tugged his sleeve down, lips pressed tight, indicating it wasn't a subject he wanted to discuss.

"Judgin' by those tattoos, you lost some people," Marx said, with a hint of understanding and even compassion in his voice.

Despair crawled across Spencer's features. "I lost everyone."

Marx paused before asking, "Bomb?"

Spencer dipped his chin once.

My chest tightened with empathy. I had never witnessed that kind of devastation, but I understood the pain of losing everyone. And the guilt, regret, and confusion that came with being the only survivor.

"Holly, why don't you grab some ibuprofen and a glass of water for him while we talk," Marx suggested.

I looked at the skillet in my hand. Right. He was going to have a brutal headache, if not a concussion.

Their voices faded as I rounded the building to my patio, the porch light coming to life at my approach. When had the bulb started working again? Had someone replaced it?

I paused in front of the door when a sweet smell teased my nose and drew my attention downward. My lips parted in surprise.

Before I went to bed last night, my flower bed had been littered with dead, shriveled-up plants. Now, there were fresh flowers in a variety of colors, and sweetness filled the air.

This explained the repetitive sound—digging in the rocky soil—and the dirt-encrusted garden tool Spencer had been holding when he attacked Marx. But why go to all this trouble? It wasn't his job to tend to my flower bed, and Mr. Whittaker would never give him permission to use business funds for a trip to a floral shop.

I admired the beautiful flowers for another second before pushing into my apartment. Riley rushed me with a concerned whine, his too-long nails clacking on the floor, and I patted his head.

"I'm okay. I promise."

Marx's muffled words penetrated the ribbon of windows as I returned the skillet to the burner. "I know that losin' everybody can make a man desperate for somebody, but Holly's been through a lot, so if you're tryin' to surprise her with flowers because you have romantic intentions—"

"I don't."

Relief swept over me as I cracked open the bottle of painkillers. Dodging advances at coffee shops and on the bus was exhausting enough. I didn't want to have to brace myself every time I stepped out of my apartment.

"Then why go to all this trouble?" Marx asked.

"Because I know what it's like to struggle with night terrors and panic attacks, and I hoped the flowers might comfort her."

Suspicion hardened Marx's voice. "How do you know she has night terrors?"

"I was working outside one night when I heard her screaming. I almost called the police, but then I looked through the window and realized she was asleep."

My throat tightened as I grabbed a glass from the cupboard. How many of my night terrors had he overheard, and did he know why I had them?

Spencer paused for a beat. "I have them too. If I can ever close my eyes long enough to sleep, I see the scattered body parts of my friends and what's left of the children sent out wearing bombs."

Oh Lord.

I couldn't imagine the horrors that replayed behind his eyelids. I didn't want to imagine. I opened the window over the kitchen sink to let in the smell of flowers and said a silent prayer for the man who offered kindness to a stranger in the midst of his own anguish.

22

I woke to sunlight streaming through the ribbon of windows on the rear wall of my apartment, warmth touching my face.

I dragged my aching body into a sitting position and rubbed at the stiffness in my neck. I was alone in the bed, my canine companion mysteriously absent.

"Why is there no . . ." Marx's flustered whisper dissolved into unintelligible grumbling in the kitchen, and the bottles of juice on the refrigerator door rattled as he closed it.

I pushed aside my blankets and swung my legs over the edge of the mattress before pausing to rub at a few more tight muscles. My entire body felt like a rubber band that had been stretched just shy of snapping in half.

Sliding my feet into my fuzzy green slippers, I parted the drapes. Marx was rummaging through my cupboards, and Riley—the traitor—was lying nearby in the hopes that he might catch a few scraps of food.

I yawned as I emerged from the bedroom. "What are you looking for?"

Marx glanced at me. "Eggs."

"In the cupboards?"

"Well, they're not in the fridge where they belong, so I figured I should check where they *don't* belong, since you hide food in strange places. I don't suppose they're in with the toilet paper."

"No, those are the Cheetos."

"Of course, what was I thinkin'?" The smile slipped from his lips as I approached. "You're still hurtin'."

192

"More stiff than anything else. Is this what it feels like to be ancient?"

"How would I know what it feels like to be ancient? I'm not that old."

"There was a hill you rolled over somewhere," I teased.

"I am approachin' the hill. I am not *over* the hill. Brat." He unscrewed the bottle of ibuprofen, setting two pills and a glass of water on the table. "You can take these with breakfast as soon as I figure out what to make."

"I don't have any eggs right now," I said, sinking into one of the chairs and drawing my feet up.

"You don't have any *anythin'* right now." He opened my refrigerator and gestured to the nearly empty shelves. "Juice, cheese, hot dogs, and puddin' cups. Where is all your food?"

"In the cupboard."

"Oh, this cupboard?" He opened the door to display the chip bags, crackers, and canned peaches. "This . . . alcove of malnutrition?"

If I wasn't mistaken, there was a hint of disapproval in his tone.

He closed the cupboard door and opened the silverware drawer. He stared at the contents for a moment, and then picked up a pink straw-shaped object. "You don't have eggs, but you have pixie sticks in your silverware drawer."

"What can I say? I love sugar."

My nickname for him brought the smile back to his lips. "I love you, too, but you're not gonna distract me from my point."

I dragged my hair over one shoulder, weaving it into a loose braid. "There's bread and jam in the cupboard."

He pulled out the items and examined the ingredients on the jam label. "Do you have nut butter stashed somewhere that we can use for protein?"

I almost blurted, "All the pantry had was peanut butter," but I caught myself. If I mentioned a food pantry, he would know I couldn't afford groceries, and then he would go out and spend a bunch of his money to stock my refrigerator.

"Nope."

He returned the jar to the counter and folded his arms, studying me. "How are you doin' financially?"

"Fine."

I wasn't going to tell him about the business troubles, or that I'd only had two photography clients in the past month. Both would gain traction eventually.

"I'm gonna assume 'fine' means not good."

"No, fine means I'm not going hungry and my bills are paid. Things aren't perfect, but . . . I'm grateful."

"Grateful is your default," he said, grabbing a butter knife to spread the jam.

Gratitude was something I practiced daily, but it didn't come naturally. Some days, it was more of a choice than a feeling.

As Marx carried two plates to the table, his gaze strayed to the ceiling. "Where is your smoke alarm?"

I pointedly avoided looking at the ceiling where the obnoxious device used to be. "It wouldn't quit screaming at me, so I took it down."

"Was it screamin' because there was smoke in the apartment?"

"I plead the fifth."

He set one of the plates in front of me. "How did you even reach it?"

"Stacked my step stool on top of a chair and climbed up."

"Why am I not surprised?" Marx shook his head with a smile as he dropped into the chair opposite me. "It's a wonder you didn't fall and break somethin'."

I nearly had, when the stool shifted perilously close to the edge of the chair, throwing off my balance.

Marx reached across the table, palms up, covering most of the distance so I didn't have to stretch, and I placed my hands in his for a quick prayer.

"Did you sleep okay last night?" I asked, folding my jelly bread in half and nibbling off a corner.

"Apart from your cat that doesn't understand the concept of personal boundaries, I didn't sleep terrible."

"Did he snuggle with your face?"

"No, but not for lack of effort on his part." He eyed Sausage, who sat beside the table staring up at him with narrowed eyes. "Why does he look like he's plottin' my death?"

"Because he probably is. Hairball homicide."

"Considerin' I had cat hair stuck in my scruff this mornin', and no small amount of it on my clothes, that's believable."

Riley scrabbled to his feet, his attention fixed on the front door. I tensed at his alert posture. Whoever he heard approaching wasn't someone he trusted.

The hard knock on the door made me jump in my chair. It was seven thirty on a Sunday morning, and the last thing I expected was visitors.

I set down my sandwich and rose from my chair at the same time Marx did. He looked through the window over the sink, while I moved to peer through the peephole the guys had installed in my door.

A man in his forties stood on my patio, his silver-and-black hair slicked back with so much gel that not a strand stirred in the morning breeze.

Biting back a groan, I unlocked the door and opened it to greet my landlord. "Good morning, Mr. Whittaker."

He cleared his throat and tried to keep his eyes on my face, something that seemed to require a great deal of effort. "Ms. Cross, I . . ." He froze when Marx appeared behind my shoulder. "Detective. I wasn't expecting you to still be here."

195

"Whittaker." Marx sank his disdain for the man into that single word, and my landlord squirmed in response.

"I just came by because . . . I heard about the incident last night, and I wanted to apologize in person."

"Which incident?" Marx asked. "The one where a man was able to attack Holly in the laundry room because the buildin' is unlocked at all hours, leavin' public areas accessible to anyone and everyone? Or the incident with your groundskeeper?"

Whittaker let out a groan of uncertainty. "Both?" His beady eyes bounced between us, and I suspected he was afraid we might sue him. "I'm glad you weren't seriously injured in the laundry room. As for the groundskeeper, that's . . . I can explain."

"We already know he suffers from flashbacks and post-traumatic stress from his time in the military," Marx said.

Whittaker nodded. "My sister's request before the cancer, before she . . ." He cleared his throat, a flicker of genuine grief in his eyes. "She passed away two months after he returned home, but before she did, she asked me to help her husband, so I gave him a job and an apartment in the building. He experienced some really terrible things during his deployment, and he's struggling to . . . reintegrate."

"'Strugglin' to reintegrate' doesn't quite cover it," Marx said. "He attacked me simply because I startled him. If it had been Holly who came up behind him—"

"No, he would never hurt a woman, and there's no chance he would confuse her for a man." Whittaker's eyes slithered over me as he spoke, and I folded my arms over my chest in discomfort.

"Stop that," Marx growled, and Whittaker's attention snapped up and away from my body.

He flushed at being caught and had the sense to step out of Marx's reach, but he didn't offer an apology. "I realize that what happened last night was . . . troubling, but please try to be understanding. Spencer needs the stability of this job. If I have to let him go, I'm afraid he'll fall apart, and I promised my sister I would look after him."

"He needs more than a job and a roof over his head. There are counselors who specifically work with traumatized veterans. If he's not seein' one, help him find one."

Whittaker nodded. "I will."

"And fix these." Marx indicated the light poles that lined the sidewalks. "There is no reason your tenants should have to walk around in the dark. And you need to install some kind of security on the main entrance."

Whittaker's lips pinched, no doubt at the cost of those repairs and changes, but he didn't argue. "I'll see what I can do."

Marx cocked an eyebrow. "Excuse me?"

Whittaker's mouth moved soundlessly before he managed, "I'll . . . make sure the problems get fixed. Thank you both for understanding." He scurried off.

Marx shut the door. "If that man looks at you like that one more time, I'm gonna knock his eyeballs out of his head."

"He's creepy, but I think he's harmless."

"He's only harmless because he's petrified of the consequences, not because he has any sense of ethics or morals. As for Spencer, I know what he's goin' through isn't his fault, but be careful around him. He's not in full control of himself."

Neither was I when I had a panic attack or flashback. I couldn't even remember part of last night.

"If we're goin' to church, I need to stop by my place and change. I didn't bring anythin' with me." Marx bent to grab his dress shoes. "What in the . . ." He tipped them and half-a-dozen pieces of cat kibble tumbled out onto the floor. "There is somethin' very wrong with your cat."

I laughed and scooped my chubby fur ball into my arms. "Don't listen to the grumpy man. You're perfect." I kissed the top of his head, and his purr rumbled to life.

Marx shook his shoes to make sure they were kibble free and then pulled them on. "Go get dressed so we can go."

I retreated to my bedroom nook to grab jeans and a sweater, then finished getting ready in the bathroom. I had no makeup to conceal the bruises that would spark unwanted questions, so I draped a scarf around my neck and hoped it would be enough.

23

*J*ordan and Marx sipped at their unlimited free coffee in the church café, and I indulged in my fifty-cent hot chocolate. This packet came with the cutest baby marshmallows.

Watching them dissolve into frothy rings reminded me of the night I re-met Jordan and we caught up with a game of truth-or-dare in the break room of the sheriff's department while I clutched the mug of marshmallow hot chocolate he'd made for me. I hadn't trusted him enough to be alone in a room with him then, but now he was a frequent mention in my gratitude journal.

I smiled and took a sip of my drink, my attention drifting over the people in the café until it snagged on a man who stood by the counter.

I had seen him on Brushwick Friday night, but I'd been such a twisted bundle of nerves at the time that I hadn't been able to place where I knew him from.

He stared at me, fear frozen on his face, as he passed a plate with a donut to his little girl. The pregnant woman beside him took the covered mug from his hand and said something.

Startled, he blinked and responded before automatically kissing her cheek. Confusion clouded the woman's soft features, but she took their daughter's hand and led her away toward the sanctuary.

He had a child, a wife, and a baby on the way. What had he been thinking, driving to Brushwick and propositioning a woman?

Despite the heat of the hot chocolate seeping through the paper mug, the warmth drained from my fingers as the man started toward us.

I considered excusing myself to the bathroom or ducking under the table, but I sat motionless in my chair, hoping he might chicken out and veer off at the last second.

Did he really want to have this conversation here, surrounded by our fellow church members? Was he going to deflect blame from himself and try to accuse *me* of something? Was he going to threaten me to stay silent to preserve his marriage and his position in the church?

You need to stay . . .

The unfinished words of my attacker replayed in my mind. Stay what—still, silent, out of his business, out of his way?

I regarded the approaching man with unease, my gaze dipping to his hands to see if there were any scratches from my fingernails. But he was wearing leather gloves—appropriate for the chilly weather and not unusual considering he was still wearing his coat.

He nodded to Marx and Jordan. "Morning, gentlemen."

Marx offered his hand. "It's Rob, right? You and your wife helped organize the group that came to the courthouse steps to pray durin' the trial."

Rob shook his hand but wouldn't meet his eyes. "Yes, sir, we did."

I had known there were Christians from our church gathered in prayer, but I hadn't known he was one of them. His involvement explained why he recognized me the moment he saw me Friday night.

Rob nodded to Jordan and then met my eyes, sweat beading his forehead. "I was hoping I could have a moment alone to speak with you."

Marx reclined in his chair, an elbow propped over the backrest, and his politeness gave way to suspicion. "What's so important you need to be alone with her to discuss it?"

"It's . . . a personal matter."

"What sort of personal matter?"

Rob wiped at the moisture on his forehead and glanced at the people around us. They were trickling toward the open doors of the sanctuary, drawn to the inviting music. "I'd really rather discuss it in private with Holly. Please."

I didn't want to have this discussion at all, especially not in private, but the desperate gleam in his eyes eroded my resolve. "One minute, right there."

I pointed to the cushions that lined the entryway. The teenagers generally gathered there, but they had all wandered off to the youth room. It was semiprivate, and I wouldn't have to be alone with him.

Rob scratched behind his ear. "I was hoping we could use one of the empty conference rooms."

Marx opened his mouth to say something, but I cut in. "It's there or nothing."

Reluctantly, Rob nodded. "Okay. I'll, um, I'll wait over there." He walked away from the table.

Marx touched my arm. "After what happened last night, are you sure you wanna talk to him alone?"

Nope, not in the least, but I said, "I'll be fine."

Jordan watched the man, no doubt analyzing his movements and behaviors, but he didn't object when I pushed up from the table. I crossed the lobby and stopped a comfortable distance from Rob.

I couldn't be sure he wasn't my attacker any more than I could be sure he had nothing to do with Cami's abduction. Erik McCallister picked her up from Brushwick and supposedly let her out somewhere else, which meant she could've gotten into anyone's car.

Rob's shy, stammering approach to women might've put her at ease enough to climb into his car in an unfamiliar neighborhood.

He flicked a nervous glance toward Marx and Jordan. "You didn't tell them."

"If I told them where I saw you and what you were doing, they wouldn't let you within ten feet of me."

He released a quivering breath and stared at the floor, hands on his hips. It took him a few failed attempts to choke out. "I shouldn't have been there."

I wasn't going to argue with that.

"I've never done anything like that before. I've driven by a few times, stopped, but that was the only time I actually . . ." His throat sounded sticky as he swallowed. "I've never gone that far before."

I folded my arms, not entirely convinced. Collin could play innocent, too, and he was as guilty as the devil. "Okay. What's this important thing we need to discuss?"

"My wife."

"I'm not gonna tell her, if that's what you're worried about. She deserves to know, but she should hear it from you."

He dropped his eyes to the floor. "Telling her would only upset her."

I wasn't an expert at romantic relationships, seeing as I had never had one, but keeping this secret from his wife sounded like a good way to destroy the trust between them. She would find out eventually, either because someone told her or because he caved and went back.

"I think not telling her is a mistake, but it's your marriage." I turned to go back to the café, then decided to take advantage of this opportunity and probe for information. "Where were you Thursday night around midnight?"

A line formed between his eyebrows. "At home in bed with my wife. Why, what happened Thursday night?"

"A girl disappeared." I snapped open the front pocket of my knapsack and retrieved the picture, showing him the half with Cami.

His eyebrows gave a barely perceptible twitch in response—he recognized her. If he denied it, I was going to let Marx and Jordan deal with him. They would scare the truth out of him.

202

"I saw her. But it was Monday, not Thursday," he said. "She was having an argument with a bald guy on the sidewalk. He got pretty hands-on every time she tried to walk away."

That must've been the conversation that made Spike angry, the one Tandi mentioned. But if he didn't want her because of her diabetes, why was there a confrontation at all?

"What happened?" I asked.

"Some guy handing out Scripture pamphlets or something tried to intervene, but the bald guy shoved him to the ground. I don't know what happened after that. I left and went home."

"The man with the pamphlets, did you recognize him?" I asked, putting away the photo.

"No, he's not from our church."

"Can your wife confirm you were home in bed Thursday night?"

"You think I . . ." He jerked as though I had slapped him. "I had nothing to do with whatever happened to that girl, and you can't talk to my wife about it. If you start asking questions . . ."

He stepped forward, and I retreated, heart skipping. He stilled at the scrape of metal chair legs on tile. Marx and Jordan were both standing now, poised to intervene.

Rob retreated, putting another two feet between us. "You don't have to be afraid of me, Holly. I would never hurt you."

"I have no reason to believe that."

Pain flashed across his face. "How can I put you at ease?"

"Take off your gloves."

"My gloves?" He looked at his hands with a puzzled frown, then, without question, peeled the leather from his fingers until both hands were bare.

There were no scabs or scratches on the tops of either hand, and some of my worry melted away. He wasn't the attacker from the laundry room.

"I don't know what this thing with the gloves is about, but I'm not a bad person. I would never hurt anyone," he said. "I'm not that kind of man."

Was he really that naïve?

"You don't think paying a woman to use her body is hurting her? You went to that street to rent and enjoy a human being like a Redbox movie."

He flinched.

"Do you honestly believe any of those women wanna be there?"

"I . . . I mean, I guess I assumed they chose . . . to do what they're doing. It's not like they're being trafficked."

"No little girl dreams of becoming a prostitute when she grows up, of selling her body night after night to keep a roof over her head and food in her stomach. But somewhere along the way, someone or something convinced those girls it was their best and only option. Beneath the callouses that help them survive and face each day, their spirits are bleeding and broken, and instead of helping them, you went there to cause more pain."

"I swear to you, I've never done anything like that before. It's usually just . . ."—he struggled to form the words—"videos."

My stomach twisted. I didn't want to hear about his addiction to explicit videos. Why was he admitting that to me, of all people?

"No one gets hurt," he hastened to say.

"*Everyone* gets hurt. Your wife, your kids, your relationship with God. And you don't know anything about the people in those videos. They could be as unwilling as . . ." My throat closed against the rest of my words. *As unwilling as I was in the videos Collin made of me.* "You need to talk to someone about your . . . habits."

Rob's shoulders slumped, the tears spilling over as he blinked. "I'm a Christian man. I'm not supposed to struggle with things like this. Who am I supposed to talk to?"

Nausea churned in my stomach as I tried to wrap my mind around how a man who claimed to love and follow Jesus could do the things he was doing. But then a quiet voice slipped through my thoughts, reminding me that there was no such thing as a perfect Christian, only a perfect savior.

"I've tried to stop, but I can't, and I am so . . . so ashamed," he admitted.

I was tempted to walk away and let him figure this out on his own, but dealing with it alone was what led him to Brushwick.

"Everyone struggles with something," I said. "Even Christians. I can't help you with your video issue, but shame is . . ." I tightened my arms around my stomach. "It's something I'm intimately familiar with. Shame thrives in the dark and grows in the silence, isolating you and convincing you to do things you wouldn't ordinarily do."

Like downing a bottle of pills, I thought, remembering that morning on Marx's couch, the softening pills shifting in my palm.

"It will keep you trapped right where you are, unable to ask for help, and unable to break free of your habit, your temptation, your struggles."

"What do I do?" Rob asked, his voice cracking. "How do I deal with it?"

I stared at the spiral carpet as I pondered my answer. I wasn't a counselor or a pastor. I could only speak from my experience.

"You don't deal with it alone," I said. "Some battles are so hard, so overwhelming, that they can only be fought and won with an army. But for that army to fight alongside you, they need to know what they're fighting. You need to confide in people you trust so they can pray for you and support you when you feel like giving in or giving up." I glanced at Marx, grateful that he was there for me when I needed someone. "But I can't be one of those people, Rob. I can't . . . hear the things that—"

"I understand. It was insensitive of me to even bring it up. I wasn't thinking about what you've been through."

I shifted my shoulders in discomfort. "I know that the moment you think about speaking to someone, that shame curls into a panicked ball inside you, determined to scare you into keeping it secret. But don't let it hold you prisoner. Talk to someone, okay?"

He nodded. "Thank you, Holly. For your advice. And for being there that night. If I hadn't seen you, I might've gone through with it."

"I'm not sure you should be thanking *me* for that last one." I left him to rejoin Marx and Jordan in the café. Judging by the tightness in Marx's jaw, he'd overheard some of the conversation. "How much did you hear?"

"Enough to know I'm never leavin' you alone with any man in this church," he said, grimacing. "I don't trust a single one of them."

I grabbed my hot chocolate from the table as a volunteer kicked up the rubber stoppers, and the heavy sanctuary doors drifted shut. I looked between Jordan and Marx. "Time to go learn some stuff."

We made our way into the sanctuary and found seats near the back. I settled into a chair between my two favorite men and sang along to the music, trying not to laugh as a man one row ahead of us belted out the lyrics, off-key and so loud that the people on either side of him cringed every time a chorus came around.

I listened with rapt attention as Pastor Greg launched into a message about the importance of deriving our identity from a steadfast and loving God rather than a world that is opinionated, cruel, and indecisive.

"Folks, God weaves our identity into us in our mother's wombs, and when we're uncertain, we find the truth of that identity here." Pastor Greg held up the Bible. "Chosen, accepted, loved, redeemed, forgiven. Mankind is quick to offer labels, and often times those labels become another link in the chain of bondage. Failure, thief, prostitute, worthless, adulterer."

I glanced at Rob, who was seated a few rows up and across the aisle. He lowered his head, lips moving soundlessly in prayer.

"The identity the world tries to wrap you in is superficial, incomplete, and sometimes divisive, and it will never hold a candle to the identity God gives us. When you're searching for who you are, look to the Word, not the world," Pastor Greg said.

I leaned toward Marx and whispered, "What does divisive mean?"

"Somethin' that causes hostility or disunity between people."

"Shh," the woman behind us said, irritation stamped on her face.

Marx turned in his seat, keeping his voice low. "You shushin' me is louder than my whisper." He faced forward with an aggravated shake of his head.

I wanted to shrink down in my seat from embarrassment, but Jordan leaned forward with an amused whisper. "Couldn't just let that go, huh?"

"No, that is the third time she shushed me this mornin'." Marx threw a look over his shoulder at her, almost daring her to do it again, but she pressed her lips together.

We made it through the rest of the service without incident and exited the sanctuary into the crowded lobby where church members mingled.

Jordan paused halfway to the doors. "Hang on, I got a text from Sam." He scanned the message. "He reached out to the staff at the dining hall and they confirmed that Erik McCallister had his car brought around a little after eight p.m."

"And Holly was attacked around nine," Marx said.

Unease crawled through me. "But how would he know where I live? Jace and I left the party fifteen minutes before him. He couldn't have followed us."

"I think we should ask him," Marx said.

Jordan tapped his screen a few times. "He volunteers at a soup kitchen every Sunday after church, and it's not too far from here."

"A soup kitchen," I said doubtfully.

"Believe or not. According to the article, he finds fulfillment serving his community at one of the local food kitchens every Sunday afternoon."

Jordan pulled up a picture on his phone. Erik, clad in a white apron, stood behind a table of food warmers with a politician's smile that didn't match the petulant gleam in his eyes. If he was donating his time to care for the poor and homeless, he wasn't doing it by choice.

24

*H*eavensbee soup kitchen resided in a closed church, a red brick building barely big enough to accommodate the people who wandered in for the eleven o'clock meal.

Even though I had never been to this particular soup kitchen, it was similar to the others I wandered into while living on the street—the scent of savory food and body odor, loud voices, and too many people packed around the tables.

I had been homeless in this city for barely a week, battered, bruised, and well on my way to starving, when the aroma of herb chicken lured me into a place like this. Too many curious stares drove me right back out the door.

"Busy place," Marx said from behind me.

"Yep." I fidgeted with the sleeves of my coat as I scanned the volunteers behind the serving table at the far end of the room. "There's Erik."

His expensive suit from the gala had been traded in for khakis, a white T-shirt, and a stained apron that covered him from chest to thigh. He plopped mashed potatoes onto passing plates without bothering to look up from his phone.

Without saying a word, he communicated to everyone in the room that they weren't worth his time.

"He's definitely not here by choice," Jordan said.

"From what I've heard, his father bases his campaign on family values. He's one of the few who seems to be genuine. If he realized his son was doin' somethin' to spoil that image, he might not take it well," Marx replied.

I started down the aisle between tables, Marx and Jordan following close behind, and stopped in front of Erik's station. "Got a minute?"

"No. If you don't want this slop, move . . ." He peeled his eyes from his screen to spare me a disgruntled glance, and a series of emotions played across his face—surprise, annoyance, and then anger. "You again."

"Me again."

He scowled and then scooped a spoonful of mashed potatoes onto an old man's plate, half of the serving splattering onto the tile. "What do you want now?"

"More mashed potatoes," the old man said, staring at the miniscule portion that had made it onto his plate.

"Not you," Erik snapped, but he gave the man another spoonful to send him on his way. "Why are you bothering me during my *fulfilling* volunteer work?"

"I'm here to talk about what you did."

He darkened his phone screen and stuffed the device into a pocket. "I already told you I didn't do anything to your friend."

"And me?"

His gaze flickered over me. "I didn't do anything to you either. You chose not to get in the car with us, remember?"

"You can keep spoonin' potatoes, or we can discuss this in private," Marx said, his voice deceptively relaxed.

Erik considered Marx and then Jordan. "This feels like I'm gonna get shanked. Is that the plan?"

"Unfortunately, we left our shanks at home," Jordan said.

Speak for yourself, I thought. I had my box cutter, and if he got aggressive, he might just get poked.

"I'm up for a conversation if it gets me out of this." Erik tossed the spoon into the warmer and stripped off the apron, abandoning his post without telling anyone.

He peeled off his latex serving gloves, tossing them on the floor, then strode into a private side room and folded his arms as he turned to face us.

"What do we wanna discuss? Something more interesting than a missing hooker, I hope. It's common knowledge that they usually come back on their own."

"According to the valet who brought your car around, you left the gala shortly after eight," Jordan said.

"Well, I'll make sure he's fired for talking out of turn. Who are *you* anyway?"

"A private investigator."

"Then tell me, law enforcement dropout, what does me leaving that boring party early have to do with anything?"

Jordan let the insult roll off him. "Holly was attacked after the gala."

"She looks fine to me, though that purple blimp of a coat doesn't do her any favors."

"It's my understandin' that you met two girls on Brushwick. One is missin', and the other was attacked last night. Hard to believe that's a coincidence," Marx said.

"Your beliefs aren't my concern. But if you're dying to know what I did when I left the party, I got together with some friends. You're welcome to ask them, if you can figure out their names."

Marx smiled, but there wasn't a drop of warmth in it. "That's fine. I'm sure your father knows their names. We'll drop by his office and—"

"Okay," Erik bit out. "George Lyle and Joel Dominguez are the guys I regularly spend time with."

He dragged his oversized cell phone from his pocket, giving me a clear view of his right hand as his thumb glided across the screen. Apart from a faded scar, there were no marks on the back of it.

He rattled off the numbers for his friends, and Jordan made note of them in his phone. When he was finished, he asked, "Anyone else?"

"I aim for quality over quantity when it comes to my friends, so unless you want the number for our homely housekeeper, that's all I've got for you."

"I'm gonna make a few calls." Jordan stepped out of the room to contact Erik's friends.

"Where did you go after the gala?" Marx asked.

"George and I went to a club. Better atmosphere, better drinks. We hooked up with some ladies for the evening, but I wasn't really interested in their names, so you're on your own there."

Marx grimaced at his blatant lack of respect for other people.

Erik returned his phone to his pocket. "Well, this has been fun, but you private investigators and your ride-along can leave now," Erik said. "If the actual cops have any questions, they can talk to one of the lawyers we have on retainer."

I opened my mouth to ask for more details about his interaction with Cami, but Marx moved to block his exit with a curt "We're not done."

Erik smiled. "I don't know what PI books you've been reading, but you have exactly no authority to detain me."

His cocky attitude reminded me of Collin, which only amplified my feelings of dislike and distrust.

"I have no interest in detainin' you, but it's only fair I warn you before you make another mistake," Marx said.

"That implies I made a mistake to begin with, and I think I would remember that."

"You've made a number of them. Startin' with the way you treat women. That girl over there that you disrespected and threatened last night . . . that's my baby."

Erik looked back at me. "Are you two related in some nongenetic way, or does she just enjoy dating old guys?"

Marx continued as if he hadn't spoken. "Your second mistake is thinkin' I'm a private investigator you can brush off. I'm a detective with the police department, and the woman I'm days away from marryin' is the district attorney for the county, and as it happens, she's on friendly terms with your father. She would be more than willin' to fill him in on your activities, and I will be happy to provide him with proof to back it up."

That wiped the amusement from Erik's face. "You can't—"

"I'm not done."

Erik snapped his teeth together, eyes smoldering.

"Holly is beloved by the police department and the district attorney's office, and if I find out you had anythin' to do with what happened to her last night, or if you try to follow through on your threat to ruin her life, we will hit you like a freight train without brakes. Do we understand each other?"

Anger twisted Erik's face. "Tell your *baby* to stay out of my personal business, and we won't have a problem."

I stepped forward. "Jace is my friend. That makes her my business. I won't let you or her mother ruin her life by pushing her into a relationship she doesn't want."

"Jacelyn would be lucky to marry someone like me. No one else of influence is going to accept a woman in a wheelchair for a wife. I have no problem satisfying my needs elsewhere and coming home to a plush bank account."

Fury drove me forward, but Marx snagged me around the waist and hauled me back. "Easy, sweetheart. Kickin' him in the shin isn't gonna do any good."

"You don't deserve my friend. And if you go anywhere near her, I'll tell everyone the truth about you."

"I suggest you forget about Jace Walker," Marx said. "If you wanna climb the social ladder, find a different rung."

Erik's chest heaved as he glared at us. Incensed, he stormed from the room. I wanted to follow, but Marx kept his arm locked around my waist.

"Leave him be, sweetheart."

"But I have questions about what happened with Cami. He knows more than he told me last night."

"I'm sure he knows a lot more, but he's never gonna answer your questions. People like him play games but always lawyer up."

I wiggled free of his loosening grip and turned toward him, frustrated. "If that's true, then why did we even come here?"

"We came so I could make sure he understands the consequences if he comes after you again."

I yanked my rumpled jacket straight. "He's not the one who attacked me. There weren't any scratches on his hands."

I would feel better if it had been him, because at least we would know who the threat was.

Jordan rejoined us, an interested expression on his face. "Unsurprisingly, Erik's friend and alibi, George Lyle, is unavailable for questioning. His family shipped him off to a drug rehab center in California first thing this morning."

"What about the other one?" Marx asked.

"Joel Dominguez's parents say he's been out of touch for days, calls going to voice mail, no response on social media. But they did have something interesting to share. Turns out there's a fourth friend. Joel's parents said his name is David Monroe."

"Somethin' tells me Erik didn't *forget* to mention him."

"I would bet he knows something Erik doesn't want us to know." Jordan turned to me. "You up for questioning another one of these guys?"

I nodded. I didn't care how many people we had to interview on our day off. I wanted answers.

25

I brushed at the dog hair on my sweater as Jordan knocked on the door of the Monroe home. We had stopped by my place to let Riley out for a bathroom break, and some of him had hitched a ride on my clothes as we left.

I visually explored our surroundings from the front porch as we waited. The property had the potential to be beautiful, but caring for the gardens and house's exterior didn't seem to be a priority. Everything was faded and weathered, and weeds smothered the blooms in the flower beds.

The front door opened, and a barefoot man in his twenties appeared. His hair was tousled, and a bruise on his cheekbone underscored the exhaustion that rimmed his hazel eyes.

"I'm sorry, this isn't a good time for . . ." His protest trailed off when his gaze swept over the unfamiliar men and landed on me at the edge of the porch.

We stared at each other, a thread of familiarity stretching between us. I tried to imagine the bottom half of his face obscured by a car window, leaving only his nose and eyes visible.

"You're the man from the backseat."

He looked me over, almost clinical in his perusal, before the murmur of women's voices captured his attention. Brows knitted in concern, he stepped onto the porch and pulled the door shut behind him, stuffing his hands in his pockets. "What's this about?"

"I think you know," Jordan said.

David assessed the men who accompanied me. "You two carry yourselves like law enforcement, and I have no interest in speaking to the police."

"Holly and I work in the private sector, searching for missing people." Jordan offered him one of our business cards.

Reluctantly, David took it and studied the information on it, then glanced at me. "I suspected you weren't like the other girls when we pulled up beside you that night. Your attire and your mannerisms were all wrong. This is what you do?"

When he lifted the card, I nodded. "I was there collecting information on a missing girl."

David tipped the card in Marx's direction. "And you?"

Marx begrudgingly identified himself. "I'm a detective for the NYPD, but I'm not here on police business."

David glanced at a security camera mounted above the front door and sighed. "My father's a defense attorney, and he forbids any of us speak to the police without a lawyer present."

"Why would you need a lawyer?" Jordan asked.

"A precautionary measure to avoid misunderstandings and misconstrued statements. My father's defended a number of innocent people whose poor word choices landed them in the courtroom as criminal suspects. It's nothing personal, Detective, but if I talk to you, it *will* get back to my father, and I don't want to deal with the fallout."

A curtain swished in a nearby window, and I expected to see an eavesdropping face, but there was no one there.

"As I was saying earlier, this isn't a good time for visitors, so if you'll excuse me."

David turned toward the door, and I rushed forward with the picture. "Please." I thrust Cami's smiling face in front of him. "Right now there is a sixteen-year-old girl who's missing, and you might know something that could help us find her before it's too late."

He flinched almost imperceptibly. "Sixteen?"

"Yes, and we know she didn't disappear by choice because she left her medicine behind. She could die without it."

He closed his eyes and then looked up at the sky. "I can't talk with him here."

Marx grimaced. "I'll wait by the cars."

As Marx walked away, David gestured toward a seating area in the yard. "We'll have more privacy over there."

We followed him along a cobblestone path to a round table and delicate white chairs shaded by an umbrella of flowering vines. I could curl up with a book in a spot like this, as enraptured by the story as the surrounding birdsong.

"We spoke with Erik before coming here," Jordan said. "And when he gave us a list of his friends, you weren't on it. Any idea why?"

"We rarely see eye to eye on matters. But someone must've told you about our connection, since you're here."

"Joel's parents."

"They're nice people."

David drew back one of the chairs and offered it to me, but I made no move to take it. I appreciated his willingness to speak with us, but that didn't mean I trusted him enough to come within grabbing distance.

"Bit late for manners after you and your friends tried to put a price on her," Jordan said, his voice curt. He pulled out a chair for me, and then took the one next to mine.

David grimaced and sat. "*I* didn't try to put a price on her. I recommended that we leave her alone. Erik wasn't interested in my opinion, as usual."

"Did you suggest that he leave Cami alone as well?" Jordan asked.

"I wasn't with him when he picked her up, but I didn't approve of the decisions made that night. Everything went . . . sideways, and I knew someone would come around asking questions sooner or later." He shook his head. "We should never have left her."

My heart thudded harder in my chest as I envisioned a struggle turning deadly and Cami's body being dumped to hide the evidence.

"What did you do?" I asked.

217

"Nothing, and I guess that's what has been eating at me for days. I did absolutely nothing, and no one has seen her since. I asked around, hoping she was somehow okay."

"You spoke with Dorina and Clayton," Jordan said. "They told us a man with a bruise on his cheek came around asking about Cami, though not by name."

"Saturday morning. I spoke with several people. I never asked any of their names, but no one had seen her, and that's when I knew something was really wrong. I told Erik we should call the police, but he said it wasn't our problem."

"Did your friends hurt her?" I asked. "Where did they leave her? Maybe she's still alive and needs help."

"She was in the alley behind the Velvet Ribbon, a wealthy members-only club. But you won't find her there. Someone took her."

"Who took her?" I demanded.

"I don't know. He was wearing a hooded sweatshirt with a scarf covering the bottom half of his face. He scooped her up and put her in his car. Black, I think."

Jordan leaned forward in his chair, suspicion in his voice. "What exactly happened Thursday night?"

"I can't tell you any more than I already have. I'm sorry. I hope you find her." He pushed up from the table, and the breeze twined around him before reaching me, carrying the scent of flowers and . . .

Froot Loops.

The air caught in my lungs as the scent dragged my mind back to the laundry room, to the man who pressed me down into the washing machine.

"Your cologne," I squeezed out.

David frowned. "It's aftershave actually. Bergamot."

My hand moved reflexively to the bruises on my throat. David caught the movement, and for a moment, he seemed to stop breathing. I was sucking in more than enough air for both of us.

"Holly." Jordan leaned toward me. "What's wrong?"

David stuffed his hands into his pockets, but not before I noticed the shallow scratches from my fingernails, where I'd tried to pry his hand from my neck.

"You were wearing that aftershave in the laundry room, when you attacked me," I said, trying to conceal the tremor in my voice.

Jordan's eyes widened. "Wait, what?"

"I recognize the smell of his aftershave, and there are scratches on his right hand from my fingernails, the same hand that was around my neck."

Jordan shot to his feet. "*You* attacked her?"

David stepped back, hands raised. "It's not what you think."

"Yeah? Then tell me what kind of guy sneaks into a building, follows a girl to a basement, and grabs her like that."

"I was trying to protect her."

I caught Jordan's wrist, silently pleading with him to sit back down. Putting David on the defensive wasn't going to help us get the answers we needed.

Jordan sank back into his chair, but his body language indicated he was ready to tackle the man if he tried to run. "Explain," he gritted out.

David released a breath and lowered his hands. "After Erik and Holly spoke at the gala, and she threatened to expose his activities if he didn't break off the arrangement with Mrs. Walker, he was livid. He wanted her scared into silence, into backing off, but he wouldn't risk it himself. He demanded that George or I do it." He gripped the back of the chair, staring at the scabs on his hand. "I knew that George would put her in the hospital. He and Erik have no reservations about roughing up people they think of as . . . less. Homeless people, prostitutes, the mentally ill." He glanced back at the house. "Introduce drugs and alcohol, and they turn into a pair of hyenas, so I volunteered."

"And then you followed her from the gala and waited for a chance to jump her?" Jordan demanded, no less angry now than before the explanation.

"Yes, but I did everything I could to avoid hurting her." David looked at me. "I only intended to restrain you long enough to warn you off."

"Why not talk to me?"

"I was weighing my options when you came out with the dog. When you put him back inside and went into the other building, I considered trying to talk to you. For so long, actually, that when I finally realized talking was too much of a risk, I didn't have enough time to scare you into silence before your friend came back."

"What risk was there to you?"

David's fingers tightened over the back of the chair. "Erik knows all of our secrets, including one that would convince my father to disown me."

"You owe Holly more of an explanation than that," Jordan said.

David blew out a breath and lowered his head. "I go with Erik and the guys to pick up girls, but I don't . . . engage."

There was a weightiness to his words, a shame, and I kept my voice quiet as I asked, "You're gay, aren't you?"

Tears pooled in his eyes. "Please don't tell anyone. My family is already in shambles from my father's affair and my mother's . . . struggles."

"We're not gonna tell anyone," I assured him. That would only serve to hurt him, and he was already wrestling with it. "Why is Erik so desperate for that arrangement with my friend's mother?"

David seemed relieved by the subject change. "His father, much like mine, is strict when it comes to presenting a certain image. Congressman McCallister promotes family values. When he found out Erik was regularly using escort services, he cut him off financially. Erik is hoping to marry into money that his father can't control."

"Getting cut off doesn't seem to have curbed his appetite any," Jordan said.

"No, he can't afford to entertain high-end ladies anymore, but there are other options."

"Which brings us back to Cami," Jordan said. "Tell us everything that happened that night."

David shook his head. "I won't betray my friends."

"It doesn't sound like they're your friends," Jordan replied.

"I'm sorry, I can't."

"If you tell me the truth, I won't press charges for the laundry room." I ignored the disapproving glance Jordan threw my way.

I believed David when he said he was trying *not* to hurt me, and I didn't think he would come after me a second time, especially after Marx instilled some fear into the ringleader.

David hesitated. "If Erik knows the information came from me . . ."

"We're not the police," Jordan reminded him. "We're here for answers, not incriminating evidence."

David pondered that for a moment, then dropped back into his chair. "I was waiting outside the club with George. Joel is usually with us when Erik picks up a girl, but he bailed an hour earlier, saying he didn't feel well. Erik pulled into the alley with Cami in the passenger seat. I didn't think it was right, surprising her like that, but when we invited her to join us a few nights before, she refused because there was more than one man in the car. Cami freaked out when she realized there were three of us instead of just Erik, and she tried to leave."

"And you stopped her?" Jordan asked.

"Erik grabbed her, and George suggested heroin to relax her. He uses it recreationally, and he'd gotten some from a dealer in the club. I can't . . . won't tell you who the dealer is."

"We don't care about your friend's addiction or his dealer. We just wanna find Cami." Jordan motioned for him to continue.

"They assumed that, being a prostitute, Cami would welcome the drugs. But she didn't. She got really scared, said something about her dad."

Her deceased dad or her stepdad? I wondered, but I didn't want to interrupt with a question.

"When she refused to take it, Erik insisted. There was a struggle, and the next thing I knew, Cami was lying on the ground, bleeding from a gash on her head. I told Erik we needed to take her to a hospital, but then a car pulled into the alley behind us. We panicked and got into Erik's car, but as we were driving away, I saw the driver scoop Cami up and put her in the back. And then . . ." He cleared his throat. "We drove away."

Anger sharpened my voice. "You saw some stranger stuff an injured girl into his car, and you just drove away?!"

"Yes." A tear splashed onto his cheek as he blinked. "And I regret that more than you could possibly know."

Jordan elicited a few more details from him while I silently fumed over the man's inaction. It was in my bones to protect people, and yet this man ran away while a girl was kidnapped.

"And what about Friday night?" Jordan asked.

"You mean with regards to Holly?"

"No, with regards to Dorina, the older black woman in the auto repair shop on Brushwick."

"I saw her pull Holly into the shop, and she's one of the people I spoke with Saturday morning. Those were my only encounters with her."

"How did you get this?" Jordan indicated the bruise on his cheekbone.

David hesitated a beat too long before answering. "It must've happened in the alley with Cami. She was frantic."

"What about your friend Joel? Any idea where we can find him? We'd like to talk to him."

David shifted in his chair and fixed his attention on the table. "Joel can't possibly know anything about what happened that night.

He left early. And if he's not at home and not answering his phone, I don't know what to tell you."

Jordan started to ask another question, but something crashed inside the house. A door banged open a second later, and a heavyset woman in an apron rushed out.

"Mr. Monroe, your mother's having one of her episodes. She threw the kitchen blender at me," the woman panted. "And she's started in on the dinner glasses." A shattering sound punctuated her announcement.

David dragged himself from his chair, as though this was a common occurrence he'd grown weary of dealing with. "I'm sorry, I need to go." He turned and followed the apron-clad woman into the house. The door closing behind them did little to contain the sounds of a domestic war zone.

"Do you believe him?" I asked, rising from my chair.

"I don't know. He's lying about the bruise for sure, but if his mother makes a habit of throwing things in the house, that might explain that. An unidentifiable man in a black car being responsible for Cami's disappearance seems convenient, though."

I fell into step beside him. "But why would he lie?"

"I don't know. Honestly, the only thing I'm sure he was telling the truth about was not intending to hurt you." Jordan paused when we were almost to the cars and fished his phone from his pocket, the screen bright with an incoming call. "I'll catch up in a sec." He swiped a finger across the screen and pressed the phone to his ear. "This is Jordan."

I rejoined Marx, who leaned against the passenger door of his car with his arms crossed. "Being a detective is a lot harder than I expected. Everyone lies and keeps secrets."

He smiled. "It's human nature."

"Slow down, Hope, I'm having trouble understanding . . ." Jordan trailed off, listening, and my back straightened at the mention of Hope's name.

Something must be wrong.

"Who is Hope?" Marx asked.

"She's related to our case."

"She wasn't in the section of your notes I read through."

"That's because she's not a suspect. She's the one who brought us the missing person's case. She works with Cami over on Brushwick."

Marx's forehead creased, and he opened his mouth to say something more, but Jordan spoke first. "Okay, stay inside, we'll be right there." He disconnected. "We need to go." To Marx, he said, "Hope doesn't trust the police, so I think she'll be more receptive to our help without you there."

"Holly was attacked last night. She doesn't need to be runnin' off into another potentially dangerous situation."

"Marx," I said, biting back a sigh. "We just—"

"Had this conversation, I know. But you bein' involved with things like this worries me, and I can't help that."

"I need you to trust me, to let me be . . . me."

His expression softened. "I always want you to be you, sweet pea, but I also want you to be safe."

"Jordan's gonna be with me, and if it makes you feel better, I'll add a Taser to my Christmas list."

"It's cute that you think I'm gonna wait till Christmas." To Jordan, he said, "Keep her safe."

Jordan dipped his head. "That's always my goal."

I hugged Marx and then hurried toward Jordan's car. Marx watched us go with palpable reluctance and worry, but even though the possibility of danger scared him, he stood back and let me choose my own path.

26

*J*ordan filled me in on the situation we were walking into. Another attempted kidnapping; only this time the victim was a child.

During the brief window of time when Hope's son was playing alone outside, a man in a white van pulled up alongside the curb and lured him away from his toys with candy. It is terrifying how quickly and easily a predator can manipulate an unattended child.

The toy dinosaurs the five-year-old boy had been playing with before the incident still lay in the grass.

"Are we sure her son's okay?" I asked, stepping around the unwrapped sucker stuck to the sidewalk.

"Yeah, she said an elderly neighbor saw what was happening and started shouting. The guy drove off empty-handed."

Thank you, Jesus.

I followed Jordan down the sidewalk to the apartment building, taking in the layout. It was two stories, with the sidewalk rolling up to the entrances of the lower-level apartments. There must be a stairwell in the alley for tenants to reach the second floor.

Jordan raised a hand to ring the doorbell, but the button was missing. He reached through the locked metal gate instead, like I had done with the repair shop, and rapped on the wood door behind it.

A shouting voice from above us cut through the beat of music pulsing from one of the apartments. I tipped my head back in time to see a wad of clothing break apart in the air and come raining down.

I sidestepped a man's shirt. "Someone's spring cleaning."

A woman ranted in Spanish, and a man shouted back, their argument spilling out of the upper-floor window and onto the street.

A shoe hit the edge of the windowsill and dropped straight for us. I stepped out of its path, and it bounced off the sidewalk into the grass. A second sneaker immediately followed, launching through the window like a missile and soaring through the air until it connected with a car.

Was this how shoes ended up tangled over power lines?

Jordan pounded on the door again and then stepped closer to me, prepared to shield me from falling debris. "If Hope doesn't let us in soon, we're gonna have to go. I don't want either of us standing here when this lady decides to throw her boyfriend out the window."

Hope's interior door opened, and the pale girl who stood on the other side of the metal gate without a trace of makeup was barely recognizable. "Now you see why I don't bother putting plants or decorations on my porch."

She unlocked the gate and pushed it open, inviting us in. Dressed in holey jeans and a baggy sweatshirt, she looked the most relaxed I'd seen her.

I stepped inside. "Do they fight a lot?"

"They do this about once a month, and then they make up." Hope rolled her eyes. "I don't care as long as they don't damage my stuff and don't scare Tyler."

Hope's apartment was about the size of mine, with worn carpet and water-stained walls. A quarter-sized hole had eroded in the center of one of the ceiling water stains, and a bucket sat on the floor beneath it.

Hope followed my attention. "Every time they run the shower upstairs, it leaks through. When she's done kicking her man out, she tries to flood my whole apartment."

That didn't sound safe.

"How's Tyler?" Jordan asked.

She folded her arms. "Mad that I slapped the sucker out of his hand, but he don't understand that crazy people can make their own candy with drugs in it, and it don't bother them one bit, handing it out to kids."

Jordan's mouth tightened. "Can you go over the events one more time?"

"Tyler was playing with his dinosaurs in the grass. I heard the fighting start upstairs, so I came in to grab the bucket for the living room. I heard Gloria next door yelling for me, so I came running back outside. This van took off, and Tyler was standing there with a sucker I didn't give him. I slapped it out of his hand and brought him inside. Then I called you."

"Did you recognize the driver?"

"He might've been a little familiar, but I didn't get a real good look. I was focused on my baby, you know?"

"Do you have any idea where you might've seen him before? At your son's day care, in the neighborhood, on Brushwick?" Jordan asked.

"How should I know? And even if I did meet him while I was working, I've been with a lot of men over the past five and a half years, and I try real hard not to remember their faces."

She stared us down, that defensive glint in her eyes as she braced for judgment and cruelty. I couldn't blame her for not wanting to remember the faces of the men who used her.

"Mommy!"

The child's voice drew everyone's attention to a closed room along the hallway, and Hope walked over, cracking the door. "Everything okay, little man?"

Water splashed, and a boy asked, "Can I have more bubbles?"

"I'll be in to wash your hair in a little bit, and that'll make some more bubbles, okay? And then we'll have some lunch." She blew him a kiss, caught the invisible one he sent back her way, and then closed the door. "I gotta make him something to eat."

She navigated the hallway cluttered with toys and a pair of dirty dinosaur socks, and we trailed behind.

"Could the van driver have been Tyler's dad?" I asked hesitantly, afraid the question might open an old wound.

She let out a protracted *ttt* sound through her teeth. "Him I would remember, but no, not a chance. He's still back in Connecticut, and he don't even know about Tyler. And if he did, he wouldn't exactly rush in to take care of us. He was a senior who convinced an idiot freshman he was in love with her. Guess I was stupid and desperate enough to fall for it."

The tension in my stomach released when she confirmed that Tyler wasn't conceived through abuse.

I paused at the edge of the kitchen, surprised by the state of the room. Half the tiles from the wall behind the sink were missing, along with a couple of cabinet doors, but it was the gaping hole in the outer wall sealed with plastic and an unfolded pizza box that won my attention.

The plastic breathed around the cardboard, bubbling and crackling with the breeze. It would do nothing to keep out cold air or intruders.

Jordan paused beside me. "What happened to the wall?"

Hope grabbed a mug from the doorless cupboard. "Used to be a window there. The frame was rotted. One day when I was out with little man, some idiot decided to bust in." She filled her mug and returned the coffee pot to the burner. "Guy stole what he could steal, then he left. Took pretty much everything that wasn't glued down."

"Won't the landlord fix the window?" Jordan asked.

She waved a hand at the pizza box. "I put in a request four months ago. Nothing else to do. Everyone around here knows—

you complain, you lose your roof. And I'm not dragging my baby to a shelter."

Her landlord sounded worse than Mr. Whittaker.

"I know this place ain't the greatest, but I'm working hard to save up enough so we can move somewhere nicer. If I can keep from getting robbed again." She glanced at the bathroom with worry. "I gotta get him outta here before something worse happens. Last month a four-year-old got killed in a drive-by. The guy two doors down sells drugs at all hours."

She set her mug in front of her and rested her hands on the portable island.

"After what you said about somebody in a white van trying to grab Dorina last night, and now this . . . I'm scared."

"Has anyone seen any vehicles or people hanging around the neighborhood kids lately?" Jordan asked.

"You think this was some kiddie perv, that it's got nuttin' to do with the other creep in a van?" Hope shook her head as she grabbed a loaf of white bread, some chocolate spread, and a tub of marshmallow crème. "I haven't heard nuttin' about someone like that in the neighborhood, and there's a lotta people with families. That kinda word spreads."

"It's possible he was trolling multiple neighborhoods, and he happened to see your son outside alone."

"I left him alone for less than five minutes. That guy didn't happen across him in that short amount of time." Worry lines creased her face. "I didn't see him, but he must've been waiting somewhere nearby. He could've taken my boy, and I never woulda seen him again."

"Let's assume your suspicions are right and it wasn't a coincidence that he picked your son. That means it was personal and someone wanted to scare you or hurt you by going after him," Jordan explained.

"I go outta my way *not* to tick people off. I don't want my baby to grow up without his mom. He'd get stuck somewhere with someone who cares more about drugs and drinking than taking care of him."

From what little she'd told me of her childhood, it sounded like she didn't want her son to end up with someone like her mother. Hope was young, and she didn't have the best role model, but she was fighting hard to give her son a better life.

"If this wasn't random, there has to be someone. An ex-lover, a disgruntled guy you met at work, someone who's afraid you might go to the press and ruin their reputation," Jordan said.

"The only problem I had got himself killed last year."

"Who was the problem?" I asked.

She slapped the bread on a plate and began slathering it with chocolate spread. "The guy who took all me and Cami's hard-earned money every night."

"You mean your—"

"We don't say the *p* word around here, or any other p-related words my son might repeat around his friends. He doesn't know, and I don't want anyone else to find out and treat him different."

"How did your problem get himself killed?" Jordan asked.

"He was roughing me up 'cause I needed to call off and take care of my sick baby. Some guy came in and roughed him up a little harder, left some creepy note stuck to TJ's corpse. Can't say I shed any tears when they carried that body bag out."

An odd expression crossed Jordan's face, and I could see him working through something in his head. "TJ, as in Terrence James?"

"Yeah, that's the one. Real charmer, till you got to know him. I don't think there was a person around who was sad to see him six feet under."

Terrence James. That name sounded familiar. Where had I heard it before?

"After he died, Spike started circling?" Jordan asked.

"Spike's always trying to recruit new girls. He made a play for me and got mad when I said no. He started in on Cami too. Even tried to set us up to get roughed up so he could swoop in and play the 'if you were my girls, I woulda protected you' card. Except I stabbed his boy with the knife I carry in my purse, and he gave up the whole plan."

Spike was sounding more and more terrifying with every detail.

"What happened to him?" Jordan asked.

"Spike? Nuttin'. His boy? Got himself locked up for something or other." She shrugged and placed the top piece of bread onto the sandwich, cutting it in four triangles.

"Would Spike retaliate by coming after your friends and your son?" I asked.

Hope cocked her head in thought. "I wouldn't put it past him, but that was like six months ago. He ain't much for thinking about things too long or too hard." She sighed and dropped the knife into the sink. "Maybe you were right and this was just a freak thing."

"Tyler might remember something the man said or did. Maybe we could talk to him after his bath," I suggested.

"I don't wanna make his day any scarier than it's already been. If you wanna talk to somebody about the guy, Gloria's—"

"Mommy! Bubbles!" Tyler called.

Hope sighed. "I gotta clean his hair before the water gets cold. Gloria's next door, but she don't hear too good, so talk loud."

She brushed past us down the hallway and closed herself in the bathroom.

I looked up at Jordan. "This Terrence James you two were talking about, what if the guy who killed him is targeting the girls and their families now?"

"That's not possible."

"I know Dorina didn't work for him, so it's not a perfect fit, but you guys always say it only has to make sense to the bad guy."

"I'm not saying your thought process is wrong. I'm saying it's physically impossible for it to be the same person. The serial killer who murdered Terrence James is currently serving time in a psychiatric facility." He paused before saying, "Thomas Mathis."

My jaw dropped. "As in my friend, Thomas Mathis, the one I write letters to?"

"One and the same."

There went that theory, and it explained why Terrence James's name sounded familiar. I never asked Thomas for the details about his crimes, but I heard some of the victims' names in the media.

Thomas hadn't been in control of himself during the psychotic break that led him to murder, but he still remembered every horrifying detail carried out with his hands, and he was struggling to forgive himself and accept God's forgiveness.

I sent him an encouraging letter each month. His responses usually included something about our faith, questions about how things were going in my life, and a halfhearted attempt to dissuade me from contacting him again. He didn't feel he deserved my kindness, but he was going to get it anyway.

"They eat like you do," Jordan commented, nodding to the jar of marshmallow crème.

"Except I wouldn't bother with the bread. I prefer a spoon as my jar-to-mouth delivery method."

Jordan grinned. "I know. I've seen it."

I stared at the sandwich that had been portioned to fit little hands. "Do you really think what happened with Tyler this morning could be a coincidence?"

Jordan rubbed at the back of his neck. "The timing does seem suspicious, but there are a lot of pedophiles and a lot of white vans."

"There are also a lot of men who kidnap women, so using that logic, Dorina and Cami's incidents could have nothing to do with each other."

"Two women who work in the same field, on the same street, two nights apart versus a child playing in his front yard blocks away.

I don't know how or if any of this connects, but if it does, we'll figure it out."

"We should talk to Gloria and see what she can tell us about the incident. If nothing else, we can give the police information about a predator in the area."

"Let's swing by my place for lunch after that. I'm starving."

"We could have some canned vegetable soup and toast with your snazzy new toaster," I teased.

"Hey, that's a nice—"

A terrified scream ripped through the air, and the bathroom door whipped open. Hope stood there, eyes wide.

"That came from the alley," Jordan said, resting a hand on his gun as he approached the back door. He brushed aside the lace curtain to peer out, then looked back at Hope. "Stay inside."

He opened the door, and I followed him out into the alley. An older woman stood beside a dropped bag of garbage, a hand clasped over her mouth. When she saw us, she lowered her shaking hand and said something in Spanish.

I couldn't understand her words, but there was no mistaking the fear in them.

"Do you know what she's saying?" I asked Jordan.

"Spanish wasn't very useful in Kansas, so I never took it."

The woman pointed to something hidden behind the dumpster and tried to make us understand. "Muerta. Muerta!"

My stomach sank. That was one of a handful of Spanish words I recognized—dead. Someone or something was dead. I followed the direction of the woman's trembling finger.

Barefoot, stretched out on her back, a teenage girl lay motionless. I rushed to her side and knelt. Even through the strands of dark hair draped over her face and the bruises staining her dark skin, I recognized her.

Cami. I wrapped my fingers around hers and squeezed, but there was no response. She was as still as a corpse.

God, please no.

233

Jordan crouched beside me as he spoke into his phone, filling the dispatcher in on the scene. He pressed two fingers to Cami's wrist and waited. When one of her eyelids fluttered, relief stretched through my chest. She was alive.

27

$\mathcal{H}$ope bounced her foot on the floor of the hospital waiting room. Tears hovered along the rim of her lower eyelids but refused to fall.

There had been no word on Cami's condition since nurses rushed her into the ER. She'd barely been clinging to life when they loaded her into the ambulance, and the minutes of waiting without news stretched into an hour.

My eyes drifted to the ceiling tiles as a silent prayer left my heart and fluttered heavenward. *Father, please give the doctors the wisdom and ability to help her.*

Kneeling over Cami's still form in that alley had been as difficult for Jordan as it was for me, but I suspected the reasons were different. I couldn't bear to watch a young girl die before she even had a chance to experience the beauty of life. But the echoes of pain in Jordan's eyes told me he'd been thinking less about Cami's bruised and broken body and more about mine the day they found me on the floor of the warehouse.

He was going to tell me to walk away from this case and leave the criminal investigation to the police. I wasn't sure I could do that.

A doctor strode into the waiting room, and Hope and I straightened with anticipation, but he passed us to reach a couple in the far corner.

Hope sagged against the back of the chair. "This is torture."

"I'm sure someone will be out to talk to us soon."

Hope tipped her face toward the ceiling, as though that might shield her tears from gravity. "I should've kept a closer eye on her."

Tyler squealed with delight, and we looked over to see Jordan performing slight-of-hand magic tricks for him by the wall. Tyler giggled every time the quarter appeared where he didn't expect it to.

I smiled as I watched the two of them absorbed in their goofiness. Jordan would be a wonderful father someday. He would teach his children to be compassionate but firm. And considering his martial arts, they would be able to flip and pin an intruder by the age of eight. Playground bullies wouldn't stand a chance.

Sadness chased away my smile at the idea of him finding love and starting a family. He was an amazing man, and that day was inevitable, but I dreaded losing him.

Jordan's eyes met mine over the boy's head, and his brows dipped in concern. I forced a smile, but he could read the insincerity in it, and that only tugged his eyebrows lower.

"Do it again," Tyler insisted, clapping his hands. Jordan obliged, sending the boy into another fit of giggles.

"I wish he had a dad for things like that," Hope said, pain threaded through her words. "It ain't fair that all he's got is me."

"It seems like you do really great with him."

"Great." She huffed. "I can't even be home for him when he wakes up at night from a bad dream. There's a babysitter there to hold him 'cause his mom's out on the street. Now we're at the hospital 'cause my friend got snatched and beat up." A tear spilled onto her cheek, and she swiped it away. "This ain't the kinda life I want for him."

"What kind of life do you want for you?"

"I gave up dreaming about a better life for me a long time ago. It's all for him now."

Her admission pierced my heart. "You both deserve to be safe and free from all this. You may not realize it, but you're worth more than any dollar amount anyone puts on you."

Her eyes narrowed as she studied me, and I mentally retraced my words to figure out how I'd offended her.

"Someone said something like that to me a year ago, some cop with a Southern accent. He told me I got value beyond measure." She shook her head, as if she couldn't wrap her mind around the concept.

A Southern cop?

"Do you remember his name?"

"Some old guy with green eyes."

Marx. My heart warmed as I imagined him saying those words to her, trying to impart a little light into her dark days.

"Sometimes I think about what he said, when I'm walking to a guy's car, and I wonder, but then . . ." She sighed, her shoulders slumping. "If he knew the first thing about me, he would take his words back."

"He wouldn't, because they're true."

"Maybe for someone like you, but I ain't never been valuable in my life," she said, a soul-deep sadness in her eyes.

Had no one ever shown her love? I had my family for the first nine years of my life, and now I had a new family—a hodgepodge of people who fit together into something beautiful.

"Your mom named you Hope. That must mean something," I said.

A bitter twist of her lips. "I asked her about that once, why she named me Hope if she hated me so much. She said she didn't pick the name. She told the nurse who helped deliver me to write something on the certificate, that she didn't care what. The nurse suggested the name Hope, and my mom said, 'Sure, whatever.' And here I am."

I closed my eyes. Even if that was how events played out, there was only one reason to share those details with her child: to hurt her.

"Mom never stopped resenting me for ruining her life when I was born, like I had any say in her getting knocked up in high school. And then I went and got pregnant when I was fourteen. She said she wasn't feeding another mouth. It was either an abortion or the street."

I followed her gaze to her adorable little boy. "You chose him."

"He's the best thing in my life, and I don't regret him for a second. I know I kept him for selfish reasons, but . . . I wouldn't change it."

"What do you mean 'selfish reasons'?"

She picked at her nails. "I wanted somebody to love me."

My throat tightened at her heartbreaking admission. I wanted to tell her that God loved her, had loved her from the moment she was conceived, but I didn't think she was ready to hear that.

"We all wanna be loved," I said. "There's nothing wrong with that."

"Yeah, maybe. I just wish I could offer him better. A home without holes in the walls, a mom who's home at night, maybe even a family. But I don't want my mom anywhere near him."

"Are there any friends back home that might help you start fresh?"

"Nah. I had a best friend, but . . ." She drew in a breath, as though to steel herself, then released it. "I was close with her family, till I overheard her dad talking in the hospital after the accident. He blamed me and said they woulda been better off if I never walked through their front door. He wasn't wrong." She sniffled and rubbed at her nose. "I realized then that I had nobody. And now the one real friend I've managed to make is probably gonna die too. I must've been some kinda awful in my past life to deserve all this."

"You don't deserve any of the bad that's happened. Sometimes people are cruel, and all we can do is hang on to God and the hope that tomorrow will be better."

"Tomorrow's only ever more of the same."

I studied the little boy who barely resembled his mother. "Is there no chance you and Tyler's dad could reconnect?"

"I doubt he even remembers my name. I was trailer trash, and he was Mr. Popular. Besides, no decent guy is gonna want anything to do with a girl like me."

"That's not true, Hope. The world wants you to believe that, but you can start a new life, build new and beautiful relationships. What you've done and what you've been through doesn't need to define the rest of your life."

"What do you know about it?" she snapped, and the venom in her voice stung. "You with your job that lets you keep your clothes on and your picture-perfect life."

I swallowed and looked away. I could understand why she might assume my life was perfect. She saw my façade of togetherness rather than the pain and trauma I was still working through.

"Girls like you can say all kinds of nice, uplifting things, but that's where it ends, 'cause you can't understand what it's like to be where I am. There is no starting fresh. Who's gonna hire me when the only job on my résumé is . . ." She glanced at her son and lowered her voice. "This is all I know how to do. It's what I've been doing since I was fourteen. TJ might be gone, but I'm not free. I'll never be free."

"Hope—"

She held up a hand. "Nah, I don't wanna talk about this anymore."

Tyler bounced over to us. "Mommy, there's a candy machine. Can I have snack?"

"Sure, baby. I think I got a few quarters." She took his hand and let him lead her across the hall to the vending machine.

Jordan sank into her empty chair, and I turned my face away as I dried my tears with the sleeve of my shirt. "You all right?"

I sniffled and nodded.

"That's not too convincing," he said.

"I'm fine. I just . . . I wanna help her, but I don't know how. She's so angry and hopeless. And given her life, I don't blame her."

"You can't fix her life, Holly, and you can't save someone who isn't ready to be saved. All you can do is be a source of encouragement and consistency in the chaos. Ultimately, she has to decide to fight for what she wants. Like you did."

"I did?"

He nodded. "The easiest path is the one you know, which in your case was running and hiding. But you chose to fight for a new life. As for the rest of us, all we could do was remind you it was possible and be there when you were ready."

"It took almost a year for that to happen."

"Change takes time."

My attention drifted back to Hope as she crouched in front of the vending machine with her son. If she had been thinking about Marx's words for the past year, maybe that change was already starting to take place.

"If you're good here, I'm gonna go visit the hospital chapel." *And pray a little harder for Cami and Hope.*

"Okay. Try not to steal any more Bibles." He flashed me a dimpled grin that coaxed a smile from me.

"No promises." I pushed up from the chair and grabbed my bag, setting off in search of solitude to pray.

28

Soothing music and twinkling flameless candles created an air of peacefulness in the small chapel. The room was dimly lit, with a porthole window at the front of the room.

There was nothing overtly religious about the space. The only trace of God was the piece of Him I carried with me as I walked down the aisle toward the front row. But my prayers and worship had never been restrained by church walls. Both poured out of me wherever I happened to be, and today it was in a space that resembled a ship cabin more than a church. But at least there were chairs.

I sank into one and closed my eyes, searching for God.

"Lord, give me the words to help Hope. I know I don't have the power to save her, but if I can offer even a sprinkle of brightness, help me do it. She needs You more than she knows. She has so many wounds, so much brokenness."

One of the rear doors opened, and I peeked over my shoulder in time to see a man slip into the back row. The hood of his sweatshirt shadowed his face, and he made no move to remove it before bowing his head.

I was under the impression that removing your hat or hood was the appropriate thing to do in a sanctuary, but then, I struggled to understand the etiquette for most situations.

Like now. Was I supposed to say hello to the only other person in the room or awkwardly pretend he wasn't there?

With my luck, I would offer a polite greeting, and he would assume I was flirting and then ask for my phone number like the guy on the bus. Mmm, pretending he wasn't there sounded like the better option.

I faced forward in my seat and tried to relax, but my body refused to let down its guard with an unfamiliar man in the room. My eyes remained open, posture stiff, as I forced my thoughts back to prayer.

Please strengthen Jordan's faith and trust in You, Lord, so he remembers to turn to You when struggles come. He's so passionate about helping the lost and overlooked, a man after Your own heart, and right now, he needs help and encouragement. Watch over—

An unintelligible whisper drifted from the back of the room and slithered down my neck. Out of the corner of my eye, I could see that the man's head was still bowed beneath his hood. He hadn't moved, not even as far as to lean forward, and yet unease puddled in my stomach.

More than likely, he was a grieving man seeking his own private moment with God, but experience taught me to be wary. I reached for the pepper spray in my bag, gripping it in my palm, and then released a measured breath as I forced my agitated thoughts to focus.

Watch over Tandi on the street tonight, and please bring Cami through the trauma she's experienced. She's gonna need a lot of support and love, heavenly Father.

The man's chair creaked, his legs bouncing out of rhythm with each other as his hands rubbed at his knees. Was he a drug addict craving a fix, someone uncomfortable with faith, or . . .

I studied him out of the corner of my eye. Could he be the hooded man from the alley who abducted Cami?

No, that was ridiculous.

No criminal would be foolish enough to follow his victim to the hospital.

Collin did, my memories shot back, and I remembered the sound of his voice as he questioned one of the nurses in Darby. She thought I was in an abusive relationship, like the one she'd escaped years before, and she lied to give me a chance to slip away.

If Collin was brazen enough to do something like that, who was to say this man wasn't?

Sweat dampened my palms at the possibility. But why would he be in the chapel? Was he searching for forgiveness . . . or another victim? That last thought sent a shot of adrenaline straight to my heart. I was alone in the room with him.

You're leaping to conclusions, I chided my imagination. A lot of people wore hooded sweatshirts, myself included, and they weren't automatically violent kidnappers.

Ringing shattered the quiet, and I jumped so hard I nearly tipped over the chair. I grabbed my phone from one of the side pockets of my bag and answered it without checking to see who was calling.

"Hello?"

Jordan's voice filled the line. "Hey, got an update. She's in stable condition."

"That means Cami's gonna live?"

"She's pretty banged up, but according to the doctor, she was unconscious because her blood sugar was through the roof. Whoever took her didn't give her insulin. She should come around soon. And the detective arrived."

The mysterious man rose from his chair, revealing a scarf over the lower half of his face, and pushed through the door into the hospital corridor. There was no doubt in my mind now. He was the person who scooped Cami's limp body off the ground and placed her in the back of a car.

"Jordan, he's here." I flung the strap of my knapsack over my head and burst through the door in pursuit.

"Who's here?"

"The guy David described, the one who took Cami. He was in the chapel with me, but as soon as he heard me say Cami's gonna live, he bolted."

Alarm sharpened Jordan's voice. "I'm coming to you. Do not—"

"I'm gonna follow him."

"Do *not* follow him, Holly!"

"I'll be careful."

"Hol—"

I snapped my phone shut, attention fixed on the retreating figure in a sweatshirt and jeans. His pace was brisk, which, given the height difference in our legs, left me scampering to keep from losing him.

I had no intention of catching up with him and giving him an opportunity to hurt me, too, but if he'd driven here, I might be able to see his vehicle. Jordan could run his license plate and find his identity.

The man threw a nervous glance over his shoulder and jerked when he spotted me. Skirting a nurse, he ducked through the nearby door into the stairwell.

Crap.

I sprinted to the door and peered through the rectangle window, my breath fogging the diamond-patterned glass. My fingers curled around the lever handle to plunge it down, but fear seeped out of my bones and into my muscles, paralyzing me.

Stairwells were isolated and dangerous, ideal places to attack someone.

What if he was waiting on the other side of the door? He clearly had no qualms about brutalizing a girl and dumping her in an alley like garbage, which meant he wouldn't have a problem shoving me down the steps or carrying me off to his kidnapper van. But there was a chance he was already gone, running for an exit, and the only thing on the other side of the door was an empty stairwell.

The guys wouldn't be afraid to follow him.

But I couldn't make my fingers press down on the handle. I was too terrified of being abducted and imprisoned again.

"Holly!"

Jordan's voice jarred me from my internal struggle, and I turned to see him jogging toward me, worry and anger warring for control on his face.

I peeled my stiff fingers from the handle and backed away. "He took the stairwell."

Jordan rested one hand on his gun and pushed the handle down with the other, thrusting the door inward and propping it open with a foot. There was no one waiting out of sight to pounce.

Jordan listened, tipping his head to catch sounds from above and below. Silence resounded. Not even a footstep. The man must've already exited onto another floor.

Jordan let the door spring shut and fixed me with a frustrated scowl. "I asked you not to follow him."

"I didn't even come close to grabbing distance. I was extra careful. I was hoping to see his license plate so we could figure out who he is, but he spotted me and panicked."

Jordan rested his hands on his belt. "I get that you wanna help, but please don't chase after potential threats by yourself. If that was the guy who took Cami, you saw the condition she's in. He could do the same thing to you, and I can't . . ." Painful memories swam in his eyes, and he averted his gaze.

Any argument I might've offered died. He was the one who carried me to the hospital after they found me in the warehouse, the one holding me when I stopped breathing. I wished I could take the burden of those awful memories from him.

"I'm sorry," I said. "But I'm okay, and I'm gonna stay that way."

He visibly swallowed and nodded.

A man standing by the nurses station twenty feet away cleared his throat. Judging by his suit and the badge clipped to his belt, he was the detective assigned to Cami's case. "If you're done running sprints through the hospital, I need to speak with both of you."

29

*A*dam Chamberlin was an older and apparently overworked detective. Exhaustion pulled the dark skin beneath his eyes into puffy folds, and the entire breadth of his forehead wrinkled with every expression. He reminded me a little of a pug.

He rubbed a knuckle beneath his bearded chin as he absorbed everything we told him about Cami, the break-in at her apartment, and the man in the chapel.

"It's an unusually cold April, and it's not unusual for people to wear hoods, hats, and scarves." He gestured to the scarf around my neck as an example, and a slight frown pulled at the corners of his mouth.

I pinched the material together to hide the bruises on my neck, but it was too late. He'd already seen them.

He met my gaze, and the question he asked didn't match the one that glinted in his dark eyes. "Why did a man in a hooded sweatshirt and scarf seem so suspicious to you?"

"There was a witness to Cami's abduction, and he described a man in a hooded sweatshirt with a scarf over his face as the man who put her in the back of his car," I explained. "But it was his behavior that made me notice him first. Nervous, sort of twitchy, and he took off the moment he heard me say Cami would live."

"What's this witness's name?"

"David Monroe," Jordan answered. "We have his address, if you need it, but he refused to speak to us until he knew we weren't the police. His dad is a defense attorney, and he has a rule about speaking with the police."

"I know the type." The skin around Chamberlin's mouth drooped in annoyance. "Is there anything more either of you can add to the description of the man in the chapel?" He glanced at me as he quoted, "'White guy with brown eyes' isn't much to go on."

"He was taller than me but shorter than Jordan, and he was mostly covered, like he was afraid he might be recognized."

"Something tells me you *would* recognize him. You don't look like a cop and you're not physically intimidating. Yet in an instant, he identified you as someone he needed to run from."

Jordan leaned forward in the waiting room chair, elbows propped on his thighs. "The supposed burglar from Cami's apartment got up close and personal with Holly when he tripped and fell on top of her. He would know her if he saw her, and if he overheard us talking, he knows we're private investigators searching for Cami."

"I can't rule out the possibility that the two incidents are related, but drug-related burglaries are common in that area. A kidnapper returning to the home of a girl he abducted two days prior is very *un*common." Chamberlin paused in thought. "That would explain why he recognized you and ran, though."

He jotted something in his notebook.

"I'm gonna have Ms. Chen's apartment searched for prints, hair, and DNA. If the burglar and the man in the hospital are the same man, we'll have a better chance of finding hair or fingerprints at her apartment than we will in a busy hospital. However, I will pull prints from that stairwell door." He clicked his pen on the notebook. "I'll need samples from both of you to test against what I find; that way I know what to ignore and what to pursue."

"Why do you think he came to the hospital?" I asked.

Chamberlin chewed on my question before answering. "If we're assuming the man in the chapel is Ms. Chen's kidnapper, it's likely he thought she was dead when he dumped her in the alley. When an ambulance brought her to the hospital, he must've followed to see if she was gonna pull through. He seemed to recognize you and followed you into the chapel. Did he give any indication he intended to hurt you?"

"No."

"Then I would guess he was hoping to overhear something. When you said Ms. Chen would live, he ran, most likely because he's afraid she can identify him."

"Do you think he'll come back and try to finish what he started?" I worried.

"I don't know enough about this man to venture a guess, but I'll have an officer posted outside her room just in case."

Some of my worry eased. Cami would be safe.

"If he followed the ambulance to the hospital," Jordan began, thought creases lining his forehead, "then he was watching and waiting for us to find the body. And his vehicle might be on traffic cameras, tailing the ambulance all the way here."

Chamberlin nodded. "I intend to check. I'll gather security footage for the hospital and the parking lot as well. Did either of you notice anyone loitering when you found Ms. Chen in the alley?"

I shook my head. "I was too focused on the screaming woman and then finding Cami's body."

"I didn't see anyone who seemed out of place. A few gawkers in the apartments, but that's to be expected when someone starts screaming."

"And why were you two there?" Chamberlin asked.

Jordan explained about Hope requesting our help to find Cami and Dorina's run-in with the masked man in a van, which inspired Hope to call him when a similar van approached her son.

Chamberlin frowned. "I haven't heard about any other attempted kidnappings."

"The victim works as a prostitute too," Jordan said. "She won't report it."

Chamberlin sighed. "There's not much I can do for her then. As for the predator who approached the boy, I'm not sure there's enough commonality to safely say it's related to Ms. Chen. I'll look into any reported incidents with kids involving a white van, and I'll keep an eye out for it in the video footage."

He rubbed at his lips.

"What interests me is the fact that this girl came to you, asking for help to find her friend, and two days later that friend is dumped behind her apartment. There's something to that. A personal message, a threat, a sign that he found out she involved an investigative agency, and it made him angry. I'd like to speak to Hope. Did she come with you to the hospital?"

"She's here somewhere with her son. About my size, with pink hair. But I don't know if she'll talk to you either. She's . . ."

"In the same line of work as the other two women?" Chamberlin guessed.

I nodded. "Have you spoken to the doctor about Cami's condition?"

"Apart from a head injury, her wounds are superficial. They'll let me know about drugs when they get her tox screen back."

"Can they tell if . . . if she was . . ." A lump formed in my throat, choking off my words.

"If she was what?"

"Sexually assaulted," Jordan clarified. "We'd like to know what kind of predator we're dealing with."

"I see." Chamberlin slanted a look my way, and I had a sinking feeling that my inability to say those words had told him more about me than I wanted him to know. "You shouldn't be dealing with him at all. This is a criminal investigation now. But to answer your question, the young lady's occupation and the fact that she was working the night of her abduction makes it impossible to say without speaking with her."

Of course, that made sense. Hopefully, she would wake up soon. "I'll see if I can find Hope for you." I grabbed my knapsack and stood.

"In a minute." Chamberlin motioned for me to sit, his gentle expression assuring me that I wasn't in trouble. When I sank onto the edge of the chair, he leaned forward to study me. "I would be remiss if I didn't ask what happened." He indicated his neck.

"Oh." I readjusted my scarf. "Those are, um . . . they're . . ."

"Finger bruises," he supplied. "Mind telling me who grabbed you by the neck?"

I appreciated that he didn't assume Jordan was responsible, but I didn't like the intent way he watched me, waiting for an answer I couldn't give him.

"I promised I wouldn't press charges against the man who did it, as long as he told us what happened to Cami the night she went missing."

"A man who claims to be a witness to Ms. Chen's abduction did this to you?" He waited, but I didn't confirm it. "Ms. Cross, I understand doing what you need to do to solve a crime, but a man who was willing to hurt you is also willing to hurt another woman. Like my victim."

"He didn't hurt her."

"I'd like to confirm that for myself."

I rubbed my hands on my thighs. "You already have his name, and Jordan can fill you in on what we learned from him about Cami's kidnapping, but I'm still not pressing charges."

Chamberlin glanced at Jordan. "You should convince your friend to change her mind."

Jordan pressed his lips together, still frustrated by the promise I had made, but unwilling to go against it. "Holly never breaks her promises. She won't start now."

I rose from my chair. "I'll let you two talk." I needed to find Hope, and I needed to find food. My slice of jelly bread was long gone, and my stomach was starting to cramp.

I didn't have much cash on me, only enough to grab a few things from the vending machine that would ease the discomfort.

Hope was chatting with a doctor down the hall, her little boy crawling between her ankles and making soft dinosaur growls. I waved at him, and he waved back with his arm tucked close to his chest like a T-Rex.

I smiled and retreated into the alcove with all the vending machines, buying a bag of cheesy crackers. I pinched the bag to open it, when movement brought my attention to the doorway.

A familiar man with wiry red hair stood there, his wide body plugging the exit like a cork. The sight of him triggered a flood of anxiety, swiftly followed by irritation.

My first instinct was to retreat, but there was nowhere to go in this cramped space. "What do you want?"

"The same thing I always want. A story that will have my followers and fans salivating for more."

Addison Miles was a self-proclaimed journalist with no reservations about splashing other people's deeply personal business all over the internet. During the trial, I had become a regular and unwilling subject on his blog.

"I have nothing to say to you."

"You might wanna rethink that," he suggested. "Your name has only been out of the papers for a couple of months, and here you are mixed up in some hooker murder."

"How . . ."

"I heard about the body dump over my scanner." His lips curled into a self-satisfied smile. "I figured there might be some juicy details to be found here at the hospital, and I was right. I overheard most of the conversation between you two and the detective."

"If that's true, then you know she's not dead, so there's no story."

"I heard you mention two other prostitutes who might've been targeted by the guy who roughed up the victim. A man targeting prostitutes. There's definitely a good story there, and I'm gonna be the first person to write about it."

"You're assuming a lot, and I'm not telling you anything." I tried to squeeze past him, but he shifted his weight into my path. The trickle of anxiety in my abdomen expanded, curling around my spine. "Please move."

Addison pulled his phone from his pocket and showed me the recorder app. "Answer a few questions for me, and I'm gone."

"You can't keep me in here."

"It's a public place, and it's not like I'm restraining you. You can leave whenever you want."

Except I would have to push through him to do it, and he outweighed me by a couple hundred pounds. I was tempted to try it, if it meant escaping this space that seemed to be shrinking in on me with every passing second.

"A lot of serial killers start by targeting prostitutes. If these women are all from the same area, it could be his hunting ground," he said. "He could be there right now, stalking another victim."

The blurry reflection of the man in the repair shop window flickered through my mind. I had assumed he was watching me, but what if he'd been watching for the woman he intended to grab later that night?

If the man stalked Dorina because he specifically wanted her, she could still be in danger. But I doubted Clayton would let her out of his sight anytime soon.

Addison released a frustrated puff of air when I didn't respond. "I tried to help Marx keep you safe on the day of your testimony. That should earn me some good will here."

The rush of anger caught me by surprise. "Good will? After the worst trauma of my life, you dragged my name through the mud. You published lies."

"If you had given me the exclusive I asked for, I wouldn't have had to rely on other people's opinions and stories. I gave you plenty of opportunities to speak up. Now it's old news. No one cares what really happened between you and Wells."

Bile rose in my throat. "Please move so I can leave." If he refused to let me pass, I could call for Jordan. He would unwedge the big man from the exit.

"Why you takin' up the whole doorway?" Hope demanded from somewhere behind him. "Buy your snacks and get out of the way. It ain't a cafeteria."

Addison turned sideways, and I caught a glimpse of Hope standing in the hallway with her son. Past her, I could see Jordan's back as he spoke with Chamberlin in the waiting room.

Hope looked from me to Addison. "Oh, I get it. It ain't about the food. You're just a lowlife who corners girls in little rooms so they can't walk away from you."

Addison blinked. "You don't know what you're talking about."

"I know she doesn't wanna be in there, you were blockin' the exit, and her boyfriend's got a gun. The hot one over there with the muscles." She twirled a finger in Jordan's direction.

Addison scrutinized her. "If you know who her boyfriend is, then you know her. By the looks of you, you're one of the other prost—"

"You say that word in front of my son, and I'll slap you so hard you won't remember your own name," Hope said, covering Tyler's ears.

"Am I supposed to be scared of you?"

She stepped closer to him, piercing him with a look that made *me* twitch, and I wasn't even her target. A chilling smile thinned her lips. "Yeah."

Addison swallowed and pressed back against the door frame. "Whatever. I'll find sources elsewhere." He turned and hurried away.

Hope dropped her hands from her son's ears and muttered, "Guy needs to brush his teeth before his breath knocks somebody out. Smells like somethin' died in there."

Tyler threw up his hands in a dance as he sang, "Brush, brush, brush those teeth, or they'll all fall out and land at your feet, and you can't be a dinosaur with no teeth!"

"That's right, little man."

"I'm not a man, Mommy. I'm a raptor."

Some of the tension drained out of me. "I can't believe he actually ran away from you."

"I've been in a lot of standoffs, and the crazy murder stare works on most people. No one wants to fight with somebody who might stab them with a rusty screw they found on the sidewalk. And that guy had coward written all over him."

"Maybe I need to learn how to make that face."

Hope snorted. "Yeah, right. You're too nice for anybody to believe it. But you got capable people around who can watch your back." She indicated Jordan with her thumb. "Now that death breath is gone, I need a favor."

"What do you need?"

"The doctor said I can go see Cami, but I don't want"—she pointed a finger at the top of her son's head—"to see how bad it is. I was wondering if you might watch him."

"Sure. Detective Chamberlin wanted me to let you know he needs to talk to you before he leaves."

Hope folded her arms and peered over her shoulder at the older detective. "You trust him?"

"It's the first time I've met him, but I get the impression he's good at his job." He was no Marx, but there was nothing about him that made me question his morals or capabilities.

"Good at his job, huh? I bet he's hoping to resolve this mess with as little effort as possible. He'll lock up some crackhead and call it a day."

"He seems like he genuinely wants to help."

"Sure he does. But he can figure things out for himself, 'cause I ain't talkin' to him."

I bit back a sigh. Chamberlin wasn't going to be able to help her if she refused to work with him. Jordan and I would do what we could without stepping on the detective's toes, but he had more resources than we did.

Hope kissed Tyler's forehead. "Be a good little raptor. Don't destroy the hospital or bite any nurses."

Did her child make a habit of biting nurses?

As soon as Hope left, Tyler turned his big brown eyes on me. "What kinda dinosaur do you wanna be?"

"I don't know. What kind of dinosaur *should* I be?"

He squinted in thought. "A Hollysaurus Rex."

"What's a Hollysaurus?"

"She's a giant with long arms and hair that's on fire. And she gets snacks for the little dinosaurs."

I bit back a laugh. "And what does this little dinosaur want for a snack?"

He bounced onto his toes. "Neminems!"

I glanced at the bag of M&M's nestled between the popcorn and kale chips in the machine. "Are you sure you don't want kale chips?"

His heels dropped back to the floor in confusion. "What's a kale?"

"I'm pretty sure it's green dirt."

"Ew."

"Definitely ew," I agreed.

I popped the quarters into the machine, and the candy dropped to the bottom. As I grabbed it, my phone rang. When I saw the caller ID, a mixture of surprise and unease flooded me.

Cami's mother.

30

$\mathcal{T}$yler followed me back into the waiting room, where Jordan and Chamberlin were finishing up their conversation. He plopped on the floor beside his backpack and dragged a book from inside, flipping through the pictures as he ate his candy.

I set my bag of crackers on a chair and approached the men. "We have a couple of problems. Hope said she won't speak with you."

Chamberlin frowned. "Any particular reason?"

"In short, trust issues. I'm not sure she can tell you much more than she told us anyway. She's certain she doesn't have any enemies, and that this has nothing to do with her."

Jordan rested his hands on his belt. "What's problem number two?"

"Addison Miles is poking around, pushing his nose into things and throwing around phrases like *serial killer*."

Chamberlin rubbed at the skin between his eyebrows. "Just what I need. A conspiracy theorist spreading rumors and inspiring fear."

"I tried to tell him his theory makes no sense because no one's dead, but I don't think he cares."

Jordan grimaced. "I'm really tired of that guy, and after what he put you through in January, I'm surprised he had the nerve to speak to you."

"He's not my favorite person. But on a positive note, Cami's mom called me back."

"I wasn't aware you reached out to her," Chamberlin said. "I was about to have someone track down the number for Ms. Chen's next of kin."

"I called her yesterday, before we knew much, and she just got back with me. All I told her is that her daughter's here in the hospital. I figured I would leave the specifics for you, since I don't know how all that works with the investigation."

"I appreciate that. Since you spoke to her first, what was your impression when you told her that her daughter is here?"

The woman had burst into tears over the phone, and I couldn't understand a lot of what she said.

"Relieved, I think. She's on her way, but she lives out of state, so she won't be here until closer to midnight. But I'm worried about who might come with her."

"I haven't had a chance to look into Ms. Chen's friends and family yet, so you'll need to be specific," Chamberlin said.

I glanced at Tyler, who chattered to himself as he turned the pages of his book, and then lowered my voice. "Hope told me that Cami ran away from home because her stepdad was abusive. He used to lock her in a closet until she repented for whatever sin he thought she'd committed."

Chamberlin's jaw hardened. "Good to know."

"I'm not sure what rights he has as her stepdad, since she's still a minor, but I don't think he should be alone with her. He punished her because he didn't like the way she dressed. If he finds out what she's been doing to pay her bills . . ."

"I'll pull him aside for a conversation before he gets anywhere near her, and an officer will be here soon."

If the idea of a minor working the streets bothered him, it didn't show. Maybe it was a tragedy he encountered so often that he'd learned to compartmentalize his feelings.

"I need to check the hospital video footage, but I would appreciate it if you would keep me apprised of any more information you glean from Hope, or anyone else who might be reluctant to speak with me." He passed each of us a card. "Also, Ms. Cross, I would rather not find myself working two kidnapping cases, so please don't chase after potential suspects on your own."

I caught Jordan's satisfied smile before he lowered his head in an effort to hide it. They were allowed to tail bad guys, but I wasn't?

"And text me the number for Ms. Chen's mother, please." Chamberlin left the waiting room in pursuit of evidence, and I forwarded the number to him.

Snapping my phone shut, I stuffed it back into the side pocket of my bag and dropped into a chair. All I wanted to do at this very moment was devour my bag of crackers.

I popped open the bag and tilted it toward Jordan. "Hungry?"

He snagged one. "Sorry our canned vegetable soup for lunch didn't work out. Why don't we try something different for dinner?"

"Canned ravioli?"

He grinned and popped the cracker into his mouth. "Something not from a can."

"Sounds adventurous. I wanna check in on Hope and Cami before we go, though."

Tyler made a thoughtful "hmm" as he tried to make one of his M&M's disappear behind his own ear, only to find it still stuck to his palm.

"Now you've got him doing it." I smiled up at Jordan. "Where did you learn to do magic tricks?"

"At Oma's bed-and-breakfast." He crouched beside me, watching his protégé. "I spent a lot of time there after your family's funeral, helping out to keep my mind off things. There was a guest staying there for a few nights, and we were talking in the kitchen over cookies. He said he could make one of the cookies disappear, and I said I could, too, then proceeded to stuff the whole thing in my mouth."

I laughed, imagining ten-year-old Jordan with his cheeks puffed out like a chipmunk's.

"Turns out, that's not what he meant. He offered to teach me some sleight-of-hand magic, and it became a nice distraction."

"I like your cookie disappearing method more. It's tastier."

He grinned. "That's what I said."

I ate the last cracker and turned the bag upside down, sprinkling the crumbs into my mouth. I was so hungry that I could have licked the inside of the bag clean.

"I'll go see if Hope wants us to drop her at home or if she wants to stay." I crumpled the bag in my fist as I got up from the chair. "Will you watch Tyler for a few minutes?"

"Yeah, we'll be right here." Jordan motioned Tyler over. "Come here, big guy, let's read that book together."

Tyler popped to his feet and dashed over, hopping into Jordan's lap. He beamed with excitement. Hope was doing a great job with him, but seeing the way he soaked up male attention like a sponge, I understood why she was concerned about him not having a father in his life.

I tossed my trash in the can by the door and made my way to Cami's hospital room. She'd been placed in a private room, no doubt at Chamberlin's request.

Hope had dragged a chair over to the bedside, her back to the entrance. I knocked on the door frame, drawing her attention from her phone.

She looked past me with concern. "Where's Tyler?"

"Detective Chamberlin left to check on camera footage, so Tyler's hanging out with Jordan for a few minutes," I explained. "Sorry if he's a little multicolored when you take him home. He's eating M&M's."

"He talked you into candy, huh?" She sat up straighter in the chair. "Kid's a little manipulator when it comes to sweets. No denying it's cute, though."

I'd known I was being manipulated with the Hollysaurus comment, but hospitals were hard for people, especially kids, and a bag of candy would bring him a little joy.

"Cami's mom finally called me back," I said. "She's on her way here now."

"Yeah? Is she bringing that creep she's married to?"

"I hope not. But even if he shows up, Detective Chamberlin is having an officer posted outside the room."

"I still think her stepdad's got something to do with all this. The guy's a serial killer in the making. It's only a matter of time before he starts killing hookers to cleanse the earth or something. Like men got no part in the fact that prostitution exists."

I dragged another chair over and sat beside her. "I hope you know that not all men are like the ones who come to Brushwick. Some of them are good."

"Like your handsome friend in the waiting room?" She tossed her pink phone into her lap. "You're lucky, you know. I've had a lotta guys look at me in a lot of different ways, but never the way Blue Eyes looks at you when you're not paying attention."

"What do you mean?"

"Like you're the most precious thing in his world. The man even fixes your funky marshmallow drink the way you like it."

I smiled. "We're just friends."

"That guy would fall on a sword for you."

She had no idea how close that statement was to the truth. Only instead of a sword, it was a skinning knife wielded by a giant.

"I guess I get why you're not together, though." She shifted, flinging one leg over the arm of the chair. "I overheard what you and the big guy were talking about, so I looked you up."

Oh boy.

There were a lot of articles drifting around on the internet, some of which supported me while others shredded me, but all of them shared too much of my personal history with the public.

"And what did you find?" I asked hesitantly.

"The big guy's got some entertaining perspectives. Garbage, but entertaining. I've known you a whole three days, and it's obvious he ain't got a clue. I'm not sure what the whole story is, but I got the highlights. Grew up in foster care, ran away, got kidnapped by your psycho foster brother last year. I read that he almost tortured you to death."

I forced down the lump in my throat. "That pretty much sums it up."

"Guess your life ain't as picture-perfect as I thought, so . . . sorry I snapped at you or whatever."

"Thanks."

Silence descended between us as our focus shifted to Cami. There was a white bandage over the wound near her hairline instead of the Band-Aids that had been there when we found her in the alley.

I thought back to the moment we found her. She'd been wearing the clothes she had on the night she disappeared, the blue blouse spattered with dried blood, but there hadn't been any on her face or neck.

I had a head injury similar to hers once, and there was so much blood that I could've passed for a character in a horror movie. Had her kidnapper cleaned her up and covered the gash? That kind of care didn't fit with leaving her body in an alley next to the trash.

Unless he prefers his victims clean, like Collin. The unwanted thought turned my stomach.

I took in the bruises on Cami's arms and wrists. I didn't see any restraint marks to suggest he'd kept her tied up, so he must've subdued her in some other way, a way that would likely show up in her blood work.

"This wasn't supposed to happen."

Hope's statement brought my attention back to her. "What do you mean?"

Grief softened her features. "Some nights are rough, but it's never something ice packs and some vodka and orange juice can't fix. It ain't never been this bad. What if she don't make it?"

"She'll pull through."

"Yeah? You see that in your crystal ball?" When I raised my eyebrows at her snarky response, she puffed out a breath and ran her fingers through her hair. "Sorry. I'm so used to people treating me like trash, it's second nature to get in their face first."

"I understand that."

"Yeah, 'cause you're so confrontational."

I smiled at her sarcasm. "We all respond to the world based on what we've been through. I never used to let myself get close to anyone because I knew I would have to leave them behind to stay ahead of my foster brother. I had no idea what I was missing until I started to let people in."

"I ain't so good at letting people in." She folded her arms. "I was better when I was around Livy's family. They made me feel like a different person, like somebody who mattered."

"You do matter."

"Not to them. Not anymore." Tears hovered along her lashes. "I wish I could go back and fix the mess I made, but they'll never forgive me."

"People are a lot more forgiving than you think."

"Maybe in your world." She released a sigh. "Did you know Cami wanted to be a singer? She's got a real nice voice."

As much as I wanted to stay on the topic of forgiveness, she clearly didn't, so I followed her lead. "No, I didn't know that." It fit with some of the pictures in Cami's star collage, though. "What do you wanna be?"

"Now I don't know. Before I got knocked up and ran away from home, I wanted to be one of those fancy flight attendants. Ugly uniforms, handing out peanuts and pretzels, cleaning up turbulence vomit . . . the whole nine yards."

"That sounds . . ."—I tried to find a positive word to describe her dream job, but there wasn't one—"terrible and not at all dreamy."

She laughed. "Yeah, but I wanted to go places, see the world. I wanted to do more, *be* more. Now, looking back, that girl from the trailer park would be a step up from this."

I reached over and took her hand. "This isn't the final destination of your life, Hope. You can choose a different direction."

She stared at my hand, confusion and questions swirling in her eyes. "Why do you care so much?"

"I remember what it feels like to have no hope for my future. My entire life, all I wanted was to feel safe and loved, but all I could see was an endless cycle of running, hiding, and struggling to survive, and I was weary of it all."

"Seems like you got it together now."

"I had a lot of help. I still have . . . issues, and I don't always know how things are gonna work out or if I'll make it through the day without a panic attack, but I do know I'm heading in a better direction."

Moisture glittered on her eyelashes. "I want that, but I'm not sure it's possible for someone like me. I got a lotta regrets and a lotta baggage."

"If I can break a fourteen-year cycle and build a better life, so can you." I pressed my lips together, unsure whether or not I should continue. "I know you may not be ready to hear it, but the biggest key to my survival and my healing is God."

She smeared a tear across her freckled cheek. "You're one of those Bible thumpers?"

"I have never thumped anyone with a Bible. Only a skillet. And a toaster. And a . . . tree branch. And there was that wooden knob from a bed."

She laughed again, slouching against the back of her chair. "Sounds like you get into more scrapes than me."

"It's a talent."

"So you're religious but not a pacifist."

Oh, I would pass a fist right into a creeper's throat without hesitation, but hopefully I would never be in a position to need that self-defense move again.

"I prefer to think of myself as a Christian rather than religious," I clarified. "It's not about rituals or strict rules. It's about . . . a relationship."

"Livy was a Christian when we met. I made fun of her for talking to invisible people on the playground." She grunted in amusement. "Not really sure how we became friends."

My phone alerted me to a text, and I wiggled it from my pocket. "Jordan says there's a woman here wanting to take your son home. Sally Gunther."

"That's his babysitter. I asked if she could watch him early so he don't gotta stay at the hospital. Places like this ain't good for kids. He needs his toys and his books, and in a few hours, he's gonna need his bed." She pushed up from the chair. "I'm gonna go kiss him good-bye. You guys don't gotta stay here 'cause of me. I'll get a ride home later."

She left the room, and I leaned forward to grasp Cami's limp fingers. "We're gonna find out who did this to you."

Jordan appeared in the doorway a minute later, and I stood, eager to escape the sterile atmosphere of the hospital. It was time for dinner and a breath of fresh air.

31

I bounced on my toes to stave off a shiver as we waited in line at the pizza stand. The glorious smell of sweet sauce and salty cheese curled through the air to tease my nose.

A tall red-haired woman crossed the sidewalk to greet a man in line ahead of us. The hug was awkward, and they bumped noses before figuring out how to make it work. Probably not their first meeting, but still rife with expectation and nerves.

He struck me as an architect, and she was . . . a cupcake baker. Yes, he made stunning buildings that survived forever, and she made stunning cupcakes that survived five minutes. I would eat all the tasties if I owned a bakery.

We inched forward as a woman and her two kids left the line with plates of pizza.

I looked up at Jordan beside me. "Before we met . . . again, I mean, did you have expectations?"

The moment the last word left my lips, I regretted the question. Of course he'd had expectations, and our reunion had fallen short of what he imagined. I had overheard that much.

"I had eighteen years' worth of expectations," he admitted. "I knew you were gonna be beautiful. There was no doubt in my mind about that."

My cheeks burned, and I dropped my eyes to my shoes. "You couldn't know how I was gonna look."

"I remembered what you looked like when we were kids, and you favored your mom, so I had a pretty good idea."

"I don't think I look like her." My mother had been stunning. She could've been a model, but she chose to be a veterinarian and mother in a small town in the middle of nowhere Kansas. I had her hair and her eyes, but little else.

"You do, and she's why I expected you to be taller."

That brought my head up. "Really?" I straightened my spine and shoulders, doing my best to reach that ever-elusive five foot two inches. "How tall?"

"Five eight, maybe five nine." He stuffed his hands into his jacket pockets. "I guess I overestimated."

"Only by a few inches."

He laughed. "Or seven."

"Disappointed?"

"Not even a little bit." Warmth softened his face. "When I saw you standing at the foot of the ramp outside the sheriff's department, I couldn't have cared less about your height or your looks. I was focused on the fact that my best friend was alive and in front of me after all those years."

I could only imagine how precious that moment had been for him. It would be like opening my door to find Gin on my patio after almost twenty years.

"Two slices of sausage and pepperoni for me," Jordan said, as we reached the food truck. "And one slice of mushroom and pineapple for the lady, I'm guessing."

"Yes, please."

Jordan passed the vendor a ten-dollar bill and accepted our plates. I thanked both of them, said a silent prayer, and bit off the end of my pizza.

Amazing.

I nibbled at my slice as we walked the sidewalk under the streetlights. "You know, for the record, I wasn't disappointed when I met you again either."

"You didn't remember me, so there was nothing to be disappointed about."

"I had some memories of you when we met again, like playing catch in the yard."

He hissed in a breath. "Yeah, I knew then that you were not gonna make it in professional football."

"What gave it away?"

"Oh, the little things. Your inability to catch a ball, throw a ball, or stay focused when a butterfly drifted by. And then there was that cute fidgety bounce when you were waiting for me to toss the ball."

"You were taking too long, and for all you knew, I could run a ball to the end of the field and score a point. I'm fast and sneaky."

He folded his pizza to take a bite. "You wouldn't make it two feet. None of the guys would be willing to tackle you, but they wouldn't have to because they could pick you up and bench-press you with their pinkies."

I had seen some of those guys on TV, and I didn't think he was exaggerating. Some of their biceps were thicker than my stomach after an afternoon of all-you-can-eat cheese dip.

"So, you know about my childhood after tragedy separated us. Tell me something about yours," I said.

"There's not much to tell. I was never interested in the things most people my age were interested in. I spent most of my time watching detective shows and studying criminal investigation."

"Because of what happened to my family." Sadness pierced my heart. "Losing them changed a lot for you."

"It did, but it's nothing to be sad about. If I had spent my years partying and playing sports, I wouldn't have been there the night Edward brought you back to your family's house."

And Marx and I would've died. He'd saved our lives, but he had to take a life to do it, and for someone with such a compassionate heart, it must be a heavy weight to carry.

"I'm glad you were there, but I'm sorry for what you had to do."

He chewed slowly, giving himself time to gather his thoughts. "Edward Billings is the only person I've ever killed. A monster, by anyone's definition, and if I had to do it again to save your life, I would. In a heartbeat. But ending a human life, no matter how evil it is . . . sometimes it's hard to deal with. And in those moments, I have to remind myself that if I hadn't killed him, I wouldn't have you in my life." He tilted his head. "Of course, Marx wouldn't be in my life either, and that doesn't sound terrible."

"Hey!"

He grinned. "I'm kidding."

"Did you make any friends after me and Gin?"

"I made more enemies than friends."

"How do you make enemies in Stony Brooke? It's so small you can yell from one end of town to the other."

"True, but not everybody likes the sheriff, especially when he keeps arresting them for making dumb, reckless decisions."

Ah, that made sense.

Jordan nodded to something ahead. "I got a basic one of these when I was eleven."

I followed his attention to the green scooter parked in a designated drop-off area by whoever had used it last. Various forms of public transportation were popping up across the city, including electric scooters people could rent using an app on their smart phone.

"Ever ridden one?" Jordan asked.

I eyed the two-wheeled contraption. "No, and I don't have a burning desire to spend the next six months in a full-body cast."

"I won't let you fall and break anything."

"I don't know. It took me twice as long as everyone else my age to figure out how to balance on a bike without the training wheels. This seems like a bad idea."

"A few weeks ago, you told me you wanna try new things and discover what you like. This is my friendly encouragement for you to follow through."

"I am not gonna like that."

"You never know until you try."

I pulled at my bottom lip with my teeth. "Okay, but you have to try ketchup on your macaroni and cheese next time."

"That's . . . disgusting, but it's a deal."

268

I tossed my pizza crust and plate into the trash and brushed my hands off on my jeans. This was going to go badly. I was certain of it.

Jordan swept the kickstand up and positioned the scooter beside me. "Place one foot on the floorboard, and leave the other one on the ground so you can kick off while holding the throttle. This"—he pumped the lever—"is the brake."

"Kicking, throttle, brakes. Got it." I stared at the scooter, then flicked a questioning glance at Jordan. "What's a throttle?"

"The thing that helps you control your speed."

"Oh." I placed my left foot on the scooter and gripped the handlebars. "Should be easier than driving a car, right?"

"As long as you don't take out trash cans like bowling pins or drive the wrong way on a one-way street, you're golden."

I narrowed my eyes at him. "Who told you about the one-way street?"

"I will never reveal my sources." He moved to stand beside me. "Go slow so you have time to find your balance."

Blowing out a nervous breath, I pressed my thumb on the throttle and kicked off the sidewalk. The quiet hum of a motor ignited, and the scooter coasted forward.

I wobbled as I tried to arrange my feet on the floorboard and tilted too far to the right. I yelped, visions of falling off and rolling across gritty asphalt into traffic flashing through my head, but Jordan's firm hands braced my sides.

"I've got you."

I knew he was going to catch me somehow, but the pressure of his hands on my waist still sent a shock of unease through me. Even with three layers of clothes between his skin and mine, it felt too intimate.

His hands fell away as soon as I stopped wobbling, just in time for me to lean too far the other way. I was about to throw out a foot to right myself when he nudged me straight again.

"I'm terrible at this."

"No, you're *new* at this. You can run for hours without missing a step because it's something you do all the time. This is unfamiliar territory, and your body needs to learn how to adapt to . . . whoa, watch out for the parking meter."

I swerved. "Who put that there?"

"Someone who's clearly never seen you drive."

I wobbled around a corner and veered to miss a worm wriggling his way across the sidewalk; I nearly ran into Jordan. "Sorry."

He jumped out of the way. "Did you just swerve to miss a worm?"

I laughed at the feigned outrage in his voice. "Maybe." A car pulled out of an alley, and I squeezed the brake, planting a foot on the ground before I could tip over. I puffed out a breath. "I survived."

"That wasn't too terrible, was it?"

"Surprisingly, no." I dismounted and gripped the handlebars to steer it between us on the sidewalk. "How many times did you fall over before getting the hang of it?"

"Five or six. By day two, I had a good grip on how to balance and maneuver. You'll get better with practice too."

We walked beneath a strand of outdoor lights, and I smiled up at the glow. What was it about strands of lights that made everything feel warmer and more cheerful?

"Thanks for coming out with me," Jordan said.

"Thanks for the pizza. And the new experience."

We slowed as a little girl with beads in her black hair flounced over to us in her pink romper, the heels of her sneakers lighting up with every bounce. She waved a hand at the grid of circles she and another girl had drawn on the sidewalk and flashed a gap-toothed smile. "You wanna try?"

"How do we play?" I asked.

The other girl, who must've been her sister, hurried over to join her and said, "It's like hopscotch, but . . . with bubbles. We, um . . . we call it . . . we call it bubble hop."

I smiled up at Jordan. "Wanna play bubble hop?"

"I'm game." He tugged up his sleeves and studied the fifty or so circles the girls had drawn. "Looks challenging, but I think I'm ready."

The girls giggled and scampered to the end of the grid, grabbing up containers of bubbles. There was quite a bit of distance between some of the circles. I had no doubt Jordan could spring between them with ease and grace if he wanted to, but he chose to hop clumsily, eliciting gasps and encouraging cheers from the girls.

"You can do it!"

"You're almost there!"

I parked the scooter in one of the designated areas and caught up with him on the grid, pushing him just hard enough to knock one of his feet out of a circle.

"Oh no!" the girl in the romper shouted. "You gotta start over, Mister!"

Jordan grinned at me as he stepped off to the side. "Cheater. And I suppose I'm not allowed to pay you back for that."

"Nope. No touching. You don't have permission."

He laughed and went back to the beginning. I reached the finish line, and the girls blew bubbles as fast as they could, filling the air with celebration. Jordan joined me a moment later, and happiness warmed my chest as iridescent bubbles danced in the air around us.

I blew one toward him, and it popped in front of his face. We high-fived the girls for their awesome creativity, then continued on our way as they tried to pull other passersby into their evening fun.

Watching them stirred up memories of an unfulfilled promise.

When it's safe, I'll find you.

271

Memories of that long-ago day seeped through my mind like fog—the frantic search for the little girl who shared my room, the tree with the calloused eyes, the rope looped around an innocent child's neck.

These girls couldn't be more than six or seven, around the same age Cassie had been when I begged her to run as far and as fast as she could from the Wells's home, with the promise that I would find her when it was safe.

I never saw her again.

"Jordan, can I ask you for a favor?"

"Always."

"A long time ago, I gave my word that I would find someone. I wanna keep that promise, but I don't know where to start."

"Who is it?"

"A fellow Collin survivor." I caught the subtle clenching of his jaw at the mention of my foster brother. "Her name is Cassandra Ward, and she was six the last time I saw her. She ran away, and I don't know what happened to her after that."

"I'll see what I can find out."

"Thanks," I said. If anyone could locate her and reconnect us, it was him.

"You ready to go home for the night?"

It had been a long day, and I was tired, but I couldn't go home and rest. Not yet. "Actually, do you mind dropping me off at the agency so I can use the internet?"

Cami's case might be in the hands of the police now, but I wasn't ready to step back and wait for Detective Chamberlin to piece it all together.

32

The guy's a serial killer in the making. It's only a matter of time before he starts killing hookers to cleanse the earth.

Hope's assessment of Cami's stepfather didn't seem too far off as I stared into the cold, flat eyes of the man on my computer screen. There was no emotion in them, even as he smiled into the camera.

Was it possible he graduated from locking his stepdaughter in a closet for her "sins" to targeting women who worked the street?

I jotted his name in my notebook under "suspects" and then snuck a peek at Jordan's computer screen.

We were stretched out on the lobby floor of the agency with Riley sprawled contentedly between us. Jordan was sifting through records while I browsed social media profiles.

I grabbed one of the purple peeps from the package on my left and tossed it at him. It bounced off his ear and landed on his laptop keyboard.

"Real mature," he said with a smile. He tossed it back, and I caught it. "Did I use the last of your marshmallows in the chocolate milk? Is that why you're eating stale rabbits?"

"They're not stale." I bit off the bunny's slightly crusty ears. "And yes, I'm out of minis. Temporarily."

"I guess it's back to carrots and celery."

Maybe when I was literally starving and had no other options. "Anything on this guy whose name screams, 'I kill girls for fun'?"

Jordan grinned. "I think his last name is pronounced Killinger, not Killing'er. And yes, Cami's stepdad, Peter Killinger, has a criminal record for disorderly conduct, resisting arrest, aggravated assault, and destruction of property."

"Doesn't sound like someone I would wanna live with."

"He definitely warrants further investigation."

"What about Spike?" I licked the sticky sweetness from my fingertips and flipped through my notebook to find the section about him. "Rob saw him arguing with Cami Monday night, and Hope said he tried to manipulate them into working for him by arranging an attack. That's someone capable of kidnapping. Shouldn't we talk to him again?"

"There is no *we* in that scenario. I'm not taking you anywhere near that guy. If the investigation points us in his direction, *I* will go and talk to him. Alone."

I didn't like the sound of that. "He's dangerous. You should bring backup."

"If I bring you, my sole focus will be on protecting you, not questioning him. The only person I might consider taking with me is Sam. He's armed, and he's a formidable presence."

"He's a good choice."

Jordan's fingers stilled on the mouse pad, and he regarded me with concern and suspicion. "You never agree that easily. Promise me you're not planning to sneak off and talk to Spike on your own."

"I promise."

He relaxed. "Good. I doubt he's involved anyway. I can't picture him hiding behind a hood and scarf or running away from you at the hospital."

Good point.

"My primary person of interest right now is Joel Dominguez. There are too many questions surrounding him," he said, opening another window on his laptop.

"But he was gone before the incident with Cami in the alley."

"Which means he's unaccounted for during that time. According to David, this isn't the first time Erik picked up a girl for the group, but Joel leaves early on the one night something ends up going wrong, only for a mysterious man to show up in his place. And the entire time Cami was missing, *he's* been missing."

274

"You think he came back in disguise and kidnapped her? Why would he do that?"

"Why do guys like this do anything?"

"Wouldn't his friends recognize his car or the way he moves?"

"Maybe they did recognize him, and they're lying to keep him out of trouble," Jordan said. "David practically squirmed when I asked him about Joel. Erik gave us his name before defaulting to 'talk to my lawyers.'"

"But if Joel had Cami and David knew it, why would David go to Brushwick looking for her yesterday morning?"

"No one's been able to get a hold of Joel, not even his parents, so the only way for David to confirm that he returned Cami to the place where Erik picked her up was to go there. When he found out no one had seen her since the night before, he became agitated."

I turned the theory over in my head as I stared at my notebook. "But he might've been upset because he did nothing to stop a kidnapping, and finding out she was still missing the next morning could've amplified his fear and guilt. That would stress out anyone with a conscience."

"True, which is why Joel is a person of interest, not a suspect. I'm checking all public records. You wanna check social media?"

"Sure. What does he look like?"

As a licensed private investigator, Jordan had access to information and databases most people didn't, so I wasn't surprised to see Joel's driver's license photo on his screen when he angled his laptop toward me.

Joel, twenty-three, had raven-black hair and brown eyes. He wasn't a large man, at least as far as I could tell from the details in the picture.

I launched into a search for him on Facebook. "Do I ever get to use your fancy credentials to snoop on people?"

"No, but if you have a problem with someone, I hope you would tell me so I can look into him."

"Why are you assuming my hypothetical problem is a guy?"

"You were there when I mentioned that you tend to attract weirdos, right?"

I smiled and rolled my eyes, but I couldn't argue. I attracted weirdos like picnic baskets attracted hungry bears.

Popping the last of my marshmallow peep into my mouth, I released a contented sigh. I enjoyed working alongside Jordan to find and help people. It gave me a sense of purpose.

It took me a while to find Joel's Facebook page. It must've been set to private, because I couldn't see anything but a handful of useless details and his primary photo.

"Nothing here."

"Joel does have a black vehicle registered to his name, which is what David claims the kidnapper was driving," Jordan said. "And his father owns a prominent construction company. I'll see if I can pull together a list of unfinished properties the company is working on."

"Why?"

"If any of them are delayed because of contracts or material issues, they're an ideal location to keep someone. Detective Chamberlin might be able to find evidence or, considering this guy may have tried to grab more than one woman, another victim."

"*If* Joel is our guy. I still think it could be Cami's stepdad. He could've found her on Brushwick and followed Erik's car Thursday night."

"I'll check into his whereabouts, but one important thing about investigative work is keeping an open mind. If we focus on one of these guys too much and we're wrong, we could miss the guilty suspect right in front of our faces."

I grabbed another marshmallow, squishing it between my fingers. "This kidnapper, whoever he is, what do you think he wants?"

276

"I wish I knew, because it might help me make sense of all this." He propped himself up against the reception desk, arms draped over his knees. "My gut is telling me there's a connection between Cami's abduction and Dorina's attempted abduction. Both victims are women, working in the same field, the same street, attacked a night apart. But the vehicles don't match, the way the man concealed his identity is different, and the victims are drastically different in age."

I pushed myself into a sitting position across from him. "What if he didn't expect Cami to get sick, and when she did, he came back for a different woman the next night?"

"Setting aside the differences between the crimes for now, I can see that. His attempt to grab Dorina goes awry because of Clayton, and he goes home empty-handed."

"And then this morning, Cami is left in the alley behind the apartment building of yet another woman who works in the same field on the same street, and then someone approaches her son."

"Maybe Tyler was never the target. What if he happened to be outside when the man came by for Hope?" Jordan said. "She fits with the other victims. They're all different ages and races, but it's possible the draw for this guy is simply the act of prostitution."

Most serial killers start by targeting prostitutes, Addison had said. I had ignored his theory because Tyler didn't fit and no one had died, but considering things from this angle, maybe he wasn't completely off the mark.

"If he's targeting these women solely because of their profession, what are the chances, out of all the women on Brushwick, he would pick three who are friends?" I asked.

"I would say it's highly unlikely."

I could call Sam, my statistics-loving friend, and ask him for the probability, but the conversation would spiral into a lecture on how I could've become a statistic myself by wandering around Brushwick.

Solid pass on that lecture.

Or was it . . . hard pass?

"So this guy chose these girls because they're connected, or he has some connection to all of them," I said, tugging at my bottom lip with my teeth as I struggled to come up with a theory. "A mutual . . . client, maybe?"

"We can't rule it out. Hope is certain she has no enemies, Dorina didn't offer up any names, and Cami . . . hopefully she can tell us something when she comes around. These women aren't the most forthcoming, and I have a feeling this guy is in the details we're not hearing about."

"Addison threw out a wild theory about the man possibly stalking his victims, and I think he could be right. This guy drove past Hope's apartment building, and Cami wasn't on Brushwick when he grabbed her. He has to be following them."

"I would say that's likely." He turned his wrist to see the time on his watch. "I'd rather not take David's word for what happened with Cami, so I'm gonna go see about security footage in and around the alley where she was supposedly kidnapped. Considering how upscale this club is, they should have exterior cameras, and hopefully one of those cameras captured the kidnapper or the license plate of his vehicle. I wanna get to the club a little before it opens at nine, so I should get going."

A night club—an overcrowded place where people went to flirt and dance to deafening music while passing around drugs and alcohol. Even the thought of being there tickled my anxiety.

"Um, do you mind if I stay here and do some more research?"

Understanding softened Jordan's eyes. "I didn't figure you'd feel comfortable in that environment. That's the only reason I didn't ask you to come with me."

I cleared my throat and dragged my computer into my lap. "I'll be more productive here, I think." Mostly because I wouldn't be hyperventilating in a bathroom.

Jordan closed his laptop and pushed to his feet. "I'll call Chamberlin on the way and let him know about our suspicions. If he thinks there's a chance this man will come after these women again, he'll reach out to them."

When he hesitated, questioning his decision to leave me alone after everything that had happened, I patted Riley's back. "We're good. And I'm not gonna take a cab anywhere. Promise."

"Okay. I'll be back as soon as I can. Call me if you need me."

He took his gun and his investigator's license with him, and Riley and I stretched back out on the floor for a long night of scouring the internet for information.

. . . .

I scrolled through the latest entry on Addison Miles's website, my irritation expanding with every sentence.

The man had wasted no time in publishing his blog post about a madman slinking through the shadows, hunting for prostitutes. He even sprinkled a few references to Jack the Ripper throughout the piece, drawing parallels that didn't exist.

> And who, outside of an officer approaching retirement, is investigating these crimes against the working women of Manhattan? Holly Cross, a supposed survivor of kidnapping herself. You might recognize her name from some of my previous articles, "All Is Not Wells with This Trial" and "Cross-Examined."

I rolled my eyes. The man was witty with his article titles, I'd give him that.

> Ms. Cross is currently employed by JGH Investigations, a private investigative firm in East Harlem, but she couldn't

provide any information during my interview with her, which suggests she's either withholding information or has no leads on this man terrorizing the women on our streets. I don't know about everyone else in this city, but I question the qualifications of the private investigators working these cases.

I groaned and dropped my forehead on the carpet. Did this man have a particular dislike for me, or did he drag everyone through the mud?

Riley whined and licked my ear sympathetically, and I turned my face toward him with a sigh. "I don't hate him. I don't. I just really dislike . . . everything about him."

Addison Miles had no interest in the truth, and he would publish anything that increased his readership. But why did he have to mention the agency? We were never going to get any clients if people thought we were too inept to connect two dots.

The phone rang in my office, and I lifted my head to cast it a wary look. What were the chances it was a potential client after this article posted? There were already six hundred views and a rapidly growing list of comments.

I checked the time on my computer screen—well past closing—and decided to let the call go to voice mail.

I perused the comments on Addison's post, hoping someone might leave a clue. There were a few readers who shared conspiracies, a handful of people who left less than supportive comments about me, and then there were the rare but disturbing statements like "Prostitution is a sin, and the payment for sin is death. DEATH."

I made note of the semihomicidal and scary religious-sounding statements. I perked up at the next comment.

There's this guy who trolls the neighborhoods in a white van with a cross painted on the side. He chats up the girls and gives them snacks and those religious booklets, but I've seen the way he looks at them, like he's disgusted.

I'd forgotten about the van across the street from Cami's apartment. That was the vehicle that was missing when we came out of the building.

I read the message again, and something clicked in the back of my mind. Rob mentioned a man with Scripture pamphlets crossing paths with Cami Monday night, and the man I met at the food pantry had chattered on about his mission in poor communities.

What was his name? I rummaged around in the cobwebbed part of my brain where names were stored, but came up empty.

Opening my phone, I started a text to Jordan with the new possibility, but someone rapped on the front door.

Riley's head snapped up from his paws, and he rose to his feet, but he relaxed when he recognized the young woman standing on the sidewalk.

Hope chewed at a fingernail as she waited, her leg jiggling. She was still wearing the clothes she'd had on at the hospital, and exhaustion and tears made the skin around her eyes puffy.

Pushing up from the floor, I unlocked the door and opened it. "What happened? Is Cami okay?"

She forced herself to stop gnawing at her nail and gripped her phone in both hands. "She ain't awake yet. I was hoping you might have like two seconds so we could talk."

"Sure, come on in." I secured the door after she entered and walked back to the reception counter. "You want some tea or hot chocolate? I can make some."

"Nah, I ain't gonna be here long."

A dog barked outside, and Riley trotted over to the door. He cocked his head curiously when the bark came again.

I tucked my fingers into the back pockets of my jeans. "What's up?"

Hope blew out a breath. "I was desperate when I came here asking for help, and you were super nice, but . . . you can drop the case or whatever. Cami's fine now, and I just want things to get back to normal."

Her request caught me by surprise. "Cami's not fine, and whoever did this to her is still out there. We need to find him."

"No offense, but you two couldn't even find Cami, and you knew you were looking for her. You're never gonna find somebody whose name and face you don't even know."

"Jordan's tracking down a lead, and I'm—"

"Just let it go, Holly," she snapped, then sighed. "I'm sorry, but I need all this to be over."

"Then help us figure out who he is so it *can* be over. There's some connection between this man and the three of you."

"The three of us?"

"Cami, Dorina, and you."

"Nobody tried to grab me."

"We don't think he was driving through your neighborhood because he was interested in your son. We think he was there for you."

"You two and your theories." She shook her head. "Even if you're right, I can take care of myself. Dorina's got Clayton, and Cami's got a cop at her door, so . . . we're good. You did your good deed trying to help a lost cause. Now you can move on to a client who can pay you."

"Hope—"

"See you around, Nancy Drew." She unlocked the front door and shoved her way out.

I stared after her in confusion. Her change of attitude didn't make sense to me, and its irrationality kindled a spark of frustration. Was this how Marx felt when I made an emotional decision he didn't agree with?

An annoyed breath escaped my lips. I couldn't let the conversation end there. Whether she wanted our help or not, I couldn't let her walk away without explaining the risks to her safety. This wasn't a threat that would go away if she ignored it.

I touched Riley's head. "I'll be right back." I threw open the door and jogged to the alley Hope had taken the other night.

It was empty.

I hesitated to follow, but I wouldn't be gone long, and Riley would guard the agency from burglars. I sprinted to the end of the alley and paused to take in both directions.

Movement in the shadows drew me to the right, and I turned onto a side street. The cold night air bit at my skin through my sweater, and I rubbed at the goose bumps on my arms. I should've grabbed my jacket from the wall hook.

"Hope?"

A flash of pink receded around a corner. Where was she going? Surely she wasn't planning to return to Brushwick tonight.

I watched for threats as I followed at a more cautious pace, praying I wouldn't get mugged. I had nothing to give a mugger unless they wanted my shoes.

The sound of a door latching made my heart skip. Had that come from the alley Hope turned into? A taxi would've waited for her in the parking lot, not in a dark alley near the end of the block. Who was she getting into a car with?

I broke into a run, determined to catch her before the vehicle could pull away. I barely rounded the corner when a patch of slick newspaper snatched my feet out from under me, and I crashed to the ground with a yelp.

Pain radiated up my tailbone, and I rubbed at the small of my back as I gathered my legs beneath me.

My breath caught at the horrifying sight in front of me. A white utility van sat ten feet away, the front end facing the other direction. My eyes grazed the license plate before settling on a round puncture in the rear left door . . . about the size of a bullet.

This wasn't just any van. It was *the* van.

One of Clayton's shots might've hit the hubcap, but the other one must've hit the door while it was open.

Fear pounded through my veins. Was Hope restrained and gagged in the back? Had the man been waiting here to grab her when she walked by?

A part of me wanted to rush forward and throw open the doors to rescue her, even as the sensible part of my brain screamed that I was in danger.

If I was right about what happened, the kidnapper was still here. Before I could decide whether to attempt a rescue or flee and call the police with the van description and license plate, a body slammed into my back.

An arm locked around my waist, and a hand clamped over my mouth to muffle the scream that burned up my throat.

33

*P*anic punched me in the chest, stealing my breath and scattering all rational thought. I flailed, desperate to break free of the arm locked around my rib cage. My attacker stumbled off balance and then reared back, pulling *me* off balance.

My sneakers left the ground, and I sucked in air through my nose as I clawed at the gloved hand over my mouth. The man hauled me toward the back of the van, his voice a hiss in my ear.

"Calm down."

I launched a frantic attack, like the chaotic tornado my mom used to jokingly accuse me of being—arms and legs flailing, clawing at and ripping whatever I could reach.

If he intended to stuff me into his murder-mobile, he was going to feel the pain of that decision for weeks afterward.

"Get . . . the doors," he grunted.

At his command, someone slipped out of the passenger side of the van and emerged from the shadows. Shock stole the fight from me.

Hope.

Her expression remained flat as she opened the rear doors and stepped off to the side. "I don't see why you gotta go grabbin' her. She ain't a part of this."

"You . . . made her . . . a part of this," he panted.

The enclosed compartment of the van stretched out in front of us, a dark box with only one way out. I kicked and thrashed, desperate to keep him from shoving me inside. He staggered and then overcompensated, causing both of us to pitch forward.

The air whooshed from my lungs as he dropped on top of me, pinning me to the metal floor.

His heavy breaths ruffled the hair on the top of my head as he demanded, "Zip ties. Glove compartment."

No.

The last time zip ties touched my skin, I had been tortured for hours. If he tightened that plastic around my wrists and ankles, I wouldn't be able to fight him off.

I wasn't going to be locked up in some abandoned construction site or dank basement for however long it took Marx to track me down and kick in the doors.

I slammed my head into my attacker's face, and he rocked back with a groan, giving me a chance to squirm out from under him. I barely made it to my hands and knees before he gripped my ankles.

Dragging in a lungful of air, I released an ear-piercing scream. Someone would hear me. Someone *had* to hear me. He wrenched me back toward him, and I belly-flopped, the impact reducing my scream to a squeak.

The man slapped a hand over my mouth again, his fingers digging painfully into my cheeks. "The duct tape too."

"Come on, Ollie, let's just leave her and take off before someone sees something," Hope suggested, her voice coming from behind the van.

"*She's* seen something, thanks to you. This is all your fault."

"My fault?" Hope hissed back. "You're the one who snatched my best friend."

"Cami's not your best friend. You killed your best friend, remember? Now give me the stuff."

A strip of wiry plastic and a roll of duct tape thumped on the floor beside my calf. With an irritated sigh, the man released my mouth and leaned down to grab them. As his weight shifted, I bucked my hips, knocking him off balance.

I didn't have much leverage, but I thrust a foot into his chest, and he fell backward. Not giving him a chance to recover, I slammed a second kick into his chest, and he tumbled out of the van, smacking the ground with a pained grunt.

I crawled out after him, cold water seeping into my sneakers as my feet splashed into a rain puddle. Before I could leap over my would-be kidnapper, he lunged up from the ground, his fingers locking around my wrist.

"Let go!" I yanked and twisted until my arm slid free inside my sweater sleeve, but the man still clutched a fistful of the material. "Hope, please . . ."

Hope backed up against the side of the building, her expression unreadable. She wasn't going to help me.

My sleeve stretched, but I couldn't pull it from his grip. I would have to leave my sweater behind. Shrugging it over my head, I pirouetted out of it, leaving it dangling from his fingers.

I stumbled and fell, pain lancing up my right wrist as I threw out my hands to break my fall. Wincing, I clambered up and squeezed between the van and the building, taking off for the street.

"Cut her off!" the man shouted, charging after me.

I pushed my soggy feet and strained muscles as fast as they would go, lungs burning with every gulp of air. If I could make it to the agency around the corner, the reinforced glass windows and door would protect me. Riley would protect me.

The rumble of an engine made my heart stutter. The van had turned onto the street with its lights off.

No, no, no.

I rounded the corner and bounded over the uneven slab of sidewalk that tripped me up the first few evenings I took Riley out for his bathroom break, but my pursuer missed the cue. He stumbled and crashed to the ground behind me.

Jordan's car was in the parking lot, and he stood on the sidewalk in front of the agency, attention on his phone. I couldn't catch my breath to scream or even call out his name, so I ran straight for him.

He turned at the sound of my footsteps, hand instinctively dropping to the gun on his hip. I was moving too fast to stop, and I plowed into him, knocking him backward.

He threw a hand against the door to steady himself and wrapped his other arm around me.

"Holly? What . . ."

Brakes squeaked as the van stopped in front of the abandoned building next door to pick up my would-be kidnapper. The passenger door slammed, and the vehicle shot down the street.

34

*J*rolled up the sleeves of the sweatshirt until I could see my fingers. I had never realized how long Jordan's arms were until now. What was that, five rolls? Six?

Jordan kept a change of clothes in the office, and I was grateful to have something to cover my tank top. My sweater was probably lying in an oily puddle in the alley or being stuffed into an evidence bag.

Rest in peace, favorite sweater.

A knock on my office door made my pulse jump, but it slowed when I remembered that I was safe. The threat had driven away.

I stepped around Riley and twisted the lock on the knob, opening the door. Jordan stood there with a mug in one hand and an ice pack in the other.

He took in the sweatshirt that hung like a sack from my shoulders. "And now I know what my sweatshirt looks like as a dress. I'm sorry I don't have any pants that'll fit you."

I glanced at my damp, dirty jeans. "They'll dry."

"You look tired."

I was beyond tired. The adrenaline that had sustained me during the fight and allowed me to outrun my pursuer was gone, and all I wanted to do now was take a nap.

I took the ice pack Jordan offered and sank into my oversized chair, wrapping the coolness around my throbbing wrist.

"Detective Chamberlin is on his way over, and officers are trolling for the van," Jordan said.

I doubted my description of a utility van with a possible license plate, give or take a number, would be very helpful in a city with more than eight million people. The chances of them finding it were slim.

But I did know one thing for certain—the van wasn't the one Jordan and I saw parked across the street from Cami's apartment. There was no cross on the side, and the shape was more rectangular. That made me question the religious-zealot angle I was contemplating earlier.

Jordan passed me a mug of hot tea, and I read the message the company had stamped on the tag.

"I like you a lot, but I'm chai."

Each tea bag had its own unique phrase, and I could imagine Jordan sifting through them to avoid the flirty ones that said things like "Hey cu-tea!" and "You are steaming hot."

I rested the mug on my knees. "Thanks."

Jordan dropped into my desk chair, concern shining in his eyes. "I know I've asked half a dozen times already, but are you sure you're all right?"

I shifted my wrist. "Yeah, it's a little swollen, but it'll be okay." It wasn't broken, but my rough landing irritated an old injury.

"I don't just mean your wrist."

I hadn't missed the worry in his eyes when I plowed into him wearing nothing but a tank top in the frigid weather. I assured him the man hadn't tried to hurt me, but the worry remained.

"It's only a few bruises. I'm fine."

"Your idea of *fine* concerns me. If he had gotten you in that van . . ." A muscle flexed in his jaw, and he looked down at his hands. "Maybe Marx was right, and having you work here is too dangerous."

Wait, was he trying to fire me?

"If it's not safe for me, then it's not safe for you," I reasoned.

"It's different, and you know it. I'm not saying someone wouldn't try to intimidate me into backing off a case, but they're not gonna see a hundred-and-eighty-pound, six-foot man and think, 'I'm gonna stuff him in my van.'"

"You don't know that."

"Speaking from a man's perspective, I do. Guys like the one who grabbed you have no interest in a fight they think they might lose. The perception, true or not, is that women are easier targets."

"Well, he misjudged me, because he lost anyway."

A smile touched his lips. "Yes, he did. But what about the next time we find ourselves in the middle of a case someone doesn't want us investigating? Or a case that involves criminals and predators."

I understood his fears, but there was nothing I could do to allay them. I couldn't change the fact that I was five two and a hundred pounds.

"You would be safer if you did photography full-time," he said. "Your office would still be yours, but you wouldn't need to be involved in the investigations."

I bristled. "I have the same drive to protect people as the rest of you, and that isn't gonna change because God made me sample sized."

His lips twitched as he tried to keep them from curling up at the corners. "I know, and I know you won't stand on the sidelines when someone is in danger or missing, but I had to try. But if you insist on continuing to work risky cases, we need to restart your self-defense training."

I stared at the swirls of dark stretching from the tea bag in my mug. Resuming training meant learning how to break out of holds. It meant being physically restrained, which was more than I had been comfortable with over the past year.

Jordan leaned forward to catch my gaze. "You know Sam and I would never hurt you, and we'll go at a pace you're comfortable with."

"I know, but I can't promise I won't freak out and hurt you."

"I'll wear long sleeves."

I tucked my lips between my teeth as I considered it. "Can we wait until my body doesn't feel like it's been through a taffy puller?"

Because right now, everything hurt.

"We can ease back into it after the wedding, if you're ready." Jordan pushed to his feet. "Why don't you rest until Chamberlin gets here. You look like you're gonna pass out in your tea."

He tugged my throw blanket out from under Riley's front paws on the floor and draped it over my legs, the simple but kind gesture warming me more than the mug of steaming tea.

"Thanks," I said.

"I'll be in my office if you need me."

"Jordan." When he turned back to me, one hand on the door, I said, "I don't wanna have this argument every time something bad happens. I'm gonna help people one way or another, and I want you to be on my side."

He was quiet for a moment. "I won't ask you to quit again, but I won't stop worrying about your safety either."

I supposed that was the best I was going to get from the men in my life. At least I had people who cared enough to worry.

He closed the door behind him, and I took a few sips of the unsweetened tea before setting it on the bookshelf and curling up under my throw blanket.

My attention drifted to the window blinds behind me. I parted them with my fingers and stared at the oily smudge from Hope's hand the night she showed up on our doorstep. She'd seemed so scared and worried.

The memory of the desperate gleam in her eyes when she tried to pay me to find her friend collided with the reality of the woman who climbed out of the kidnapper's van in the alley, the woman who tossed duct tape and zip ties to him so he could tie me up.

She cried for Cami in the hospital but offered no objection when the kidnapper accused her of murdering her own best friend.

She was a contradiction, and I wasn't sure which side of her was real.

I should've realized something wasn't right, but the idea of her working with him didn't make sense. Why come to us in the first place if she was involved with the man responsible for Cami's abduction?

I let the blinds fall shut with a weary sigh and stared up at the lights on the ceiling. What would've happened if the man had succeeded in zip-tying me and locking me in the back of the van?

The terrifying possibilities ping-ponged around in my head as exhaustion tugged my eyelids shut. What kind of monster was he? What had he done to Cami before he left her in that alley?

I released a breath and pushed the questions from my mind, trying to relax. I melted into the softness of my chair and listened to the soothing rhythm of Riley's snores as he guarded the floor at my feet.

A soft creak from somewhere in the room tripped a mental alarm, and my eyes popped open. Darkness pressed in from every direction like a veil, and fear bloomed in my chest. What happened to the twinkly lights on my ceiling?

My office door creaked again as it rested against the frame, unlatched. I stared at it as I tried to remember whether or not Jordan had pulled it shut when he left.

I pushed aside my blanket and rose from my chair, when a flicker of movement in the darkness made me freeze beside the desk.

"Riley?"

A shape moved toward me, the shadows clinging to his features until he was barely a foot away. The mask hugging his face left his eyes visible, and the icy blue irises sent a chill all the way to my bone marrow.

"No," I whimpered.

He pulled a zip tie from his pocket and stretched it out in front of me. "Let's have a little fun, shall we?"

He fastened the plastic ribbon around my wrists and yanked it so tight that it bit into my skin. Panic exploded inside me, and I yanked and twisted, desperate to escape what I knew was about to happen.

I flung myself away from Collin, only to find myself plastered against the back of my reading chair, cowering from nothing. Chest heaving, I visually dissected every inch of my office, but no one was waiting in the shadows to attack me.

The lights on the ceiling still twinkled, and there was nothing cutting into my wrists. The tension drained out of me with a muffled whimper, and I dragged a shaking hand through my sweat-dampened hair.

It was only a nightmare. Or a night terror, judging by the ice pack lying on the floor across the room. I must've flung it in my sleep. But the dream was so vivid that the last few tendrils of panic refused to release my chest.

Hushed voices from outside my office tightened those tendrils even more, until I recognized Marx's bottled fury.

"How did this lunatic manage to get her alone in a dark alley?"

When had Marx gotten here?

I touched the mug of tea on the bookshelf, surprised by the coolness of the ceramic. I had been asleep long enough for the contents to reach room temperature, which was enough time for him to make it here from his apartment.

A beat of silence stretched before Jordan replied, "She was lured out of the building by someone we both believed was innocent."

Riley nuzzled my leg with his snout, agitated by my distress, and I rubbed his head. "I'm sorry, buddy. I'm okay. It was only a bad dream."

"Holly is safe for the moment, so we can think about this calmly and rationally," Sam said, surprising me yet again. Who *hadn't* arrived while I was asleep?

"Is that your way of sayin' I'm bein' irrational?" Marx snapped. "Somebody tried to kidnap my baby. Anythin' short of arrestin' every van owner in the city feels rational to me."

"You're thinking like a dad."

"What's your point?"

"Anger and vengeful impulses won't help us find this guy or figure out if he's gonna make another grab for Holly." Sam paused before asking, "The woman who lured Holly out of the building . . . you've met her before?"

"Briefly," Marx confirmed. "We met shortly after Thomas Mathis murdered her pimp. She had no part in it, and if you're hintin' at what I think you're hintin' at, Thomas wouldn't be involved in somethin' like this, even by proxy. Even in the middle of a psychotic break, he would've never condoned the abduction of a child or a teenage girl, and he certainly wouldn't condone somebody abductin' Holly. Her letters might be the only thing keepin' him sane."

I pushed aside the blanket and padded to my office door, cracking it open. The men were gathered around the reception counter, and the only man missing was the only one I had expected to see—Detective Chamberlin.

"Hi," I said, widening the door.

Relief chased away the anger in Marx's expression. He covered the distance between us, scanning me for injuries with every step, and then folded me into his arms. "I'm glad you're okay, sweetheart."

I rested my head beneath his chin, craving the comfort he provided. But I couldn't ignore the sense of guilt that crept in. Jordan's call to fill him in on the incident had ruined another romantic evening. I couldn't let this become a regular occurrence.

I drew back, strands of my sweaty hair snagging on the scruff he'd grown over the weekend. "I'm sorry for interrupting your evening with Shannon."

He frowned. "That's twice in two days that you've apologized for somethin' like that, and I don't like it."

I blinked at his response.

"I love Shannon, and I love spendin' time with her, but just because we're gettin' remarried and movin' back in together doesn't mean time spent with you is suddenly an interruption or an inconvenience."

"I don't . . ." I struggled to find words to express my concerns. "I know how long you've waited to have her back in your life, and I don't wanna get in the way."

Marx cupped my face, a glimmer of sadness mixed with the tenderness in his eyes. "You always fail to understand just how much you're loved, sweetheart. Your presence in our lives is a gift, and you couldn't be in the way if you tried."

"But Shannon didn't want kids, so how is she gonna feel about your not-quite daughter hanging around and calling you away at all hours? Won't it cause problems?"

"You can drop the *not quite*, and Shannon didn't wanna *raise* children, but she wanted me to have them. She's happy you fill that void in my heart, and even happier that she didn't have to raise you and risk screwin' you up."

I smiled at that.

"She doesn't begrudge me the time I spend with you, and she is in no way threatened by you. In fact, she asked me which guest room you would prefer and if you had a bed cushion for your dog. She doesn't even like dogs, but she wants you to feel at home whenever you come spend the night. She even bought marshmallows, which you would never have found in her cupboards before."

That was true. I had searched her entire kitchen the last time we were there, and there wasn't a marshmallow to be found, not even a stale one that rolled out of a previous bag to hide in the corner of a drawer.

"I know that Shannon and I movin' back in together is a big change, and that for most of your life, change meant losin' people and havin' to figure out how or if you fit in. But you couldn't lose me if you tried. You're my family, and that doesn't change with my address. Okay?"

I nodded.

"Good. I don't wanna hear any more apologies." He released me and grabbed the clothes from the reception counter, handing them to me. "Jordan told me you needed a change of clothes, so I brought some of the stuff you left at my place."

"Thanks. I'll be right back." I retreated to my office to change, grateful for dry jeans and a sweater with sleeves that I didn't have to roll up every other minute. I folded Jordan's sweatshirt and handed it back to him in the lobby. "Thanks for the loan."

Marx retrieved a box from the counter. "And this is your early Christmas gift, which I expect you to carry with you any time you're walkin' somewhere alone."

Oh, I loved presents. I removed the lid and studied the contents. "Is this . . ."

"A Taser."

I had been joking about putting this on my Christmas list, but here it was. "It's not gonna kill anyone, right? Because I don't wanna—"

"No, it's not gonna kill anybody, but it'll take their breath away as well as their ability to come after you. This one can be used in direct contact and up to thirty-five feet away."

I lifted the Taser from the box and turned it over in my hands. "Have you ever had to shoot anyone with one of these?"

"No, but I have been on the receivin' end, so I know it works."

My eyebrows lifted. "What did you do to get tasered?" I couldn't imagine him doing anything criminal. Maybe he was arresting a bad guy, and he got tasered by the guy's overly aggressive girlfriend.

"It's tased, not tasered, and I didn't do anythin'. It's part of our law enforcement trainin'. And I'd rather not experience it twice." He pushed the front of the Taser away from his stomach.

"Sorry." I returned it to the box and set it aside before I accidentally zapped someone I cared about.

"I'll teach you how to use it after I get off work tomorrow. I don't want you weaponless if somebody comes after you again." He turned to face the others. "Now, somebody tell me who I need to hunt down."

"We have a few potential suspects for the kidnapper, but nothing solid," Jordan replied. "Holly's the only one who's seen this guy up close and interacted with him." He deferred to me with a nod.

Appreciation welled within me. "I picked up a couple of details while the guy and Hope were arguing in the alley. He's the one who took Cami Thursday night, and judging by the bullet hole in the back of the van, we can safely assume he's the one who tried to take Dorina Friday night. The van is exactly as she described. A rear compartment that's cut off from the front seats."

"This man abducted one woman, tried to abduct another the next night, and then you tonight?" Marx asked, the lines of concern deepening on his forehead.

"I don't think he planned to take me. Hope tried to throw me off the case, but I followed her to the van."

"Maybe that *was* the plan," Jordan countered. "She happened to show up after I left, said some things that piqued your curiosity, then walked right to the van, where he was able to come up behind you."

"They couldn't have known I would go after her, and he only grabbed me because I saw the license plate. Hope tried to talk him out of it. I don't think she really wants to be a part of this."

"I understand why you wanna believe that, sweetheart, but sometimes the heart blinds people to the truth," Marx said, and by *people* I wasn't sure whether he meant me or himself.

My heart occasionally confused victims and villains. I had never expected Rachel to help my foster brother, and I certainly hadn't anticipated this turn of events.

"Some people are skilled enough to deceive everyone around them," Sam commented, a flash of pain in his eyes for the partner he'd lost. "It's not your fault for believing she was innocent in all this."

"But it doesn't make sense that Hope is helping this guy," I said.

"It doesn't make sense to *us*," Jordan amended. "But there must be a reason that makes sense to her."

"I don't fit with the victims, though. I don't . . . do what Cami and Dorina do, so what would he want with me?"

"We don't even know what he wants with them, but you were on Brushwick by yourself. Maybe he saw you and assumed you were one of the working girls."

I mentally sifted through the faces I'd seen that night—Spike, the man who took Tandi away, the men in the cars, the distorted reflection in the shop window.

Fear fluttered in my stomach. What if Jordan was right and this guy made the same assumption Erik made? But Hope knew I worked here, and if they were in this together, she would've told him that. Unless we were completely wrong about why he was picking these women.

Trying to figure all this out was making my head hurt.

Sam cleared his throat. "On the subject of the van, the van license plate is registered to an elderly gentleman from Connecticut. He claims he recently sold his van to a man who responded to his online ad."

Hope was from Connecticut. Yet another connection, however tenuous, between her and the man she called Ollie. A little more of my belief in her innocence died.

"The buyer paid him five thousand in cash," Sam continued.

Marx let out a low whistle at the amount of cash the man had on hand. "What's the buyer's name?"

"Jack Sparrow. Obviously fake."

"Why is that obviously fake?" Marx asked.

"Because Jack Sparrow is a fictional pirate," Sam clarified. "My sister is addicted to those films. It's not unusual for me to wake up to the sound of sword fighting."

"If it helps at all, Hope called him Ollie," I said. "I know it's probably a nickname, but it's something to call him other than kidnapper guy."

Marx smiled. "I think you're the only one callin' him that."

"One thing's for sure. Ollie the kidnapper guy is an amateur," Sam said. Was that a hint of amusement in his voice? "Out of three attempted kidnappings, he only succeeded with one."

"And Cami was drugged and injured at the time," I added, which reminded me—Jordan had gone to Club Velvet to discover exactly how the abduction went down. "What did you find out at the club? Did they let you see the camera footage?"

"It took some persuading. There are two cameras, one covering the front of the building and one covering the alley. At 12:32 a.m., a black car parked at the edge of the front camera's range. It's hard to say, but I think it might be a sedan. Four minutes later, the car turns into the alley, parking out of frame. The alley camera captured some of the scuffle between Cami and the three guys. And at the same time that the car turns into the alley, the three guys climb into their car and take off. A man with a hooded sweatshirt and scarf over his face enters the frame, scoops Cami off the ground, and carries her back the way he came."

That was consistent with David's statement as well as what I witnessed at the hospital.

Jordan frowned. "What I can't figure out is why this guy wore a mask and drove a van when he made a grab for you and Dorina, but he used a scarf and a black car when he abducted Cami."

300

"Planning," Sam offered. "If you're planning to kidnap someone, you come prepared—a mask to conceal your identity, gloves to avoid fingerprints, a van to conceal and transport the victim. If you're surveilling, you do everything you can to blend in and go unnoticed. The police do the same with unmarked vehicles. Taking Cami at that very moment may have been spontaneous."

And he couldn't waltz into the hospital in a ski mask and gloves, so he did his best to conceal his face with a hood and scarf.

"You think the fact that he was wearin' a mask and drivin' the van means he was plannin' to take Holly tonight," Marx said.

"It's possible, but it's also possible he was simply *prepared* to take her if Hope failed to convince her to stop investigating," Sam said. "It's hard to gauge his intentions, but when she saw the van and the license plate, taking her to keep that information from getting out might've felt like the only option. Now that he knows we're on to the van, I wouldn't be surprised if he dumped it." He turned to Jordan. "Did you get a plate number for the car?"

"No, it wasn't clear from that angle."

The front door swung open, and Detective Chamberlin lumbered in, his features more tired than earlier. His eyebrows inched up when he saw Marx, and his tone took on a questioning note. "Rick."

Marx extended a hand. "Good to see you again, Adam."

"Likewise." Chamberlin clasped his hand. "Should I be concerned that you're here? Did someone die?"

"Not that I'm aware of. I'm here for Holly. You remember me mentionin' her when our cases overlapped last fall."

I could see the pieces connect behind the detective's eyes. He looked from Marx to me and shook his head. "How did I miss that connection when we spoke earlier?"

"Sounds like you're slippin'. Time for retirement," Marx teased.

Chamberlin scoffed. "Like I could afford to retire." He returned his attention to me. "I understand you had a rough night."

Tonight didn't even come close to the rough nights I'd been through, so I wasn't sure how to respond to that. "I guess. Did the surveillance video at the hospital give you anything on the man in the chapel?"

Chamberlin hesitated. "Ms. Cross, I'm here because you were attacked. This isn't a meeting to exchange information in an ongoing investigation."

"So, you don't wanna know what I found out while having a rough night?"

Chamberlin glanced at Marx, who shrugged and said, "If you want her to tell you somethin' more than 'I have nothin' to say,' you need to give her a reason to work with you."

"You don't trust cops either, I take it," Chamberlin said.

"I trust that one and that one." I pointed to Marx and Sam. "They earned it."

"Okay. I'll cooperate with you, if you cooperate with me."

"Deal." I folded my arms. "You go first."

He pulled his smartphone from his jacket pocket, slid his finger over the screen a few times, then turned it toward me. "Is that the man you saw in the chapel?"

I studied the small photo of a man in a hooded sweatshirt with a striped scarf. "That's him."

Jordan peered over my shoulder. "That's the same scarf the guy was wearing in the club surveillance video, the one who put Cami in the back of his car."

"This man left the hospital parking lot in a white van. I was about to head over to the club and view that footage when I got your call. I have a zoomed-in image of the scarf, and you can see some initials stitched into the material, but it's grainy. Tell me what you see."

I squinted. "J. D.?"

"Looks like a J. O. to me," Jordan said.

Chamberlin grunted. "I can't tell either. But I'm gonna show this to Joel Dominguez's parents first thing in the morning to see if they can or will identify this scarf."

"Did you get anything more from David or Erik?" I asked.

"They both lawyered up the moment I identified myself, like I figured they would. Now, if we could—" His phone rang, and he checked the caller ID. "Excuse me, this is the hospital."

Nerves knotted in my stomach as he stepped back outside to take the call. Unless he had another case involving someone in the hospital, it had to be about Cami.

God, please let it be good news.

Chamberlin disconnected the call, his expression impassive, and returned the phone to his jacket as he strode back inside to talk to us. "Camilla Chen is awake."

I sent a silent thank-you heavenward and turned to Marx. "We're gonna go to the hospital to see Cami. If it's not too much trouble, would you mind taking Riley home for me?"

Marx flicked a glance at Jordan, his manner both questioning and demanding.

"I'll be by her side until she's in her apartment with the door triple locked," Jordan assured him.

"Then yes, I'll drop Riley at your apartment. Should I bring clothes to stay the night?"

I grabbed Riley's leash from the hook on the wall and passed it to him. "Only if you really miss my lumpy couch."

"As it so happens, I don't."

If someone came lurking around my apartment tonight, I suspected Spencer would greet them before they could so much as trample one of his freshly planted flowers.

Marx clipped Riley's leash to his collar, and my canine grinned with excitement at the prospect of going outside. "Call me when you're home so I know you're safe. I don't care how late it is."

"I will."

He kissed the top of my head and followed Sam and Chamberlin out. I shrugged on my jacket and grabbed my cell and knapsack. Hopefully, Cami would be willing to speak with us. We needed to find out what she knew about her kidnapper, and someone was going to have to break the devastating news that her best friend betrayed her.

35

I sat on the hallway floor outside Cami's hospital room, staring at the colored specks on the tile as minutes dragged by. Jordan watched the closed door from his position against the opposite wall.

The officer had slipped away for a bathroom and coffee break while Chamberlin was in the room interviewing Cami.

"Still hurt?" Jordan asked, tipping his chin toward my right wrist.

I hadn't realized I was rubbing at it, my thumb unconsciously tracing the pale scars. I drew my knees into my chest. "Not so much. The ibuprofen and ice pack helped with the swelling."

He abandoned his position by the wall and came to sit beside me. "I'm talking about the scars."

I had told him the story behind those permanent marks once, and I could see by the glimmer of sadness in his eyes that he hadn't forgotten.

"No, they don't hurt," I said, tugging my sleeves over my wrists. "The whole van thing has me thinking about the past. Ollie was gonna use zip ties to restrain me. I've only ever been zip-tied one time before."

A moment of silence stretched before he said softly, "I'm sorry."

"For what? Being there for me to plow into when crazy people were chasing me? Making me feel safe afterward so I didn't have a panic attack? Or was it the chai tea you made for me but forgot to add sugar to? Because you should definitely be sorry for all of that. It's unforgivable."

He rested his head back against the wall and smiled. "How could I forget the sugar?"

I gave a theatrical sigh. "It's like you don't know me at all." I tried to keep a straight face, but a quiet laugh snuck out.

The hospital room door clicked open, and a woman in dress slacks and a wrinkled blouse emerged, a badge from children's services hanging around her neck. Chamberlin followed, disappointment pulling at the corners of his mouth.

"I'm sorry, Detective," the woman said, as he pulled the door shut. She scraped graying strands of hair behind her ears. "Runaways aren't very trusting, and after all she's likely been through, I'm not surprised she doesn't want to speak with either of us. Authority figures are the enemy."

"I'm trying to help her, not convict her of something," Chamberlin grumbled.

"I know. There's a chance she'll be more open after her mother arrives. If you decide you want to try again before that, call me and I'll try to be here to facilitate."

She passed him a card and offered us a smile laced with fatigue before walking away. My caseworker had always been exhausted, too, but I had never reflected on why until now. Maybe her workload had been too heavy, the families and children too difficult to deal with, the suffering of others too disheartening.

I should reach out to Keri.

Maybe it would comfort her to know that one of the children she worked with for years had landed on her feet. I didn't end up in prison, prostitution, or a grave from an overdose like so many others.

Jordan stood and offered me a hand up. My stiff, aching body protested, but I let him help me to my feet.

I tugged my sweater back down over my jeans. "I'm guessing it didn't go well."

"No matter how I try to approach her, she won't talk to me," Chamberlin said.

"She's been through a lot."

Chamberlin considered me. "As I understand it, you've been through similar circumstances. Rough home life, time on the street."

"Kidnapped?" I offered when he paused.

He dipped his head in acknowledgment. "I wasn't gonna say it, but yes, it crossed my mind."

"What are you getting at?" Jordan asked.

"Ms. Chen might be more forthcoming with someone she can relate to, someone nonthreatening."

When both men looked at me, my gaze bounced between them. "As in *me* someone?" I shook my head reflexively. "I don't know how to interview a victim."

I had only ever been on the other side of that questioning. Granted, it had happened often enough that I should have the entire interview script memorized. But I didn't.

"Just do what you do best," Jordan suggested.

"Eat marshmallows?"

He grinned. "The other thing you do best. You have this way of making people feel comfortable and cared about simply by being you. She might open up without you having to ask a bunch of questions."

I doubted she would trust me any more than she trusted Chamberlin and the social worker, but I could at least check on her.

I took a moment to scrounge up some nerve and then pushed into the hospital room. My sneakers, still damp from the puddle, squished across the tile, every step dredging up doubt—what if I said the wrong thing, asked too many questions or not enough questions, or forgot to ask about important details?

Be a friend, not an interrogator, I told myself as I approached the bed.

"Hi, Cami."

Her head lolled toward me, her eyes glazed and her lips chapped. She blinked at me, confusion puckering the edges of her black eyebrows. "You're not Hope. Who are you?"

"I'm Holly."

"Are you another social worker?"

"No, nothing like that." If I told her I was a private investigator, would she confuse me with the police? It might inspire distrust, and it wasn't worth the risk. "Someone came to me and asked me to find you when you went missing. She gave me this." I wiggled the worn photo from my bag and handed it to her.

She stared at it, her blink lethargic, almost drugged. "Where's Hope?"

"Um . . . we think . . ." The words refused to leave my tongue. I couldn't tell her that her best friend was involved with her kidnapper, not when she was in this condition. "I think she's with the man who took you."

She squeezed her eyes shut, a silent expression of grief. "You have to find her."

"We're trying, but we don't know anything about the man she's with. Can you tell me anything about him?"

"I don't remember his face. He had . . ." She gestured to her mouth and nose. "A scarf and a hood."

"Do you remember anything after what happened in the alley?"

Tears gathered in her eyes, and she looked at the bruise in the crease of her arm. "They . . ." Her breath hitched. "They drugged me."

I tucked my fingers into hers. "I'm sorry they did that to you. You didn't deserve it." Hopefully, the video footage from the club would be enough evidence to convict those men, no matter how much money they had to throw at lawyers.

"My dad died of an overdose." A wet spot spread across her pillow as the tears flowed down the side of her face. "I'm afraid of drugs."

That was what she'd been trying to tell the men, when she started shouting about her dad. She didn't want to die like he did.

I squeezed her hand. "You're safe now, and you're gonna be fine."

She licked her dry lips. "I don't know how I got there, but . . . there was a room. With blue walls, and a . . ."—she twirled her finger in the air—"big swirl on the ceiling."

That didn't sound like a house under construction. Painted walls and stylish plaster on the ceiling suggested a completed building, which meant the list Jordan was compiling of stalled construction projects would be useless.

"Did the man hurt you at all?" I asked, bracing for her answer. I wasn't sure I could stomach the details.

"I don't know. I don't think so. I didn't really see him after that first time. He left water and food, but it made me . . . really tired."

He must've drugged the water to keep her sedated, which would explain why he didn't bother to restrain her. He trusted the sedative would be enough.

"I tried to get out of the room, but the door was locked. I wanted to tell him I needed my insulin, but I kept . . . falling. I was so dizzy and . . . sick."

"Did he talk to you?"

"There was a voice, when he was cleaning my head." She grazed the bandage with her fingers. "He said, 'This isn't personal. It's not even about you.'"

A commotion erupted in the hall, and a woman's distraught voice cut through Jordan's and Chamberlin's calm tones.

"No, you let me see her right now!" A stocky black woman shoved her way into the room. "Cami."

Cami's eyes widened a fraction, and there was a sliver of hope mixed with the fear in her voice. "Mom?"

I stepped aside as the woman rushed to the bedside.

"Oh, my baby. My baby girl." She gathered her daughter into her arms, and Cami rested her chin on her mom's shoulder, her worried gaze on the now open doorway.

I watched for her stepdad, too, ready to step between him and the bed, but it was Jordan who appeared. He gave a slight shake of his head, and I relaxed.

"Are you okay? Who did this to you?" Cami's mom demanded, taking a visual inventory of her daughter.

"I'm okay."

Her mom released a shaky breath. "I want you to know that there have been some changes. I moved to a new town, and I finally worked up the courage to leave Peter."

Cami's breath hitched. "He's gone?"

"He's gone, baby, and I am . . ." She couldn't stop touching Cami's face as she cried. "I am so, so sorry I didn't leave him sooner. I'm so sorry."

Cami began to sob as she sagged weakly against her mom. "I wanna come home, Mom. Can I? Can I come home?"

"Of course you can come home."

I slipped out of the room as they cried and clung to each other. My own eyes stung with tears, and I blinked them back as I rejoined the men in the hall.

I relayed the details I'd managed to get, then turned to Chamberlin. "Did you get Cami's blood tests back?"

He nodded. "There were traces of heroin as well as a heavy duty prescription sleep aid with a name I can't pronounce."

"He used his own sleep aid to keep her drugged?" Jordan asked.

"More than likely."

"I wonder if Peter Killinger has a prescription for it," Jordan said. "His marriage falling apart could've sent him off the deep end, and he might've come after Cami."

I doubted that. "She said the man told her this wasn't about her, and after everything that happened tonight, I think it's got more to do with Hope."

Chamberlin's eyebrows pinched. "It's time you filled me in on the events this evening."

"Hope came by the agency," I began, launching into her visit, the attempted kidnapping, and the conversation I overheard.

The wrinkles on Chamberlin's face deepened as he absorbed the details. "Ollie could be a pet name that has nothing to do with his legal name, but I'll check into it."

"What about Hope?" I asked.

"I'll see what I can dig up on her first thing in the morning. Maybe we'll make some headway before she and her partner try to grab another woman."

"You don't know that she's his partner."

"You would be surprised how often a wife or girlfriend is complicit in the victimization of other women, Ms. Cross. Because they're desperate for the love and attention a man promises, because they're subservient to him, and sometimes because they enjoy the thrill as much as he does. It's twisted and it's sad, but it's reality."

I didn't want to believe that, but something Hope said about Tyler's father flitted through my mind. She'd slept with him because he told her he loved her, and she'd been desperate to believe it. She'd chosen not to abort her son because she wanted someone to love her. Could another man have used her desperation for love to manipulate her?

But there was so much about that theory that didn't make sense, starting with the fact that she didn't approve of him taking Cami. If they were partners in crime, how did that work?

Chamberlin stuffed his notes into his pocket. "I suggest we all try to get some rest tonight and hit the ground running in the morning."

I blew out a flustered breath and sagged back against the wall as he walked away.

Jordan leaned beside me. "You okay?"

"I'm not ready to believe Hope's been playing us this whole time. I can't accept that, not without proof."

"You told me yourself, she's not like you. She's crossed lines to survive that you never would, so who's to say where that ends? I know you empathize with her, but we don't know her or what she's capable of."

"I know," I said, but I had seen the longing in her eyes for a better life. A nurse breezed past us into the hospital room, and I looked up at Jordan. "Do you think Chamberlin will arrest the guys who attacked Cami outside the club?"

"He strikes me as the kind of guy who doesn't give free passes to anyone, no matter how much money there is in their bank account."

The nurse's bemused voice came from the hospital room. "Who wrote this? Did either of you write this?"

Curious, I popped my head into the room to find the nurse staring at the dry erase board on the wall intended for staff use only. Someone had written a message in black marker:

Help me, Nancy.

My heart skipped. Jordan questioned the nurse about who had been in the room and when, but I knew who left that message—the only person who called me Nancy.

I pulled out my phone and called Hope's number. It took a moment to connect, and then the trash can beside the door began to ring.

Oh no.

I reached into the otherwise empty can and pulled out a pink cell phone, my thumb grazing the screen and bringing it to life. A picture of Hope and her son appeared.

I ended my incoming call and saw the most recent one she'd received. It was from Cami's number.

"Jordan." I showed him the screen, and his brows dipped as he studied it.

"I didn't see Cami's phone in the alley, and there was no place to stash it in her clothes, which means either someone found it or the kidnapper has it."

"Why call Hope?"

"That's a good question, especially since the call lasted just shy of two minutes. It wasn't an accidental dial. Whoever was on the other end of this line had every intention of talking to her."

And the call was at 7:30, well before Hope came to speak with me at the agency. My attention drifted back to the message on the whiteboard and then to the doorway, where the uniformed officer's elbow appeared. He was back at his post.

I took the phone from Jordan and gave it to the officer with instructions to pass it along to Chamberlin. After a quick explanation, I started down the hall toward the exit.

Jordan jogged to catch up with me. "You wanna tell me where we're going in such a hurry?"

He wasn't going to like the answer to his question, but there was only one place I could think to go to get more information.

"Hope's apartment."

36

*J*ordan scanned the encroaching shadows for threats as we huddled on Hope's patio.

"I'm not sure this is a good idea, Holly."

I wasn't sure it was a good idea either, but after finding the message on the whiteboard, what other option was there?

I reached between the bars and pounded on Hope's apartment door with the side of my fist. "If Hope really does need help, then maybe we can find answers here. Sally might be able to tell us something."

The babysitter was supposed to bring Tyler home so he could play with his own toys and sleep in his own bed, so she should be here.

"I know you don't think I should trust Hope, but I have to follow my instincts," I said.

"She helped a man try to kidnap you two hours ago, so no, I don't think you should trust her."

"She left a message asking for help."

"We don't know who wrote that note on the whiteboard."

"She calls me Nancy Drew, and she addressed the message to Nancy."

Jordan sighed. "Even if she did leave that message, if she truly needed help, why not say something when she came to the agency afterward?"

"I don't know." The possibilities flitted through my head until a detail I had glossed over at the Agency sharpened. "The phone."

"What phone?"

"When she came to tell me to back off the case, she had a phone in her hand, but she left hers in the hospital trash can."

"She picked up a burner."

"Or he called her at the hospital, told her to toss her phone, and had her meet him somewhere so he could give her a phone he could monitor."

Jordan couldn't hide the skepticism from his voice. "If she's not complicit, why would he give her a phone at all?"

"So he could listen in. When we were talking in the lobby of the agency, there was someone outside walking their dog. I heard it bark. And then I heard the exact bark again, but faint like . . . an echo."

Thought lines creased his forehead. "An echo like what comes through the phone speaker when a caller is close by."

"Yes. I think he was on the other end of the line, listening to make sure she didn't say anything he didn't want her to. And considering I could hear the dog from the lobby *and* coming through her phone . . ."

"The person on the other end was right outside the agency." Jordan bit back a curse at the realization.

"I don't think she was leading me into a trap, Jordan. I think when she failed to convince me to drop the case, and I followed her, he followed me. And then I saw the van he's been driving, the bullet holes linking him to Dorina's attempted kidnapping, the license plate."

"But what could he be holding over her to force her to help him?"

Both of our gazes drifted to the smashed sucker on the sidewalk, and I said, "The safety of the person she cares for more than anything in this world."

Concern rippled across Jordan's face. He'd been performing magic tricks for that little boy hours ago, delighting in his laughter and wonder. He hammered on the door with the side of his fist, mindless of any complaints it would draw at this hour, while I squeezed between the bushes and the building to peek through the window.

I squinted through slatted blinds at the dim interior, my breath fogging the glass. The place was tidy, except the glass of spilled milk on the floor.

"Jordan."

I leaned, straining to see more, and spotted a handful of scattered orange slices. Jordan crunched through the mulch and peered over my head, tension threading through his voice. "We need to call the police."

"For spilled food?" I wedged my fingers under the windowpane and heaved, but it didn't budge.

"They can do a wellness check."

"*We're* doing a wellness check right now. I'm not waiting for them." I stumbled out of the bushes and back to the front door, wiggling the knob. Locked. "I'm going around back."

I jogged through the alley toward the back of the building, puddles splashing around my feet. I rounded the building and found the back door that led into the kitchen. Also locked.

I slapped the door in frustration. Something was wrong—I could feel it in the pit of my stomach—but I couldn't get inside. I backed away from the door, and something crinkled beneath my shoe. I lifted my foot off the tangle of plastic wrap, tape, and cardboard.

Was that a plastic-wrapped pizza box?

My gaze darted to the hole in the kitchen wall. Someone had ripped through Hope's makeshift covering and dragged it into the alley, leaving an opening into the apartment.

She'd been worried it would leave her vulnerable to another burglary, but I had a feeling something much worse than a burglary had happened here.

"Crap," Jordan breathed, when he saw the uncovered hole. He pulled out his phone to report the break-in.

An overturned bucket had been pushed up against the building to use as a step stool, and I climbed up to see into the kitchen. Except for a nightlight in the hallway, darkness consumed the interior.

"Hello!" I shouted.

A muffled sound drifted back to me as Jordan explained the situation to the dispatcher. It might've been a cry, but it was nearly drowned by ambient noise.

"I think someone might be hurt." I planted my hands on the boards that had been used to frame in the window and hefted myself up, ignoring the twinge in my wrist.

"Holly, you can't go in there." Jordan motioned me out of the opening. "Hop down."

I tucked my legs into my chest and then swung them out the other side, dropping into the kitchen. When Jordan released a frustrated sigh, I replied, "You said hop down."

"You know that's not what I meant."

I ignored his exasperation as I wiped my hands on my puffy coat and then searched for the light switch. He ended the call with the dispatcher and pulled himself up into the window frame, contorting to fit through the narrow passage.

He landed beside me with a grunt and rolled his shoulder. "If a man came in and out this way, he can't be very big."

"If it was my would-be kidnapper, he's not. He's bigger than me, but Sam could flick him off his feet."

"That could be why he had so much trouble subduing you and Dorina." He drew his gun, keeping it trained on the floor. "Anyone in here?"

A muffled whimper came from deeper inside the apartment.

"Stay behind me," Jordan said, quashing my urge to dart past him and help whoever was in need. He took the lead with me on his heels.

The desperate plea led us to the bathroom door, and Jordan rested a hand on the knob. Bracing for any threats that might be inside, he flung it open.

My heart skipped at the sight.

A woman lay on her side on the floor, arms behind her back, duct tape wound around her head and ankles.

I tried to slip past Jordan to help her, but he nudged me back. Stepping around the bound woman, he trained his gun on the closed shower curtain, and then whipped it open.

Empty.

"Okay." He stepped out of the bathroom so I could squeeze in.

I dropped to my knees beside the babysitter. "You're gonna be okay. I'm gonna try to get you free, okay?"

Fear and relief glittered in her liquid brown eyes as I rummaged through my knapsack for my box cutter. I pushed out the blade, locking it in place.

"I'm gonna check the rest of the apartment. Shout if you need me," Jordan said. He disappeared from the doorway, his footsteps almost silent as he moved from room to room.

I doubted he was going to find Tyler nestled beneath his blankets, hugging a stuffed dinosaur.

I readjusted on my knees. "Try to stay still."

I pulled at the tape in her hair, loosening it so I could slice through it with the blade. When the last fiber gave, I peeled it from her face, wincing as I ripped out strands of her hair.

She sucked in a breath before releasing a sob.

I leaned over her to find plastic binding her wrists behind her back. Nausea pooled in the pit of my stomach, and sweat slicked my palms. The memory of sawing through my own restraints with a pair of scissors pushed to the front of my mind.

But I couldn't let myself fall into that memory and leave this woman in this position. Wiping my sweaty hands on my jeans, I began cutting at the zip tie, careful not to nick her wrists.

"Who did this to you? Did he hurt you?"

She released another trembling breath. "He was wearing a mask. I was in the bathroom when I heard a noise. I thought it was Tyler messing around in the kitchen, but when I opened the door

318

to come out, there was a man. He shoved me back inside and tied me up at knifepoint." She whimpered and stretched her wrists as I went to work on her feet. "We were only back from the hospital for a couple of hours before he broke in."

That meant she'd been lying here, tied up, for about four hours.

A sound came from behind me, and I whirled toward the doorway with the box cutter.

Jordan held up his hands. "There's no one else here." His gaze dipped to the mutilated zip tie on the floor, and his eyes shimmered with compassion when he looked back at me. "We're good."

I tucked away my tiny blade, heartbeat staggering back to a normal rhythm. "Tyler?"

Jordan's jaw hardened. "Gone."

Sally pushed herself into a sitting position against the vanity cabinet, rubbing at her raw wrists. "He took him. He grabbed the Benadryl from the medicine cabinet, and I think he put some in Tyler's Kool-Aid. They hung around for fifteen minutes or so, and I heard Tyler say he was sleepy."

The man could easily maneuver Tyler out the kitchen opening and into his van if the boy was half-asleep from Benadryl.

Fresh tears dripped down Sally's face. "Why did he take him? What am I gonna tell Hope?"

I suspected Hope already knew. She'd been at the hospital when this man broke in and took her son, and it was around that time that she received the call from Cami's number. I could imagine the caller informing her that he had her child, a terrifying revelation that would spur Hope to do whatever was necessary to save her little boy.

. . . .

I sat on the couch beside Sally, gripping one of her hands in mine. The poor girl was a wreck and working her way through an entire travel pack of tissues.

Officers milled around the apartment, speaking in hushed tones as they searched for evidence to point them in the man's direction. Jordan had led an officer around back to explain our part.

Chamberlin stepped through the open front door. The expression on his face when he saw me on the couch was hard to read, but there may have been a sliver of exasperation.

The man had known me for half a day, and I was already on his last, sleep-deprived nerve.

He motioned for me to join him, and I had a feeling I was about to be scolded for interfering or trespassing or some other lecture-worthy offense. I released Sally's hand and rose to meet the detective by the front door.

He scratched at the bristles on his chin. "While I appreciate you helping that young lady over there, you are not a cop, and you walked into a potentially dangerous situation."

"Actually, we sorta fell into it. Through the hole where the window used to . . ." I trailed off when he stared at me with an unamused expression. I cleared my throat and folded my arms. "Sorry if we complicated anything."

"We can work around it this time. But it's best if civilians leave the police work to the police, simply because we're better equipped to handle it. Your best plan of action in situations like this is to call 911 and wait somewhere far from danger."

"Tried that," Jordan said as he returned.

I rolled my eyes. There was zero chance I would leave an innocent person bound and gagged in terror for another ten or fifteen minutes until the *official* help arrived.

"I see she's not easily persuaded," Chamberlin replied.

"Nope. If there's even a one percent chance she can save someone in distress, she'll take it."

"I suppose it's a good thing I'm learning what to expect now, since I'm sure our paths will cross in the future," Chamberlin said, and I had no doubt he was dreading the day our paths crossed again.

"How was he even able to get in through the alley? Wasn't forensics collecting evidence from where Cami was dumped?" Jordan asked.

"They finished up about thirty minutes before this happened. More than likely, he was waiting for them to clear out so he could find a way in."

"Hope had nothing to do with this. She was still at the hospital when he broke in," I pointed out.

"I know. The officer posted on Ms. Chen's room filled me in on her upsetting phone call and abrupt exit. He thought it was odd that she left, since she'd told him a few minutes before that she planned to stay until Ms. Chen regained consciousness, which, as you know, didn't happen until after nine p.m."

"We're on the same page now, right? Hope is a victim, not an accomplice," I said.

"With the abduction of her son and the phone call that rattled her, it's clear this man is pulling the strings," Chamberlin said.

I narrowed my eyes at his choice of words. That wasn't the same thing as "she's innocent." He was still clinging to his suspicion that she was involved with the kidnapper.

"Can you tell where the call came from?" Jordan asked.

"It originated from the cell towers in this area, and we were able to track Ms. Chen's phone here, but it hasn't been—"

"Detective." A male officer stepped up to the doorway without entering the house and held up an evidence bag with a glittery cell phone in the bottom. "Found it in the dumpster around back."

Chamberlin grimaced and nodded his thanks. "I suspected as much. He took the boy, made the call, and dumped the phone."

"What are you gonna do about Tyler?" I asked.

"An AMBER Alert has already been issued, but if the information passed along to me from the officer you spoke with is accurate, then the child's been missing going on five hours. Finding him won't be easy."

"The kidnapper probably used the van. Are you guys still searching for it?" I asked.

"It's been located. Forensics is scouring it for evidence now. If the boy was in there, we'll find something. There's no way he had time to clean it before he dumped it."

"Where did he dump it?"

Chamberlin stared at me, visibly debating how much he was willing to share. "A patrol officer located it in the driveway of an off-the-market rental property. No one appears to be in the house, so we're reaching out to the property owners for permission to search the premises."

Permission? A child had been abducted, and they were waiting around for someone to say they could go in?

"What's the address?" I asked, as innocently as I could manage.

The first hint of a smile curved Chamberlin's lips. "I'm afraid I can't tell you that. You might drive over there and accidentally fall through another window."

Jordan tried to hide his smile.

"I appreciate the information you've both provided. I'll follow up if I have questions. You two are free to head home and get some sleep."

Chamberlin walked over to the couch and sat beside Sally, pulling a travel pouch of tissues from inside his jacket. He offered them to her, and she accepted them with a shaky hand as she crumpled her last tissue in her fist.

I didn't agree with Chamberlin's assumptions about Hope, but at least he was kind and patient. Hopefully, he was as good at discovering the truth and solving cases as Marx was.

37

I stared out the passenger window, my thoughts whipping by as fast as the streetlights as we cruised toward my apartment.

I couldn't wrap my mind around the man in the mask. He had tried to abduct four people, but only succeeded in taking two, and he left Cami in a public alley where she would be found. He had two women incapacitated and at his mercy, but he didn't abuse either of them.

What was his motivation?

I tapped my fingers on the passenger door in growing frustration.

"You're trying to work things out in your head, aren't you?" Jordan's question drew me from my thoughts.

"How can you tell?"

He pulled his eyes from the road to look at me. "Your lips quirk to one side and you squint, like you're trying to intimidate your thoughts into obedience."

Relaxing my face, I admitted, "They're unfortunately not intimidated. There are so many questions, and I can't work out the answers."

"We'll figure it out."

"In time?"

His expression turned grim. "He hasn't killed anyone."

Yet. The word hung unspoken at the end of that statement. Cami had almost died. He may not have intended to kill her, but kidnapping her and leaving her trapped with no access to her medication nearly had.

"The question nagging at me is, what does he want with Hope?" Jordan turned onto another street. "Everyone he's targeting is someone she's connected to or cares about, which means this is somehow about her. She's a single mother with no money, no valuable connections, who works as a prostitute. Why is he so interested in her?"

"Maybe he was one of the guys who paid for her time, and now he's got some fantasy in his head that they're something more. Maybe he wants her all to himself."

He let out a skeptical grunt. "If he wanted to eliminate her friends to have her all to himself, he could've killed them. Kidnapping them doesn't accomplish that."

"Maybe it's not about some twisted sense of love. Maybe Hope was wrong when she said she didn't have any enemies."

"She was pretty adamant."

"Yeah, but just because you're unaware of something doesn't mean that *something* doesn't exist. I had no idea I had Edward as an enemy until he tried to kill me."

"You had amnesia. She doesn't. If she knew there was someone who might come after her, wouldn't she have said something?"

I shifted in my seat to face him. "She left her childhood behind when she ran away. She could've left behind bad relationships that, over the past five years, evolved from bad to what we're dealing with now."

"I suppose five years of bitterness could grow into hatred, even a desire for revenge, but what could she possibly have done when she was fourteen years old?"

"Killed someone."

Jordan jerked the steering wheel on reflex, and then straightened it, glancing at me. "She killed someone?"

Oh, I must've forgotten to share that detail after everything that happened.

"That's what *he* accused her of doing. I thought it was an offhand remark, a jab, when he told her that Cami wasn't her best friend, that she *killed* her best friend."

"You think there's any truth to it?"

"I don't know. I think the evidence points to them knowing each other before all this started. The Connecticut connection, her calling him by name. And she told me that the only other best friend she had was a girl named Livy, back before she ran away, and something happened to her."

"Something like what?"

"She didn't give me specifics, but there was so much sadness and grief around the memory of her friend. She mentioned an accident, and that Livy's family would never forgive her."

Jordan tapped a thumb on the steering wheel. "Accident or not, this guy may blame her. We need to find out what happened to Livy. It might help us identify this guy."

"But all we have is a nickname and a state."

"Hope told you she ran away when she was fourteen, right? If the death of her friend was a catalyst for her running away, we're looking for the tragic or suspicious death of a teenage girl in Connecticut in 2012, most likely named Olivia. It might take a while, and maybe nothing will come of it, but it's worth a shot."

Jordan guided the car into an opening at the curb in front of my apartment complex.

Concern darkened his expression when he noticed the light shining through my kitchen window. "Are you expecting company?"

"Marx must've forgotten to turn off the light after he dropped Riley off," I said as I unfastened my seat belt. "Do you think Sam could find out anything about the house where the van was found?"

"I'll text him. But even if he finds the address, we can't go there. If the police have it cordoned off, there would be legal repercussions for trespassing."

I sighed. If only Marx were the investigator on the case. I could usually pester some information out of him. It was going to take some work to soften up Chamberlin.

"I'm gonna see if Jace is still awake. She won't mind if I hang out for a bit and use her Wi-Fi to do some research on Livy," I said.

"Will she mind if I join you?"

"No, but she might challenge you to a pillow duel over best friend status, so enter at your own risk."

He grinned. "I think I can hold my own."

I punched out a text to her and waited. Jace was always late to bed and late to rise, but it was almost one in the morning. She might have already called it a night, which was what my body wanted to do. Unfortunately, there were too many questions buzzing around in my mind for me to sleep.

She sent a reply instantly.

"We're good to go."

Jordan rounded the car to open my door, and I looped the strap of my bag over my head as I climbed out. My feet were as heavy as cement blocks as we climbed the steps to the main apartment building, and by the time we reached the top floor, I regretted dismissing Jordan's suggestion to take the elevator.

Jace whipped open her apartment door, greeting us in blue plaid pajama bottoms and a Star Wars T-shirt with an ugly green toad creature on it. "Greetings, bestie, and . . . guy who randomly tags along."

I grinned and walked in, Jordan trailing behind.

"Is this research you need to do about your missing girl?" Jace asked, swinging the door shut.

"Related to it." I plopped onto her couch and wiggled my laptop from my knapsack. It automatically connected to the familiar Wi-Fi, and I folded my legs, nestling the computer into my lap.

"Who wants coffee?" Jace asked, then pointed at me. "Obviously not you."

"I'll take decaf, if you have it." Jordan dropped onto the couch at the far end, giving me space to stretch out if I wanted to.

"*If* I have decaf? I have one addiction," Jace began. "It involves every flavor and caffeine-level of coffee available."

"And shoes," I put in.

"And shoes," she conceded. She spun and wheeled into her kitchen to brew a pot of grossness.

Jordan rested an ankle over his knee as he used the browser on his phone to search for any articles about Hope's childhood friend, while I scrolled on my laptop.

I skimmed an article about a fourteen-year-old girl who died in a car accident, but then I noticed the small print beneath the title. It was only from four years ago. I backed out and continued searching.

Jace wheeled out of the kitchen and rolled up to the couch with a tray of drinks in her lap. She passed me a hot tea and then held out one of the two remaining purple mugs to Jordan.

"Colleen from the library was getting rid of these, and I decided they would be perfect." Mischief teased her lips. "This one just needed a slight adjustment."

Jordan took the mug and read the writing on the side before turning it toward me, amusement in his eyes.

Engraved into the mug was the word "Besties," the twin to Jace's mug. But she'd taken black permanent marker and added a twist to Jordan's. It now read "#2 Bestie."

A laugh bubbled out of me. There were no lengths she wouldn't go to in order to assert her best-friend dominance.

Jace grinned and lifted her mug to her lips. "You can take comfort in the fact that the coffee is delicious."

"Points for creativity," Jordan said. He blew across the top of the scalding liquid once before setting aside the mug, his focus on his phone screen. "I think I've got it. Fifteen-year-old Olivia Kendrick tragically drowns in family lake."

He leaned over so I could see the screen. The state, year, and name were a match. And the anniversary of her death was tomorrow.

"See if you can find the obituary," Jordan said. "It should have her surviving family members listed."

This had to be the friend Hope lost as a child. There were too many connections for it not to be. I pulled up the obituary on my laptop.

"Olivia Kendrick, fifteen, is survived by her mother, Amelia, and her father . . . Oliver Kendrick."

"I'm guessing he goes by Ollie."

What had Hope overheard her friend's father say? That he blamed her for the accident and their lives would've been better without her in them?

Jordan's phone vibrated with an incoming call. Going on two in the morning, there was only one person it could be, and I wanted to hear what he had to say.

Jordan answered. "Hey, Sam." Silence stretched as he listened, offering a grunt of acknowledgment every now and then. "Okay. Thanks." He darkened his phone screen, his expression grave.

"What is it?"

"The house where they found the van is handled by a management company. They received permission to search it. Someone's been squatting there, and they found a room upstairs with blue walls and a swirl of plaster on the ceiling."

"The room Cami described."

"There's evidence she was kept there. Her shoes, a bloodstained rag. But they also recovered a green stuffed dinosaur in the room."

My heart squeezed. "Tyler."

The man had kept both of his victims there, but after I saw the van and escaped, he must've abandoned the vehicle and the location to stay ahead of the police. They could be anywhere now.

"There's one more thing," Jordan said. "While the property is handled by a management company, it's owned by a wealthy couple with over a hundred properties throughout the surrounding states. Amelia and Oliver Kendrick."

Was it smart or reckless for Oliver to use one of his own properties to hold his victims? It was less likely that someone would stumble across them, and in the case of discovery, he could use the fact that the house was vacant to deflect blame: *Of course my prints are in the property I own, but it's been vacant, and anyone could've trespassed.*

"We have to go talk to them," I said. "If Oliver has Hope and Tyler, he could be holding them in any one of those hundred properties. And the police will need to do interviews, get warrants, and worry about the whole jurisdiction thing."

"I know, but we can't leave Chamberlin out of the loop. This is his investigation. I'll call him before we head out first thing in the morning."

"But morning could be too late."

"For all we know, *now* could be too late. We can't base our decision on that. And we're both exhausted. I can't make a two-hour drive to Connecticut at two in the morning, and if there's any chance these people are innocent, we're not banging on their door at four a.m. on the anniversary of their daughter's death."

All good points.

"I'm gonna use the restroom, and then I'll walk you home." Jordan pushed up from the couch and disappeared down the hall.

I closed my laptop and tucked it back into my bag. "So how are things with you and Sam?"

"Good. There haven't been any promises of forever made yet, but a girl can hope," Jace said, a twinkle in her eyes as she sipped her coffee.

Muffled ringing came from the bathroom, followed by Jordan's hushed voice. Had Sam discovered something important that he wasn't comfortable relaying through text?

I strained to overhear the one-sided conversation, but all I could make out was something about a decision that endangered lives. Jordan emerged from the bathroom a few minutes later, his expression grim.

"Is everything okay?" I asked.

"That was David."

"What did he want?" Especially at this hour.

"To clear his conscience."

"He withheld information, didn't he?"

"Yep." Jordan sighed and gripped the back of the couch. "Turns out we were right, and he was worried his friend Joel might be behind Cami's kidnapping."

Jordan explained how Joel's behavior leading up to the kidnapping seemed more strange than suspicious—bailing on planned activities, vague allusions to a girl he liked but wouldn't name. It was after the kidnapping, when he responded to David's text with, "I'll be out of touch for a while. I'm with my girl," that David became concerned. All of that combined with the fact that Joel owned a similar car to the one the suspect drove and was conveniently absent during the kidnapping, I understood how he came to the wrong conclusion.

"Turns out Joel eloped with a female escort they used to see. He sent David a wedding photo, which he forwarded to me." He called up the image and turned his phone so I could see a smiling Joel with his arm draped around a pretty blonde woman.

"What information did David withhold?"

Jordan grimaced. "During the abduction, he snapped a picture of the kidnapper's license plate. It's blurry but legible. Once he realized his friend wasn't involved, he forwarded that to me too."

"What do we do with it?"

"*We* go to bed. Sam's gonna run it for me so I don't have to go back to the office, and we'll go from there."

I shook my head in exasperation. If David had been truthful earlier, we might've been able to identify the man and prevent Hope and Tyler from being taken. David didn't strike me as a bad person, but he was letting his so-called friends lead him down a dangerous path.

"Ready to get some sleep?" Jordan asked.

330

I gathered my things, hugged Jace, and headed home. I hated the idea of waiting until morning to speak with the Kendricks, but by the time we reached my apartment, I was minutes away from collapsing in exhaustion, and Jordan didn't look to be faring much better.

I unlocked my door. "Will you call me if you find out anything tonight?"

"I doubt we'll know anything until morning. Try to get some rest. I'll be back in about five hours so we can get an early start."

"Okay. See you in the morning."

When I stepped inside, Riley greeted me as though he hadn't seen me in days, even though it had only been hours. Sausage poked his head out of his box to acknowledge with a chortle the arrival of the food giver, then snuggled back down to sleep.

I smiled and walked to my refrigerator for a pudding cup. I opened the door and gaped at the stocked shelves that had been nearly bare this morning.

"Did I black out and rob a mini mart after breakfast?"

There was a carton of eggs, a box of butter, a jug of milk, lunch meats, and so much more. A glass sat in the center of the top shelf with a label taped to it that read, "Sweet tea for my sweet pea."

Even without the familiar nickname, I recognized Marx's chicken scratch writing instantly, and I smiled at the cute message. We were going to have to discuss him buying all these groceries and leaving them in my refrigerator, though.

I noticed a slip of notebook paper beneath the glass, and I lifted the tea to pull it out and read the soggy message. "If you can let yourself into my apartment and leave something, so can I."

I looked from the note to the groceries. "It was one marshmallow. I left *one* marshmallow." And then I'd eaten it to eliminate the evidence. I looked down at Riley, who was basking in the coolness of the open refrigerator. "Your grandpa is an over-giver. But I love him for it."

I snagged an apple to quiet the rumbling in my stomach and prepared for bed. I opened my gratitude journal, but propped against my pillows in cozy pajamas, I barely managed to put one complete thought on the page before sleep dragged me under.

38

*J*ordan's eyes were bloodshot as we started the drive to Connecticut at seven in the morning, and he had a thermos of coffee big enough to kick-start a village.

I offered to drive while he caught up on his sleep, but he only smiled and sank behind the wheel. He might've taken me up on the offer if I hadn't been yawning while I said it.

Maybe.

I studied every black car we passed, but none of the license plates matched the car from the alley. I didn't really expect them to, but I hoped.

The black sedan was registered to Amelia Kendrick, Livy's mother, but the assailant in the video footage was inarguably male. Had he driven back to Connecticut before we even knew what license plate to look for? That would explain why none of the patrol officers spotted the vehicle overnight.

We passed the "Welcome to Connecticut" sign along the side of the road, and I glanced at Jordan.

"This is our first road trip together," I pointed out.

"I'm not sure a two-hour drive qualifies as a road trip."

Two hours was long enough for me. Any more than that and I would need to take breaks to keep my claustrophobia from overwhelming me.

"Do you think Riley will be okay?" I asked.

"He's a former police dog who gets to spend the day at a precinct, surrounded by cops. He's in heaven."

I didn't want to bring Riley with us because I wasn't sure how long we would be gone, so he was spending the day with Marx and Michael. I had crouched in front of him to explain the rules of his trip to the police station before we left.

"No tackling bad guys, no biting bad guys, and no breaking your leash and chasing after weirdos." I assumed the sloppy lick to the side of my face meant we were in agreement.

Marx wasn't thrilled about our destination, and neither was Chamberlin, but we needed to speak with Mrs. Kendrick about her car, the accident that took her daughter's life, and how her husband handled the loss.

I didn't look forward to bringing up such a painful subject on the anniversary of their daughter's death, but I had a sinking feeling that Hope and her son couldn't afford for us to put it off until tomorrow.

As we neared our destination, my nerves buzzed. Neither of us had any idea what to expect from this meeting.

"At the first sign of trouble, we call the police," Jordan said, turning into the driveway. "I don't wanna take any chances."

The Kendrick home was smaller than I anticipated. A single-story brick cottage at the end of a short driveway, the yard lined by blossoming bushes.

There was no black sedan in front of the house, but it could be hidden behind one of the closed garage doors.

A woman knelt in the grass out front, tending to a beautifully arranged rose garden. At the approach of our car, she sat back on her legs and lifted her head, a wide-brim hat shading her face.

She finished pressing the dirt around a newly planted bush and then pushed to her feet to greet us as we climbed out of the car. "Can I help you?"

Jordan's warning glance reminded me to stay close as we crossed the lawn. "Are you Mrs. Amelia Kendrick?"

"I am." The woman was in her late forties, with wisps of ash-blonde hair escaping her hat. Her eyes were heavy with grief as she regarded us. "But whatever you're selling, today isn't the day for it. You can come back tomorrow."

"I wish we could wait until tomorrow, but it's important." Jordan introduced both of us as he offered her one of our business cards. "We're trying to track down a missing woman and her son, whom we believe to be in danger."

Amelia tugged off her dirt-stained gloves and took the card, scanning the information. "I'm sorry they're missing, but I don't understand what this has to do with my family."

Jordan visually scanned the windows and property. "Is your husband here?"

"He's not in any state to speak with anyone right now. Today is the anniversary of our daughter's death, and we mourn in our own ways. Planting rose bushes is what I choose to do."

"Why roses?" I asked.

"Our daughter's name was Olivia Rose, and I add a new bush every year. This one will have orange blooms, her favorite color." Tears misted her eyes, and she blinked as she fought to compose herself. "I'm sorry, I'm not sure how I can help you."

Jordan nodded to me, and I passed the photo of the girls to her, leaving it folded down the center so it only showed Hope's face. "This is the young woman we're trying to find."

Confusion creased her forehead, but it only took a second for recognition to smooth away the lines, and then her hand flew to her mouth. "Hope," she breathed through her fingers. She drank in the details of the image, touching it as though she could feel the softness of Hope's hair and the delicate planes of her face. "She's grown up so much over the past six years. Where has she been?"

"New York," Jordan said.

"And she has a child?"

"A five-year-old son."

"Five? But that means . . ."

"She was pregnant when she ran away," I confirmed.

Amelia shook her head, fingers pressed to her lips. "Please tell me the father isn't one of her mother's boyfriends. We worried about her living in the same trailer as some of those men, but she wouldn't talk to us about it."

My stomach tightened. "She told me the father was a boy from school, someone she liked."

"Good, that's better than the alternative." She lost herself in the picture again, as though longing to pull Hope through the photograph and into her arms.

There wasn't a doubt in my mind that Amelia Kendrick loved and missed Hope. But what about her husband, Oliver?

Jordan hesitated to break the moment. "I know this is a difficult day of the year for your family, but if we could ask you some questions."

Amelia inhaled sharply and nodded. "Of course. Whatever I can do to help. Please." She led us into the house and into a living room off the entryway. "Make yourselves comfortable. I'll be back in a minute."

I studied the beautiful living room. The wallpaper was a pattern of gold and green flowers that stretched all the way up to the high ceilings. Detailed engravings and delicately carved legs added elegance to every piece of furniture, and the artwork on the walls was signed.

The house might not be as big as I expected, but they had clearly funneled their money into the design.

I perused the family pictures on the wall. They all centered around their daughter—celebrating at her birthday party with her parents, grinning over her sand castle, wearing a kindergarten graduation gown, swinging alongside a little blonde girl with big brown eyes and a bright smile.

Hope.

The tinkling of ice cubes in a glass preceded the man who appeared in the arched doorway. His graying hair was mussed, stubble darkened his jaw, and the pungent scent of liquor wafted from the glass in his hand.

He was the older, grief-stricken version of the man from the birthday photo. Oliver Kendrick.

"Amelia told me we have company," he said, and there was something familiar about his voice. "Apparently, you have something important to discuss with us."

He studied us as he entered the room, and Jordan moved closer to me, keeping himself between us. He glanced at me for confirmation, but I couldn't be sure he was the man who grabbed me in the alley. Between the darkness and the ski mask, the mental image of my attacker was fuzzy.

But it had to be him, didn't it?

Oliver passed us to reach a table lined with half-empty bottles. He uncapped a bottle of liquor and poured more over the ice cubes in his glass.

"Today of all days, you feel the need to stop by," he said, a bitter edge to his voice.

"We apologize for the timing, sir," Jordan said. "But we need to talk to you about Hope Carmichael."

The man's shoulders tensed. "That's a name I haven't heard in a while." He added a little more liquid to his glass, as though to fortify himself for the impending conversation, and then recapped the bottle. "Why are you asking about her?"

"She's missing," I said.

"She's been missing for six years," he said, turning to face us. "She ran away after . . . the accident."

Was his hesitation to mention the accident because it dredged up painful memories, or did he stumble over the phrase because he believed it was more than an accident?

"Did anyone report Hope missing when she ran away?" I asked.

Oliver's lips pressed together, the tilt of his mouth tugging at a memory I couldn't quite grasp. "We were focused on our own family at the time—grieving and dealing with other issues that arose." The ice cubes clinked in his glass as he lifted it to his lips for a drink. "Gloria, her mother, never bothered to report her missing.

Not surprising. The woman has always been the epitome of selfish."

Amelia bustled into the room with a tray of glasses filled with dark liquid, her gardening hat absent and her hair swept into a tidy bun. "I hope you like sweet tea." She plucked the glass of liquor from her husband's hand and replaced it with tea.

He grimaced but didn't complain. "I was telling them about Hope's mother."

"Gloria, yes, she was . . . is . . . well . . ."

"She's irresponsible and an unfit mother," Oliver filled in, when his wife couldn't find the words to describe her. "She's been in and out of bad relationships for as long as we've known her."

Amelia's lips pinched, but she didn't disagree with her husband. "Hope used to spend more time here than she did at home. When she confided in Livy about her home life and Livy shared some of her concerns with us, we welcomed her."

She held out the tray, and I accepted a glass. The moment I took a sip, my tongue tried to curl away from the unpleasant flavor that mingled with the black tea. What did she sweeten it with, antifreeze?

"We tried to provide Hope with clothes and school supplies, but her mother would turn around and sell everything," Oliver said, his tone conveying his distaste for the woman.

"That poor child had nothing." Amelia sank onto the elegant sofa, eyes shining. "Oliver and I, we would've adopted her if we could've, but of course, that wasn't possible without getting children's services involved and dragging her mother through court. Still, when she . . ." She plucked a tissue from the box on the coffee table and dabbed at her eyes. "When Hope ran away, I felt like I lost two daughters. I don't understand why she chose to leave, especially at a time when we needed each other the most."

"She, um . . ." I glanced at Oliver as I set my glass of tea on the table. "She overheard you in the hospital after the accident, when you were upset."

An array of emotions played across Oliver's face before regret settled, and he sank onto the edge of the nearby chair.

Amelia shifted toward him on the couch, tissue clutched in her fist. "What did you say, Oliver?"

He closed his eyes. "I was angry, grieving, and I needed someone to blame. I never really thought it was her fault, but—"

Amelia sucked in a breath. "We were the only stable people in her life, and you . . . she ran away, pregnant and heartbroken, because you made her think she lost us too." She sniffled and dabbed at her nose with the tissue before turning back to us. "You said she's missing and that you're searching for her. What can we do to help you bring her home to us?"

"The problem is, we don't think she's just missing. We believe someone targeted her and took her," Jordan said. "Unfortunately, that means we can't find her by tracking her movements. We need to figure out who took her so we can track his."

Amelia paled. "Took her? Who would do something like that?"

"We believe it's someone who knows her, and judging by a comment he made to Hope before she disappeared, he's someone who knows what happened to your daughter."

"Livy's death was in the paper. Anyone who read the article knows she drowned," Oliver said.

"This person seems to think Hope killed Livy," I clarified, eyeing the man whose features were familiar but elusive.

"Are you suggesting I had something to do with this?" Red infused Oliver's face. "That I kidnapped a girl my wife and I think of as a daughter? To what end?"

Jordan held out his hands in a pacifying gesture. "We're not accusing you. We're just trying to connect the dots, and this is where the dots have led us."

Oliver leaned forward in his chair and slammed his glass of tea on the coffee table, brown liquid splashing onto the lace table runner. "We had nothing to do with whatever happened to Hope, and I've heard enough. You remember where the door is. Let yourselves out."

Amelia reached over and laid a hand on his forearm. "Oliver, please. Set aside your pride for a moment. If there's even the smallest chance they can find Hope, that we can make this right and have her in our life again, I wanna take it."

"The man who took her is driving a car registered to you." I looked at Amelia, and then to Oliver. "And Hope called him Ollie."

My words seemed to blow out the flame of Oliver's anger, and he blinked as Amelia's face paled. They exchanged a long, meaningful look, and then he said, "Call the school and find out if he's there."

Amelia scrambled off the couch and rushed from the room without explanation.

"Find out if who is where?" Jordan demanded.

"Our nephew, Julian. He attends a special school about two hours from here. We took him in when he was six, after my sister decided she couldn't handle him on her own. She left him with us and moved to France."

"What does that have to do with Ollie?" I asked.

Oliver rose from his chair. "My father's name was Oliver. When our daughter was born, we named her Olivia out of respect for him. My sister gave birth to a son after a five-month mistake with a married man, and she named him Julian Oliver. Julian for his father and Oliver for ours."

I locked eyes with Jordan. The scarf the man at the hospital had been wearing had initials stitched into the fabric: J. O. Julian Oliver.

"When we took Julian in, he wanted to be called by his middle name. In hindsight, I surmise it's because it was closer to Olivia's name, but I had called him Julian for six years. I couldn't make the transition. But the girls called him Ollie." He pointed to the picture of the girls swinging. "If you look closely, you can see him in the background, watching them swing."

I approached the photo and squinted. Inside the bushes behind the swings, the face of a young boy stared out, a hideous anger and hatred twisting his expression.

"Thirty seconds after I took that picture, Julian sprang out of the bushes and shoved Hope off the swing," Oliver said.

I turned back toward him. "Why?"

"He hated her from the moment Livy befriended her and brought her home. He viewed her as competition for Livy's attention."

"That doesn't sound normal."

"It isn't. Within the first few months of living with us, he became overly attached to our daughter, to an unhealthy and sometimes concerning degree. He followed her everywhere, insisted on being a part of everything she did. Discussing appropriate boundaries with him didn't work, so we had him evaluated. He was diagnosed with borderline personality disorder and social anxiety."

"What's borderline personality?" I asked.

"In general, I don't know. In terms of Julian, his entire identity was wrapped up in his relationship with Livy. He needed to be with her, and he had no idea how to handle being alone. And then there were the dramatic mood swings, anger, impulsive behavior. The smallest thing could set him off, and we couldn't figure out how to calm him."

"He blamed Hope for his separation from Livy even before the accident," Jordan said. "I imagine that only worsened after she died."

Oliver nodded. "Yes. And unfortunately, he was in the hospital room with me when I made that statement about Hope, and I think, in his mind, it validated his own feelings. He spiraled after the funeral and tried to kill himself. He didn't know what to do without Livy, and with his social anxiety, he couldn't form new relationships. After the suicide attempt, we had him committed for his own safety. The past six months, he seemed so well adjusted that we pulled him out of the institution and enrolled him back in private school with therapy three times a week. We thought he was improving."

Oliver opened the drawer of a cabinet, rummaging through the contents, but stilled when Jordan asked, "What happened the day Livy died?"

He released a breath and gripped the edges of the drawer. "The girls wanted space from Julian, so they paddled out to the middle of the lake and left him on the shore. They were supposed to wear life jackets, but they didn't. Amelia and I were in the garden when we heard screams, and we ran to the lake. Livy was nowhere to be seen, but Hope was struggling to stay above water. I dove in and pulled her out, and then I went back for Livy. I tried CPR, but she . . ."

Grief strangled his voice.

"I'm so sorry," I said, my heart aching at the scene of a father desperately trying to pump life back into the body of his little girl.

"I regret what I said in that hospital room. I didn't mean it. What happened that day was an accident. Hope said they were dancing to some silly pop song they were singing, and she lost her balance and fell overboard. Livy tried to help her back into the boat, but she slipped and hit her head before falling into the water herself."

Jordan frowned. "You said Julian was on the shore. Did you notice if he was wet?"

Oliver pulled a picture from the drawer and then closed it, a line between his brows. "He was, but I assumed it was because he tried to save Livy when she fell in."

He might have tried to save Livy. But he also might've swum out into the lake with the intention of knocking Hope into the water without a life jacket. That was something a jealous kid struggling with hatred and impulsive anger might do. A sideways glance at Jordan revealed that he was wondering the same.

"We still need to frame and hang this one in the other family room with the rest of his pictures, but this is Julian on his eighteenth birthday, two months ago. That's when we gave him the car." Oliver handed Jordan the picture.

"I don't recognize him." Jordan angled the picture so I could see it, and my mouth went dry.

The tilt of the boy's lips and the color and shape of his eyes were similar to Oliver's, which was why the older man looked vaguely familiar.

I knew this boy.

I had stared into those eyes in the hallway of Cami's apartment building, when the masked man fell on top of me, and I had spoken with him before. The memory of helping him gather his belongings from the café floor flashed through my mind. He had seemed so nervous and unsure of himself.

It's okay to be a little abnormal, and it's okay to struggle with things, I had told him. Not the best advice for a young man planning to kidnap three women and a child. That kind of abnormal was not okay.

"This is him. I saw him at the café when Jace and I were discussing Cami's diabetes, and he's the one who broke into her apartment. I recognize his eyes."

Amelia burst back into the room, clutching the phone to her chest. "He hasn't been at the school for the past two weeks."

"Why didn't they tell us?" Oliver growled.

"He's eighteen."

"We're paying the tuition!"

"Please," I cut in. "He has Hope and her son, and I'm afraid he's gonna hurt them. We need to figure out where he took them."

"Before he grabbed Hope, he targeted the people closest to her. He kept one of the girls in an off-the-market rental property you own in New York City," Jordan explained.

"The one our management company contacted us about in the middle of the night," Oliver said.

"They told us something about a suspicious van being parked in the driveway and the police requesting to search the house, but no one's gotten back to us about what came of the search," Amelia added. "He held a girl there against her will?"

"Until he realized the van and house might be compromised, yes," Jordan confirmed.

Oliver's face lit with understanding. "He could've moved Hope and her son to one of our other unoccupied properties. I have a list in my office. I'll be right back."

Amelia pressed a hand to her chest and closed her eyes. "Oh, Ollie, what've you done?" She curled her fingers around a cross pendant and murmured a prayer.

I paced the living room rug as we waited for Oliver to return with the list. He jogged back into the room and thrust a sheet of paper at Jordan.

"Seven vacant properties as of this morning."

My hopes sank as I peeked at the list. "He could be at any one of those locations. We'll never find her before he follows through with whatever he's planning to do."

"He's not gonna take Hope to some random house," Jordan said. "He tried to take away everyone she cares about so she would feel the loss and loneliness he felt when Livy died. And today is the anniversary of that day. He's gonna take her someplace that means something."

"The last place they were all alive together."

Jordan's attention snapped back to the grieving couple. "Where's the lake? We didn't see it when we drove up."

"We moved after Livy's death," Oliver answered. "The estate has been vacant since then. We have the property cleaned and maintained regularly, but we couldn't bring ourselves to put it on the market."

"What's the address?"

Oliver turned to his wife. "Melly."

She walked to a desk to retrieve a pen and paper. She jotted down the address and then rummaged through a nook in the desk. "My keys to all our properties are missing."

Oliver's jaw clenched. "He must've taken them when he was here for Easter. I'll get mine."

As he left the room, Amelia handed Jordan the slip of paper with the family name and business logo imprinted across the bottom. "I can hardly believe this is happening."

Oliver returned with three keys and offered them to me. "One for the main house, one for the guesthouse, one for the shed by the lake."

"Thank you." I tucked them into my jeans pocket.

"Should we call the police?" Amelia asked.

"Yes. Give them the list of addresses, including the one for the house we're going to," Jordan said.

Amelia touched my arm. "Please. Bring Hope and her little one home safe. And be gentle with Ollie. He needs help."

Her nephew needed more help than we could give him, and all I could do was assure her that we would try to keep everyone safe. But if he spiraled into a violent rage, Jordan would do whatever was necessary to protect innocent lives.

39

The address on the slip of paper led us to a rural area, down a long private drive to a house that could've doubled as a hotel. Everything appeared to be well tended, and yet there was an air of abandonment that hung over the place.

Through the large windows, I could see the plastic sheeting that covered the furniture. Amelia and Oliver had left everything behind when they downsized. Too many memories attached to this place and its contents, I supposed.

I folded my arms against the chill in the morning air and scanned the endless rows of windows for movement. "Do you think he has them in the house?"

"If this is the right place, I think he brought her here because of the lake. Let's scope out the property, and then we'll check the buildings." He closed his door with a soft click.

"You really think he's gonna kill her?"

"After everything he did leading up to this, I don't think his goal is to talk out their problems."

I couldn't wrap my mind around the idea that the skinny young man with social anxiety I met in the café, the boy who blushed when he called me pretty, could have murderous intentions.

But if he could hold a woman captive and drugged for days, kidnap an innocent child, and manhandle me into the back of his van, underestimating him based on first impressions would be a dangerous mistake.

I started around the house, noticing the old swing set that matched the photograph on the Kendricks' wall. I could almost see

Hope and Livy giggling as they pumped their legs to soar higher, racing to see who could touch the sky with their feet first.

I looked out at the endless stretch of land, beyond the fenced-in area that must've been the garden, to the guesthouse. A black car sat in the driveway.

"Jordan." I pointed to the car, but then something pulled my attention past the guesthouse to the lake. Movement on the water.

We were too far away to make out the details, but someone was rowing a boat toward the center of the lake.

"I doubt the house cleaner decided to take the boat out on a forty-degree morning," he said. "Come on."

We took off toward the lake, skating in the dew-slicked grass as the flat yard dropped into a slope. I nearly lost my footing, but Jordan snagged my arm to rebalance me. He tugged me behind the wooden shed set back from the lake.

I shot him a questioning look, and he whispered, "I saw sunlight reflect off something near his hand. Could be a watch, could be a gun."

I peered around him at the lake, which was small enough in circumference that it might be more accurate to call it a large pond. The rowboat glided toward the center, ripples expanding from the oars that Hope plunged into the water.

"That's far enough," a man said, his voice stretching across the lake to reach us. He rose in front of Hope's petite frame, back to us, and wrenched her to her feet so hard the boat rocked.

Hope staggered. "Ollie, please don't do this."

He ignored her plea as he handed her a black object. "Put this on, zipper facing me."

Puffs of steam escaped my mouth as my heart galloped in my chest. "What is that? What is he making her put on?"

"I think it's a weighted vest," Jordan said, his height allowing him to watch the scene over my head. "If she goes into the water with that on, she won't be able to swim." Jordan grabbed his phone and dialed the police.

But they weren't going to get here in time. Ollie could push her in at any moment, and she would sink to the bottom like a boulder. How far down was it? There was a pond in our hometown that was twenty feet deep in the center—more than deep enough for a person to drown.

I tuned out Jordan's one-sided conversation with the dispatcher and tried to focus on the events unfolding on the boat.

"I'm sorry for what happened to Livy. I miss her, too, every day," Hope cried. "But this won't bring her back."

Ollie zipped up the vest. "Livy was the only person who understood me, the only person who ever loved me. And she's gone because of you. You took my whole world from me, so I'm taking your whole world from you."

"Please. Please don't hurt my son."

"That's up to you." He pushed her closer to the side of the boat. "Now, climb over and get in."

Hope's chest heaved as she stared at the water, and then she curled in on herself and stepped back, shaking her head. "I can't."

"Then you don't love your son any more than you loved Livy."

"He needs me."

"He'll be better off without you." He shoved her toward the side, and she stumbled and fell forward.

I gasped and grabbed Jordan's arm, anticipating a splash, but Hope caught herself on the edge, gripping it with both hands as the boat rocked.

Anger tightened Jordan's expression at the way Ollie manhandled Hope, and he stuffed his phone back into his pocket. "The police are coming."

"We have to do something."

"I know. Let me get a better view." He inched around the shack and reappeared a moment later. "There's nothing we can use to get out there, no other boats, and the dock doesn't extend that far."

"We can swim if we have to."

"Holly, that water is freezing."

I would accept hypothermia if it meant Hope could go home to her little boy. Tyler didn't deserve to lose a mother who loved him, only to land in a foster care system that shuffled him from one neglectful placement to the next until he aged out.

"Maybe I can talk to Ollie, distract him long enough for the police to arrive," I said.

"No. We don't know if he has a gun."

"He won't shoot me." I sank more certainty into my voice than I felt. "I'm not his target any more than the other women were, and he didn't kill them."

A muscle flexed in his jaw, but he knew there was no other choice. Ollie's self-control was hanging on by a thread, and it could snap at any moment.

Jordan drew his gun from the holster. "If I see him raise a gun, the conversation's over."

"Okay." Despite the barely forty-degree temperature and the shiver of fear curling around the base of my spine, my palms were sweating as I inched out from behind the shed. "Ollie!"

He locked an arm around Hope's neck and dragged her in front of him, both of them staggering to find their balance in the unsteady boat.

I held my hands out to show him I wasn't armed. "It's me. Holly. Can we talk?"

Ollie stared at me for a beat, confused by my presence, and then he shouted, "There's nothing to talk about! You shouldn't even be here!"

"Isn't this where you were gonna bring me when you tried to put me in your van?"

"No, I was never gonna bring you here. I was gonna come back and let you go as soon as this was over."

Come back? Had he intended to keep me locked up in the house the police discovered?

I paused a few feet from the shed. "You never planned to hurt me?"

"There was no reason to."

"You didn't intend to hurt Dorina or Cami either, did you? But you didn't know about Cami's diabetes."

"I wasn't there to grab her that night. I was just watching, working things out, but then those guys in the alley . . . they were attacking her."

"You scared them off and took her."

He nodded. "But she kept getting sicker, and she was so out of it, she couldn't tell me what was wrong. I didn't know how to make her better until I heard you and your friend at the café. I tried to get her medicine from the apartment."

"You tried to save her, and you came to the hospital to check on her, not to hurt her. Even though you're angry, you still care about people."

"People are saying I dumped her in an alley, but I didn't. I thought she was dead, but I still laid her down gently where I knew she would be found."

"You have a good heart, Ollie." I stepped closer to the shore. "Yes, people got hurt, but no one is dead. You were careful not to kill anyone. Please . . . don't cross that line now."

He tightened his arm around Hope's neck, and she cried out. "No, no, she has to pay for what she did."

"It was an accident," I said.

"Stop saying that! Everyone keeps repeating that lie!" He bellowed, and I flinched. "If she had let me in the boat instead of leaving me on the shore, Livy would still be alive! I tried to find her in the water. I tried!"

Jordan shifted in the corner of my vision, but I couldn't look at him. If Ollie knew there was a man behind the shed with a gun trained on him, he might panic.

"Holly, you have to save my little boy." Hope choked on a sob. "Please, you have to take him, you have to tell him I love him."

"Nothing's gonna happen to Tyler," I assured her.

"You can't let my mom have him. She doesn't know how to love anyone, and I don't want that for him. You have to take him, Holly. Please."

My throat tightened with tears. "Ollie, please let her go. I know you're hurting, but she doesn't deserve this."

"Stop taking her side!" he yelled. "This is her fault, not mine, and there are consequences!"

He released Hope's neck and shoved her. She toppled over the edge of the boat with a scream, and her body splashed into the water about twenty feet from the shore.

No thrashing, no desperate gasps for air—she just . . . sank.

No!

I kicked off my flats, pulled my sweatshirt and knapsack over my head, and tore through the grass onto the dock, scampering barefoot across the dried, splitting boards.

"Holly, no!" Jordan's objection breezed past my ears as I jumped off the end of the dock and plunged into the lake. The icy temperature of the water snatched the air from my lungs as it closed over my head.

I thrust toward the surface, breaking through with hair plastered to my face. I dragged in a wet breath.

The sound of shoes pounding on wood interspersed with shouting voices met my ears.

"She deserves to drown like Livy!" Oliver bellowed.

"Swim back, Holly," Jordan instructed, and I caught a distorted glimpse of him through my hair as he bent over the end of the dock, hand extended. "I'll pull you out."

He would heave me out of the water, but he wouldn't leave my side to rescue Hope while Oliver was still a threat. He would prioritize my safety, and she would die.

"I have to find her," I said, spitting out water.

"Holly, pl—"

Refilling my lungs, I dove. Bubbles and leaves drifted around me as I swam deeper, searching the cloudy depths. The lake couldn't be that deep.

Darkness surrounded me, the water seeming to squeeze my throat and chest until they burned for the oxygen. It was a familiar, terrifying sensation, being deprived of air—the pressure in my head, the fire in my chest, the dots dancing in my vision.

Panic burned through me. I couldn't do this. I wasn't brave enough to . . .

Ghostly fingers reached out of the murkiness ahead of me and grasped at my hair. The last of my breath escaped my mouth in a startled cloud of bubbles.

Hope.

She was only feet in front of me, but I was out of air. I would have to come back for her. Frantic, I kicked upward. The distance stretched, and flames of desperation licked through my chest with every second, engulfing me in a fire that water couldn't extinguish.

I wasn't going to make it. I was too deep, and the water was thickening to gelatin, slowing my movements. Panic crashed into me again, and I wanted to open my mouth and gasp, but my brain locked my lips together.

Breathe and you die, dropped into the chaos of my thoughts.
God, please, please, please.

My muscles started to cramp from the cold, and I barely managed to break free of the water. I sucked in a breath, but my spasming lungs hacked it back out.

Jordan's voice stretched over the distance, asking if I was all right, begging me to get out of the water.

"I found her," I choked out.

And now I had to swim back down into liquid terror to save her. Tremors racked my body, as much from the cold as from the fear, but I dove.

The last thing I heard before going under was a creak, followed by Jordan's harsh warning. "Stop! If your feet leave that boat . . ."

A muffled bang, like a gunshot, resounded above the surface, and then a body crashed into the water above me. My heart skipped, but I didn't slow my descent.

By the time I reached Hope, she was limp on the bottom, and the bubbles coming from her nose were almost nonexistent. I turned her back toward me and unzipped the vest, sliding it from her arms.

The weight sank, stirring up sediment, and I pushed her upward, praying it wasn't too late.

Someone snaked through the brown water toward me. Ollie. I tried to swim away from him, but he snagged my foot. A knife appeared in his other hand.

I kicked, frantic, my attention swiveling between him and the sweet oxygen my lungs ached for.

Another figure peeled through the water and collided with Ollie. The two men disappeared in a flurry of bubbles. I launched upward. Jordan could take care of himself.

I hope.

I bobbed to the surface a few feet from Hope, and relief flooded me when I found her coughing and sputtering, her chin dipping in and out of the water.

"Come on." I paddled toward the edge of the lake with her alongside me, my legs and arms threatening to seize up from the cold. Hope straightened when the bottom of the lake rose up to meet our feet, and she staggered forward toward the shore, clawing her way into the grass.

I lingered in the shallows, shivering and exhausted, and stared at the glassy surface of the lake. Seconds passed, the stillness sinking fear deeper into my bones.

Where was Jordan?

The mirrored surface of the lake rippled, and I tensed with anticipation, but the mop of dark hair that emerged didn't belong to my friend.

Ollie pawed at the side of the boat, gasping as he pulled himself up and over. He landed on the bottom with a wet thud.

I hadn't seen the knife in his hand. Where was the knife?

A horrifying possibility struck me, and I looked back at the water, half-expecting to see blood bubbling to the surface. What if he'd stabbed Jordan and left him to bleed out or drown on the bottom of the lake?

I shouldn't have left him down there alone. I needed to go back for him. My feet slid in the muck as I inched further from the shore, but before I could venture deeper, Jordan surfaced in a spray of water.

My cry of relief twisted into a scream when Ollie grabbed one of the oars and swung it at Jordan's head. Jordan dipped back under, and the thick wooden oar skipped off the water. The boat sloshed from Ollie's efforts, and he staggered, letting out a frustrated growl.

He plunged both oars into the water and began to row, the boat turning toward the patch of shore where Hope and I huddled.

Jordan bobbed up again and tracked the movement of the boat. "Go, Holly!"

Heart in my throat, I scrambled out of the lake, slipping and dragging myself through mud and algae. I urged my body to move faster, but my limbs were heavy and sluggish.

I collapsed on top of Hope, who had curled into the fetal position, her entire body trembling. As much as my body wanted to curl into a ball and rest alongside her, I knew we would die— either by Ollie's hand or hypothermia.

"Get up. We h-have to g-get up."

Grabbing my discarded sweatshirt, I stumbled to my feet and pulled at Hope's arms and clothes, trying to peel her off the ground before it was too late.

40

The mud sucked at my bare feet as I half ran, half stumbled toward the nearby guesthouse, fingers intertwined with Hope's as I dragged her along behind me.

The icy water left both of us stiff and uncoordinated, and we stumbled over rises and dips in the ground, bumping into each other.

"S-slow down," Hope protested.

I glanced toward the lake to see Ollie rip one of the oars from the boat and charge up the hill after us. Nope, slowing down wasn't an option.

I dragged her around to the front of the guesthouse and groped for the keys in my jeans. My cold fingers closed around the metal ring, but I nearly dropped it as the wind swept through my sweatshirt and triggered another uncontrollable wave of shivers that rattled my bones.

I pressed a hand to the door frame to steady myself as I swayed forward and tried to unlock the door. On the fifth attempt, the key sank into the opening and twisted.

Thank you, Jesus.

I threw open the door, and Hope rushed past me, calling for her son. "Tyler!"

"Mommy!" his small voice replied from the back of the house.

I stumbled inside and locked the door behind me, dropping against it as my legs threatened to give out. My energy level was plummeting as quickly as my body temperature, and all I wanted to do was to curl up in a warm blanket beside a fire and sleep.

But judging by the blur of movement that passed the window beside me, rest and warmth weren't going to be an option anytime soon.

The knob rattled on the door at my back, and Ollie thumped a fist against the wood. "Hope!"

If he had the keys he'd taken from his aunt and uncle, there was no way to keep him out. I couldn't hold this door shut with my body. He wasn't much bigger than I was, but he was stronger and angrier, and he would shove through me.

Hope appeared at the end of the hallway, wrapped in layers of blankets, with her son in front of her, her face pale.

God, please give me the strength to protect them.

I waved her back inside the room.

Indecision played across her face before she retreated with her son and closed the door. Furniture scraped the floor as she barricaded the entrance.

I was on my own, but I only had to hold off Ollie until Jordan caught up with him. A minute, at most.

If he made it out of the water.

No, I couldn't let myself think like that.

Ollie kicked the door in frustration. He must've lost his keys when he dove into the lake. He backtracked to the window, and an instant later, the wide end of the oar smashed through it, sending glass shattering everywhere.

I yelped and shielded my face.

He scraped the edges of the frame with the wooden paddle and climbed through the opening so clumsily that he nearly sprawled in the shards littering the floor.

I lunged for the island counter and grabbed the first weapon within my reach—a wooden meat tenderizer from a utensil pot. It was a lot smaller than the stick he was carrying, but it was either this or a rubber spatula. And slapping him in the face with one of those wouldn't do much.

I planted myself in the mouth of the hallway, clutching my tiny hammer in trembling hands. "Please . . . j-just leave us . . . alone."

Ollie's body shook nearly as badly as mine as he straightened in front of the window, cold water streaming from his clothes and pooling on the floor. Some of the water had a pinkish hue, and I noticed a hole in the sleeve of his shirt. The bang I heard from under the water *was* a gunshot; the bullet must have grazed him before he jumped in.

"Move," he demanded, wiping at the water dripping from his saturated hair onto his face. His fingers smeared the concealer he used to soften a bruise under his left eye. "Please, I don't w-wanna hurt you. You . . . w-w-were nice t-to me."

"You don't have to hurt anyone."

"I lost the one person who l-loved me. Because of her! This is *her* fault!"

"Ollie—"

"Move!" He drew back the wooden oar like a batter about to swing, and I backed up instinctively, fresh fear slicing through me.

He was going to hit me. Would he stop after one swing, or would he beat me until I was no longer an obstacle? I found myself taking another step back, torn between the desire to stand my ground and the bone-deep instinct to flee from another beating.

The last one left me with broken bones and internal bleeding.

When he started to bring the oar forward, I flung the meat tenderizer at him. The metal block thumped against his chest hard enough to rip a grunt of pain from him, but it was too late to stop the swing. I ducked, my weak, frozen legs buckling and taking me to the floor as the oar arced over my head. It slipped from Ollie's chilled fingers and clattered into the dining room.

I tried to scramble to my feet, but my body refused to obey me. My legs were as heavy and unbending as tree limbs, and I only managed to scoot through the water that dripped from my clothes.

Ollie stumbled forward on the slick tile and grabbed the hood of my sweatshirt, wrenching until it cut into my throat. I pawed at it with fingers I couldn't feel anymore, and tears blurred my vision.

God, is he gonna kill me?

A thump came from the back bedroom—the sound of a body hitting the floor—followed by a child's frightened cry.

"Mommy! Mommy, wake up!"

Hope must've collapsed from the hypothermia that was taking control of my body too. Even as Ollie tried to drag me up, the exhaustion was dragging me toward the floor, toward darkness, like a magnet.

Jordan sprang through the window opening and threw himself at my attacker. In an instant, the strangling grip on my sweatshirt was gone, and I sagged to the floor like a boneless doll.

I sucked in air through my aching throat as I watched the struggle unfolding on the floor in front of me. Two men, fighting and flailing in slow motion. I tried to focus on their faces, but my line of vision narrowed to a slit as my eyelids drooped.

I needed to save Jordan from drowning. No, that wasn't right. I needed to save him from the man with the oar. What was his name? I should know, but my thoughts were too slippery to hold on to.

Hope. I need to check . . .

And then the thought vanished from my head. Familiar sneakers rushed toward me as my eyelids fell shut. Someone shook me, and the sound of my name wobbled in my ears.

I just wanna rest. A nap. Five minutes. That's all. Just five minutes, I wanted to say, but I didn't have the energy to push the thoughts through my lips.

Wailing sirens floated somewhere in the distance, and in the back of my mind I knew that was important, but not as important as rest. I surrendered to the warm darkness, letting it wrap around me and carry me away.

41

*R*ushing water, like a heavy rain on a scorching day, filled the air with steam. The earth vibrated and shuddered against my back as I tried to peel away the damp, sticky layers of clothes. I was too hot, and my skin needed to breathe. Arms tightened around me, and a voice whispered something into my hair.

I clutched at the fragments of memory, trying to make sense of them, as I pulled on the dry clothes one of the nurses had grabbed from the hospital donation box.

Everything that happened between the shoes coming toward me and the voices of the paramedics in the ambulance was foggy. Bits and pieces came into focus, but most were lost. I hated the feeling of lost time.

Usually it meant something terrible had happened to me, something my mind was too afraid to remember, but apart from hypothermia and a sprained wrist, I was in perfect health. It was hypothermia, not trauma or drugs, that left my memory in pieces this time. And Jordan was with me, so I could trust that no one had hurt me.

I squeezed into the borrowed sweatshirt. Judging by the fit and the Care Bears holding hands around a rainbow, its previous owner had been a child. It barely met the waist of the skinny sweatpants that scrunched around my ankles.

Either the donations for women my size were in short supply, or the old woman in grumpy-cat scrubs was mocking me.

"Knock, knock," Jordan said from the other side of the curtain that separated my bed from the adjoining patient.

"You can come in."

The hooks screeched along the metal bar as he opened the heavy curtain. Jordan was wearing borrowed clothes as well, but he was average size, and he looked cozy in his sweatpants and sweatshirt. Except for the patterned bruise fading into his hair.

Jordan's mouth twitched in amusement as he took in my outfit. "A Care Bear sweatshirt and polka-dot socks. Somehow perfectly you."

"They don't have a lot of clothes in my size." I tugged at the hem of the sweatshirt self-consciously and then folded my arms over my stomach. "Everything is so short."

"Maybe this will help you feel better." He retrieved a pudding cup and spoon from inside the pouch of his sweatshirt.

"Pistachio!" I took the delectable offering and wiggled back onto the bed, polka-dotted feet dangling. "Thanks. For the pudding and for remembering it's my favorite."

Jordan dropped onto the end of the bed and studied me in that worried way of his.

"I'm okay," I assured him, peeling back the pudding seal with my left hand, since the brace on my right wrist made small movements feel clumsy. "I'm a little chilly and sore, but mostly normal. You?"

"A bruise, but that's about it." He gestured to the darkening bruise on his forehead that matched the pattern of the meat tenderizer I flung at Ollie, who must've gotten hold of it during their struggle and landed a blow.

"Does it feel tender?" I asked, biting back a mischievous snicker.

It took him a moment, and then he huffed a laugh. "Funny, but yes, that utensil holds true to its name. Thankfully, he didn't hit me hard enough to do any real damage."

I swirled the spoon through the green pudding. "Out of curiosity, did it start raining while we were waiting for the ambulance?"

"You're probably remembering the shower. You passed out from hypothermia, and I knew none of us were gonna make it if we didn't get warm, so I carried you and Hope into the bathroom, turned the room into a sauna with a scalding shower, and wrapped us all in towels until help arrived."

The arms that held me, the shuddering against my back—despite the fact that he was freezing, Jordan had cradled me and tried to keep me warm.

"The cops arrived shortly after that, but the ambulance was about eight minutes behind them. It was a rural area, so there weren't any emergency vehicles close by, and with hypothermia, every minute counts," he explained.

"I remember being really hot at one point, which doesn't make sense."

"It does, actually. Hypothermia confuses the mind. At that point, most people strip down to cool off, too disoriented to realize they're freezing to death."

Anxiety fluttered through me. "Did I . . ."

"No." He offered me a reassuring smile. "The protocol is to get out of the wet clothes and into dry ones, but we didn't have any dry clothes. And for the record, I would never let a disoriented and confused woman strip in front of me. It's not exactly the gentlemanly thing to do."

Relieved, I released a breath. "Thanks."

"I did have to hold you pretty tight to keep you from trying, though, so I'm gonna need a pardon for crossing the border without permission again."

I smiled. "Consider yourself pardoned." I scooped a bite of pudding, but asked before popping it into my mouth, "What about Hope? Is she okay?"

"Yeah, she's good. But we need to talk about you jumping into that lake."

Ah, the inevitable scolding.

"I couldn't let her drown, Jordan. She deserves a chance at a good life, and her little boy loves her so much. I didn't want him to lose her."

"I know. But let's discuss crazy rescue tactics before taking the plunge next time, okay?" His brows drew together in concern. "You could've died today."

I couldn't promise to discuss things next time, because if it was a situation like Hope's, when a few seconds could mean the difference between life and death, I wouldn't waste time discussing options.

I dipped the tip of my spoon in the pudding and savored the taste. "Have you heard anything about Ollie?"

"His headache won't be much better than mine. When I realized you were passing out, I gave up trying to restrain him and knocked him unconscious."

"Ollie is doing fine," a female voice said.

Amelia Kendrick and her husband stood in the doorway, every bit the well-dressed, wealthy couple I expected to meet this morning. Oliver wore pressed slacks and a polo, as though he'd been out golfing this morning rather drinking his way toward oblivion, and Amelia wore a silk sundress and heels.

Her shoes clicked against the tile as she approached the curtained area. "I understand we have you to thank for diving into the lake to save Hope."

I squirmed, uncomfortable. "Um, I did jump in, but . . ."

"Yes, she dove in after Hope and rescued her," Jordan chimed in.

"Hope told us everything," Amelia said. "The attempted kidnapping, the events at the lake, at the guesthouse. We're so sorry for what you've both been through these past few days. I can't even imagine."

"We are beyond grateful for what you've done for our family." Oliver stepped forward, a glow in his eyes that hadn't been there this morning. "We understand there will be legal repercussions for Julian . . . *Ollie* . . . but he'll get the help he needs, and we have a second chance with Hope."

He offered me a bundle of flowers that must've cost a fortune. I gaped at the bouquet and then looked from my pudding cup to my sprained wrist and then back to the flowers. How to . . .

Jordan took the half-empty cup from me, freeing up my left hand.

I accepted the flowers and buried my nose in the sweet scent. "Thank you. These are . . . incredible."

"Hope has agreed to come stay with us, and she's going to bring that sweet little boy of hers." Amelia pressed a hand to her chest. "I can scarcely imagine what it will be like to have little feet running around the house."

I drew in a breath, hesitating, and then said, "I don't know how much Hope has told you, but she's been through a lot since she ran away from home. The world takes advantage of a child with nowhere to go and no way to live. She's been treated terribly, and she's got a lot to heal from."

Amelia's eyes glistened. "We know, and we will do whatever it takes to help her."

"She told us she came to you and asked you to find the friend Julian kidnapped and that even though she couldn't afford to pay you for your services, you agreed to help. We want to make things right." Oliver withdrew a folded slip of paper from his slacks and passed it to Jordan.

Jordan blinked. It was a check for . . . how many zeros was that? "Mr. and Mrs. Kendrick, this is . . . I can't accept this much money. It's . . ."

"Consider it payment for services rendered, restitution for damages and trauma, a bonus for going above and beyond, and a little extra for the next hopeless case that knocks on your door." Oliver clapped Jordan on the shoulder. "And your hospital bills are covered."

Jordan stared at the man, speechless.

Amelia rested a hand on my forearm. "Come visit Hope anytime. I'm sure she would be delighted to see you. And she's going to need good friends she can talk to."

"I'll do that. Oh, I think the keys you gave me are at the guesthouse. I dropped them."

"We'll have the cleaner pick them up. Take care, both of you."

The couple left the room. They seemed like such kind and generous people, and I wished Jace's parents could be more like them. She deserved the same unconditional love from her mom and dad.

Jordan released a long, slow breath as he studied the check. "I joined you on this case expecting it to cost us when we didn't have anything left to give. But you were right. God always comes through."

"And then some." I leaned closer to see the amount—$25,000—scrawled across the check. "Now we can afford to replenish the hot chocolate and marshmallow stash at the office."

Jordan laughed. "Yeah, I think we can afford to do that. And you're cashing your paycheck." He looked over at me and smiled. "You have pollen on your nose."

"I do?" I rubbed at my nose. "Did I get it?"

"Some of it. May I?" At my nod, he rubbed a gentle thumb over the side of my nose to remove the evidence of the flowers I had buried my face in a minute ago.

A tap of knuckles on the door frame captured our attention. Hope lingered in the doorway with her son, who appeared unscathed from his time with Ollie.

"I was trying to catch you before you left," Hope said. "Tyler wanted to say good-bye."

Jordan bent down as the little boy surged forward for a hug. Hope smiled at the pair before walking over to me in an outfit that wasn't much better than mine. I laid the flowers on the bed and hopped down.

"I'm not real good at the touchy-feely stuff," Hope began. "But, uh, you saved my life. There ain't a lot of people who've been kind to me, but you were, even when I was nuttin' but horrible. And you helped me when you had no reason to, so I guess what I'm trying to say is—"

I threw my arms around her and pulled her into a hug. She stiffened for an instant before hugging me back and burying her face in my hair.

She choked on tears. "Thank you, Holly. Thank you for being the kinda person who cares about everybody for no reason."

"There is a reason," I said. "You remember what that Southern detective said?"

"That I got value beyond measure."

"He was right, and I see that value in you. And in your son." I drew back to look her in the eyes. "I am always here when you need me, and I will always have enough love in my heart to care for you."

She rested her forehead against mine. "You are such a strange person. I don't understand you."

"Well, when you're ready to understand, I have a really good book for you to read. But maybe don't thump anyone over the head with it. I think that's called assault."

She laughed. "I'll keep that in mind. I thought you might wanna know, I called the hospital to talk to Cami, and she's going home with her mom. They're gonna try to start over."

"And you?"

"We're gonna try to start over too. Amelia and Oliver are giving us a place to stay, and I won't have to . . ." She glanced at her son and reconsidered her words. "I think maybe I can get a job at a movie theater or something. Sell tickets and popcorn instead of something else."

"And someday you'll work your way up to being a flight attendant," I said.

She smiled, the faintest glimmer of hope in her eyes. "I'm still not so sure about dreams, but . . . maybe." She noticed the brace on my arm, and the smile disappeared. "I'm sorry you both got hurt. I hope you know I didn't have a choice in that alley when Ollie grabbed you. He had my son. I tried to talk you out of the case 'cause I didn't want you to get hurt."

"I know."

"I always knew Ollie hated me when we were kids, but I didn't know he'd do something like this. Sometimes he was real awkward, and other times he was downright mean and creepy. He scared Livy sometimes, and we wanted to get away from him that day. We wanted a few minutes without him as our shadow."

I caught Jordan's eye before asking, "Did Ollie tip the boat?"

Hope looked over her shoulder at the doorway, checking to make sure it was only the four of us, then said, "He waded into the lake and swam out. He went under seconds before the boat rocked. It shouldn't have rocked like that by itself."

"You told the Kendricks you were dancing, and that's why you fell overboard."

"I didn't want them to lose anybody else." She shrugged as the tears spilled onto her cheeks. "I don't know if Ollie did it on purpose or if it was an accident, but . . . it happened, and Livy died. That was all that mattered."

"I'm so sorry."

"Is what it is, you know? I'm glad it's over." She held out a hand for Tyler. "You ready to go get some lunch, little man?"

Tyler threw his arms around my legs. "Bye, Hollysaurus."

I ran a hand over his hair. "Bye, raptor." To Hope I said, "Keep in touch."

"For sure."

My heart overflowed as Hope and her little boy left the room to start their new life with a family that loved them.

God brought everything together—Hope and the Kendricks, the money for the business, Cami and her mother—and it all started with Hope finding our lipstick-stained business card on a sidewalk.

42

Nine Days Later

*T*he tape roller crackled as I taped up the last box of pillows and then smoothed the strip into place with my hand.

I had never packed my belongings like this before. I usually stuffed what I could into my duffle bag, which was what I had done with my clothes when I moved out of Marx's apartment.

Did I tape the bottom of this box?

I squinted, trying to remember, but I had taped so many boxes today that it all melted together in my memory. I guess we would find out if there was a pillow avalanche when Sam picked it up.

"Three boxes of pillows," Marx observed, and I turned to see him leaning against the door frame of the spare room.

"You bought them for me."

He smiled. "True enough. Your room at the house is bigger, so you'll have plenty of room for all these colored bags of stuffin'."

"Pizza's here," Sam called from the kitchen.

"I hope you're in the mood for fungus and fruit," Marx said.

"Always." We abandoned the stacks of boxes in my old bedroom and joined Sam at the peninsula for lunch. I wiggled up onto one of the stools. I was going to miss sitting at this counter for breakfast and late-night macaroni and cheese with Marx.

I opened the pizza box, and the aroma of herbs, tomatoes, and pineapple filled the apartment.

"Sam, how many slices do you want?"

He scowled as he grabbed a paper plate. "If you touch my pizza, I'm not eating it."

Unfortunately, he was completely serious. I grabbed one of my slices and plopped it on my plate, waiting for them to do the same.

Once everyone had food, I stretched a hand across the counter, my fingertips a hairsbreadth from Sam's, and then took Marx's hand so we could pray.

Sam wasn't much for spirituality, but his only protest before bowing his head was a sigh.

"Dear God," I began, "thank you for this apartment, for all the hope and joy and healing we experienced inside its walls. Thank you for the memories. I pray that you bless whoever lives here next. Thank you for this food and these two men I love. Amen."

Marx kissed the top of my head, an unspoken expression of his love in return.

Sam swallowed, his Adam's apple dipping and rising slowly as he stared at his pizza. "Despite how irrational, impulsive, and stubborn you can be, I . . ."—he cleared his throat—"love you too."

I smiled and popped a piece of pineapple into my mouth. My rigid friend was going to have to get used to speaking that four-letter L word if he ever wanted to move forward with Jace. She was as demonstrative as a person could be.

We chatted about old times as we ate our lunch, reminiscing about the hole Jordan had put in the wall, the baking mishaps, the baseball game we watched on the couch, which Marx had passed along to me. As much as I liked my eggplant couch, the middle of it had started to cave in.

Sam folded his empty plate and tossed it into the trash. "If you wanna give me your keys, I'll put the rest of these boxes in your car. Mine's full."

Marx tossed him his keys, and Sam pocketed them as he strode into my bedroom to grab the last few boxes.

A strange sound came from the room, and a round pillow rolled into the doorway.

"Holly," Sam said, exasperation tightening his voice.

Yep, definitely forgot to tape the bottom of that one. I hopped up to help collect the escaped pillows and tossed them toward the box, missing more than I made.

Sam scooped up one of the square ones that hit the edge and bounced off. "You're terrible at this."

The next pillow nailed him in the face, and I laughed. His stony expression cracked with a smile, and he threw the pillow into the box.

As he taped up the box and carried it out, I roamed the apartment, revisiting the memories that had formed in each of the rooms. Marx's bedroom where I mismatched his socks, the bathroom where we threw toilet paper, the spare bedroom where I walked in to find that Marx had brought Riley home to help me feel safer, the kitchen where we made brownies at ten o'clock at night, the living room where we sat and watched movies until the early hours of the morning.

A floorboard creaked behind me, signaling Marx's approach. I folded my arms against the sadness wrapping around my heart. "I'm gonna miss this place."

He rested his hands on my shoulders. "Me too. But it's not the walls or the roof that make a place a home. It's the people. And we're gonna make so many new memories that your little head won't be able to hold them all."

I leaned back against him and tipped my face upward. "My head is not—"

"Mmm hmm."

Sam returned. "There's two boxes left. You wanna grab the second one so we can head out?"

"I can grab it," I offered. It was only filled with pillows.

"You won't be able to see over it," Sam replied, and I crinkled my nose at his reasoning.

"You can lock the door behind us," Marx suggested.

Begrudgingly, I followed them from the now vacant apartment, pausing to take one last look around before flipping off the light.

"I see someone finally evicted you," a familiar, crackling voice said from behind me. Mrs. Neberkins. "Moving your drugs and human trafficking to another location?"

"No, I'm gettin' married," Marx said.

"To a mail-order bride, no doubt. What is she, fifteen?"

"Fifty, actually, but close."

I locked the door and ducked around the boxes to see her. "Hi, Mrs. Neberkins."

She blinked at me and then lifted the glasses on the chain around her neck, sliding them onto her face to study me. "Holly? But I thought . . ."

"I'm alive and well. Marx didn't kidnap me, traffic me, or bury me under a bush. He's one of the good guys."

I could see the wheels of thought turning behind her oversized glasses, and then she wagged a finger. "Stockholm Syndrome. I've heard of it before. You're in love with your kidnapper."

There was no convincing this woman that there wasn't a conspiracy around every corner. On impulse, I wrapped my arms around her frail shoulders—so at odds with her fierce personality—and hugged her.

Trying not to choke on the perfume that plumed from her housecoat, I said, "Good-bye, Mrs. Neberkins. I hope things work out with Henry."

She blinked owlish eyes at me as I released her. "How . . . are you three spying on me?"

Amusement lifted my lips, and I ignored the barrage of suspicious questions she fired at our backs as we descended the steps. When I reached the landing, I glanced back at Marx's apartment door.

Life was about moving forward, not standing still and not going backward. But it was a bittersweet moment, saying good-bye to my home away from home.

EPILOGUE
The Wedding

The scent of flowers hung in the air, a rainbow of loose petals tumbling down the temporary aisle as the breeze swept through the park.

I tried not to fidget as I stood in front of the arbor in the sparkling blue gown Jace had fitted for me. The sheer sleeves, peppered with sequins, reached my wrists, and the skirt flowed down over my legs to the ground.

I studied the faces seated in the folding chairs as Marx and Shannon stood before the preacher. The guest list was small, amounting to about twenty people, and I only recognized a handful.

Ms. Martha offered me a discreet finger-wave and a wink when our eyes met, and I caught Jace's delighted grin in the second aisle seat before returning my attention to the happy couple.

"I knew, from the moment you stepped out of that painfully long line at the coffee shop and swooped in to drive away the persistent man interrupting my studies, that I wanted to spend as much time with you as possible," Shannon said.

Shannon was beautiful on an average day—tall, with olive skin, defined cheekbones, raven hair, and deep gray eyes—but today, she was stunning with white flowers woven into her wreath of hair and a white silk dress that flattered her curvy figure.

When I first met her, she reminded me of an elegant but distant queen. Over time, though, she began to thaw, warming to the people around her.

"I regret all the time we missed out on these past few years," she continued. "But even in that time apart, my heart longed for you. From this day forward, I intend to savor every moment we have together and to embrace this unique family we've created for ourselves."

She reached forward to take Marx's hands, and I leaned a little to the left so I could see him. The joy in his green eyes was so intense that I could feel it twining around me.

Certain of my place in their new life together, a part of their unique family, I let go of my worries, feeling nothing but happiness for Marx.

Behind him, Sam stood as best man, but his eyes weren't on the couple between us. His attention was on Jace, who was watching the ceremony with longing. I couldn't read Sam's expression, but I had a feeling those promises of forever my best friend was hoping for weren't so far off.

"Shannon, you are my first love. Aside from Mama, of course," Marx said, and laughter rippled through the small audience. Ms. Martha dabbed at her eyes with a handkerchief even as she beamed. "No matter what the years may bring—laughter or tears, health or sickness—I am grateful for a second chance to share those moments with you."

My eyes wandered over the audience again and connected with Jordan's. Admiration and affection warmed his blue eyes, and he smiled. Heat crept into my cheeks, and I looked away from him, only to glance back and offer him a shy smile in return.

"The rings," the preacher said, recapturing my attention, and Shannon turned toward me.

Oh, Marx's ring. Right.

He had taken off his wedding band of twenty-something years for this ceremony, and it was my job to pass it to Shannon so she could slide it back onto his finger.

I looked at my dress and then at Shannon's bouquet in my hands. "Hold these for a second?"

The corners of her lips lifted into a hesitant, worried smile as she grabbed the ribbon-wrapped stems I thrust toward her. "Holly . . ."

"I have it." I whipped up one side of the dress, eliciting a few murmurs from guests that quickly turned to laughter, and reached into the back pocket of the jeans I wore beneath the dress. I retrieved the ring and held it up. "Got it."

The hesitation in Shannon's expression vanished, and she gifted me with a rare full smile. "Never a dull moment."

Past her, I could see Marx trying to restrain a laugh, Sam shaking his head, and the preacher gaping at me in astonishment. What was I supposed to do? The dress didn't have pockets.

They exchanged their rings and kissed before gliding back down the aisle together as husband and wife.

Sam approached and gestured for me to join him. "We follow them down the aisle."

"Oh." I fell in step beside him, and we trailed behind the bride and groom. "Is it so unusual for a woman to wear jeans under her dress?"

"Yes, but it could've been the purple rain boots that caught everyone by surprise."

I looked down at the barest tip of my boots that appeared with every step and then up at the dark clouds. "It was supposed to rain this afternoon."

"So you brought shoes to keep your feet dry while the rain drenched the rest of you?" He offered me his usual I'm-puzzled-by-your-reasoning look.

"I couldn't juggle flowers, the ring, *and* an umbrella. I picked shoes. I'm tired of having wet feet." Between lakes and puddles the past two weeks, I'd had my fill of soggy feet.

"And we're ignoring the fact that gravity would pull the rain *into* your boots."

"I have plenty of dress to duck under."

He considered the gown. "True. Just don't throw it over your head in front of the preacher again. He wasn't expecting the jeans, and you nearly gave him a heart attack."

The poor old man did look stricken.

"I'm glad Jace convinced you to wear the dress, even with your unusual layers underneath," Sam said. "You look very nice."

Sam didn't offer compliments often, and I smiled in appreciation before addressing a different, more important issue. "I saw the way you were watching Jace during the ceremony. Are you . . . planning something?"

He slanted a look my way, then past me as Jace headed toward us. "We'll talk about that another time. I'll see you at the dining hall." He strode over to join Jordan, who glanced my way before shoving his hands into his pants pockets and giving Sam his full attention.

We hadn't seen much of each other this weekend.

Yesterday morning I had a photo shoot, and my evening was consumed by one final dress fitting. I spent most of this morning getting my hair and nails done with Jace before getting dressed. She insisted on makeup, but I drew the line at face paste. It made me look like a Barbie.

My nails were a pretty iridescent purple, though, which was a little trippy if I stared at them for too long.

Jace snagged my arm with hers as she rolled up beside me. "*You* are riding with me. Girl time. The boys can ride together."

She released me and started through the grass, struggling a bit with the soft ground, but I knew better than to offer help.

"I've been meaning to ask. Did you meet Erik McCallister at the gala?" she tossed over her shoulder, and I tensed.

I hadn't told her or Sam that Jace's mother was trying to arrange a relationship between her and the unpleasant man. Maybe I should have, but the situation seemed to resolve itself after Marx's talk with Erik, and I was afraid the news would only hurt them.

"Um, yeah, I met him. Why?"

"I showed up for family dinner as ordered last Friday night, and I overheard my mother in her office, talking about how relieved she was that they didn't set me up with him. Did you know him and one of his friends were arrested for attacking and drugging a girl?

What kind of lowlife does that?" She paused, then added, "Other than Edward the serial killer Billings."

I rubbed my hands together as we walked. "I actually met him before the gala. He propositioned me on Brushwick because he thought I was a prostitute."

"Are you kidding me? What a creep." She rotated toward me so abruptly that I almost collided with the side of her wheelchair. "He didn't try to hurt you, did he?"

How to answer that.

"Not directly, no. But he thought I was party-crashing the gala to blackmail him, so he threatened me."

"Seriously? Why didn't you say something? I would've taken out both of his ankles for that. No one gets away with threatening my best friend."

"Marx set him straight, and I didn't have any problems with him after that."

"Good, but I still wish you had told me." She straightened her wheelchair, and we continued toward the parking area. "Did you confront your mom after overhearing that conversation?"

"Oh yeah. I told her I'm in love with Sam, and I'm not interested in seeing anyone else."

Maybe I hadn't needed to threaten Erik's reputation after all. Jace caved to so many of her mother's demands, but she might hold her ground in the relationship department.

"Love, huh?"

Jace threw me a warning look. "Don't tell him I said that."

I smiled. "Your secret's safe with me."

We climbed into her car and cut across the city to Shannon's house, where the reception was being held. I unhooked my seat belt and contemplated the tall stairway to the front porch. How was Jace going to get up there?

"Well that could be a problem," she said, leaning over to see the steps. "I don't suppose there's a ramp around back."

"Not that I remember."

"I am not crawling up those steps in this dress."

As if on cue, Jordan and Sam came down the steps to meet us. Sam rounded the car to open Jace's door and crouched in the opening.

"There's no ramp. Do you mind if I carry you up while Jordan gets your chair? The party's on the first floor."

Jace, my independent friend who preferred to tackle all things physical on her own, took one last look at the steps and puckered her lips. "Yeah, I can roll with that."

I grunted in amusement at her pun and stepped out of the car onto the sidewalk beside Jordan, grabbing my knapsack. He shut the door and opened the back to retrieve the folded wheelchair.

Sam scooped Jace into his arms, seemingly effortlessly, and nudged the driver's door shut.

She hugged his neck. "I could get used to this kind of treatment. Take your time with that chair, Jordan."

Sam actually smiled as he carried her up the steps.

Jordan slung the folded wheelchair under one arm. "I noticed it's a little hard to walk in that dress. I can run this up and come back to give you a lift to the top."

"A lift?"

"I'm thinking piggyback ride."

"Well . . . stop thinking it." I hiked up all the excess material, and trudged up the steps toward the porch, praying I wouldn't trip over a loose bit of skirt. How did women in history do anything more than walk across a room in these fluffs of fabric?

Jordan reached the porch a second after me, and Sam lowered Jace into her wheelchair. She wiggled into a more comfortable position and then cruised into the house.

The decorations inside were simple yet elegant, the way Shannon preferred things. White and cream flowers adorning every flat surface, cream candles and white tablecloths over the entryway tables, white cake on the plates of people wandering around the first floor.

Good thing I brought some color with me, I thought, mischief curling my lips.

"This looks familiar," Jordan said, directing my attention to the crooked picture frame on the wall right inside the door.

I inhaled and gravitated toward it, my heart warming. My Christmas gift to Marx hadn't been stuffed in a box in the attic to collect dust. It hung where he would see it every time he left for work and every evening when he came home.

"Something tells me he's gonna want you to visit pretty frequently," Jordan said.

Ms. Martha, passing from the kitchen to the living room, spotted us in the entryway. She gasped and bustled forward, sweeping me into a hug before I could brace myself. She squeezed me to her chest and exclaimed, "Oh, baby, it's so good to see you. It's been too long."

Even here, far from her Georgia kitchen and baked goods, she smelled like cookies and comfort. The first time I met her, it had been Christmas, and the two would be forever intertwined in my mind.

I slipped my arms around her, sinking into the abundant love that overflowed from her. "Hi, Ms. Martha."

She released me and cupped my face the way Marx did, studying every detail with the same green eyes. "Sweet girl. You know you're as good as my grandbaby, and it would do my old heart good to be called Grandma at least once. If you're not uncomfortable with that."

Grandma. I rolled the word over in my mind. I had never known my grandparents—they passed away before I had a chance to meet them—but I had always wanted some. I couldn't adopt my cute photography clients with their matching sweaters, but I would happily adopt this cuddly, cookie-baking woman as my grandma.

"Can I call you Gran?" I asked with a smile.

"Ooh, yes! I am so happy." She turned and hollered over her shoulder, "Gus, our grandbaby's here. Come say hi!"

Gus ambled out of the kitchen with a slice of cake, his gruff voice a perfect match for his gruff appearance. "We don't have a grand . . . oh." He looked me over and then nodded. "Holly."

"Mr. Gus."

"He'll warm up eventually." Ms. Martha . . . Gran . . . slid her hands from my cheeks and wrapped an arm around my shoulders, leading me away from my friends. "Right now, he's just grouchy that it's a dry reception."

I eyed the dark clouds through a nearby window. "I was expecting rain too." But I wasn't upset that the clouds were hoarding their raindrops.

"I know. I noticed those cute little rain boots under your dress. But in this instance, dry means no alcohol."

Concern welled in my chest. "Is Mr. Gus drinking again?" His alcoholism had nearly destroyed his family, and he'd been sober for almost ten months.

"No, no, but some days the demon is harder to fight than others. He knows that if he gives in this time, though, he'll lose me and Richie both." She gave my shoulders a gentle squeeze. "But you don't need to worry about that. I wanna hear everythin' that's happened since our last video conversation. I hope you've been stayin' out of trouble."

I puckered my lips between my teeth and glanced back at Jordan, who grinned. Staying out of trouble wasn't exactly how I would put it, but I wasn't about to tell her about the case involving crazy kidnappers and daring lake rescues.

I told her about my photography instead, and we made plans to bake s'more brownies together before they headed home to Georgia. I slipped away to find Marx and Shannon, but I stumbled into the path of a gawky man in a green plaid suit and yellow shoes before I could spot either of them.

He'd been sitting in the second row at the wedding, and I caught him staring at me more than once.

Time to evade.

I started to step around him, when he blurted, "Hi-lo." His cheeks turned pink as the mangled word slipped out. "I mean . . . hi. Hello." He cleared his throat and extended a hand, like he expected me to shake it. "I'm Sully."

"Put your hand down," Marx said, approaching the two of us.

Sully snatched his arm back. "Right, that was stupid. Sorry. I'm just thrilled to meet you, Holly. I'm your hero."

I blinked, and Marx shook his head.

"No, that's not . . . you, *you* are *my* hero. Or heroine." His face pinched. "That makes you sound like a drug, which I know you have nothing to do with despite that couple you stayed with as a kid. It's not like you're a closet drug dealer or anything. I mean that would be . . ." He visibly swallowed, the words clogging in his throat. "Completely off point."

"Breathe before you pass out," Marx told him, before draping an arm around my shoulders and leading me away.

I looked over my shoulder as Sully muttered, "I did it. I actually talked to her. I sounded like an idiot, but I did it, and she didn't run away, and Marx didn't smack me off my feet. That's progress." He stared at the floor for a beat before deciding, "I need cake."

"Is that guy okay?" I asked.

"No, but that's normal. He's pretty much our computer forensics team, and he spends all day in front of a computer. The last real woman he spoke to was probably his mother."

"Oh. How does he know about my second family?"

"When Edward was comin' after you, and we were tryin' to piece together your history, he was the man helpin'. He knows quite a bit about you, but he's a good guy."

How much was quite a bit? Did he know about Collin? The videos? Was he a witness that Shannon called to the stand during the trial? I dismissed the flurry of questions, because truthfully, I didn't want to know the answers.

"I'm gonna grab you some cake and sparklin' apple juice. You can sit beside me, right there." Marx pointed to a slice of cake at the banquet table they had set up in the living room.

I rounded the table and took the folding chair beside his. Checking to make sure no one was watching, I reached into my knapsack and pulled out a bottle. I flicked up the lid and shook rainbow sprinkles onto Marx's slice of cake and then balanced a mini marshmallow on top.

Perfect.

Stuffing the evidence back into my bag, I noticed a man leaning against the far wall, watching me. Brown eyes, brown hair, with a baby cradled in his arms. Michael Everly, Marx's partner.

"You didn't see that," I said, gesturing to the now brightly colored cake.

Michael smiled and strode forward with his baby girl, who slept soundly despite the voices chattering around her. "I may have been distracted, making me an unreliable witness, but I don't think there's gonna be too many suspects."

True enough.

I rested my arms on the table. "How's baby Grace?"

"Sleeps all day, cries all night." He watched his sleeping daughter with unbridled love. "But still the greatest blessing in our life."

Marx nodded to his partner as he returned to the table. "Where's your better half?"

"At home, taking advantage of the quiet house. She wanted to come, but she's exhausted. I told her to rest."

"Good, she needs it." A slow smile stretched Marx's lips when he saw his cake. "I don't remember the marshmallow bandit bein' on the guest list."

"The bandit and I are like this." I crossed my fingers. "She's around here somewhere. Want me to find her?"

"Oh, I think I know exactly where she is." He swapped our cakes. "And if one of us is gettin' a cavity tonight, it's not gonna be me. I've got plans."

I swiped a finger through the buttercream frosting and sprinkles, popping it into my mouth. "Where are you and Shannon flying for your second honeymoon?"

"A cottage on the beach. No courtrooms, no robberies."

"No dead bodies?"

He grunted. "Let's hope not."

I dug into my cake, enjoying the sugar rush as much as the flavor. Soft music from a speaker on a side table cut through the chatter, and Shannon sashayed toward us in her gown, holding out her hand.

"Husband, may I have this dance?"

Marx set down his fork, took her hand, and rose from his chair. She led him to the small clearing made by the guests, her movements graceful as they glided into a slow dance.

I watched them as I nibbled at my cake, their happiness burning more brightly than the candles that lined the tables.

Jordan sank into the vacant chair beside me, pushing aside Marx's untouched cake. "We haven't had much time to catch up this weekend, but I thought you might like to know. I found something."

I cleaned the creamy sweetness from my fork. "Something like . . . a lost sock?"

"More along the lines of information. On Cassandra Ward."

I dropped the fork to the table. "You found Cassie?"

"Not yet, but I have a lead."

Hope flooded my chest. Even if it took weeks or months to track her down, a lead brought me one step closer to fulfilling the promise I had been holding on to for fifteen years.

The End

Take a picture of your book beside something Holly-ish and post it on social media with:

#ccwarrenshollynovel

Dear Reader

I wanted to express my thanks to all of you who took precious time out of your day to read this novel. If this is the first book you've read by me, I hope you'll go back and start the journey at *Criss Cross*. The experience is so much richer when you watch the characters and relationships grow.

If you think you would enjoy excerpts from future books (as well as publication dates and the occasional short story about my life), I would love for you to sign up for my newsletter.

If you're not an email kind of soul, then you can find updates on book progress and interactive questions on my Facebook author page, Instagram page, or my website. If you want to chat with other readers about my books, check out the Facebook group "C.C. Warrens' readers: Mysteries, Mischief, and Marshmallows."

If you love these stories, I hope you'll take a moment to share your thoughts and feelings on Amazon, Goodreads, and BookBub. I know everyone asks you to write reviews, and if you're an avid reader like me, that's a lot of reviews. But trust me when I say, as an author who has poured out her heart into every book she's ever written, your reviews are cherished.

I would love to hear from you, so feel free to reach out through any of my social media sites, my website, or through email. Have a beautiful day!

About the Author

Jesus and laughter have brought C.C. Warrens through some very difficult times in life, and she weaves both into every story she writes, creating a world of breath-stealing intensity, laugh-out-loud humor, and a sparkle of hope. Writing has been a slowly blossoming dream inside her for most of her life until one day it spilled out onto the pages that would become her first published book.

If she's not writing, she's attempting to bake something—however catastrophic that might be—or she's enjoying the beauty of the outdoors with her husband.

How to Connect

Facebook.com/ccwarrens
instagram.com/c.c._warrens/
Website: ccwarrensbooks.com/
Email: cc@ccwarrensbooks.com

Made in United States
Troutdale, OR
03/29/2024